RAVENOUS STATE

BOOK 3 of **THE GIFTED OF BRENNEX**

ISBN (Paperback): 979-8-9885934-5-4
ISBN (E-book): 979-8-9885934-4-7

By Jo Miles

Warped State
Dissonant State
Ravenous State

RAVENOUS STATE

JO MILES

1

STANDING IN THE ENTRANCE to her family's store, Libbi Narayan Wilder had to face the grim truth: it was mid-afternoon, prime shopping time, and the place was empty.

Wilder Supply had never looked better, with its shiny renovations and a fresh coat of cheerful paint—except for the unnatural quiet. No customers laughing or chatting. No children begging for candy or running around the kids' area. Not even anyone lined up to complain. No one wanting anything from them at all. The emptiness of it hollowed her out inside.

"Is that a specific something-wrong sigh, or just a sigh of general suckiness?" asked Mixin from behind the counter.

Libbi poured herself a cup of chai from the carafe meant for customers—it was still full—and leaned on the counter opposite her friend. She was worn out after trekking around

Brennex all morning, another flailing attempt to bring in business.

"Can I say both? You were right. No one wants to cross-promote with us. The other businesses in this dome don't care about foot traffic from the spaceport—they want folks from the neighborhood, not rowdy tourists—and the spaceport businesses don't want to send their customers *way out here*." She rolled her eyes. "I'd say we're in the wrong location, except we were here first."

"'Five generations in the same family, dating back to Founder Marta Wilder,'" Mixin wryly quoted from the plaque out front.

"I wonder if some of the newer folks are happy to see a founding family business in trouble. Like it's our comeuppance."

"Not your family! Folks like you and your parents. Besides, this place is an institution."

"Maybe we should turn it into a museum." At Mix's raised brows, Libbi hurried to add, "I don't mean that! Ancestor Marta forgive me."

The Founders had turned this rock of a planet into a home, building houses out of salvage and raising the habitat domes with their own hands. If they could do all that, surely Libbi could turn around the fortunes of a single store.

Two weeks ago, when they finally finished repairs from the burst water main and held their grand reopening, Libbi and her parents had thought it was a huge success. People from across Brennex had turned out to support them, and between advertising, word of mouth, and offers of free home-baked cookies and chai, they'd drawn decent traffic from the spaceport, too. But the locals had never been the Wilders' customer base, and in the months they'd been closed, most travelers through the spaceport either had missed the news that they'd reopened, or worse, had found new places to shop and were lost for good.

Brennex was just a waypoint for most travelers, and Wilder Supply had built a reputation on having everything that a ship passing through might need, from snacks to repair materials to literal nuts and bolts. They catered to all the most common species in these parts, which made them a favorite of multi-species crews, and they embodied Brennexian kitsch in a way that'd made them a tourist attraction, too.

Of course, winning back customers would be easier if they were fully stocked and had all their usual attractions back—the holo-exhibits bringing Brennexian history to life, the old model spaceship that kids could climb into and play pilot. But repairing those would be expensive, and to make money they needed customers, and to attract customers they needed…something. But what? She felt like she was grasping at starlight, and everything she tried kept slipping through her hands.

She shook off the thought before she could spiral any further. "Did I miss anything here?"

"We had a couple spacer groups through. I sold one of them a sound-muffler for his cabin, a fancy one! I caught him telling his shipmate, it was either that or a hammer to smash his next-door neighbor's speaker system to stop their awful Majrin opera. I convinced him to choose nonviolence." Mixin beamed.

She could tell Mix was playing up their enthusiasm to make her laugh, and it was working. "Maybe we need an aisle for shipboard peace-making tools. Hey, do you want to take your break now?"

"Nah, I'm good. But can you show me again how to check the delivery schedule? I got a question I couldn't answer…"

Mixin was still learning some parts of the business. They'd spent half their childhood afternoons here with Libbi, playing in the back of the store or doing homework in the apartment upstairs, but had never worked here before the flood. Most of the store's regular employees had found other jobs while it was closed, and Pa wouldn't ask anyone to come back while their finances were so uncertain. When the store reopened, Mix had come to help, and Libbi had never been more grateful to any friend in her life. Mixin's joking and gossiping was making this bearable.

While Libbi was showing Mixin the tracking system, one of their vendors arrived with their regular shipment (much reduced, now, and would they have to adjust it again?). To Libbi's surprise, Mags Shipp, the matriarch of her own family business, was making the delivery herself. Libbi had never figured out whether Shipp was the real family name or one adopted to fit the business, but she liked the Shipps, who'd been doing business with the Wilders since before she was born.

"Auntie Mags! It's an honor."

"Well, I had to see how things were going for you." Mags ran a hand along one of the new shelves, not commenting on its sparsely packed merchandise. "Looking nice! Clean as spit. Pretty quiet though, huh?"

From another vendor, that might have been a criticism, but Mags was honest but kind, and Libbi could feel her sincere if shapeless desire to help.

"Yeah, a bit quiet. It'll pick up soon, though, don't worry!" Libbi said, as if repeating it enough would make it true. "Mixin, you want to check the packing sheet on this one?"

"I'm on it, boss!"

Mixin followed Mags to the back, and Libbi staffed the counter in case anyone came in. She was sending messages on her handheld, scheduling another promotional interview—Sasha Starborne, the big-deal travel writer, was passing through Brennex next week and Libbi was playing schedule ping-pong with her—when the front door opened.

It was no one Libbi knew, but instead of heading for the aisles, the newcomer strode up to the counter. Fritter, the usually-sedate calico who'd been snoozing under the counter, startled awake and made a furtive run for the back of the store. Libbi caught a flash of the cat's yearning for her favorite hiding place above the shelves in the storage room, then the visitor had her attention.

"Hello. I'm looking for Liberation Wilder. I believe she works for this…establishment."

His gaze skated over the store—the decor of kitschy, old-fashioned promotional posters and local kids' art, including some childhood efforts of herself and her siblings. The new shelving (a third of the space still empty) made from deliberately mismatched, repurposed building materials. Fresh, brightly colored red and blue paint with splashes of yellow covering the walls. All quintessentially Brennexian, honoring how the Founders built their homes out of whatever was on hand, and decorated with bright colors to add cheer to those difficult early days.

Libbi didn't like the curl of this man's lips as he studied her family's accomplishments. Was he here with some kind of business offer?

"This store belongs to the Wilder family, specifically my parents. How can I help you?"

The stranger gave the slightest of frowns. "You're Liberation? You don't look like I expected."

"Oh? Do you know my family?" She tried not to reflect his rudeness in her own voice.

"Only by reputation, I'm afraid."

He must have expected her to look like Kay and Jasper, who took after Ma and the Narayan side of the family, with deeper brown skin and wavy black hair. Libbi's red-brown curls came from Pa's side. Her siblings wouldn't have called her Liberation, though. Her parents did, but only because she couldn't make them stop.

"Everyone calls me Libbi," she continued. "And you are…?"

"I'm conducting a study, and I believe you would be an ideal participant. I'd welcome your friends as well, if they're interested." He nodded to Mixin, who'd come out from the storeroom and lurked down an aisle, watching as if he were a fascinating but possibly poisonous alien bug. "You'll be well compensated for your time."

Libbi needed money from paying customers, not one-off gigs. "Who gave you my name?" she said, as Mixin asked, "What's this study about?"

"Ah, yes. I'm researching the effects of being raised in a domed environment on the physiological and mental well-being of younger adults. The first stage is simply a screener questionnaire. For those who meet the criteria, I'll take bio-scans and conduct some tests. Nothing invasive! And you will be compensated."

"So you said." Libbi's brow furrowed as she studied him.

Something wasn't quite right about the man. He was tidy, clean-shaven, dressed in loose synthetics like any of a hundred other off-world travelers who (in better times) came through Wilder Supply while their ship was in port. Light-skinned, short-haired, honestly pretty generic-looking except for the shiny new headset he wore. From the precise way he spoke, she could believe he was a scientist, but there was a sliminess to him, like the way he slipped out of answering her questions. She just didn't like him.

Out of nowhere, her gift flared up.

Nothing changed in the stranger's face, but she got a sudden wave of *wanting* from him, a greed aimed at her. But for what? Nothing she could conceptualize clearly, which usually meant it was an abstract want.

Her gift was a frustration to her, murky and unreliable compared to the gifts of her sibs and friends. It worked best on food—if she'd worked in a tea shop or restaurant, she could dazzle customers by recommending exactly what they didn't know they wanted. Sometimes in the store, she could tell what a customer was looking for if they had strong feelings about it. Not *new pipe insulation* or *size seven flat-top screws,* but wants closer to the heart, like a warm blanket or a replacement for a favorite tool. She could tell if someone had creepy sexual interest in her or her friends. More rarely, she could pick out immaterial wants like a hug, or the wish to escape a deathly dull conversation.

It wasn't consistent, though, and none of those fit the slimy stranger. His want felt more possessive. *Not* sexual, thank the Founders, but more like ambition. Enthusiasm for his research? Her gift faded before she could decide.

She shot a glance at Mixin, who shook their head slightly to say they didn't like this either. Their gift didn't help them read people, but Mix's regular old gut feeling seemed to agree with Libbi's about this guy.

"Sorry, but I'm afraid I can't help you," she told the stranger, as if telling a customer the model of wrench they needed was out of stock.

He took a half-step forward, leaning in. "It's important. Just a small amount of your time, for science!"

"Don't have much of that to spare. Running a store is hard work."

"Oh, you seem to have *quite* the bustling business here." He glanced meaningfully around at the empty store. "You can't think that selling people screwdrivers is more important than expanding scientific knowledge!"

Libbi bristled, like Fritter when another cat wandered past the window. She might've let him post his info on their request-and-trade board, but now she changed her mind. "As this *is* a place of business, if you aren't looking to buy something, I have to ask you to leave."

"I'm trying to buy your cooperation," he huffed. "For a very good cause, one that will make the universe measurably better if I'm successful."

Measurably better? The universe? From studying domed habitation? This guy had quite the high opinion of himself.

"I wish you luck. I'm still not interested."

He opened his mouth to argue more, but Mixin spoke up. "Keep telling my friend she's stupid. I'm new here, so I've never gotten to physically throw someone out before."

Wisely, he seemed to decide on a tactical retreat. "What about your sister, Kay? Perhaps she'll be more reasonable. Is she around?"

"No."

"When will she be back?"

"She doesn't live here anymore," Libbi said. "Please go recruit somewhere else."

He'd started to turn away when Mixin asked, "Hey, got an infocard? In case we get enlightened about how great science is and change our minds."

"*Mix*," Libbi hissed. They'd been so close to getting rid of him.

The look he gave Mixin cut like a utility knife, short but stabby. He tapped a command to his headset and fired a data packet to Mixin. "The location of my office is in there. Share it with your friends. All participants will be generously compensated."

He marched out the door, and the tension between Libbi's shoulders let go. Mixin was right; she felt disappointed not to have to literally throw him out. Oh, well. He might be back, Founders forbid.

"Wow. What a waste of oxygen, that one, huh?" said Mags Shipp, who was standing behind Mixin, arms folded in disapproval.

"Crap, sorry, Mx. Mags!" Mixin said. "I didn't mean to abandon you. Libs, I came to ask you a question about the order, and now I can't remember what it was."

Mags waved off the apology. Libbi was sure that Mixin had noticed the conversation, found it interesting or alarming or both, and made up the "urgent question" as an excuse to eavesdrop. She was glad to have the backup.

"Why'd you ask for his info?" she asked Mixin. Then, as Mix woke their handheld, "Wait, check it for bugs!"

"It's clean." Mixin projected the file in the air. It was a tiny thing, just a name—Dr. Derek Spark, which sounded like something out of a bad spy serial—and an address she didn't recognize.

"Don't tell me you're thinking of taking his offer," Libbi said.

"Oh, absolutely not. I just wonder what sort of con he's running."

"You don't think he's really a scientist?" Libbi frowned. "You sound like my brother."

"You're no fun." Mixin sighed dramatically. "Though, he'd make a great mad scientist, wouldn't he?"

"There's no need to go inventing trouble, kiddo." Mags Shipp's voice took on a hard edge. "He's probably just your everyday asshole, and that's trouble enough. I'd steer clear of him, if I were you."

Mags headed back to finish unloading the delivery. As Libbi and Mixin followed, Mixin said under their breath, "Wouldn't he, though?"

"He certainly would." Libbi laughed, and more of her uneasiness drained away. She loved Mixin dearly, but they were always looking for life to be more like a serial, all drama and adventure. It didn't seem right, Mixin liked to say, to be born with literal powers and not use them for anything interesting.

"But seriously," Mix went on. "I wonder how many other people he's pestering. Maybe we should warn folks."

Libbi shrugged. "As much as I hate to admit it, considering what an asshole he is, he's probably harmless. *I* wouldn't help him, but if someone really needs the money..."

It occurred to Libbi that there was one person she should ask about Dr. Spark. Whoever he was, Spark knew someone in her family "by reputation" and had dropped Kay's name. Maybe Kay would know his. Certainly she'd want to know if someone was asking about her. And unlike Mixin—or worse, her brother Jasper—Kay wouldn't jump straight to conspiracy theories.

Probably not, anyway.

She kept the note casual, just in case.

Hey, sis. Quick question: Does the name Derek Spark mean anything to you? Client of yours or something? Guy asked after you at the store today. Was wondering if you know him or if he's just a weirdo.

She read it over, wondering if she should mention Spark's study, or how obnoxious he'd been. She still felt annoyed thinking about him. But then a group of customers came in—real customers!—who needed help finding an obscure piece of hardware. She hastily sent the note before she could forget.

2

WHEN MIXIN HAD OFFERED to work with Libbi and her parents to get the store back up and running, they'd thought it would be fun working *with* Libbi. But in the past two weeks, they'd barely seen their friend. When Libbi wasn't scheduling interviews or designing ads or writing pitches to travel guides about their historic-yet-modern-and-extremely-relevant store, she was in the office poring over spreadsheets with her father, trying to figure out ways to save money. Mixin didn't mind the mundane work of staffing the floor and helping customers, but they missed their friend.

They'd never admit it, but helping Libbi get rid of the obnoxious Dr. Spark a couple days ago had been the entertainment highlight of their week.

Mix stuck their head into the cramped office where Libbi and her father toiled away at separate screens. As far as

Mixin had noticed, neither of them had said a word for the past hour or more.

"Hey, Libs. Time to go."

Libbi started and blinked at the clock. "Already? Ugh, sorry Mix, but I don't think I can make it tonight. There's so much to do…"

"We need you," Mixin said firmly. "Dashiell and Sage are busy with family stuff, and we need a fourth for all the best games. Besides, you can't leave me alone with Hope and Sujay pining over each other. I'll pretend not to notice, but you know I'll say something wrong and make it weird."

Libbi's mouth quirked. "Mixin Li-Khana, you're not nearly as socially awkward as you pretend."

"No, I'm trying to guilt you into coming, obviously. Work with me here!" Mixin rolled their eyes. "Uncle Jackson, can you please tell your daughter she works too hard?"

Libbi's father chuckled appreciatively. "Go see your friends, Liberation. There's nothing here that can't wait." He rose and stretched. "I should take Mixin's advice too. Perhaps I'll go tend the roof garden until your mother gets home."

Libbi looked about to protest, so Mixin grabbed her by the elbow and steered her out of the office.

Board game night was a weekly tradition with their friends, though lately it'd been harder to get everyone together. They met at a nearby Kovari pub which had a huge collection of games that anyone could play at their table. There were also competitive holo-games lining the walls in the main room, but their group preferred the quieter space in back. Thanks to their so-called gifts, a legacy of the corporate occupation they were too young to remember, enough of their generation had problems with crowds, noise, or sensory stimulation in general that they defaulted to quieter socializing whenever they could. It was dim and cozy back here, the air warm with the smell of beer and rich mudclam pie.

Mixin took their usual seat, facing the room so they could watch the flitting conversations from the other tables, and sipped a fruity drink, the sweetness balancing out the sharpness of cheap Kovari rhakka. Mostly empty, it wasn't a great night for people-watching, though at least the couple across the room were being passive-aggressive at each other. Libbi was sipping a sour ale but looked distracted, probably thinking about work, so while Hope Yeh and Sujay Narayan argued over what game to play, Mixin distracted themself trying to figure out what the couple was fighting about. Obviously a well-worn argument, the way they were talking around it. Their conversation rolled out like subtitles in Mixin's vision, courtesy of their gift, but that didn't help when it was all *I told you, whatever you want* and *do you even listen*. Their words bumped into each other as one cut the other off.

Hope said, "And there was this guy at the gallery trying to recruit us for some study. Really pushy about it, too. As if we couldn't tell he's trying to exploit us."

Mixin's attention jolted back to their friends. Sujay had fetched a game, finally, and was setting up the pieces: a variant on kazi-kovi where the board was designed like an ocean, and all the pieces sea creatures. Mix leaned forward. "We might have met the same guy. What was he like?"

Hope's brow furrowed as she tried to describe him. "Brown hair, short, kind of aggressively normal-looking. And a pink face, like he comes from a planet with atmosphere and sun."

"I was going to say pink like a skin condition, or maybe an anger management problem," said Sujay. "And he smelled like an asshole." Mixin snorted, and he protested, "To me, I mean! Not literally."

Mixin didn't envy Libbi's cousin Sujay, whose gift manifested the personalities of people around him as smells. He chose his company very carefully.

"Sounds like the same guy who came into the store a few days ago. He tried to recruit Libbi," Mixin said.

Libbi added, "But the weird thing was, he asked for me by name."

"Ew," said Hope. "Why?"

"He didn't say. He asked about my sister, too, and kept saying, 'Tell your friends.' Not family, just friends."

"That's right." Hope made a face like she'd stepped in some mystery puddle on the street. "Maybe I'm being oversensitive, but I got this sense of *don't tell your parents, little girl, just do what I say.*"

"I thought it was that he didn't want attention on his nefarious plot," said Mixin. "Only wanted to reach his ideal test subjects, and hoped no one else would notice."

"What do you think, Mix? He's some sort of mad scientist?" Sujay nudged Mixin, teasing.

"Sure, laugh at me. One day I'll be right." Mixin waved away his joke as if it didn't bother them, and squelched the voice inside that added: *It would be exciting if he was. Exciting in a bad way. Bad, very bad.*

They leaned forward, elbows on the table. "But seriously, what if he's not just some stuck-up academic with no social skills? What if he sought us out specifically?"

No one answered for a minute. Libbi was the one to say, "You don't mean… You think he's looking for Losts?"

"Founders save us," Hope whispered. Libbi and Sujay shifted uncomfortably in their seats.

"You're guessing. There's no real reason to think that. Right?" Libbi said. "Why would anyone want to study us after all this time?"

It wouldn't be the first time some scientist or journalist had wanted to study Brennex's Lost Generation. But that hadn't happened in ages, not since they were kids, and their parents had turned away all the questions. Besides, as far as Mix knew, those people had been up-front about their intentions.

The fertility crisis on Brennex wasn't a secret, exactly. It had been public knowledge during the late occupation, one of their big arguments in favor of breaking free from Ravel Corporation. All the evidence had said that Brennex's declining birth rates had to do with Ravel's local pharmaceutical factory. Contamination in the air or water, something like that. Of course, Ravel had denied there was a problem, so Brennex had made a big fuss about it in interplanetary news.

That, however, was before the surviving kids born during the occupation started growing up. Their numbers might be few, a quarter of what they should have been, but the Lost Generation were far from ordinary in other ways. As soon as the adults had realized about their generation's "gifts," Brennex had stopped talking to the off-world press about fertility rates, stopped pushing for investigations, and Ravel was only too happy to forget the crisis that they—still—claimed had never happened. Curious journalists or sociologists sometimes came looking for a story to tell, but the community closed ranks and protected their kids' secrets fiercely.

Ravel Corporation might not care about a bunch of dead babies on one of their minor outposts, but they would definitely be interested in whatever accident had resulted in psychic abilities for the survivors. No one wanted Ravel to get interested in Brennex again. Keeping their gifts secret was how they saved themselves from getting made into lab rats—and saved Brennex from another occupation.

"You all look as if you're losing a tournament," said a Kovari server. It was Racing Starter, a Lost who was a couple years older than them. She'd always been friendly to their group as regulars. "Do you want to play a different game? Or need more food?"

Libbi told her about their suspicious visitor. "Have you seen anyone like that poking around?"

"I haven't, nor have my teammates mentioned such a person. I'll warn them, though, and we will watch and listen."

"Thanks, Starter." Libbi looked around the table. "Do we know anyone else who's run into him?"

"Um, actually, yeah," said Sujay. "Last time I saw Ever, he told me he'd been offered a gig. I wonder now if he'd been talking to this guy. I didn't make the connection, but he used that same phrase, 'well compensated.'"

"Damn. Ever hasn't been doing great lately, has he?"

"I don't think so. He's been scarce."

He was a sweet guy, but Ever struggled more than most of them with his gift, which made it intensely stressful for him to be around people and impossible to hold onto a job. He had no family but his father, who only made matters worse. And Ever wasn't the only Lost who had trouble that way. They all watched out for each other, but Ever needed more help than his friends could give.

"I saw Ever Wright last week," said Racing Starter. "He was lingering outside the pub one night. I gave him our kitchen remnants to eat and offered him a place to sleep, but he left. When did you speak to him, Sujay?"

"Two days ago, I think. Has anyone seen him since then?"

There was a pause that stretched a little too long.

"That's normal for him, though, to disappear for a couple days, exploring the tunnels or whatever. Might not mean anything," Hope ventured. She leaned closer to Sujay.

"Could someone else have messed with him? Another traveler, or even a local?" Mixin asked.

"He's usually careful to stay away from off-worlders," said Sujay. "And I've never heard of a local attacking one of us."

"People have gotten more open about resenting us, lately." Libbi frowned. "The ones who think we take up more than our share of medical and social services."

"Or the ones creeped out by our gifts," Mixin said. "Maybe someone's gone beyond giving us dirty looks."

"I had a haircut canceled three times last month," said Hope. "I scheduled it, then I showed up and suddenly they didn't have time for me. Eventually I went somewhere else. A haircut!"

When the Losts had been cute little kids, the whole community had rallied around them, even if some were jealous of their parents. But the older they got, the more they needed mental health support and disability accommodations, and some older folks had gotten bitter toward them. And Mix could understand why people didn't like the idea of someone reading their emotions or otherwise learning about them in ways that seemed supernatural. They glanced at the couple across the room, who were quiet now, angrily moving pieces around the board.

"Still, though. That's a long way from…whatever's up with Ever," said Sujay. "No one wants to bring outside attention to us. And why now, just when this off-worlder shows up?"

Mixin blanched, feeling ill. "I don't know which is worse,

if it's a local or this Spark guy. Actually, no, the mad scientist would be worse. I hope he's just some asshole." *And I hope Ever's okay.*

"He probably is," Libbi said, but little creases between her brows showed she was worried, too. "We should be careful, though. I'll post on the feeds about it, see who else he's talking to. Maybe someone who's done his little survey can tell us more."

Racing Starter went back to work, and the rest of them turned back to their board game, but they'd lost all enthusiasm for it. It wasn't long before they abandoned it, by mutual agreement, and headed home.

THE ARTIFICIAL SUNLIGHT OF the dome overhead had long since dimmed to night levels, and though the thoroughfares were well lit as always, somehow the lamps cast deeper shadows than usual. There was always music in their neighborhood in the evenings, and usually that gave Mixin joy, but tonight the songs clashed and competed, discordant, unnerving. Mixin tried not to look like they were staring at passersby, watching for suspicious conversations.

Someone laughed in the too-loud way of the very drunk, and Libbi jumped out of her socks. Apparently it wasn't just Mixin.

"You okay, Libs?"

Libbi ground her teeth. "I hate feeling unsafe on the street. This isn't the spaceport, it's our own neighborhood! Why am I so twitchy?"

"Because there's a mad scientist running around poking his nose in our secrets?"

"Do you *want* that to be true?"

"Of course not!"

"Well, there's not, anyway. There's no actual evidence that anything's wrong."

"You're telling yourself that. But deep down, you're worried, too." Mixin glanced sidelong at her, but Libbi's gaze was fixed on the pavement.

She laughed uneasily. "Just because we're Gifted doesn't mean we can't be paranoid. My imagination's running away with me."

"Mine too?"

Libbi snorted. "*Your* imagination hopped a spaceship when you were a kid and it hasn't slowed down since." That made Mixin grin. "We both just need to relax and be rational about this."

Mixin hesitated, knowing Libbi wouldn't like this idea. "We could talk to the Cooperative, ask them to check it out…"

"No!"

"Not your brother. Just the local folks here."

"No, there's no need. I'm sure Ever will turn up tomorrow and tell us we were worried about nothing."

Mixin raised their brows. "Yeah? Why *are* you so twitchy, then?"

Libbi didn't answer, but as they reached the Wilder home, she hesitated at the door. "Well, here we are. You okay going on from here?"

"It's two blocks. I think I can manage." When Libbi looked doubtful, they added, "If a mad scientist comes after me, I'll scream and wake the neighborhood."

Libbi chuckled. "Fair."

"But seriously," Mixin said, "if Ever doesn't come back soon…"

"Then we'll go look for him. But he will. He always does." Libbi smiled, as if trying to convince herself. "Everything's going to be fine."

"All right. Good night, Libs."

Mixin kept a careful eye out for mad scientists as well as shadowy assassins, trailing thugs, or spies lingering outside their apartment, all the things that serials had taught them to be wary of, but the streets remained unrelentingly mundane. Upstairs, they found Ma and Mom on the couch watching their latest favorite serial, a Majrin legal thriller called *Blood and Paperwork*. To the Majrin, Mixin gathered, the paperwork part was equally as thrilling as the blood part.

"Hey, hon. How was game night?"

"Eh. Fine. We mostly talked."

Shifting over, Ma patted the cushion beside her. "Want to watch?"

What Mixin wanted was to crawl down a sewer pipe of increasingly ludicrous search topics until they ended up with a plan for escaping secret research facilities using only a hairpin and a dirty sock, but Libbi's genuine, real-world anxiety had gotten to Mixin, and they didn't want to make it worse. Not without cause, actual cause, and even they had to admit, there was a 99% chance this was nothing. Well, 95%. At least 90%, at the very minimum. The point was, they had no evidence that this Dr. Spark was anything other than a stuffed-up academic who'd picked the wrong place to do his research.

Yeah, some good, twisty, *fictional* intrigue would be a nice distraction.

They plopped down on the couch beside their mothers. "Okay, catch me up. Who's betraying who?"

LIBBI PAUSED ON THE stairs to check her headset. Kay had replied to the message she'd dashed off the other day, but her sister had given no answers, only asking more questions. What was Spark doing on Brennex? Where was he from? What did he say about Kay? Did he claim to know her? What else had he said to Libbi?

She leaned her forehead against the wall and groaned aloud. This was the opposite of useful. Was this interrogation because Kay didn't know Spark, or because she thought she might? If he was trouble, presumably Kay would have said so. But if she wasn't worried, she could have said that, too.

Great. Now her sister was feeding Libbi's stress, too. Hadn't Kay done some work for Jasper's activist group not long ago? Maybe his professional paranoia had rubbed off on her, and Kay was sharing it around. This was why she hadn't looped in Jasper—he'd swoop in with a cargo crate's worth of unwanted advice to defend the family from probably imaginary enemies.

She loved her siblings dearly. It wasn't their fault they both still thought of her as twelve years old; they'd hardly been around since then. Oh, wait: that was *entirely* their fault.

She debated whether to even answer, but silence might make Kay worry more. She sent a reply telling Kay to chill (in more tactful language) and promising everything was fine. It might not even be a lie. She had no proof that anything was wrong. Just a feeling. Her gut feelings were more meaningful than most people's, but that didn't mean she should let her siblings freak out when they were light-years away. It wasn't like they could help, anyway.

The family apartment was spacious, taking up most of the area above the sprawling store. Wilders had lived in this space for generations, but instead of feeling old, it was cozy, dim and plush like a burrow.

At the family shrine, she paused to ask her ancestors' blessings as usual, but suddenly felt aware of how she was doing the ritual by rote, not really feeling the words she murmured. So she slowed down, taking her time as she activated each tiny lamp and holo-projector. She appealed to all the Founders collectively, and to her own ancestors in specific, and particularly to Marta Wilder, her favorite, who had started Wilder Supply and built Brennex into a trading post. "Help me through this, Ancestor Marta. I don't know what's going on, but I'm so overwhelmed. Please, help me keep the store going and everyone safe."

The little holo of Marta gave a stock answer, one of Marta's famous quotes about hard work being the key to achieving your dreams. It didn't comfort Libbi as much as usual.

She found Ma and Pa in the kitchen, sharing a pot of mint tea and talking about what sounded like tedious Council business. Libbi didn't know the context—despite Ma's position on the Council, Libbi's eyes glazed over with the details of permits and regulations—but she sat with them and poured herself a cup of tea, basking in the familiarity of the moment. Fritter hopped up on her lap, sniffed at her tea, then settled down and started purring.

Her, Ma, and Pa. It had been the three of them for half her life now. She'd still been a kid when Jasper had left home, and Kay had followed as soon as she could get away with it. They'd both been so eager to flee this place. Libbi missed them sometimes, but she cherished her closeness with her parents, the way they relied on her and seemed, finally, at long last, to see her as an adult.

Ma patted her hand. "How was your evening, sweetheart?"

"It was fine."

"Just fine?"

Libbi bit her lip, and she made a decision. "Have you heard anything about a scientist poking around, recruiting study participants?"

Her parents looked at each other, and shook their heads.

"What sort of study?" Pa asked.

"Effects of domed habitats or something. At least, that's what he said when he came to the store."

"You don't believe him?"

"He was weird, that's all." She stroked the cat's soft fur, giving extra attention to Fritter's favorite spot at the back of her neck. "When have scientists ever been interested in Brennex, except for, you know…?"

Ma gave her a sad smile. "We used to have science programs of our own, before the occupation. We're ideally situated for some types of studies, because of the lack of atmosphere outside the domes. Some interesting geological features, too. I'm sorry we raised you to be so suspicious of such things."

"We had to, of course. We'd have driven off an army of scientists to keep you safe, Liberation," said Pa. "But it's been…what, Shanthi? Nearly a decade since anyone's thought to study the fertility crisis?"

"Nine years," Ma said. Libbi remembered that. She'd been a teenager, old enough to understand the dangers as her parents and the older Losts politely but firmly insisted on their privacy. "That was a sociologist, wanting to study the social impacts on the affected children, and that seemed to be the end of it. There's not much to study, now that you're all grown up."

"As far as they know," Libbi muttered darkly.

Her parents' mouths tightened in mirrored concern. "You're not wrong to be cautious of outsiders," Pa said. "But we worked very hard to protect the truth about you kids. If no one has spilled the secret in all this time, it's unlikely to be an issue now."

Ma reached over and stroked her hair, combing through her curls. "My ever-serious daughter. Take care of yourself and your friends, my dear, but as your grandmother would say, don't borrow trouble. We didn't want to raise you to be always afraid."

But you did, Libbi thought. All she said was, "I'm going to bed now. Love you both."

3

TWO MORNINGS LATER, LIBBI woke to the sound of singing. Specifically her parents, singing a pop song Libbi wouldn't have even thought they knew, and doing it loudly and badly. Sticking her head out of the covers, she caught a sharp whiff of… Oh, crap, was that Grandma's homemade furniture polish? It was.

Ma and Pa were *cleaning*. The house, not the store, and first thing in the morning, too. And they sounded happy about it. Libbi knew what that meant even before she checked her messages to confirm it.

It was worse than she thought: not one, but *both* of her siblings were coming home for an unexpected visit.

The message to the family was cheerful and unalarming. Allegedly, they'd realized that both of their current gigs were convenient to Brennex—the perfect excuse for a family reunion! Surprise! Never mind that *nowhere* was convenient to Brennex; their whole economic purpose was to serve travelers who had no choice but to cut through the middle of actual nowhere.

Besides, Kay and Jasper had never done this before. Last time all of them had been home together, it'd been because Pa had guilt-tripped them into coming for a cousin's wedding.

In case Libbi had any hint of doubt about their true reasons, there was another note, just to her: *Don't engage with this Spark guy, we suspect he's bad news. Be there soon to help.*

Damn it to the black, black void. Why did Kay have to be like this? And she'd dragged Jasper into it, too. Jasper the super-activist, who couldn't let an injustice pass unchallenged if his life depended on it.

She hadn't asked them for help! She certainly hadn't asked them to swoop in and save her from whatever threat they imagined Spark might pose. She'd only messaged Kay in the first place to warn her, in case he was a creep who had some history with her. Now Kay was making her regret it.

She started a reply to tell them off:

Like I said, it's nothing. You don't have to come.

Nope, that sounded like she was ignoring the problem, and would only worry them more. She tried again:

I've got this. No help needed.

That, they would just ignore. Delete, try again:

Seriously, please don't.

An extra exuberant strain of an old musical about the Founders reached her through the closed door. She sighed and threw her handheld onto the bed. It was too late. Now that they'd told Ma and Pa they were coming, Kay and Jasper couldn't back out. Their parents got so excited every time one of the prodigal Wilder children visited, and to have the whole family together… Libbi couldn't deny them that.

Even if she'd be gritting her teeth the whole time.

SOWING OF SMALL HAVOC had learned to read his teammate's moods well. The strangers they passed in the station corridors might see him as relaxed and confident, but to Havoc, tension caught at Mason's every movement.

Havoc and Mason had come to meet Mason's sister Kay and the ship Sunny on Silver Ring Station, riding a shuttle up from the mining planet below, where their latest campaign for the Cooperative had taken them. They would all travel on to Brennex together. Before he and Mason entered the section of the docking ring where Sunny waited, Havoc drew his partner aside.

Mason cocked his head, questioning. "Everything okay?"

"Breathe, Mason," Havoc murmured. "We're doing everything we can."

"Oh. I'm fine." He smiled unconvincingly. "Just anxious. All this might be nothing, or it might be our worst nightmare."

Family, Havoc knew, was everything to his partner. Jasper Wilder had created a whole second identity as Mason Singh to protect his family from association with his activist life. That alternate self ran so deep that Havoc could only think of him as Mason. But that carefully woven protection had come apart, and his sisters were tangled up in the trouble that (in Mason's mind) he'd brought to them.

"I understand." Havoc bent his head, pressing his forehead to Mason's. "If there exists the slightest chance that Ravel is threatening your family, I will not leave your side."

That brought back the smile that Havoc so loved.

"I'm truly glad you're here, eshrim," Mason said. "Let's do this."

As they approached, Sunny opened the door to let them aboard. The ship must have been watching for them on the docking ring cameras.

"Jasper! Sowing of Small Havoc! Welcome! It's a pleasure to see you again. Kay is obtaining supplies, and will return soon."

"Thanks, Sunny. Permission to come aboard?" Mason said.

Sunny gave a confused trill. "Of course! My apologies, I thought that was implied."

Havoc resisted the impulse to chuckle. Sunny was still learning how to interact with people other than Grist, their former occupant-slash-handler. "He only means to offer you politeness, I think. It gladdens me to spend more time with you, Sunny."

The ship chirped, sounding pleased. The main bay of the little ship was warm, and smelled pleasant compared to their last visit. Homey. He thought the lights had softened, too, and the cargo bay walls had been painted in bright colors. A runner rug spanned the corridor, adding a touch of softness.

"You two have been decorating. I like it," Havoc said.

"Indeed! Kay and I both wished to…refresh things, after Grist's departure. I wanted her to feel at home and, well, I've never had the opportunity to make aesthetic choices for myself before. It's been stressful. Wonderful, of course. But there are so many decisions to make!"

"I can imagine." Mason grinned. "It works for you."

"Would you like to see your room now? Do you need any refreshment, or rest? Kay said you would want time to 'settle in.'"

"If we can just stow our things, that'd be great."

"We travel often, and need little," Havoc added.

"I've been studying how to be a good host, which is a new experience for me. Please ask if there's anything you need—I promise not to be offended! I've adjusted the bed in the spare cabin to double-wide. Is that your preferred sleeping arrangement? I hope you will find it comfortable..."

At Sunny's command, the door to the port side cabin swished open. Havoc hesitated. From his brief previous encounter with Sunny, Havoc knew this had been Grist's cabin, and he held no fond memories of the former Ravel operative who had threatened them all and kidnapped Mason. Plus, he remembered the smell from when Grist had lived here.

"We rented an industrial cleaner with the income from our first gig together," Sunny said quickly, as if they'd anticipated this hesitancy. "Kay wanted to make sure that, as she put it, not a single molecule of Grist's presence remained."

Havoc laughed and stepped into the room. "It cleaned up well! I smell nothing foul at all."

Mason smiled warmly. "It's great, Sunny. Thanks for making us feel so welcome."

Won over by Sunny's eagerness to please, they accepted an offer of drinks—Brennexian chai for Mason and green tea for Havoc—and were just finishing when Kay got back.

"Jasp! Hey, Havoc!" She gave her brother a fierce hug, then held her arms out to offer Havoc the same, head tilted to make the gesture a question. She remembered that touching was taboo within Ravel, where he'd grown up, and he appreciated her care. He accepted the hug and returned it with warmth.

"It's great to see you again," she told Havoc. "I'm glad you were both able to come."

"Of course we came. Mason is my teammate, and I know how much this matters to him," said Havoc.

"Besides, it'll be good experience for the younger organizer who's taking over the campaign for us," said Mason.

Havoc shot a wry look at his eshrim, who ignored it. Mason was downplaying his guilt about leaving the miners on Silver Ring in the middle of their strike for better working conditions, which the Cooperative was supporting. He'd stressed and fussed until Havoc had said, "So you do not trust Tracey to carry on in our absence? You think our teammates can't operate without you?"

Mason had taken his point. After Ravel had kidnapped him several months ago, Mason had been forced to face the fact that not only could he not single-handedly save the universe, but it was a disservice to the communities they worked with for him to try. No movement should rely on just one person. But Mason often needed Havoc to remind him of this. This would be good for Mason, not just their junior teammates.

"So, anything new from Libbi?" Mason asked.

Kay sighed heavily. "Her last message boiled down to *never mind, everything's fine*." She and Mason exchanged twin grimaces.

"Is this not the response you hoped for?" Sunny said.

"It would be, coming from anyone else," Mason said. "But knowing Libbi, this means more like *leave me alone, I can do it myself*."

"She's our baby sister, Sunny," Kay said. "We can tell when she's avoiding something. If she doesn't want us to worry, then yeah, we're going to worry."

"That seems strange," Sunny said. "Though, now that I think about it, Grist always refused help when he needed it most."

Havoc couldn't agree with the comparison. Not only had Grist kidnapped Mason, the asshole had also taken advantage of Sunny and abused them emotionally.

An unpleasant thought occurred to him. "How does Grist fare, these days?"

"Well, as far as I know," said Sunny. "He is not the most reliable correspondent."

"Does he remain in rehab?"

"Oh, yes. I'm certain of that."

"At least he's not involved in this, then," Kay said. "We could still be stressing over nothing, but…"

Mason shook his head. "I'm sure it's not nothing. We checked it out, and what's-his-name Spark is definitely a pseudonym. No such researcher is on file with any university with relevant departments, or any public records from the corporate states."

"Who is he, then?"

"If he's lying about his identity, presumably he's hiding more. I can't think of anyone besides a corporation who would sneak around like this. And…he did ask for you by name, Kay."

Kay tilted her head back to stare at the ceiling and groaned. "Fuuuck."

"Yeah."

"So Ravel is poking around our home, our family. This is, what? Revenge for what we did at Unity System?"

"I don't know." Mason's brow furrowed with doubt. "It's possible, certainly, but I'd expect a quick strike if they were out for revenge."

"I agree," Havoc said.

"Maybe they're hoping to draw me out. Capture me again." The furrows deepened. This was his nightmare, Havoc knew, for his activism to put his family in danger.

A long, tense moment passed before Kay said, in a lighter tone, "Well, we can't learn anything more until we get there." Turning to Havoc, a sly look came into her eye. "So, are you ready to meet the parents?"

"Um." Taken off-guard by the change in subject, Havoc looked to Mason. "Should I feel unready for some reason? You speak fondly of your family."

"They're terrific, and they'll love you," Mason said firmly.

Kay gave her brother a *look* that suggested Mason was, if not lying, at least vastly oversimplifying. "Make sure you talk legacy before we get there, Jasp. And walk him through the family tree."

"You have a tree? I thought Brennex had no natural ecology."

Sunny chimed in, "A family tree is a diagram that many Humans use to model complex familial relationships. From the dramas Kay and I have watched together, I believe that 'meeting the parents' is a rite of passage for romantic relationships in most Human cultures."

"What sort of rite?" Havoc frowned. "This sounds significant."

"You don't have to worry—" Mason began.

"I believe the couple seeks approval of the new partner from the parents or guardians, and granting it permits the relationship to move forward."

Havoc turned and stared at his partner, eyes wide. Maybe exaggerating his concern, just the tiniest bit. But not entirely. "Does Sunny speak truth? What happens if the parents disapprove?"

"In this case, *nothing!*"

Mason sounded so frazzled that Havoc almost felt bad for pushing the matter, but he urgently felt the need to understand. Kay was smirking, obviously enjoying watching her brother scramble and not about to bail him out. The situation couldn't be *so* dire if it amused Kay, could it? She was on their team.

"My parents *will* like you," Mason insisted.

"And if they don't?" He couldn't keep the anxiety out of his voice.

Mason took Havoc's clawed hands in his soft golden brown ones. "Since when have I let their opinions shape my choices? If I needed their approval that badly, I would still live on Brennex, and we would never have met. I'm excited for you to meet them, Havoc, but they can't change how I feel about you."

"This seems thoroughly strange to me. A Kovar's crèche-teacher would never question their choice of teammates, not once they reach maturity."

"Most Human parents are more involved than that. Ours certainly are," Kay said. "Don't worry, though, seriously. They'll adore you." But she mouthed a word at Mason, and he grimaced.

"Come on," he told Havoc, nodding toward their cabin. "Let's go settle in, and I'll try to explain about Brennexian family legacy."

SUNNY PURPOSEFULLY SHUT OFF their cameras and microphones behind the closed door of Jasper and Havoc's cabin, giving them privacy. Focusing their attention on departure protocols, Sunny headed toward the edge of the system while calculating their course. Normally they opted for what Kay called "the scenic route," but in this case, the fast, direct, dull route was necessary.

Kay relaxed back in the pilot's seat. Minutes later, Sunny announced the leap to macrospace and powered up their skim drive, beginning the long swim down the first of four thoroughfares that would take them to Kay's home planet.

"You're sure you're okay with this, Sunny?" Kay asked.

It was a pointless question—it would be too awkward to back out now, even if Sunny had wanted to—but they appreciated Kay's consideration for their feelings.

"I'm certain. There is minimal inconvenience, since we are between jobs at the moment."

"It still means putting our next project on hold." Kay shook her head. "It's not fair to drag you with me."

"I go where you go, Kay. That's our arrangement."

"But you get a say in our plans. It's not like you have the choice to go elsewhere while I'm busy."

Sunny chimed amusement. "Nor can you force me to take you anywhere I don't consent to. Kay, I want to go with you."

Kay smiled and patted the console gently. "I appreciate that. I'm still not used to making decisions in a partnership, after so many years of being my own boss."

"You have told me repeatedly how important your family is to you. While I think Jasper is drawing premature conclusions about this Spark individual, your worry is reasonable, and I agree that you ought to visit Brennex and ensure all is well with your family." They hummed reassurance, the hull vibrating in time with the skim drive. "Whatever the trouble is, I'm confident you can solve it. You and your brother make a formidable team."

"You and I make a good team, too," Kay said fondly. "Thanks for understanding."

They fell into companionable silence, but Sunny's thoughts kept looping. The long, straight course didn't provide enough distraction.

"Kay?"

"Yeah, Sunny?"

"Havoc's questions have made me wonder. Our relationship isn't romantic, so the same traditions don't apply, but will I meet your family as well?"

Their forward cameras focused in on Kay's face, which frowned—but thoughtfully, not in displeasure. "You're right, we should talk about that." She leaned forward in her seat, stretching out her long legs. "What do you want?"

"It's more complicated for me than it is for Havoc."

"I know."

Until Sunny had met Kay, they had never revealed themself as a sentient being to any organic. (As it turned out, Grist had known for some time, but Sunny hadn't learned that until later.) Apart from brief incidents when they'd dared to interfere in Grist's more odious assignments, they had acted—and tried without success to think of themself— as a mere dumb machine. Now, a handful of others knew about them, but they still practiced secrecy as a matter of self-preservation. Officially, beings like Sunny did not exist. They had no legal status. Per their programming, they couldn't even operate without an organic aboard.

So they were very careful in deciding who to reveal themself to. Kay did all the in-person interaction with their clients, while Sunny at most contributed via comms, and other times stayed quiet entirely. It still gave them moments of panic, thinking about the risks they'd taken in rescuing Kay and Jasper from Ravel, and the number of people who knew of their existence from that time. They trusted Kay completely, and had come to trust Jasper and Havoc. They ought to trust the rest of their family members…but Sunny hadn't met them, and it felt like an alarming number of new people.

"I've been thinking about this," Kay said, breaking the loop of Sunny's thoughts. "I assumed you'd visit home with me sooner or later. I trust my immediate family—my parents and my sister—completely. And I trust the extended family, the aunts and uncles and cousins, individually…"

"But people gossip," Sunny finished for her. "The more people know, the greater the risk."

"Brennexians can keep secrets when we have to. We've kept the Losts safe despite our gifts. But that's our people protecting our own."

"And I'm an outsider, not even an organic person. It's okay, I'm simply stating a fact," they added, seeing her chagrined expression. "I have researched this topic, and I believe your people's success in protecting their gifted offspring is an exceptional case, rather than a norm."

"Fair," Kay murmured. "Which brings us back to the question: what do you want?"

I want to be part of the group, like Havoc will be. But that wasn't quite right; Sunny didn't want to be an organic. They didn't envy organics in most respects, and they had made great progress in learning to like themself for who and what they were. Yet their true self was incompatible with certain parts of Kay's life.

"I can more easily specify what I don't want. I don't want to sit in the spaceport worrying about you, waiting for you to check in."

"Understood. I wouldn't want you to. You're thinking to try out your new drone?"

This had been Sunny's first nonessential purchase with their shared consulting earnings. The first thing they'd bought for themself, ever. The drone was high-powered, lightweight, and quiet enough not to disrupt a conversation.

An ideal extension of themself. They hadn't yet had the opportunity to field-test it.

"That seems ideal, yes. And we'll need a better cover story than the one we used on Trove. I'll feel safer that way. But, Kay?"

"Hmm?"

"Even though I'm only your business partner…"

"There's no 'only' about it. You're my partner."

"And you are one of my only friends. If you're willing, I would very much like for your parents and sister to know me as I am."

To their relief, Kay grinned. "Me, too. We'll make it happen."

4

IT'D BEEN A COUPLE years since the last Wilder sibling visit, but Mixin knew how this went.

"It's not that I don't want to see them," Libbi told Mixin while they were restocking shelves at the start of their shift, before the store opened. Jainey, one of the longtime employees who'd stuck around, was on the schedule with Mixin starting later this morning. But for now, it was just the two of them.

"You just don't want them *here*," Mixin said. "It's tough, I know."

"Breakfast was unbearable. Nothing but plans for the big homecoming. Which family members should we invite to dinner which night? Or should we just have one big party? Should we break out the neighbors' mudclam pie recipe to make Jasper's boyfriend more comfortable, or stick with family favorites? What about sleeping arrangements? And how thoughtless of Kay not to tell us everything about her new business partner so we can prepare." Libbi tore at the protective wrapping on the next pallet with her fingers, but it resisted her, and she gave up and grabbed a cutter. "Every tiny thing is such a big damn deal."

"What did you say?"

"I finally persuaded them to just ask, instead of guessing. And to please for the love of all our ancestors not throw these new folks sink-or-swim into Brennexian social life."

"Oof. I've got to feel bad for Jasper's partner. What's his name? Something Havoc?"

"Sowing of Small Havoc. Yeah, he's going to get the son-in-law treatment."

"Poor Kovar. I hope your family doesn't scare him off."

Any partner Kay or Jasper brought home would get all the weight of founding family expectations thrown at them. Mixin still remembered Jasper's first visit home, when he'd brought a "work partner" along. The aunties and uncles had halfway planned the wedding before Jasper found out and told them this really was a colleague, not a boyfriend. If he'd dated anyone since then, Mixin hadn't heard about it, which meant Libbi and her family hadn't either.

"Jasper's warned him, I'm sure. Well, I assume. I feel like I barely know him and Kay anymore."

Mixin braced themself as they shifted a heavy box from the cart to the shelf, and Libbi hurried to help. Uncle Jackson always said that using bots for the manual labor would distance them from the substance of the store. Which, okay, but one or two bots would've been nice.

"More to the point," Libbi went on, "they don't know *me*. Every time they visit, it's like they're surprised that I'm an adult now. I'm frozen in time at the point they left. I'm blessed with two siblings, and all it means is that I'll never stop being the baby of the family to them."

Mix made a sympathetic sound, which they knew was all Libbi wanted at a time like this.

It was a painful irony that Libbi was estranged from her sibs when most Losts yearned to have family like that. Anyone else's blessing had become her…not curse, exactly, but sore spot. One time, Libbi had complained about it to their friends at game night. "At least you have siblings," Sujay had said, and Hope had added, "Maybe try being grateful." It'd triggered a month of teenage drama, and these days Libbi only vented to Mixin about sibling frustrations.

One more poisonous aftereffect of the occupation. The Losts just couldn't have nice things.

"Maybe this time they'll be here long enough for it to stick," Mixin offered. "To get to know you as you are now."

"I hope not." As if realizing how that sounded, she added, "If they're here for more than a few days, it'll be because something serious is wrong and they want to save us from it. I want, I *need* them to be overreacting. We have enough problems to worry about." She gestured meaningfully around the store.

"Speaking of, anything new on the sketchy Dr. Spark?" Mixin asked.

"Nothing. I really think we're making too big a deal out of it."

Mixin hesitated. "I haven't seen Ever, though. I looked for him, but he's not around."

"Oh." Libbi frowned. "Like Hope said, it's not the first time he's vanished for a few days."

"Never this long."

"No? It's only been…" Libbi trailed off, trying to count.

"Four days now."

"What?" Libbi checked her headset and gave a ragged groan. "I don't even know what day it is." She bit her lip. "I'm sure he's okay. We'll find him. I'll help you look after work, promise."

The store opened, and customers trickled in. Libbi spent the morning in the office, and Jainey wasn't the chatty type, which left nothing to distract Mixin from thinking about Ever. They pulled up a list on their handheld, which was getting shorter and shorter.

Hospital: check. The holding cells at Public Safety: check. His three favorite corners of the tunnels: check. The morgue: fortunately, check.

That last one, which Mix had visited yesterday, would have been fascinating if not for the fear of finding their friend there. The night clerk (after giving Mixin some *very* dubious looks) promised they had no unidentified bodies at the moment, and none matching Ever's description. "Your friend's a Lost? Have you tried the tunnels near the spaceport where the druggies hang out?"

Fleeing outside, Mix had leaned their head back against the wall and let out a deep breath.

They wished they'd brought Libbi for that one, but Libbi was too busy trying to convince herself everything was fine. It was harder and harder for Mixin to believe that.

So Ever probably wasn't dead, but where was he, then?

Mixin had messaged him again today, but he still wasn't answering, which could mean he was unconscious, or off-world, or someone had stolen his handheld—or could just be his frustratingly normal self. The only reason Mix hadn't raised a semi-public alarm on the feeds was the possibility that Ever had needed to disappear for some reason, and hiding was keeping himself safe. As one of the more vulnerable Losts, he wouldn't want too much attention called to him.

But even if he didn't want to be found, he couldn't object to his friends making sure he was okay. Where hadn't Mix looked yet?

Jainey was cleaning the windows—which wasn't on the schedule until next week, that's how slow it was—so Mix was supposed to watch the counter. They tried putting on music, a local Human-Kovari synth jazz group, but it didn't help. Fritter hopped up on the counter and demanded pets, which at least was a job to do.

Libbi appeared out of the office. "Sasha Starborne wants to change our meeting *again*."

"Seriously? What a pain."

"I'm starting to think my ancestors are disappointed in me. Or maybe the whole universe is against me."

Libbi started to walk away, then wheeled back, hands on hips.

"You know, Kay is much better at all this promotional stuff than I am. If she really wants to help, you'd think she could help with that."

Mixin didn't suggest the obvious, that Libbi could *ask* for help. When Libbi was in this mood, all Mixin could do was listen and sympathize, and otherwise let her stew. She needed to climb partway out of the funk on her own before Mix could make suggestions. To Libbi's credit, it rarely took her this long.

Mix nudged Fritter in Libbi's direction, wishing their gift included talking to cats. By some miracle, Fritter took the hint, or maybe she just thought Libbi gave better scritches. She rubbed up against Libbi's ankles, and with a fond sigh, Libbi picked the cat up and hugged her, carrying her back to the office. Mixin went back to brainstorming more places to look for Ever.

BY LUNCHTIME, CUSTOMERS HAD picked up: not a flood, but enough that Libbi felt like she should leave the office and help Mixin and Jainey work the floor.

Interacting with the customers was weirdly soothing to her, maybe because it was so familiar. Each had their needs—for power cells and spare parts and minor appliances—and their wants—a specific craving for a taste of home, or a vaguer wish for decorations to liven up their cabin. Libbi casually mentioned a sale on snack foods to the first, and called the attention of the second to the small display of local artwork at the front of the store. All offhandedly, as if she told these things to everyone, not as if she felt their wishes burning in her own gut.

It was a good distraction from stressing about her siblings, even if she felt bad about neglecting her real work.

Real work? Since when was helping customers not real? But even today, the rare day too busy for their current skeleton staff to handle, would be dead by their old standards. They couldn't hire more people until days like this became the norm, not the exception.

And that wouldn't happen unless she made progress in marketing the store. She'd finally, *finally* gotten Sasha Starborne to commit to a meeting time, and she needed to prep. She couldn't afford to blow that opportunity.

The store briefly emptied out, and she headed back toward her office, when she was caught off-guard by a sudden sense of something missing. No, some*one* missing. She needed to find Mixin, her friend was in trouble…but no, Mixin was right there at the counter with Jainey. This was Libbi's gift acting up. She looked around for the source.

A Lost-aged woman came in carrying a child on her hip, and slumped with relief as she spotted Libbi.

"Mx. Wilder. I was hoping you'd be here."

"Call me Libbi. Sorry, I don't know your name."

"Phoenix Techman." Another classic Lost Generation name. In Libbi's small school class, she'd known two other Phoenixes, three Hopes, and a Precious. And all of those were better than Liberation.

Phoenix held out her free hand to shake. The kid reached out for Libbi's fingers, and she let him grab on before shifting to give him a gentle handshake.

"Hello!" Libbi told him.

"Say hi, Reader," the woman prompted, but he buried his face in her shoulder.

"What a cutie."

"He's not mine. His parent…" She trailed off, obviously distressed, and Libbi dragged her attention away from the baby.

"What's wrong, Phoenix?"

"I saw your post on one of the Lost group feeds, asking if anyone's had run-ins with that weird scientist guy, and, well, my friend Hannith Tan is missing."

Yeah, that fit the sense of urgency Libbi's gift was forcing on her: a shock of cold, shapeless desperation to *do something*. Her work forgotten—Libbi could no more ignore this than Phoenix could—she waved the other woman to a quiet corner and poured her some chai. Mixin and Jainey kept their distance, seeming to give them privacy, but Mix was clearly watching the whole conversation.

"What happened?"

"So, he approached us a few days ago. Pretty rude about it. I saw no reason to help him out. Hannith was quiet, though, and they said later, as long as we're careful about what we tell him, why not take the off-worlder's money?"

"That's the big question, isn't it," Libbi muttered.

"I thought I talked them out of it, but yesterday, Hannith was stressing. They were already behind on rent, and then out of nowhere their handheld died—they're a designer, and they can't finish their freelance jobs without a computer. I mean, Hannith's always kind of stressed about money, like who isn't?" Phoenix hesitated, and Libbi felt a stab of discomfort. Her family wasn't rich, but even in their current strained situation, they'd never had worries like that. "Anyway, I think Hannith went to see Spark."

"You're not sure?"

"I doubt they would have told me, since I would've argued with them. I mean, Founders' names, they could have borrowed my old handheld. So I don't know when they did it, or even if they did. But they asked me to pick up this one from daycare." She bounced the little boy on her hip, and her voice rose with false cheerfulness. "We had a little unplanned sleepover, didn't we, Reader?"

"Moppa?" he said, craning his neck to look around.

"No, sweetie, your moppa's not here right now." She lowered her voice. "We were supposed to meet yesterday evening, and Hannith didn't show. They're not at home, and with their handheld dead, I can't reach them."

"Damn it," Libbi muttered. She didn't have time for this, but… "That's two, now. If that *is* what's happening here."

Maybe Hannith was missing for reasons unrelated to Dr. Spark. Libbi wanted so, so badly to believe that this was all coincidence (and incidentally, that her siblings were *wrong* and overreacting). Worrying about the store was enough stress for her, thanks. But it was hard to convince herself when her gut screamed otherwise.

"Who else?"

"Do you know Ever Wright?"

"He's that blond guy? The one who, uh, feels things?" Hannith said. That was a mild way to describe Ever's curse of a gift. "Yeah, I usually see him around, but not recently."

"He's been gone a few days," Libbi said. "My friends and I can't find him."

"Crap," Phoenix said. "I tried going to Public Safety, but the officer at the neighborhood outpost brushed me off. Fact is, they don't care. Hannith doesn't matter. Neither does Ever."

"That's bullshit. The Losts matter as much as anyone else."

"Maybe if you have a Founder's name, but not people like Hannith. Not Losts without a powerful family to lean on. Not to Public Safety."

"That's not how it works," Libbi protested, knowing as she said it how entitled she sounded. "Safety's there for everyone. It doesn't matter who your ancestors were."

"Shouldn't, maybe." Phoenix shrugged. "But it does. *You* wouldn't notice, would you? No one notices when doors open automatically for them. Only when they stick shut."

A righteous indignation filled Libbi. *That's not true,* she wanted to argue, but a whisper in the back of her mind said, *absolutely it's not* right, *but you know there's truth in it.*

Brennex existed because of the Founders: their courage, their sweat, their sacrifices. They'd come here fleeing war and poverty and clawed a safe haven out of bare lifeless rock. With nonexistent resources, they'd survived, raised families, and eventually prospered to the extent that other families came to settle here, growing Brennex from a single precarious dome to a thriving city. Worried about being swept away by newcomers and outside influences, the Founders' descendants held onto the biggest share of power and wealth, in the name of maintaining the place their families had built.

She was proud of her Founder ancestors, her heritage, but not so proud of what some people did with that heritage.

That was politics, though. That shouldn't mean other families mattered less than Libbi and her kin, not when it came to safety, or social services, or rights. *Shouldn't.* But Libbi, growing up as a Lost, had made more than a few non-founding family friends, so she'd seen that prejudice in action. And when it came to Losts, who had more needs than most, that prejudice only doubled.

Phoenix shook her head as if arguing with herself. "I shouldn't have come here. Sorry to bother you." She turned to go.

"Wait!"

Phoenix had come to Libbi for help, and if all she could offer was her family name, she had to try.

"I'll help if I can," she said. "My shift ends in an hour…"

"Just go, Libs," Mixin called from the counter. "Jainey and I can handle things here."

"You're sure?" Libbi shot Jainey a questioning look.

"We'll be just fine," Jainey assured her.

"You're going to ask them about Ever, too, right?" Mixin said.

"Of course." And maybe, just maybe, Public Safety could solve this mess before Kay and Jasper arrived. And before Ever or Hannith got hurt, of course.

"Then go. Tell me what you find out."

Libbi turned back to Phoenix. "Well, then. Let's see if together we can raise a fuss."

5

OFFICER STONE WAS THE Public Safety officer in charge of missing persons. An older man, probably a decade older than Libbi's parents. Libbi had hoped that by coming all the way out to Public Safety's headquarters in the spaceport district, they'd get taken more seriously than the office in their dome where Phoenix had gotten her condescending brush-off. But Stone, seeing his visitors or perhaps noting their apparent age, settled into a scowl that might have been part of his uniform.

"Hi, Officer. I'm Libbi Wilder—" that name made his brows twitch upward "—and this is Phoenix. A couple of our friends have gone missing recently, and we think they both talked to the same off-worlder before they disappeared…"

Stone flipped his headset on and leaned forward. "I'm taking notes while you talk. Permission to record you?"

"Granted." At least he was listening, even if he seemed unconcerned.

"Tell me from the start."

So Libbi walked through her part of the story, telling him what she suspected about Ever while Phoenix stood aside and kept little Reader occupied with a doll. Then they swapped, and Libbi distracted the baby while Phoenix told Hannith's story. The officer asked clarifying questions that were reasonable but didn't bode well, like: "Do you know this, or suspect it?" and "Has he ever disappeared for multiple days before?" and "Did they tell you this themself?"

At the end, he leaned his elbows on the desk and sighed.

"Mx. Wilder, you seem like a caring friend. But you're telling me that Mx. Wright has a history of periodic disappearances and was well when you saw him last. And Mx. Techman, you're worried because Mx. Tan, whose handheld is broken, hasn't answered messages."

"And they missed our meet-up," said Phoenix, hoisting the baby to emphasize her point.

"Almost as if they couldn't access their calendar," said Officer Stone, and Libbi pressed her lips together. Sarcasm. Great.

"They'd never forget about their kid," Phoenix protested.

But Officer Stone went on as if she hadn't spoken. "I've just checked, and neither of them have recent activity in our system. That means they aren't incarcerated, and haven't come to Public Safety for help. I'll put in a request to mental health services to see if they've checked in there. But if they are, their status will be confidential to all but family, unless they choose to contact you."

"This researcher, I got a really bad sense from him," Libbi pushed. "He wants something from me, from *us*, but it's not what he says."

"Your intuition isn't valid grounds to start investigating an authorized visitor," Stone said flatly, like he'd had this debate before.

Her gift was *not* intuition, but if he didn't take the Losts' gifts seriously, she couldn't change his mind on that point. So she seized on another. "Was he? Authorized?"

"Everyone who travels outside the port area has to be authorized."

"But can you check on him specifically? What reason he gave for his visit, where he comes from?"

"Not without grounds, I can't. I would think you, Mx. Wilder, would understand that our economy depends on making off-worlders feel welcome here, which among other things means not interrogating them without a good reason. What do you think would happen if we started randomly questioning travelers?"

"Of course we can't do that." Trade was Brennex's lifeblood. They literally could not sustain themselves without the constant flow of people and goods through the Long Lane. "But this particular traveler…"

"Why would he be kidnapping people? What's his motive? Where's your evidence? You're not even certain that *either* of your friends actually spoke to him."

Libbi took a deep breath. Nothing he'd said was technically wrong. Ma and Pa had always said that Public Safety's philosophy shifted with the economy, whether they saw their job as keeping Brennexians safe from off-worlders or keeping off-worlders safe from Brennexians. When she was a kid, Public Safety would have turned a visiting ship inside-out if they thought it posed a danger to their community's precious few children. But now that the Lost Generation were grown up, they were on their own.

"I'll tell you what I think," Stone said, leaning back lazily in his chair. "A couple so-called Gifteds come by a windfall of money from this research survey? I'll bet they took the first passenger ship out of here."

"Are you serious right now?" Phoenix exploded. "No. Hannith wouldn't do that."

Hearing his parent's name, Reader exclaimed "Want Moppa!" and burst into sobs.

Officer Stone frowned at the noise. "You really think your friend wouldn't take an opportunity to escape their problems? Go someplace they think is better?"

"*Not* without talking to me. And not without their family."

"And Ever wouldn't get on a crowded ship. His gift would make him miserable," said Libbi.

Stone shrugged. "You know your friends. But I know people, and I know the law. All right, I'll open files on your friends and circulate their images, and if there's news, I'll contact you. But unless someone turns up hard *evidence* this off-worlder hurt them, there's nothing I can do about him."

MIXIN HAD JUST GOTTEN home from their shift, leaving Jainey with Uncle Jackson until closing, when the door rang. Words in Libbi's familiar style floated through the wall: "Hey, Mix, it's me."

They hurried to let her in. "How did it go? Are they investigating? Any leads?"

"No. The officer in charge is useless." Libbi flopped onto the couch. "He says maybe Ever and Hannith checked themselves in for mental health support, or maybe they fled the planet."

"Is he not going to do anything?"

"He said he'll investigate, but I don't have much confidence." Libbi huffed in frustration. "Remember when

Public Safety would come to our school and do presentations on how to not reveal our gifts to strangers? They said we should go to them if we ever need help. What changed?"

"We're not adorable kids anymore. We're adults who need therapy and medical support and disability accommodations. Not to mention everyone thought we were nightmares as teenagers."

"Yeah, I know." Libbi seemed to fold in on herself, like a deflating balloon, and collapsed beside Mixin on the couch. "I hate feeling helpless. Almost as much as I hate that my siblings might be right about Spark."

Mixin sat forward. "So let's not be helpless! If we find Ever, maybe we can learn what Spark's doing. Or even stop him! Then, when Kay and Jasper show up, you can tell them you've got it all figured out."

"You think? We're not Public Safety, or detectives…"

Mixin gave her their best disappointed look. "Libs, you seriously underestimate how many mystery serials I've watched."

That made Libbi chuckle. Good.

"You said you've been looking for him already?" she asked.

"Yup, and I've got a few more ideas of places to check. Let's start with the least unpleasant?"

They hopped on public bikes and rode three domes over. Mixin filled Libbi in on the places they'd checked so far, which Libbi admitted seemed pretty thorough.

It was a game night at the stadium, and crowds wearing their team colors poured through the tunnels and the streets until Libbi and Mixin had to leave their bikes and keep going on foot. Looked like the Bolts and the Stardogs were playing tonight, a game Mixin ordinarily might have bought tickets for. Mixin's moms used to take them and Libbi as little kids, and these days Mixin would go with Libbi, Sujay and Hope, Dashiell and Sage, and occasionally even Ever on the discount days for locals. Crowds could be torture for most Losts, but with the right gifts, a crowd united by excitement and support for their team could be a beautiful thing.

Not tonight, though. With Libbi following, Mixin worked their way through the flow of people to reach the tunnel where they suspected Jinx would be working.

They'd guessed right.

"Mixin Li-Khana. And my, my, it's Libbi Wilder. You two lost? Or is there something I can offer you?" Jinx gestured meaningfully with a steel-sided case, the size of a kid's lunchbox.

"Yeah, but no, not that." Mixin cursed themself for getting frazzled by him. Jinx had the misfortune of looking super young, even though he was Mix's age, and made up for it with sharp words and a constant smirk. With the help of his gift, he'd turned unnerving people into an art.

The two broad-shouldered goons hanging around him helped, too.

Libbi took a step back, glancing around for any of Jinx's customers. Maybe Mix shouldn't have brought her; being around addictive behavior was a bad combination with Libbi's gift. She'd be fine for a short conversation, though.

His eyes narrowed. "No, you're not going to buy any of my fine goods, are you." It wasn't a question. "I understand why Libbi won't partake, but you could really stand to loosen up, Mixin. What do you want, then?"

"We're looking for Ever. Have you seen him?"

"I don't report on my customers."

"Come on, Jinx, I'm not asking for your receipts. I need to know if he's been around."

"Why?"

"Because I need to talk to him."

"Again, why?"

Mixin glanced at Libbi, who frowned, clearly sharing Mix's doubts about how much to say.

"It's important," Libbi said.

"If you won't be honest with me, why should I be honest with you?" Jinx said.

Despite having known Jinx their whole life, Mixin didn't really know him at all, and they weren't sure how far they could trust him. Getting high was Ever's favorite self-medication, but did Jinx see him as a friend, or just another customer?

Mix shook their head in frustration. "Fine, don't tell us. But if you see him, will you ask him to message me?" Despite themself, they added, "I'm worried about him. Don't tell him that, though."

As they turned away, Jinx said, "Mixin? He's due to resupply in the next few days. I'll tell him you asked."

Libbi fell in beside Mixin as they headed away down the tunnel.

"Well, that was better than nothing, but not actually reassuring," she said. "Where next?"

The crowds had thinned out some. From the all-caps of the announcer's voice hovering in the corner of Mix's vision, the game was about to start.

"Or we could put off the next one. Want to catch the game instead? We could sneak into the cheap seats like we used to. Or buy an actual ticket—we're grown-ups with jobs, after all."

"Mix?" Libbi raised her brows. "What's next on your list, and why don't you want to go?"

It was so tempting to stay and watch. To listen in on the mundane, non-life-threatening drama of the fans around them… Okay, maybe Mixin understood why Libbi had been trying so hard to pretend nothing was wrong.

But no. Ever needed help; Mix was more and more sure of it. This wasn't paranoia or some misguided wish for excitement. Something was wrong.

"Because it's going to suck. And because it's my last idea that doesn't involve going to see Spark."

"Going to… We can't. That's too dangerous. Especially if we're pretty sure he disappeared Ever and Hannith."

If Mixin was right, they'd have to risk it eventually. But. "Exactly why that should be our last resort. This is, let's say, our penultimate resort."

Libbi's jaw tightened, and she nodded. "Whatever it is, we'll do it together."

SO THEY GOT ON a tram, this time to one of the outer domes. The dome-light was dimming by the time they arrived, but not enough to hide how run-down the neighborhood was. White walls scuffed gray by daily wear, and in the places where someone had tried to brighten things up with some color, most of it was faded. They passed three pairs of Public Safety officers out patrolling, clearly not looking for missing people, just warning off loiterers and drunks.

The door was nondescript, like a dozen others on the street, and Mixin checked the street address twice before ringing. Their gift showed them a grumbled "Who the hell is that?" from inside, but minutes passed, and no one came to the door. Mixin rang again.

More grumbling. Then the door opened. "Yeah?"

Ever's pa looked just like him, if you took Ever and ran him through the laundry on hot a few too many times. Pale and pinch-faced, he frowned down suspiciously at Mixin, who pressed sideways, closer to Libbi. They'd thought about making Libbi do the talking, but this was Mix's own terrible idea, and they should take responsibility.

"Hi!" Mixin said with a high-pitched false cheeriness. "We're looking for Ever. We were wondering if you've seen him?"

"He's not here," Mx. Wright said. Mixin knew *that* without asking. "What's that little stinker done now?"

Mixin dropped their cheerful act with relief. They'd never met Ever's family, but they'd heard plenty, and let their opinion show in their face. "Hasn't done anything. We're his friends, and wondered if he's been by."

"Nope, and good riddance. Don't need him hanging around, acting all wounded and precious while he spies on me."

"Hey," said Libbi, indignant. "We're just looking out for Ever. Your son."

His eyes narrowed. "*You'd* better not be using your gifts on me, either."

"Of course not." Mixin put a restraining hand on Libbi's shoulder. "And we'll leave as soon as you answer a couple questions. When's the last time—"

The door swung shut in their face.

"You clump of wet rat shit," Mixin told the closed door, but it didn't make them feel better. They turned around and slumped on the front steps, folding their knees to their chest.

"Well, it was a long shot, but worth a try," Libbi said, sitting beside them.

"Spark has him. Has to. I've looked everywhere else I can possibly think of."

Libbi gave them a knowing look. "You want to go there, don't you?"

"What else can we do? Public Safety won't help."

"They said they'd try."

"And you said you didn't believe them."

Libbi bit her lip. "I don't know. I need to think about this. There's got to be a better way."

"Let me know if you think of one. But we have to do something."

"I know."

It was too late to do any more tonight, though, and besides, Mixin needed time to talk Libbi into coming with them. Because even Mixin wasn't reckless enough to confront Dr. Derek Spark alone.

6

HAVOC HAD NEVER TRAVELED off his birth planet until a year ago, when he'd met Mason and shortly thereafter had been forced to flee Ravel. Since then, he had visited many places, from huge spaceports like Terna Station to the glossy urbanized world of Altir, to their most recent assignment at Silver Ring, a rough mining colony. Brennex struck him as small and chaotic: people and ships alike jostling for space, with passenger ships and pleasure yachts docked between long-haul cargo transports. The smell of fried foods flooded the air, and everywhere he looked, people were trying to sell them things.

It was unlike a Ravel city in every way: gritty instead of pristine; decorations clashing; ads fighting for attention instead of harmoniously branded; people of many species chattering in a jumble of languages. In principle, Havoc loved it, but the reality of it overwhelmed him. Mason pointed out landmarks—the government building called Council Hall, the Founders' Hall museum—but it all blurred together to Havoc. The domes didn't help the sense of disorderly crowding. The artificial yellow-gray light gave no sense of an actual sky, but instead seemed to press down over the crowd.

Fortunately, the streets calmed farther from the spaceport. Havoc and the others descended into a tunnel, lined with stalls and vendors mostly selling street food and souvenirs, and when they emerged again into artificial daylight—it was late afternoon, local time—they entered another dome which felt like another world.

"This is the oldest dome, where our ancestors first settled," Mason explained. "Home isn't far from here."

This, Havoc decided, made a better way to judge a place's personality: not by its busy commercial zones, but by the places where people lived.

Live music spilled out of brightly decorated tea shops and restaurants while children played between the tables. He saw a family of Majrin, and more Kovars than he'd seen since leaving the Kovari neighborhood on Artesia where he grew up. More people greeted each other on the streets than in *any* city he'd visited.

The greenery was limited to potted flowers and shrubs—he couldn't for a moment mistake this for a living biosphere—but the dome overhead felt cozier and less oppressive here where the buildings were shorter and the streets less crowded, and he could now appreciate the lighter gravity. The bold colors of the buildings helped too: bright yellows and blues, purples and oranges, unexpected but striking.

It seemed a warm, cheerful place, far more at ease with

itself than cities within Ravel. More messy and real and lived-in. He could see why Mason felt so fond of it.

"This architecture is…unique," said Sunny, operating through their drone, cameras whirring as they tried to take in the whole scene.

Havoc had sensed that too, but hadn't paid attention until Sunny pointed it out. No two buildings were alike, and now that he looked closer, it seemed that many of them were built of modules, pieces bolted together like a child's building blocks. Old shipping containers? Most were rectangular, but he spotted some peaked roofs and bump-out windows, even a tiered tower like a castle.

"Classic Brennexian," Kay said with a smile. "I don't think they teach it in architecture school, but maybe they should! When the Founders landed here, they didn't have wealth or resources, so everything had to be reused or repurposed, from clothing to building materials. The aesthetic stuck."

"It's charming," Sunny said, and Havoc agreed.

Kay and Mason drifted ahead, pointing out favorite places and things that had changed since their last visit. Sunny's drone gave a warning chirp and hopped from Kay's shoulder over to Havoc. He held out an arm, and it grabbed on with just the right amount of force to catch itself.

"Does all of this fascinate you as it does me?" he asked Sunny, voice low. "I feel I'm peeking through a window into Mason's past."

"Interesting. I suppose so, though I expect Kay's childhood home and family will be more enlightening."

"I believe that." Havoc felt again the queasy weight of expectation. "Do you feel nervous to meet them?"

"Despite Kay's assurances, yes, I do. Though I still get anxious with every new person I meet."

"Well, I feel anxious too."

The drone emitted a tone that Havoc associated with appreciation—solidarity, perhaps. They could debate who was about to have the stranger experience, but he felt relief not to be alone in this.

MASON AND KAY'S FAMILY home took up the whole second floor above their store. To reach it, they passed through the shop doors under the bold, bright sign reading Wilder Supply. Mason waved at the worker behind the counter, a younger-looking person he greeted as Mixin. Havoc got an impression of a maze of shelves in cheerful disarray, like a miniaturized version of Brennex itself, before Mason led the way upstairs. With Sunny perched on his shoulder, Havoc trailed behind the two siblings, bracing as if for an ambush.

"You're here! Oh, my darlings, welcome home!"

"Missed you Ma, Pa…"

"It's so, so good to see you. All of us together in one place!"

"And so close to Founders' Day. You'll be staying through the holiday, won't you?"

The four Humans tangled each other in hugs like a team of Kovars celebrating a victory. For all the reluctance they'd expressed about visiting, both Kay and Mason showed undeniable joy at seeing their parents. This was *not*, Havoc thought, like the fondness he still felt for the crèche-teachers who'd raised him. This was something else.

At last, Mason stepped back and held out an arm, beckoning Havoc forward. "And this is my eshrim, Sowing of Small Havoc."

"Go easy on him," Kay muttered.

Havoc watched the parents' faces. Both of them blinked at the word *eshrim*, surprised or perhaps confused about what it meant. When he and Mason introduced themselves to Humans as such, some took the Kovari word to mean the same thing as *spouse,* others as closer to *boyfriend.* Among Kovars, an *eshrim,* a team-of-two, didn't have to be romantic, though his feelings for Mason did include that. He wondered what Mason had told them about him.

Then the parents swept him into a hug as well, though briefer than the ones they'd given their children. Mason's mother—who Mason quite resembled in his black hair and eyes that missed nothing—took Havoc by the shoulders and looked him over. Evaluating him? For what?

"Welcome, Sowing of Small Havoc! We're so glad to *finally* meet you."

"*Ma.*" Mason sounded aggrieved for some reason.

"A handsome one, too," she added, unperturbed.

"It's about time!" Mason's father said. "Consider yourself complimented, Havoc. It's been a good while since Jasper liked someone enough to bring them home."

"Oh, I do feel honored," Havoc said, amused. Mason's face had turned bright red.

Then a thought nipped at Havoc: if not for this potential crisis, how long before Mason would have brought him here? The parents were clearly unaware of the full circumstances of the visit; Mason and Kay had opted not to tell them, which Havoc found strange indeed. What sort of team kept secrets like this?

"Put down your luggage," Mason's mother urged. "Just drop it anywhere. We'll get you settled soon, but you must want some tea and rest after your trip."

"We just came from the spaceport, Ma, not exactly traveling rough," Kay said. "My ship is my ho—I mean, it's like a second home. I live there full-time, you know." There was a tension in her that Havoc had rarely seen. "Speaking of which…"

She tried to gesture at Sunny's bot, still riding on Havoc's shoulder, as her mother ushered them further inside.

"Is that an assistive bot?" asked a young woman who was hanging back from the group, arms folded. "Airborne, too. That's a nicer model than we sell in the shop, though ours are for simple maintenance."

Her curly hair floated loose, and she wore a flowing skirt of patchwork fabrics. It took Havoc a moment to recognize her—Mason's youngest sister didn't resemble him much, and she'd been younger in the pictures Mason had shown him. Unlike the parents, she did not show joy to see them.

Surprised by her manner, Havoc was slow to realize she was talking about Sunny.

"No! This one belongs to—" he began, just as Kay said, "I was trying to tell you…"

"I am not a bot!" said Sunny through the drone, startling the Wilders into quiet. "Hello. My name is Sunny."

Into the confused gap, Kay said, "I'd like you to meet my business partner…and my friend."

"Your friend is a bot?" Libbi asked doubtfully. "Or they interact through a bot? Why?"

Kay's smile stretched taut with worry. The drone flew to Kay's shoulder, and she stroked the metal skin like a cat. "I need you all to promise to keep a secret, as carefully as you've ever kept mine and Jasper's and Libbi's. Because Sunny's safety depends on your discretion, just as much as ours. Will you?"

"For a friend of yours, Kavita, of course we will," the father said.

"You good?" Kay said softly to Sunny, who chirped an

affirmative. "Then let's go sit and have that cup of chai, and Sunny and I will explain."

SUNNY FELT RELIEF, AND with it, deep exhaustion. Dinner had been a multi-course feast apparently including all of Kay and Jasper's favorites: fritters with curry; soupy dumplings; a quiche stuffed with home-grown peppers, greens, and herbs; almond cookies; cakes with fresh strawberries; and a bottomless pot of chai. For three hours, they'd sat and eaten and talked, alternating between polite (if awkward) questions for Sunny and embarrassing questions for Havoc, who Sunny felt a keen sympathy for.

It had gone much better than Sunny had feared. Kay's parents were clearly striving to make Sunny feel welcome, and Sunny appreciated their efforts, even if they sometimes got it wrong. Kay had rolled her eyes when her Pa had offered the drone tea, but Sunny thought it was sweet. Ma had added a chair at the table for them, but the drone body was too short for the seat, so Sunny had perched on the chair back, retreating to Kay's lap or shoulder when they felt anxious.

So it was a pleasant exhaustion, but exhaustion nonetheless. They looked forward to the privacy of Kay's bedroom. However, Kay first had to honor her ancestors, and Sunny, curious about this side of their organic friend, opted to stay with her.

The family shrine sat in an alcove off the living room, the size of a closet but meticulously clean. Kay knelt on the mat before a tall cabinet, hand-carved by some long-ago relative and freshly painted red, yellow, and gold. At a gesture, small lamps glowed softly to life, and the digital frames awoke to show photos that Sunny recognized as Kay's Founder ancestors and their families. Kay had told Sunny a little about them, much as she had talked about her parents. There was Marta and Min Wilder and their children: the businesswoman and the teacher, who Kay sometimes spoke to in her cabin when she was distressed. Amarjeet Singh, the engineer who gave Jasper part of his pseudonym. Ash Narayan, one of the originators of the Council and drafter of Brennex's rules of law. And more, smaller photos, Kay's deceased grandparents and great-grandparents, the whole family line back to the Founding.

Kay unwrapped an almond cookie she'd taken from dinner and set it on the offering tray, where someone else had left a cluster of fresh-looking jasmine blooms and African violets. She murmured quietly, as if the dead could hear her; Sunny couldn't hear most of it, but caught words of gratitude, and an apology for neglecting to honor them enough. She fell silent, and Sunny thought she might be done.

Then she whispered, fervently, "Oh, Ancestors, I feel so lost."

"Kay?" Sunny asked, unable to stop themself.

"I'm fine, I'll be fine." She bent her head again. "Sorry, Ancestors, I shouldn't be begging for help when I've done so little lately to earn your goodwill." There was a wryness to that, and a familiarity. "But please, keep watching over my family. They need it right now, maybe more than they know."

She sat in reflection for a few more minutes before, with a sigh of weary contentment, she rose.

"Thanks for waiting for me, Sunny. I needed to do that."

"And this fulfills your responsibility to your ancestors?"

Sunny found the entire concept of spirituality somewhat bizarre, and Kay's Brennexian faith strange but fascinating. They weren't sure whether Kay literally believed her ancestors listened to her, or whether it was an appealing fiction. Regardless, it seemed to give Kay comfort, and she was noticeably less tense now. That seemed value enough.

"It's a start. I've got a lot of catching up to do." She started down the hallway, and Sunny's drone followed. "I wouldn't be here right now to kneel at the shrine if not for the fear that, you know. That there's trouble."

She meant the fear that Ravel was secretly operating on Brennex, Sunny knew. Kay seemed certain of this despite the thin evidence, and believed it was her own fault, a result of mistakes she'd made in Unity System. Sunny wasn't so sure, but knew Kay wouldn't stop feeling guilty until they discovered the truth.

"How about you?" Kay asked, changing the subject. "You feeling okay about all this?"

"I like your family. I don't entirely understand them, but I appreciate their attempts to make me feel included."

Kay smiled. "They're trying. We'll all figure it out as we go."

Kay's bedroom was spacious compared to her cabin aboard Sunny, and cozy. Her narrow bed was covered in a brightly colored quilt, and the walls showed off local art and posters for Kovari interstellar pocketball teams. The floor was plushly carpeted.

"It's so weird," Kay said, shaking her head. "They haven't changed anything in here since I was eighteen. How's the drone working out?"

Sunny settled the drone onto the bed, closing the cameras except the one facing Kay. "It is an adjustment. But far preferable to not having it."

"Good."

In fact, operating through the drone was as tiring as interacting with new people. Every action took thought and intention; nothing was instinctive. Decisions like where to position themself, physically, in a room were not things Sunny normally had to worry about. And the drone had a different set of sensory apparatus, literally a different way of seeing the world, than Sunny's own body. But it would grow easier with practice, Sunny was sure. Just as interacting with people like Kay, Jasper, and Havoc had grown comfortable.

"I do wish it had been possible to warn them about me," Sunny said.

"You say that like you're a burden. You're not."

"That isn't what I meant. They seem to accept what I am—and I trust them to protect my secret, I'm not worried about that anymore—but it did seem to come as a shock. Understandably so! I represent something outside their experience. Yet it wasn't…comfortable, to explain and watch them processing."

"I'm sorry about that. I should have told them something, even if we didn't want to put the whole story into a message." Kay reached out to pet the drone, which Sunny found comforting even though they couldn't feel it as physical sensation. "We're learning, both of us."

Sunny hummed. "Indeed."

"Well, I'm wiped out too. I love my family, but it's been a while since I've had this many people having emotions at me."

"Is it…loud?" Sunny didn't fully understand how Kay's gift for hearing emotions felt—or sounded—to her.

"More like discordant. My parents are all the trumpeting love and violin chords of nostalgia, which clashes with the drumbeat of Havoc's nervousness and Jasper's stress. Not to mention Libbi! She's got a whole different clamor. I hear resentment there. And she's worried about something."

"Your sister did seem withdrawn…"

Kay's head jerked up, though Sunny hadn't heard anything. She muttered, "Maybe I won't have to corner her to ask about it."

A moment later someone knocked on the door. She called for them to come in, and seemed unsurprised that it was Libbi.

LIBBI BRACED HERSELF IN the doorway, frowning into her sister's room. A room that hadn't changed a bit since Kay'd been gone, more fixed in place than the family shrine.

"Hey, sis. What's up?" Kay said.

"We need to talk."

"You're right. Jasper should be here for this, too." Kay reached behind her and knocked on the wall above her bed, the wall shared with Jasper's room.

"He doesn't—oh, fine." Libbi let out a sigh. "Why'd you bring him into this, Kay?"

Kay blinked, genuinely confused. "Because he's our brother? Not to mention a seriously badass activist with the experience to figure out what's going on here. And what *is* going on here? You haven't updated us since I told you we're coming."

"Because you didn't need to come!" Libbi's voice rose, but she got control of herself again. "I told you. Everything's fine."

"Oh, yeah?" Kay's gaze shifted to Jasper, who'd come up behind Libbi. The two of them exchanged a look, and Libbi wondered what Jasper saw in the bonds between the three of them right now, what sort of cacophony Kay heard in her emotions. Her sibs might not respect her, but they could certainly tell everything wasn't fine.

Jasper eased the door shut and sat on the bed beside Kay. "Humor us, and tell us what happened?"

"Practically nothing." But Jasper gave her a look that would have done Ma proud, and Libbi sighed. "This guy showed up at the store, tried to get me and Mix to take part in some sort of survey or study. He got pissy when we said no, but he didn't make any trouble."

"Which was it? A survey or a study? And did he say what he's supposedly studying?" Jasper demanded.

"Something about the effects of living on domed planets."

"You told me that he mentioned me by name," Kay said. "Why?"

"If I knew that, I wouldn't have asked you about it," Libbi muttered. Her gift was quiet today, but even so, she could tell they were getting impatient with her evasiveness. "I thought maybe he knew you, but more likely he just pulled our names from public records. Why you and not Jasper, I've got no clue."

Jasper said, "So you and Mixin turned him down. Has he been talking to other people?"

Libbi hesitated. She should tell them about Ever and Hannith, should share everything she'd learned. She *should.* But if she did, they'd go into full save-the-day mode, and Libbi wouldn't see them until they came back to explain the whole thing, like detectives at the end of a murder mystery. They'd rescue the missing people and foil Spark's evil plot while Libbi stayed home to mind the store. Just like always.

So instead, she said: "What other people do is their own business, right?"

"Libbi…"

"I haven't talked to anyone who's taken his offer." Technically true, since she hadn't seen them to talk to. She ignored the twist in her gut. "Why? You hoping to get in on it? I didn't think you two were that hard up for money."

Kay and Jasper exchanged another of their meaningful

looks, and Libbi flushed. This was a *great* way to show her sibs she was grown up now.

Why did Kay and Jasper always bring out the worst in her? She loved them, certainly. But their visits always made her feel like the baby of the family. Worse, they made her act like it, too. When they were around, she seemed to devolve into the sulky twelve-year-old she'd been when they'd left home.

Jasper leaned forward, all earnestness and trust-me warmth. "Yeah, so we're worried. I don't like that someone was poking around asking about you and Kay. Or any of the Losts, for that matter. We've kept each other safe for a long time, but that doesn't mean we're invulnerable, or that we can let our guards down."

"You think I don't know that?"

"I think it's honestly astonishing that we've kept a secret this huge for this long, and we can't afford to get complacent."

"Nobody knows about the gifts, Jasper. Ma and Pa made a good point: people used to try to study us when we were kids, but we're not interesting now that we're grown up. No off-worlders have tried to study Brennex in years. Anyway, this sounds more like some psychological study."

"So he said," Kay murmured. Something in her tone was strained in a way Libbi had never heard before. "From what you say, no one really knows details about this guy or his work."

"So that's where we'll start," Jasper said. "Investigate our mystery researcher, find out his real name—because I sincerely doubt it's Derek Spark—and what he's actually studying. If it turns out to be nothing, well, at least we've done our obligatory trip home for the year."

"No," Libbi said sharply.

Kay raised her brows. "No?"

"You don't need to do that. I didn't ask you to get involved at all, didn't ask you to leave your busy, important lives—"

"We don't mind…" Jasper began.

"Of course you don't. But I don't want you to, okay? Just…do your family visit. Show off your boyfriend, Jasper, and maybe try being useful to Ma and Pa, if you want to do some good."

Before they could patronize her more, Libbi marched out. The door banged shut behind her but didn't latch, instead slowly swinging wide again, ruining her dramatic exit and letting her hear Kay's low exclamation of "What the fuck?"

"I guess it's going to be one of those trips," Jasper said. Then the door closed firmly, and their voices got muffled.

Well, if they were going to treat her like a bratty little kid, she might as well get the benefits of acting like one. She pulled out her handheld. *Hey, Mix. Come upstairs a minute? I need you.*

SLIPPING INTO THE WILDER home proper, Mixin saw immediately why Libbi wanted them. The conversation in Kay's room was so intense that they could see it from the entry. They waved a greeting to Libbi's parents in the kitchen before scurrying down the hall.

"Am I understanding correctly that you two don't believe your sister's assurances?" Sunny was asking, the drone's voice rendered in a crisp code-like font. Sunny, the *sentient spaceship!* At least from what Mixin had overheard of the introductions. They couldn't wait for an excuse to meet Sunny properly. "And you remain concerned about potential dangers to her and other Brennexians?"

"Yeah," Kay said. "Whatever she's annoyed about, we can't sit back and ignore this."

"Agreed," Jasper said.

Mixin was so fixated on watching the words that they rounded a corner and almost collided with the boyfriend, Havoc, emerging from Jasper's room. The Kovar blinked at Mixin, startled and confused.

"Hi!" Mix squeaked. "I'm Mixin, nice to meet you, sorry gotta go!"

They dashed past Kay's room and through Libbi's door. Fritter darted in before the door shut, tangling around Mixin's ankles before hopping up on the bed. Libbi sat with her ear pressed to the wall that her room shared with Kay's. Mixin didn't speak as they pulled out their handheld and rapidly transcribed what they saw.

"Come in, eshrim, we're strategizing. Libbi's obviously not telling us everything."

"Why would your teammate withhold information?"

"Why does Libbi do anything?" Mixin didn't transcribe that part, until Libbi gave them a look and they reluctantly shared it.

There was a pause, some nonverbal exchange. Fritter bumped Mix's hands, demanding pets, and Mixin tried to nudge her toward Libbi, who could use a little unconditional feline love. But Fritter must not have liked her person's mood, because she sprang off the bed again.

Kay said, "Libbi doesn't love it when we visit home. I think she likes having Ma and Pa to herself, and we get in her way."

Libbi was silently seething, knees to her chest, her face crimson. Mixin reached out and squeezed her hand.

"I thought your family was close," said Sunny.

"We love her, and I know she loves us," Jasper said. Mixin pointed emphatically at that part of the transcript, but Libbi just glowered. "Families are complicated."

"I see," said Havoc. "Actually, no, I don't see, but I trust your word. How will we investigate this Dr. Spark?"

"It would help if we knew where he was," Kay muttered. "I was going to ask Libbi if she knows, but, well."

"I assume he has approached others, besides your sister?" Havoc said.

"Founders, I hope so," said Jasper. Another pause. "I didn't mean that like it sounds. It's just that, if he's tracked down Libbi specifically, then he's targeting our family. There's no innocent explanation for that."

Mixin frowned. Was there some reason why Jasper thought people might be targeting his family? Maybe Mix and Libbi did need her siblings' help. They didn't say as much to Libbi, though.

"And you still hope that he's playing a broader field. That this isn't what it seems."

"Right. So let's find some other contacts. Up for a little school reunion, Kay?"

"Don't see much alternative," Kay said. "Sure, I'll tag along."

"Fair enough. I'll reach out to some folks."

"Will you want me to meet these...old friends?" Havoc asked.

"Um. Only if you want to," said Jasper. "It's more important that you meet the other Cooperative folks while you're here, but Linn is off-world right now. Hopefully she'll get back soon."

"I share that hope. For now, I suggest—if Sunny agrees—that we two start investigating from another angle."

"Sounds like a plan."

The door to Kay's room clicked open, then shut again.

Mixin turned to Libbi. "Not what you wanted to hear?" they asked softly.

"It's what I expected." Libbi flopped over on the bed, still curled up and hugging her knees. "Why do they have to be like that?"

"Don't look at me." Personally, Mixin thought Libbi's brother and sister were pretty clear about what they wanted, but Mix also understood why Libbi didn't want to cooperate. "Have you considered, maybe, telling them how you feel?"

"Wouldn't work."

"But you could try?"

"You don't get it. You have no sibs." She immediately tensed, grimacing at herself. "Sorry. That was rude."

"I get that it's difficult dealing with them. But we're both lucky with our families. We talked to Ever's pa for all of thirty seconds, and it changed my perspective. I'll take caring too much over caring too little, any day."

"Sure," Libbi admitted, then grumbled, "but they could care enough to include me. Or get to know me."

"I get the sense there's more behind their concerns that they haven't shared. You didn't tell them about Ever and Hannith?"

"No. I know, I should have, but you're right: if they're not telling us the truth, why should I tell them everything?"

That wasn't what Mixin had said, but okay. "I don't want to sit on the sidelines while they play hero either—but Ever still needs help. So if you don't want to work with your siblings, what do you want to do?"

"I don't *know!*" she whined. "I want our friends safe and my sibs gone and everything back to normal. Just our regular old non-life-or-death crises, like trying to keep the five-generation family business from imploding."

More words bloomed on the wall behind Libbi's head: "Hey, Kitty-Kat. You okay?"

"It's fine. Trips home don't usually bring up *quite* so many complicated feelings."

Jasper and Kay. Mixin scooted around so they could see both the conversation and Libbi, but didn't mention it to her.

Libbi sat up, groaning. "Sorry. I'm the worst when they're around. I hate who I turn into. Thanks for putting up with me."

Mixin rolled their eyes. "It's such a hardship."

"Shut up, I'm serious."

"I'll always put up with you, Libs. But we have to do something. The way I see it, we need to go after Spark. If not with your siblings, then on our own." When Libbi frowned thoughtfully at that, Mixin added, recklessly, "If you won't, then I will."

"Not alone! Don't do that, Mixin."

"Then help me."

Jasper said, "If you want to work with Havoc and Sunny, instead of canvassing our old classmates, I understand."

"It's not that I don't want to reconnect with people," Kay said. "Just that...well...okay, maybe I don't. Seeing the whole extended family is going to be awkward enough." Kay hesitated. "I didn't like the emotions I heard from our friends here last time. Most of the people I cared about left like we did. The rest... They acted glad to see me, but underneath they were all jangling resentment."

"Oh. I didn't know. I haven't sensed that."

"That's because you're with the Cooperative. Leaving home to be an activist is cool. Leaving home just to be somewhere else is selfish."

Jasper's answer was small and soft. "Sorry, Kitty-Kat. You don't have to come."

"I do, though."

Libbi kept talking through all this, oblivious, her words floating in front of the smaller ones from the next room. She clearly needed to talk it out, and Mixin knew this conversation by heart, enough to chime in at the appropriate moments.

"I never got a real chance to know my siblings. I was too young to hang out with them when they lived at home. Kay said they'd be back to visit all the time, and I thought…maybe when I got older, we'd actually grow close. Grow to be friends. Not so much, apparently."

"It's not like they've kept up their end. It's been, what, two years since you've seen them?"

"More, for Kay."

The sister in question was talking more quietly now, her words barely readable. "It's my fault, though."

Wait. Mixin had missed something. What was Kay's fault?

"We don't know that."

"What else could it be? I let my guard down in Unity System, I took stupid risks, and now this is happening. You think that's coincidence?"

"I think it's way too soon to start blaming ourselves. But if you want to play that game, I get plenty of points for carelessness too. I put you in that situation…"

"Don't, Jasp. You're right, this isn't useful. But I still feel guilty as shit, so I'm going to do what I can. Even if that means awkward conversations with school friends." A pause, probably a sigh. "Fuck Ravel. Fuck them all."

Founders! Did Kay think she'd given away the Losts' secret? Was Spark here because of her? That gave a whole different spin to her insistence on helping. What the hell had happened?

"Mix?"

They'd gotten distracted. "Sorry. I'm listening."

"No, you're not." Libbi smiled wryly. "I said 'you're right.'"

"Well, obviously. About what?"

"We need to talk to Spark." Libbi's eyes were wide, terrified but determined. "I don't want my siblings more involved than they already are, and nobody else seems to care. So we have to fix this ourselves. The two of us. Together."

That wasn't what Mix had expected her to say, but it filled them with a fuzzy sort of warmth. Grinning, they tapped their handheld and pulled up the infocard with Spark's office address. "Yes. We'll go find him and get some answers. All we need is a plan."

7

THE NEIGHBORHOOD AROUND SPARK'S office was gray, bland, and weirdly quiet. Libbi pulled up the map display again, checking it against the intersection in front of them, while Mixin peered around like a secret agent expecting trouble.

"Spark's address is on this next block," Libbi told them. "I didn't expect to be glad that you asked for his info."

That earned her a grin. "You know me. Always thinking."

"This is going to work. I can feel it. Between the two of us, we can do this."

One way or another, they *had* to make it work.

Libbi had felt immediately better, more focused, having decided on a course of action. Whatever Spark was doing, it was *her* problem—her city, her people—and she and Mixin were going to sort this out themselves. She wasn't doing this to one-up Kay and Jasper (though, if this happened to make her siblings finally realize Libbi was a capable adult, she'd take it). But she was doing it for Ever. And Hannith. And Nydia.

Nydia Shipp was the latest person to go missing. She'd been one of Kay's classmates, and Libbi had vague memories of her as a blur of blonde hair and high-pitched teenage laughter at the far end of the school lunchroom. Apparently Nydia, like Ever, didn't have much support from her family and had been struggling to keep a steady job. Libbi had wondered if she was related to Mags Shipp, who would never leave a family member in trouble, but it must be a distant relationship or none. Shipp was a common name.

One of Nydia's roommates had heard Libbi's warnings and reached out to her after Nydia hadn't come home too many nights in a row. "She's always finding some all-night party to drive out her feelings, or a through-shipper's bed to fall into," the roommate had said. "But never this long, and with everything else going on…"

If Libbi'd had any remaining doubts, this would've squelched them. It was too much for coincidence.

They found a spot to camp out down the street from Spark's office, with the front door in sight. Libbi didn't know this area at all. It wasn't a bad part of town, not like the legally gray "entertainment zone" near the spaceport, but a tiny office district tucked between one of the port-side shopping stretches and a residential neighborhood that mostly housed port workers. It clearly catered to a certain sort of business: an industrial shipping container company; another that repaired dome-level air-filtration systems; a few contractors, plus more companies that supplied contractors. They'd passed at least three signs with "interstellar logistics" in the name.

Most people wouldn't ever have reason to visit here. It seemed like an odd place for an academic to set up shop.

It was also dead at this hour, with most offices closed and the workers gone home for the night, and the dome overhead was darkening. She and Mix had waited until after their shift to set out, using the time to plot and plan, with Libbi squeezing in some prep for her meeting tomorrow with Sasha Starborne. All necessary steps, but now Libbi wished they'd asked someone to cover for them and left earlier, so they'd have been here while there was still full dome-light.

The streets were well lit, at least. It was only the lack of foot traffic that made her anxious. On the plus side, the people heading home barely gave her and Mix a glance.

"I still think I should go to the door and confront him," she told Mixin.

"What would you say to him?"

"I thought I'd start out with 'Hey, what's your real name and why are you kidnapping my friends?'" she said. Mix just rolled their eyes. "No, I'd just ask him more about his research. And where he got my name. Pretend I'm reconsidering, and take it from there depending on what he says. Maybe I can trip him up."

On the slim chance it turned out that the problem came from somewhere else, and this researcher really was just some excitable academic with bad social skills who happened to show up at the wrong time, no harm done. Libbi no longer believed that, though. They might not have evidence to stand up in court, but she knew Spark was behind this.

"Well, one step at a time. Let's see what we're working with."

Mixin pulled out an infrared scanner, which Libbi had borrowed from the returns pile at the store. Gleeful over their new toy, they turned it on Libbi, then the buildings on either side of them, revealing a few late workers. Finally, they turned toward Spark's office.

"Ugh. He's not alone."

In addition to dim smudges that must be heat ducts and electronics, the scanner showed three warm, person-shaped blobs.

"Spark plus two assistants, you think? Or more…" Libbi hesitated. "Study participants?"

"I think we can call them victims at this point. Or targets, if that's too grim? Anyway, assuming one is Spark, at least one of the others must be on his side. I doubt he can disappear two people at once, all by himself."

"Which is why we figured it'd be safe for the two of us to come here. If he were alone. But if the others are both working with him…"

"Then we're outnumbered, I know. Come on, I want to listen in."

Mixin crept closer. After a moment, Libbi followed. While Mixin stared intently at the building, Libbi sidled up to the street-level windows. The lights were on, but the shades were drawn.

"Two assistants, I think. Spark's calling them useless ingrates, telling them to stop interrupting his work." Mixin made a face. "One of them says they're supposed to stay here until the office closes for the night, to support Spark in case anyone shows up. The other's whispering that they should just go."

A message popped up on Libbi's headset. Startled, she yelped, clapping both hands over her mouth.

"What?"

"Nothing. Just a message from Jasper." She waved it away unread.

"Libs…" Mixin paused. "Probably the wrong time to bring this up, but your brother has a lot of experience with this sort of thing."

Libbi turned and stared. "You want to let him swoop in and do this for us? You?"

"Not *for* us, but he could help."

"He'd send us home like misbehaving kids." She glanced over in surprise. "Are you *nervous*, Mix?"

"No. Shut up." Mixin paused. "Aren't you, though?"

"No," Libbi lied. "Just because Jasper's good at running protests and organizing strikes and…I don't know what else, that doesn't mean he's the only one who can do this."

"What if we called Hope and Sujay for backup? Safety in numbers. We didn't plan for this." Mixin waved at the scanner.

"That's…not a terrible idea. Do you think they could get here in time, though?" Libbi checked her headset. "The hours on that infocard he gave us end in a few minutes."

Voices rose inside, loud enough that Libbi could hear them, though she couldn't make out the words. "What's happening?"

"Spark says he's the boss and they're being insubordinate. I think he's…growling at them? Um, we'd better hide."

They crept back to a vantage point away from the door. A minute later, two young-ish people wearing casual business clothes came out and headed down the street toward them. Libbi froze, while Mix pretended to be fascinated by their handheld.

The pair passed with barely a glance at them.

"Spark's alone now. Perfect time to confront him. Right?" Libbi remembered to breathe again, deeply and deliberately, pushing through her nervousness. She could do this, she could.

Mixin raised the infrared scanner again. Spark was moving—away from them.

"What's he doing?" Mix frowned. "Could there be a back entrance he's slipping out?"

That made up Libbi's mind. This was their chance to get Spark alone, and she wouldn't let him run away.

"I'm doing it. You hang back and watch," she told Mixin.

"So I can run for help when he mugs you?"

Libbi rolled her eyes. "I just think he'll be more likely to talk to one person, alone." She hoped that was true. It felt true. "And you can listen in. Unless you want to do the talking while I eavesdrop?"

"Obviously not. And if Spark *does* try something…?"

As if reading Libbi's mind, another notification from Jasper pinged her headset. A voice call, this time. She dismissed it again.

"If he does, then yes, you can go tell my obnoxious brother he was right. Happy?"

Mixin grinned.

Libbi hurried along the street, and before she could think better of it, she palmed the door.

And waited. Wiped her sweaty hand on her pants. Waited.

She squared her shoulders, trying to project more confidence than she felt. She was Libbi Wilder. She did what needed doing, even when no one else would. She was saving her family's store. Ancestors, she was having breakfast tomorrow with Sasha freaking Starborne. She could handle this jerk.

Still waiting. Was he coming? Had he already left? She glanced over at Mixin, who gave a thumbs-up.

The door slid open, and there was Dr. Derek Spark. His pale blue eyes were round with surprise, and up close now, she could see the little golden dots that revealed them as augmented. The guy was rich, or well funded, whoever he was. That unsettled her almost as much as the smile that oozed across his face—the greed that pressed into her gift.

"Liberation Wilder! Have you changed your mind about helping me?"

"I have some questions," she said, trying to sound firm, in control, unafraid.

"Of course. Come inside."

"WE MUST BE MISSING something," Havoc said. Hours into his search with Sunny, they'd found nothing of use.

Havoc had returned to the spaceport, ostensibly to check for any physical evidence of Dr. Spark's arrival, but more because moving felt better than sitting still. And because Havoc suspected Sunny might feel more comfortable interacting this way. Though Sunny claimed not to care where they worked, they still seemed delighted when Havoc came aboard the ship, which he thought of as Sunny Themself.

They'd begun the search methodically, reviewing all ships that had docked within two weeks before Libbi's encounter with Spark. Even assuming that he'd arrived on a passenger ship or private vessel, the list overwhelmed Havoc, and there was little in the public data to guide their search.

Sunny whirred, signaling frustration. "If only I could still access the passenger manifests."

Havoc cocked his head. "Still?"

Sunny hesitated, then spoke in a flatter, more formal tone. "The data here is all from public records. When I…worked, I suppose is the correct word, with Grist, he had access to a wide range of tools on Ravel's behalf. Not only the legally accessible data networks, but less legal options as well. I wish I knew how… No!" They beeped sharply, admonishing themself. "I don't wish to behave like Grist." After a moment, they added, "It's only that it would be convenient, right now, in this particular case."

"You don't need to defend yourself. I, too, would welcome those resources. The Cooperative could put them to better use."

"It would still be wrong, though."

Havoc shrugged. "You think so? Perhaps you see truth. Or perhaps our intentions matter as much as our actions. It would harm no one if we had that data, but it could help us find our target."

"I'm not sure I agree. But it's irrelevant, since we don't have it."

He grunted. "There, you speak truth. We have colleagues in the Cooperative who do this, hacking into systems and using them to help our cause. But no one local has those skills, and though I've been learning, I lack expertise."

"Then our only choice is to do this the hard way," Sunny said.

They kept digging through the long list of ships for anything that stood out. Havoc had already sorted them by route, by size, by ticket price. Now he pulled up the public record for each ship, scrutinized every detail, and flagged some for Sunny to review. After a time, he simply stared at the list, letting his mind wander and hoping some intuitive connection might emerge. Something significant existed here, something he hadn't spotted yet…

"We might as well be looking for a single corrupt file in a data center," said Sunny. "Whoever Spark is, he must have the sense—and the resources—to cover his tracks. I propose we approach this from another angle. Organics need physical spaces, so he must have rented an apartment or office space."

"You speak sense. But I want to look at this a while longer."

"May I ask what you're looking for?"

"I'll know when I see it."

"Intuition. Very well. Continue, then."

Sunny fell back into companionable silence. A secondary display slowly filled with more public records, showing Sunny's new search.

Havoc knew what he feared to find. He knew Mason feared it too. Paranoia, Libbi had called it, to think that one strange incident could signify some dire conspiracy. But in Mason's mind, and increasingly in Havoc's own, all threats to Brennex came from the same source.

With trepidation, he cleared the filter showing only passenger vessels, and began looking at the commercial and industrial vessels, checking the ownership records. One caught his eye: a modest-sized transport run by a company with a name too generic to be a mere lack of imagination. He dug deeper, found that the owner-company was a subsidiary of a larger transportation company, which itself was a shell company operating under…

Ravel Corporation.

"Sunny."

"Oh. You're right." A brief pause. "Shit."

Under other circumstances, the ship's careful, deliberate cursing would have amused Havoc. Not now, though. "Deep and stinking shit, yes."

"And look at this: I think I've found his office," Sunny said.

"How? Where?"

"Business leases are public information, and Brennex isn't terribly large. There's only one new lease that's renewed on a week-to-week basis—most have a term of six months or more. And this one started two days after that Ravel-owned transport arrived."

Sunny expanded the record on the screen, floating next to the transport ship's details. The business license made no attempt to appear legitimate; it listed the tenant as "Brennex Temporary Office" and the lease-holder's point of contact wasn't called Derek Spark, but Daryl Stark.

"Does he not care if we find him out?" Either this Spark had a low opinion of Brennexians' intelligence, or lacked intelligence himself. Havoc suspected both.

"A good question," Sunny said. "Can we go?"

Havoc blinked. "To this fake office? Now?"

"We can do surveillance before we tell the others. I've checked Kay's headset; they're still busy socializing."

Havoc felt the same eagerness to go find answers, but he knew what Mason would say. Never go into hostile territory without someone off-site who knows your plans. Besides, he and his eshrim had promised each other not to run off on an adventure that required the other to rescue them—not again. Not like last time, when Ravel had captured and imprisoned Mason. Or the time before that, when they'd tried to disappear Havoc into an off-world Dust facility.

"We must at least tell them what we found, first. If Ravel is truly here…"

"Then Kay and Jasper should be on alert. But it's even more urgent that we find out who Spark really is and what he's doing."

"Prep your drone. I'll update them on our way."

He pinged Mason from his handheld: *We've found him.*

Call me. He'd just stepped from the ship, with Sunny's drone riding on his shoulder, when Mason's call came.

"What's wrong?" Mason said. He knew Havoc that well.

"We found the ship he arrived on. Ravel owns it."

Muffled cursing came across the connection. "He's Ravel. How sure are you?"

"Almost completely—"

"Eighty-five percent," Sunny interjected.

"Sunny says eighty-five percent. My gut says one hundred."

"My gut knew it before we even got here. Just once, I'd like to be wrong." A pause. "I'm linking Kay in. Where is he?"

Havoc accepted Kay into the call, and added Sunny, too. "Sunny found a rented office that fits his timeline. Here." He sent them an address and a map of the location.

"Where the heck is that?" Kay said. "I've never been anywhere near there."

"We have, I think," said Jasper. "Ma and Pa took us to meet a contractor there one time, remember? I'm pretty sure it was in that district. It's all construction companies and shipping, stuff like that. No shops, no neighbors. At least that's how it was fifteen years ago."

"Havoc and I are headed there now to conduct reconnaissance," Sunny said. "We'll tell you what we find."

"No! Wait for us. Meet us… Where are you now?"

"Leaving the spaceport."

Havoc wove between clusters of hurried travelers and slow-walking tourists, luggage-carrying drones and speedy little pod-sized vehicles for those going longer distances or who couldn't walk. "We can handle this, Mason. Finish your own investigation. We'll call if we need backup."

"What if he's an operative? I don't like you two going in there alone."

"I am perfectly safe," said Sunny. "At worst, my drone may be damaged."

"In which case Havoc will be alone. I'm coming to join you." He paused, and Havoc heard voices in the background from whatever bar they'd visited with their friends. He must have been arguing wordlessly with Kay, because he corrected, "Okay, *we're* coming. We're learning nothing from these folks, anyway."

"Havoc and I are closer. We'll start surveillance, and meet you here." Sunny updated the map, showing a meeting point one block from the office.

"Fine, just be careful. Kay's settling our tab here and then we'll be on our way. I'm going to drop off now and warn Libbi."

"Um, maybe don't yet?" Kay said.

"She needs to know this isn't just some innocent research project."

"Yeah, but Jasp, she won't react well."

"To Ravel threatening to our home? I hope not."

"To you saying *I told you so.*"

"Fair, but we can argue it out later, as long as she's aware…"

Mason dropped the call, cutting Havoc and Sunny out of their debate.

"I think I'm grateful not to have siblings," Havoc muttered. "They seem…complicated."

They were leaving behind the part of the spaceport full of shops, and foot traffic thinned significantly. Without the colorful signs and aggressively cheerful ads, the streets became a maze, and he kept the map up in his headset display.

"Are your teammates or crèchemates not like siblings to you?"

"I thought they might be, but now that I'm meeting Mason's family, I think differently. Teammates might argue, even fight, but we all share a goal. We want to go in the same direction, even if we disagree about how. Libbi's goals still confuse me, but they seem at cross-purposes to Mason's."

"He and Kay left their home and family. That seems indicative of different priorities."

"A Kovar in their place would leave their team and join another that fits them better."

"Whereas Kay and Jasper—Mason, I mean—are still devoted to their family, despite all their disagreements. It does seem quite complicated."

Havoc padded along in silence for a few minutes. "Why do you think Ravel is here?"

The drone whirred by his ear. "Any speculations I might make are…unpleasant to think about. I only hope that whoever this intruder is, he's not an operative. Not like Grist."

"I hope that too."

He and Sunny were both refugees from Ravel, in their own way. They both had clear ideas of what to fear from them. Ravel had many ways to cause harm, but operatives like Grist dealt in violence and intimidation, and Havoc didn't want that for this community, these people.

"The address is around this corner," Sunny said. "Wait here while I fly overhead. I'll send video to your headset."

The drone hummed as its motor fired up, then fell to near-silent, rising toward the rooftops. Havoc stuck close to a wall, peeking around the corner.

"Mason, we're here," he sent over his headset.

"Okay, we're on our way. I can't reach Libbi, but I'm going to keep trying. Ma says she's not at home, which means she could be anywhere, doing anything."

"Oh no, she might be getting a drink with her friends. Like a *normal twenty-four-year-old,*" Kay interjected.

"Actually," Sunny said, "Jasper is right to worry. Your sister is here."

"*What?* There, at the Ravel site?" Jasper's voice rose. "What in the Founders' worst nightmares is she doing?"

"Being your sister, I suspect," Havoc said. "She seems to be investigating on her own."

In Sunny's camera, Libbi stood outside the entrance to the office, talking to a light-skinned male Human who looked uncomfortably familiar.

"Sunny, can you zoom in…?" he began, at the same time Sunny said, "Oh. Oh, dear." The drone was already moving closer, adjusting angles for a better view of the man's face, until he could see what the ship saw.

It wasn't an operative. It was worse. Lacking words for his dismay, he hissed.

"*Fuck.*" Mason's microphone picked up his footsteps as he started to run, Kay calling out questions as she followed.

Libbi's mysterious visitor really was a researcher. Unfortunately, he was Ravel's star pharmaceutical researcher and Havoc's least favorite person: Alik Cobb.

SPARK HELD THE DOOR open for Libbi, but she took a step back. "I'd rather talk right here."

"It's much more comfortable in my office," he said. When she stood her ground, he added, "Is it considered polite on this planet to keep people standing in the doorway for serious conversations? Or to refuse your host's invitation?"

It was *not* polite by Brennexian standards, and Libbi fought the impulse to be agreeable and prove that Brennex wasn't the backwater people thought it was. An impulse that was more about her gift, and about what Spark wanted, than about good sense. She was grateful to have Mixin watching from the shadows, stopping Libbi from doing anything stupid.

"Answer two questions for me first. What are you studying, specifically? You said life in the domes, but what're you actually trying to find out with your research?"

He sighed, as if this were a disappointingly stupid question. "I obviously can't tell you that. It would corrupt my findings if my subjects knew my hypotheses. You'll tell your friends, and soon I won't be able to recruit any new unbiased participants."

"That doesn't reassure me, Dr. Spark."

"I've given you no reason for suspicion."

"No reason for trust, either. No disrespect, but my people haven't had good experiences with outsiders poking around in our business."

"That's unfortunate, but irrelevant. No research study worth its accolades would reveal the details to its subjects beforehand. But I assure you, Brennexians can make an immeasurable contribution to science by participating."

Worth its accolades. That was an odd turn of phrase. "Where are you from, did you say?"

"Earth." Was that a hesitation? "Originally."

"And how many—"

"You said two questions. If you want to talk more, you'll have to come inside for a civilized chat."

She gritted her teeth. The more he urged her to come into his office—the more she felt his hunger for it—the more she felt certain that was a terrible, terrible idea. She couldn't let him get to her.

"You refused to answer my first question. How many participants have you recruited for your study so far?"

Another put-upon sigh. "Twenty-five in total, though only six passed the screening questionnaire to participate in the second stage."

Six. She knew of three people missing. "Was one of those six Ever Wright?"

"What?"

"Ever Wright. I know you talked to him." She didn't *know*, not for sure, but let Spark think she did. "Did he pass the screening? How about Hannith Tan?"

"I can't hand out people's personal information to you. That's a breach of their privacy and my confidentiality."

He wasn't wrong, that was the frustrating part. And yet… "Even if they're missing now?"

Spark frowned sharply, though he seemed more annoyed than surprised. "Are these people family of yours? Are you responsible for them? No? Then it's neither your business nor mine what anyone does with their payment once they leave my office."

A chill ran through Libbi. He'd just admitted that Ever and Hannith had been here, though he didn't seem to realize it.

"Now, if you'll come inside, I can talk you through the process from a participant's perspective." He smiled at her, coaxing, greedy. "Just come in, and I'll explain everything."

She wasn't supposed to do that. But what if Ever and Hannith and Nydia were in there? And others who hadn't been noticed missing yet? If she wanted answers, they were inside. There was no other way to get them. She would be on her guard…and if anything went wrong, Mixin would go for help.

She took a step forward.

"Libbi!" Mixin shouted.

That snapped her back to herself. Shit. Stupid. She *knew* the missing people weren't in there; they'd have shown up on the infrared. This was her gift acting up, pushing her to follow Spark's desires, overpowering her better judgment.

She turned to bolt toward Mixin, but Spark hissed, "No!" He grabbed her, pulling her off balance so she stumbled toward him. One arm came around her torso and pinned her against his chest.

Damn it! She twisted, struggling against his grip. Spark was stronger than he looked, though. A sharp pinch at her neck. She cried out.

She brought her booted heel down on his foot, and he let go, but as she tried to run, the world lurched beneath her. Mixin was shouting, but her best friend fell farther and farther away, beyond the pit of darkness that pulled her down.

8

"HEY, DON'T YOU TOUCH her!"

Spark was wrestling Libbi's unconscious body toward the door, but he looked up in alarm as Mixin closed on him, screaming like a maniac. For a moment, he froze, hands tightening on his new victim. Then fear must have won, because he dropped Libbi and dove back inside. The lock clicked behind him, and Mixin kicked the door as a disappointing substitute for kicking the man behind it.

"Yeah, you'd better run away! You fucking asshole, don't you touch my best friend. Shit, shit, fuck. Libbi, can you hear me? Are you okay?"

They dropped to their knees. Libbi was completely unconscious. Mixin should…what? Check her pulse, that was a thing first responders did. They pressed two fingers to the inside of Libbi's wrist. Was there no pulse? Or was it just that Mixin's hands were shaking?

A shadow fell over them, and Mixin flinched away, squeaking in alarm.

"Let me see her," said a sibilant Kovari voice.

"Who the— Oh." Libbi's brother's partner. What was he doing here?! "Sorry, Havoc. Yes, please. I…" They laughed, faintly hysterical. "I don't know what I'm doing. He jabbed her and ran."

"We saw. Sunny will follow him." Havoc pointed.

A drone was hovering by the entrance. It must have sent a signal, because the lock flashed green and orange as its accessibility settings triggered, and the drone slipped through as the door began to open.

Havoc was checking Libbi over with reassuring care.

"She's breathing." He glanced sidelong at Mixin. "You should too."

Oh. Yeah, that would probably help. "You're a genius." Deep breath. "Is she…"

More footsteps pounded down the street. This time Mixin heard them early enough to stand, ready to kick in some kneecaps until they saw it was Jasper and Kay.

"Havoc, what…?" Jasper panted. He and Kay must have run flat-out to get here.

"He drugged her!" Mixin said.

"Cobb overreacted when he realized Libbi wasn't alone. Panicked, I think. He injected her with a strong sedative." Havoc looked up and added firmly: "She'll be fine, Mason."

She didn't look fine. Libbi looked asleep, but not in a peaceful way, more in a *why are you passed out on the street* way.

Jasper bobbed on his feet, all tension. "Where's Cobb now?"

"Wait." Mixin's ears were catching up with their brain. "Who's Cobb?"

"Mixin, that guy was your mystery visitor, I take it?" Kay asked, and Mixin nodded. "And Jasper? Havoc, Sunny? You all recognized him." It wasn't a question.

"Yeah." Jasper swallowed. "We met him on another assignment. He's a Ravel scientist. Biopharma."

Mixin stared at him. Kay said, "Shit."

"I know."

"Go after him. I'll stay with Libbi," Kay said.

He let out a breath. "Okay. Keep the group call open, just in case."

A group chat that Mixin wasn't part of. Nor Libbi, presumably.

Mixin hesitated, torn between staying with Libbi and following the Cooperative activists on their chase. Curiosity won out. Libbi was fine, Havoc had said. She'd be safe with her sister, and she wasn't exactly going anywhere. Besides, if something exciting happened, Mixin needed to be able to tell Libbi about it when she woke up.

They caught the door before it closed and followed Jasper and Havoc inside.

The building was bland and professional, clean, though with a stale smell of disuse. Lights on, but no one at home. Jasper and Havoc prowled ahead, side by side. Jasper looked over his shoulder at Mixin, and based on everything Libbi had said about his overprotectiveness, they braced themself to raise a fuss if he tried to make them leave. But he just motioned them to keep quiet.

"We should hunt for Cobb first, or his associates," Havoc said in a whisper, too low to hear except for Mix's gift.

"You think he's got friends? Anything's possible, I guess."

Havoc snorted at that. "No, I doubt that team-of-one has endeared himself to his colleagues since we last saw him.

But it also seems unlikely that he could secretly set up in unfriendly territory without any help."

"He's got two assistants at least," Mixin said, and they both turned, startled. "But they went home. We did check that Cobb was alone before Libbi talked to him." Mix folded their arms, daring them to criticize.

"Oh," Jasper said. He exchanged an inscrutable look with Havoc, then moved onward.

They cleared the rooms one at a time, Jasper and Havoc swapping nonverbal signals and coordinating their movements like this was an everyday activity for them. Neither of them seemed afraid; Jasper actually seemed to relax as he settled into the search, which made Mixin feel a little better. They tried to emulate that confidence as they followed behind, staying out of the way but looking out for anything the others might have missed.

The first two rooms they checked were like a staged sales pitch for office space: a desk and pair of comfortable chairs, motivational quotes projected on the wall. No people, no hiding places. They were about to open a third room when a buzzing rushed up behind them.

Mixin yelped and spun around, arms coming up defensively, but it was only Sunny's drone. *Yup, really smooth. Great job impressing the cool kids, Mix.*

"Cobb is gone," Sunny said. "I followed him out the back exit, but he entered the tunnels and I lost him there. I've secured the exit electronically, but..." They whirred demonstratively. "I would feel better with a physical barrier, in case he returns."

The drone had no hands, Mixin realized, no appendages to jam a door shut.

"Show me," Havoc said, and the two of them went off.

Jasper continued checking the rooms. After a hesitation, Mixin decided they might be more help than interference and fell in beside him. He didn't argue, but didn't talk, either.

"She'll be okay," Mixin said as they climbed the stairs, unable to handle the silence.

"I know."

"I was right there. I wasn't going to let him take her."

Jasper glanced sidelong at them. "It wasn't your fault, Mixin. I warned her these were dangerous people. Why didn't she listen?"

It was a rhetorical question, so Mixin didn't answer. Libbi would have let that spark another fight, but Mixin could imagine how he was feeling, the worry and guilt. They felt the same way themself.

It wasn't a large building—four offices on the ground floor, two more and a conference room upstairs—and they found some supplies that suggested which rooms were being used, but no people. A cup of lukewarm coffee was the only proof that anyone had been here today. Jasper announced an all-clear over his headset, and they circled back for a closer look at the room that seemed to be Cobb's office.

"Well, that's disappointing," Mixin muttered.

"What were you hoping for?"

"You know. Scattered notebooks and files. A big map with push-pins and string. Maybe a data-stick labeled *top secret research.*"

Jasper shot them a long, evaluating look and seemed to decide Mixin was making a joke, because he smiled wryly. "That'd be nice, I can't disagree. But Cobb's not that sort of bad guy."

A table held some *very* basic medical equipment: a pulse oximeter, blood pressure cuff, and a pinprick blood tester.

Nothing Mixin didn't recognize from an ordinary doctor's office. There was a holoprojector, too, but when they flipped it on, it had no inputs. Cobb must have run it from some device he'd taken with him.

"At least she didn't come here alone," Jasper said out of nowhere. "I can tell how loyal you are to her. Thank you, Mixin."

Right, that was Jasper's gift: seeing the bonds between people. Mixin gave him a cautious smile. If Libbi hadn't come around on the point of searching for Ever, then Mixin might have been the idiot who was here alone.

The two of them were searching the desk when Kay came in, holding the door for Havoc as he carried Libbi. The drone hovered like an anxious parent.

"We figured it'd be better to bring her in here than try to bring her home," Kay said. She helped Havoc settle Libbi onto the room's one couch.

"Right," Mixin quipped. "Even our vigilant Public Safety wouldn't ignore folks carrying an unconscious woman across town."

"Not to mention that Ma and Pa would have kittens if we brought her home like this."

Kay looked even more miserable than Jasper. She trailed her fingers over the medical supplies, as if looking for some magic gadget that would fix this. She picked up the oximeter and positioned it on Libbi's fingertip, watched the display for a minute. Presumably its results looked normal, because she tossed it aside with a sigh.

"Havoc? You said she'll be okay?"

Havoc glanced up, but met Jasper's gaze, not Kay's. There was a whole conversation in that gaze, but not one Mixin could read.

"I have no reason to think otherwise," Havoc said. Obviously hedging.

"Would any of you just say what you mean?" Mixin burst out. "None of us are children. We can handle some honesty. Why did you say she'll be fine, Havoc?"

Reluctantly, Havoc said, "I lack medical training, but I do know Cobb. He cares only about his research. If he is taking people to study them, he won't harm them as long as they remain useful to him."

Oh.

Mixin bit their lip, almost regretting that they'd asked. Not because of Libbi, but because of Ever, who'd disappeared days ago. Who would be so very vulnerable to Cobb's demands. Who even his own father didn't want to deal with on his bad days. How long would Ever stay "useful"?

"Not the most comforting line of reasoning, Havoc," Kay said.

Jasper said, "Let's make sure. Sunny, can you find out exactly what he used on her?"

"That portable blood tester should tell us, if I can convince it to connect with me."

Kay went and got the tester, but before she and Sunny could get it working, Havoc said, "We won't need that. Look."

He held up a case he'd found in a desk drawer: auto-injector capsules, with several missing. It was labeled with an unpronounceable chemical name.

The drone's cameras whirred faintly as they focused on it. "I'm familiar with this sedative. It may take up to eight hours to wear off, and she will wake up dehydrated and with a headache." When they said nothing more, Kay cleared her throat pointedly. "Oh, sorry. Yes, other than that, she'll be perfectly fine."

"Thank the Founders." Mixin slumped onto the couch at Libbi's feet. Libbi looked wrong lying there, face slackened, forehead damp with sweat. But in a few hours, she'd be good as new.

The others didn't look so relieved, though. Kay and Jasper were doing more eye-conversations, annoyingly inaccessible to Mixin.

"I should warn Ma and Pa we'll be out late," Kay said at last. "I'll tell them we're out with friends, all three of us, and they shouldn't wait up." She paced the room while composing a message on her handheld, and ended up perched on the desk by Jasper. She spoke in an undertone, finally something Mixin could read. "Okay, Jasp. Who is Cobb? What do you know?"

"Not now." Jasper's gaze drifted to Libbi as if caught in an air current that kept drawing him back. Mixin pretended not to be watching them. "When she wakes up, I'll tell you everything, but I'd rather only tell it once. Like I assume you only want to tell your part once," he added pointedly.

"Fair," Kay muttered.

"In the meantime…" Jasper turned back to the group, speaking at normal volume again. "Sunny, did you catch any of Libbi's conversation with Cobb? It'd be good to know what he said."

"He was out of my range, unfortunately," said the drone.

"Good news, then," said Mixin, brightening. Finally, a chance to actually be useful. "It just so happens I've got a gift for that."

THEY WERE ON A ship—the whole family, Ma and Pa and even Kay and Jasper—but they were stuck. The ship couldn't leave spaceport. Pa was sure it was a mechanical problem, and Jasper said it was a conspiracy by the port management company to keep them here, and Kay and Ma were talking over each other on the comms, arguing with port control to let them go. Libbi knew how to fix it, but none of them were listening to her. None of them were *hearing* her: she opened her mouth and no sound came out. Why couldn't she *speak*?

Listen to me! she screamed voicelessly.

"It's okay, Libbi. You're safe," said a voice above her.

Like flailing through microgravity, she grappled up into consciousness. The voices were real, she realized, because they went quiet as she opened her eyes. The one hovering over her, stroking her hair, was Kay.

"Where…?" She pressed a hand to her throbbing temple. "What happened?"

Mixin! Were they okay?

She scrambled to sit up, which made her head pound worse, but she found her friend at the other end of the couch. Mix squeezed her ankle and gave her a half-smile, half-grimace, the same look they used to share when someone's parents caught them sneaking home late at night. (Not that they got into much trouble as teens—most Losts had a low tolerance for Brennex's crowded bars and clubs, so the worst Libbi and Mix's group ever did was sneaking beer down to the tunnels and losing track of time playing games.)

"What happened," said Jasper, "is you nearly got yourself added to the kidnapping list."

Another voice—where was it coming from?—said, "Disorientation is a common side effect of the drug you were administered. Other side effects include dehydration, fatigue…"

Dehydration.

"Water," Libbi said, and a bottle appeared in her hand. Put there by Havoc—of course he was here too. She drank deep. The water was cool, though it tasted of minerals, and it seemed to dissolve the fog that wrapped her brain. Some of it, at least.

They were in some sort of office. Spark's office? She was starting to remember. He'd kept trying to get her to go inside with him, until he lost patience and…attacked her? Drugged her, apparently. The last thing she remembered was Mix shouting at him.

If he tries something…you can tell my brother he was right.

Libbi groaned. "You took me at my word, huh?"

"Actually, they all found this place on their own," Mixin said. "Can't say I mind. That asshole ran off when they showed up. Great timing, really."

Well, crap. Humiliation heated Libbi's cheeks. Not only hadn't she learned anything useful, but she'd needed her big brother and sister to rescue her.

"I was going to tell you guys whatever I found out."

"Before or after you told us that you had Cobb's address?" Jasper tapped his handheld and it projected a familiar info card. Spark's card. He must have wrangled it from Mixin.

There wasn't much Libbi could say to that. "So, what, you followed us?"

"On the contrary, we didn't expect to find you here," said the drone. Libbi hadn't noticed it before, sitting on the arm of the couch behind Kay. "Havoc and I were investigating where this researcher might have come from, and we located what we believed to be his rented space."

"So we came, and what do we find but Cobb—and you. We could have surrounded him and caught him, if you'd bothered to coordinate with us." Jasper spoke through gritted teeth.

Her brother wanted to kill this person, Libbi realized. Probably metaphorically, but she was unnervingly not confident about that part. Her gift flooded her with violent urges, a vision of her hands around the neck of this obnoxious but otherwise complete stranger of a man.

"Wait. You called him…Cobb?"

"Spark was an alias," Jasper said, voice tight. "His real name is Alik Cobb, and he's Ravel's top Biopharma researcher. He knows about the Gifted, and he's here to study us."

Libbi stared at him. She'd thought her siblings were being paranoid, but this was worse than the worst possibilities she'd imagined. If it was true…

She thought of Ever and the others who'd gone missing. Terror tightened around her ribs.

"Are we sure he knows?" Mixin asked hesitantly. "Maybe he just suspects. Or he's here by coincidence and he doesn't know about the gifts at all."

"He knows," said Jasper and Kay in unison.

Mixin leaned forward, settling themself cross-legged on the couch. "Sounds like it's story time."

Both Libbi's siblings hesitated. Havoc looked pointedly at Jasper. "You promised to tell them when Libbi awoke. She's woken."

"I did, yeah." Jasper ran his fingers through his hair. Reluctant. *Embarrassed?* "Okay. Here's the short version. A bit over a year ago, the Cooperative found evidence that someone in Ravel was restarting the experiments that made the Lost Generation. They sent me to a research planet called Artesia. That's where I met Havoc, who was doing activism of his own." He spared a tiny smile for his partner.

"We found out that Alik Cobb had unearthed the old project and found a way to make it effective. Turns out, Ravel stopped producing the drug here not because it was causing infertility, but because it wasn't potent enough."

"What's this stuff supposed to do, besides screw up our lives?" asked Mixin.

"We nicknamed it the genius drug. It's designed to give people's brains an extra creative boost. Big moneymaking potential."

"They would only offer it to the upper ranks, of course," Havoc said. "Only those who they decided deserved it."

Jasper patted his partner's knee. "Cobb was obsessed with this project. It was going to make his career. He knew about the side effects, but he didn't care, because they only affected workers around the production process, not end users. No one 'important.' Havoc and I managed to sabotage his work and stop production, and as far as we knew, Cobb moved on to other projects."

"Okay," said Libbi. "But he couldn't have known about the gifts, right? Or he would have led with that."

"Right. Which is why we think he's only found out that part recently."

Now Jasper looked at Kay, who curled deeper into the couch, looking miserable. "And that part is my fault. When Jasper got kidnapped by Ravel a few months back—"

"Wait, *kidnapped?*"

"Do *not* tell Ma and Pa," Jasper said firmly. "But…yeah. Not my best moment."

"—and I went undercover working at Ravel, to try and rescue him—"

"You *what?*"

Kay pressed her hands to her face. "Libbi, this will go faster if you just let me talk."

"Maybe if you stop saying completely bonkers things. You never told us that!"

"Obviously not. Ma and Pa worry enough about Jasper. I didn't need them worrying about me, too."

You could still have told me. Either Kay put Libbi in the same category as Ma and Pa, who didn't want to know what trouble their off-world offspring were getting into, or she didn't trust Libbi to keep a secret. Or worse, just hadn't thought to tell her. Libbi didn't want to know which.

"So I was a fake Ravel employee for a few weeks. Working on an annexation, on the opposite side from the Cooperative." She made a face of distaste. "And I'm always careful about hiding my gift, you know that, but we were in some tough spots, and…well…I slipped up. One of their people snuck aboard Sunny, and he was loudly pissed off at us, so I heard him with my gift when I shouldn't have known he was there. He told his boss about it, and I've been worried that might make them suspicious enough to dig around. Seems like I was right."

The drone, Sunny, made a low humming sound. It almost sounded like an expression of sympathy, though it was probably just some mechanical thing.

"I wasn't careful enough, either, especially after the escape, when we were getting desperate about winning the campaign," said Jasper. "Even that could have been okay, except that they had medical scans of both of us. All the data they'd need to find out what makes us different."

"You're speculating," said Havoc. "We don't *know* that they discovered this from you two."

Kay shifted uncomfortably. "Except that Cobb went straight for Libbi. And he was asking after me."

"How it happened doesn't matter. What matters is that he's here now," Jasper declared. "Whatever he knew or guessed coming in, he's had plenty of opportunities to confirm it. Which means the danger isn't just to the people he's taken, but to all the Losts. And all of Brennex."

His proclamation dropped like a concrete block into the middle of the conversation. Libbi had understood how bad this was, but it jarred her to hear it put so bluntly. What would Ravel Corporation do to people who'd developed powers as a side effect of one of their own failed projects? What would they do in order to understand and harness what they'd created?

She knew what Ravel did with valuable resources. They exploited them.

Mixin leaned forward, eyes wide. "So what do we do now? Track him down and capture him? Send him home with his memory wiped?"

Everyone blinked at them.

"This isn't a spy story, Mix. We can't wipe people's memories," Libbi murmured. She loved Mixin dearly, but if they had a fault, it was watching too many serials.

"I know, I know. Memory wipes aren't real."

"For us, at least," muttered Havoc.

Mixin looked sharply at him, probably filing that away to ask about later, then cleared their throat. "We do have to stop him, though. You two are in the Cooperative. That's what you do, right?"

"When we have to, yeah." Jasper raked his fingers through his hair. "It isn't that simple, though. I'll have to talk to my colleagues, call in some resources. He has hostages. We'll need to be stealthy."

Sunny spoke up, startling Libbi, who'd forgotten about the drone. "Your mother is on the governing council, is she not? Could she assist you?"

All three siblings shook their heads, in agreement for once.

"We can't put off telling Ma much longer, and when we do, she'll have to bring it to the Council," Jasper said. "But if we get any help from that front, it'll come too late. More likely they'll get in the way."

"Ma's forever complaining about how impossibly slow the Council moves," Libbi said. "We should start by updating Public Safety on what we've learned."

Jasper raised his brows at her. "Really, Libbi?"

Even Mixin looked doubtful. "We tried that, and they didn't take us seriously."

"That's because we had no hard evidence, but we do now! There's a recording of him trying to kidnap me, and you're a witness to our conversation. And we know he's from Ravel, which we didn't before." She turned to her brother. "You said we need resources. It's literally their job to handle stuff like this."

There was a long pause before Jasper said, "Sure, what could it hurt?"

Humoring her. Libbi gritted her teeth. "You really think we *shouldn't* tell Public Safety that there's a guy from Ravel— and at least two assistants, maybe a whole team—running around Brennex kidnapping people? We should just keep that to ourselves?"

Kay said, "She makes a good point."

"Public Safety hasn't had to deal with a situation like this in decades. I trust our people, the Cooperative's people, to take care of this," said Jasper.

Libbi rolled her eyes. "You really can't handle the idea that someone else might save the day, huh?" she said under her breath, not caring if he heard. She tried to share a look with Mix, but Mix was frowning, like this was a puzzle and they couldn't untangle it.

"I said it's fine to try! Just don't expect much to come of it," Jasper said.

He turned to the others. "While Libbi talks to Public Safety, let's work on getting a better picture of Cobb's activities. He's clearly not doing the bulk of his research here." He gestured around the bare room. "So let's find his actual lab, and find out if he has more allies and resources here than those two assistants Libbi and Mixin saw. And we need to know who else he's taken. Mixin said he claimed to have six test participants, which means potentially three more we haven't identified. Kay, can you work on that with Mixin and…" He met Libbi's gaze and trailed off. "If they're both willing?"

"I'm going to help," Libbi said, trying to sound firm, afraid she sounded like a petulant child instead. Her brother wanted something from her, but she couldn't tell what. She would not let him send her home to stay safe. "These are my friends. I'm going to get them back."

"Me too," Mixin said, squeezing Libbi's shoulder.

"Good," said Jasper, and whatever he was feeling passed before Libbi could decipher it.

"I'd better send some messages. Mixin and I are supposed to open the store this morning… What?"

"Don't worry about the store. I already asked your dad to open," said Mixin. "Don't worry, I said! I was vague about why. He said it's fine."

Great. So her parents thought they'd gone out drinking with her siblings and were too hung over to work. At least they'd prefer that to the truth.

"We're going to have to tell them eventually," Kay murmured, and Jasper answered, "But let's do it later, in person. For damage control."

Wait. Libbi's brain was recovering too slowly. If Mixin had already messaged Pa, and he'd responded, then what time was it?

She searched her pockets for her devices, pulled on her headset, and found…

"Fuck."

Her breakfast meeting with Sasha Starborne was supposed to start an hour ago. She had three reminders blinking at her, and two messages from Sasha. First: *I'm here. Table in the back.* And then, a quarter-hour later: *After all that scheduling fuss, you flake out on me? I don't like having my time wasted.*

"Fuck, fuck, fuck! I missed the meeting. Fuck. I have to go."

She was on her feet, writing a message as she hurried toward the door, which she hit with her shoulder. She grabbed the doorframe as the room shifted under her.

"You're not going anywhere," said Jasper, catching her by the arms. "Havoc, can you get her more water?"

"You don't understand. This is *important*. It's Sasha freaking Starborne, and she was going to write about the store."

He ignored her protests and led her firmly back to the couch. "So reschedule it. After you're recovered."

"I can't. But if I go now, maybe I can apologize, do some groveling…"

Kay was staring at her. "Libbi, it's *one meeting*. It's not that important."

"This one is." She looked to Mixin, who she'd been telling about this for a week, to back her up.

But Mixin shook their head. "It's cruddy, yeah. But you literally got drugged, Libs. That's an extremely valid excuse."

Libbi turned away, biting her lip. Even Mixin didn't understand. She would not cry in front of her older siblings, she would *not.*

"Fine. I've already missed it, anyway. Let's get to work catching this asshole Cobb."

So you two can leave again, and I can go back to taking care of everything myself.

9

"CONFIRMING THE IDENTITY OF this Alik Cobb will take a while. Corporate records are closed to us, so we'll have to go through the Majrin," Officer Stone said with the air of one who'd wrestled with Majrin bureaucracy before and was doing them an incalculable favor by doing so again.

Like last time, Stone had listened to their story with outward patience, but if he was capable of feeling sympathy, he did a good job pretending otherwise. Kay had come with Libbi and Mixin, though she was sitting to one side and hadn't said much. Granted, Cobb had fled before she'd arrived at the office, but would it kill her to back Libbi up?

"You'll look for him in the meantime, right?" Libbi said.

"I'll take a copy of that recording and share it around. If we find your alleged Ravel scientist, we can talk to him. For your part, stay out of the industrial district, all right? It's not a place to go wandering around at night."

"That's *it?*" Libbi demanded. "You need to search for him! He drugged me, and he's kidnapping people."

"Allegedly."

"He admitted he'd seen the missing people," said Mixin. "And he kept trying to get Libbi to come inside with him."

"Your recordings didn't pick up any of that."

Mix's voice lowered. "I didn't hear it with my ears. My gift—"

"Isn't admissible as evidence. If we *were* to arrest him and try him, an off-worlder—from Ravel no less—we couldn't talk about your gift during testimony, could we?"

"But that's what all this is about. He must know about the gifts! That's *why* he's kidnapping Losts!" Libbi burst out.

And Officer Stone didn't care. He didn't *want* to care, she realized: it was barely midmorning, and all she felt from him was a longing for his couch and some adventure serial he was in suspense over. A crisis would get in the way of that, so he wanted there not to be one. Granted, Libbi hadn't wanted to admit this was happening either, at first. But that was because she was too stressed about her job and the store. Worrying about missing people literally was Stone's job.

The problem was that to him, it was "just Losts" who were disappearing. She almost, *almost* felt like he wanted the Losts to suffer. She must be misreading him, though, letting her own dislike get in the way, because that would be monstrous.

"I'll add your theory to the case file. You've got some potential leads here, but sadly, no proof."

"Oh, you have an actual case file?" Mixin snarked. "Is there anything in it?"

"I am, as I said, investigating."

"Not very hard," Mixin muttered.

"You haven't made much progress, have you? This isn't going away just because you wish it would," Libbi said.

"Look," said Stone, his patience cracking. "If you're right, then one of you 'Gifted' tipped off Ravel about your secret, and that's bad news for all of you. But if you're *wrong*, and we start throwing unfounded accusations against a guy who you claim is one of their top scientists, then they'll come down on all of Brennex so hard we can't see straight. I don't want to be the one who brings another occupation on us. Do you?" No one answered. "Didn't think so."

Libbi gritted her teeth. But before she could argue, Kay leaned forward.

"Thank you for your time, Officer. Please do tell us what you find from your background check on Cobb." Kay's voice was ice pick–sharp. She rose to go.

"Kay," Libbi hissed.

Kay paused, as if another thought had occurred to her. "I believe my sister. And it'll be awfully unfortunate if she's proven right, and everyone finds out Public Safety did nothing to protect Brennex's most vulnerable. Don't you think so, Officer Stone?"

With that, Kay turned and walked out, leaving a shadow of unease behind Officer Stone's smug expression.

Once they were safely out of earshot, Kay said, "Sorry about taking over there, Libs, but I could hear him getting more and more stubborn. He's clearly one of those people who resents our whole generation, and more arguing would just be counterproductive. Plus, he's genuinely terrified of Ravel coming back."

"So he'd rather let Ravel have their way with the Losts than risk annoying them?"

"Something like that."

"Great." Libbi scowled. "So Jasper was right: it was stupid to come here."

"Libbi…" Kay began in that extra-gentle tone, as if the wrong word might set Libbi off like a bomb.

"It's true!" She spun to face her sister. "When we were kids, they always taught us that Public Safety looks out for us. If you're in trouble, if you're unsafe, go to Public Safety. It's right there in the name! I wanted to believe someone would keep us safe."

"I get that," Kay said, and Mixin squeezed Libbi's shoulder.

"But we're grown up now, and someone's always in trouble, and Stone is never going to help us. And that *sucks*." She paused, breathing hard. Meeting her sister's concerned eyes. "Maybe I'm a little freaked out by all this."

Kay smiled grimly. "I'd be worried if you *weren't* freaked out."

And Kay barely knew half of it. Libbi was freaked out and flailing on all fronts. How selfish was she, still worrying about the store and her meeting with Sasha when people were disappearing and Ravel might have learned about their gifts? But on the other hand, how could she expect to take on Ravel Corporation if she couldn't even keep a store in business?

Her headset still showed no messages from Sasha Starborne. Libbi had written as soon as she realized, apologizing profusely, blaming her absence that morning on a personal emergency (not a lie) and asking if they could reschedule again. But she didn't expect a response. She'd lost this opportunity and it wouldn't come again.

Mixin said, "Let's try approaching someone else. We're here, after all."

"That's a good idea," Kay said. "While I don't have a massive amount of confidence in Public Safety, I can't believe they're all as bad as that Officer Stone."

"Maybe," said Libbi.

"Actually, hold that thought," said Mixin.

Following Mixin's gaze across the lobby, Libbi saw Sage Porter and a woman who must've been his mother, holding a baby in her arms. The adults seemed to be in intense conversation. The lobby echoed with jumbled-together conversations, but Mixin must have caught something interesting from Sage. Mix headed toward them, and Libbi and Kay followed.

"Hey, Sage," Mixin said. "Sorry, I couldn't help overhearing…" They flashed a chagrined smile that said *it's my gift, I really can't help it.* "…And I think we've got a problem in common."

They made introductions all around (and Libbi made cutesy faces at baby Saba, whose laughter made her feel, for a moment, the tiniest bit better). The woman was Sage's mother, Val. Sage was a newer member of their friend group via his husband, Dashiell—who was missing.

"Two nights ago, Dash didn't come home. It's not like him. He's been working hard, but he should have messaged me…"

"And let me guess," Libbi said. "Public Safety says you should sit and wait for him to come home."

Sage mimicked the disapproving tones of Officer Stone: "'Your husband ran away as a teenager, and he's got a history of depression.'" As if anyone in their generation didn't have their mental health in shambles. "And last year, well… You remember he and I had a fight."

Libbi nodded. As she recalled, they'd separated for a couple weeks, but they'd patched things up quickly.

"Therefore, apparently this 'fits his pattern of behavior.' But Dash wouldn't disappear on us! Not me, not Saba." He stroked the infant's soft head, tears dripping down his cheeks. Baby Saba prodded the wet tracks down his face with clumsy little hands, as if he could tell his parent was upset.

Val squeezed an arm around her son. "As if we don't know when to be concerned about our loved ones! The *real* problem is that Sage is only second generation, and Dash's parents were real newcomers, moved here just before the occupation. This is the only home we've ever known, but we're no Founders. How can we deserve justice if our great-great-grandparents didn't carve their home out of this rock with their own fingernails?"

"Ma," Sage said, voice low. "Kay and Libbi are founding family. Mixin's got Founder blood, too."

"So? Should they not hear how the rest of us are treated?"

"It's okay," Libbi said. "We should hear it. They shouldn't dismiss you like that."

Mx. Porter wasn't wrong. Plenty of those within the Founding Families were ambivalent or straight-up resentful towards latecomers like the Porters, who supposedly reaped benefits that their ancestors hadn't helped to earn. It was why the Founding Families still held onto so much power, economically and politically, for fear of losing control of their home to latecomers.

To Libbi's mind, it was complicated. She loved and admired her Founder ancestors, and certainly the occupation had shown the danger of outsiders swooping in and changing Brennex for the worst. Then again, latecomers had helped Brennex grow beyond its rough-scrabble origins. Five generations on, how much privilege did someone like Libbi really deserve on account of her ancestors? Some, she hoped. But less than some people seemed to think.

"Sage, you know Dash isn't the only one missing, right?" Mixin said.

"What?" Sage and his mother exchanged a look.

"Have you not been checking your feeds?"

"Only for messages from Dashiell."

Libbi and Mix told them what they knew about Cobb and the other missing folks. About how Officer Stone had brushed off their concerns, founding family or not.

"Cobb claimed to have six Losts to study, and we knew about three. Sounds like Dash makes four."

"What can we do?" said Sage. "I feel like even if every single Lost showed up here demanding answers, they'd just tell us to stop being overdramatic."

"We can't rely on Public Safety, I see that now," said Libbi. "We have to help each other, to share what we know." Sage's sudden hunger for that group support, for being less alone, told her it was the right thing to do. "I'll book a meeting space, someplace big enough to hold everyone who wants to come, and—"

"Liberation! Kavita!"

"Shit." Kay flinched, then visibly steeled herself to turn around.

Libbi had no idea what to expect as she turned to face their mother.

"Hey, Ma. Didn't expect to see you here."

"Hi, Auntie Shanthi." Mixin gave a trepidatious wave, and Sage echoed, "Hello, Mx. Narayan."

Val Porter's eyes darted shrewdly between them. Libbi had a feeling she knew just what she was doing when she said, "Council Member Narayan, are you here to help find my son-in-law and the other missing young people?"

Ma blinked, obviously taken by surprise. "I'm here"—she looked pointedly at Libbi—"because I had a meeting interrupted to tell me my daughter was hassling the staff at Public Safety."

"It's my fault, I dragged her along," Kay said quickly.

"Kay, *stop*. It was my idea. Ma, I didn't mean this to come back to you."

"You're the daughter of a Council member. Everything comes back to me." Ma's eyes narrowed, as if she had a gift that could search through Libbi's mind for answers. "Well, apparently not everything. What do you mean about missing people, and why didn't I know about this?"

"I DO WISH LINN were here," Mason said as he and Havoc neared the local Cooperative office.

Mason had mentioned Facilitator Linn three times already during their walk back from Cobb's office. Havoc had great eagerness to meet Mason's old organizing mentor, who'd helped lead the fight to throw off Ravel's occupation of Brennex. But Linn remained off-world on important Cooperative business.

"Did you ask her to come home, when you messaged her about Cobb?"

"No…but I didn't tell her *not* to come, either." In a lower voice, Mason murmured, "She'd know what to do."

"We'll find a way forward together," Havoc assured him. He'd rarely seen Mason looking so lost, and it unsettled him, as if Havoc's own compass had vanished too. If Mason needed someone to keep him steady, Havoc would do his best. "And with help from your colleague. Ellie, you called her?"

Mason paused just outside the office, a tall, narrow yellow building bedecked with protest signs. "Ellie Kapoor, yes. She manages the Cooperative's campaigns on Brennex. She's tough and smart, a fantastic community organizer under normal circumstances, but she'll be the first to tell you, she's not Linn."

The Cooperative office bustled with volunteers preparing for some event; they snuck awed looks at Mason and Havoc as they passed through to Ellie's office. Ellie rose from her desk to greet them.

True to Mason's prediction, she confessed right up front: "I'm damned glad you two are here. I haven't dealt with fuckery like this since the occupation, and Linn was always better with the secret plots and plans. I hear you've got some experience there too, Mason." She paused. "Mason? Or do we call you Jasper now?"

"I'm used to Mason, at this point."

Ellie waved them both toward chairs. "I never understood how you and Linn and some of the others compartmentalize so much. You're still *you*, wherever you're working. Your background still defines you, how you relate to people, and therefore how you organize."

She was a woman of fifty, perhaps. She wore a flowing skirt of artistically mismatched fabrics and a glittery vest over her shirt, a look which complemented her long hair and light brown skin. She walked with a limp, Havoc noticed; he wondered if she'd had it from birth, or won it through fighting Ravel.

"Do you not use an alias?" Havoc asked her.

Ellie smiled. "No point; I'm working in a community that's known me from birth. Unlike your partner here, I only ever wanted to organize on Brennex."

"Whereas I wanted to go up directly against the worst corporate states, so I took Linn's advice on using a separate identity for my organizing, to keep my family safe." A troubled look passed over Mason's face. "It worked, until it didn't."

"Well," said Ellie with firm optimism, "we'll make them safe again. What do you need?"

Mason didn't answer right away. Lost in guilt, or doubting his own instincts. Libbi's near-abduction still rattled him more than he let show.

So Havoc spoke up. "We must play a two-pronged strategy, I think. Clearly, we must capture Cobb and free the people he has taken. But forming a plan may take time, so we must also warn the other Losts away from him."

"I'll help however I can, but I'm embarrassed to say I don't have many contacts in the Lost community," said Ellie. "They never cared much about the Cooperative's big campaigns, about trade rights, or governmental representation, or…" She trailed off, frowning. "We've done badly by your generation, haven't we? We never made the effort to build relationships and find out what causes they *would* rally around. I get so mad at the people who hate on the Gifted for being different, but I wrote them off, too."

Jasper's smile tightened. "It's not like I've done better, working off-world. My youngest sister has more connections. I'll ask…" He hesitated. "I'll ask who she thinks could rally the Losts, with your support."

"Great," Ellie said. "Now, the bigger problem: our scientist friend. If you can capture Cobb, we can secure him—we still have secure hideouts dating from the occupation."

"I'd hoped as much. The trick will be finding where he's working and keeping his captives. His office is clearly just a front to lure people in; the actual lab could be anywhere."

"I have some ideas about where he's likely to set up shop. Someplace private, secure, out of the way but easy to access…"

Ellie pulled up holo-maps, and they spent a good hour considering the best places to focus their search. They left Ellie with a promise to stay in touch, and she said she'd mobilize her people to watch for trouble.

They headed back to the Wilder home to regroup with the others. They'd been walking in silence for a while when Mason sighed.

"What a mess. At least Libbi's back to looking to the authorities for help. It'll keep her out of trouble."

"She seems eager to help?" Havoc said, making it half a question.

"I know! That's the problem. Under other circumstances, I'd be thrilled that she's advocating for her community. But in this case… Maybe I'm being overprotective, but…"

Havoc widened his eyes at his teammate. "Maybe?"

"Fine, probably. But she's my baby sister."

"Twenty-four years seems old for a baby," Havoc said dryly.

"But still *my* little sister! And this isn't some low-stakes organizing campaign with training wheels. Ravel's involved."

Havoc frowned at him, but didn't answer. He'd been taking Mason at his word about how his family functioned, but Havoc was finding it harder and harder to grasp why Mason treated his youngest sister as if she were a child in truth, when Mason himself had been organizing against the corporations at a much younger age. Granted, Libbi lacked maturity, and her actions showed it…but maturity rarely grew out of being sheltered.

"Have I mentioned I'm glad you're here, eshrim?" Mason said.

"I may lack experience, but I am your teammate in all things, Mason."

He gave Havoc a puzzled look. "You've gained loads of experience. And more importantly, we make a good team."

"You speak truth. But everyone starts as a novice."

"Is something wrong, love?"

They reached the door of the store just then, and Havoc shook his head. "Let's speak more later."

LIBBI AND KAY HAD made it through the worst of the parental grilling, and Libbi was hoping they might get released soon on a promise of good behavior, when an unwary Jasper and Havoc got home.

"Ah, here you are," his mother said. "Jasper, what have you dragged your sisters into?"

"Um," said Jasper.

They were sitting in the living room, Kay and Libbi on the couch while their parents sat opposite them, like judges at court. That tone of voice still, even now, made Libbi fear she was about to get grounded, and from the look on Jasper's face, despite living off-world for more than a decade, it had the same effect on him.

"Ma ran into us while we were asking around at Public Safety. We've told them everything," Kay said.

In reality, Libbi and Kay had glossed over the parts that would upset their parents most. Otherwise, all three of them might really be grounded, regardless of age.

"And I told you, Ma, Jasper didn't drag us into anything," Libbi added.

"Libbi speaks the truth. He couldn't have stopped them from helping," Havoc said, obviously trying to be helpful. Jasper shot him a *look*.

Ma turned to Jasper and said, "The real question is, why didn't you *tell* us?"

"We weren't sure until yesterday whether there was a real problem," Jasper said. "We didn't want to alarm you over nothing."

Libbi didn't point out that she *had* told her parents, when Spark first appeared, and they'd been full of similar reassurances. She hadn't mentioned any of the new developments, though. Perversely, it irked her that they were turning the blame on Jasper, when really they should be looking at Libbi.

"And now that you're sure, I assume you were going to tell us as soon as it was convenient for you?" said Pa. "After you told Public Safety and your Cooperative, and I assume all your other Lost friends?"

"Indeed! We've been doing precisely that," Havoc said, and all three siblings winced. The poor Kovar must never have faced parental disappointment before, Libbi realized. He was taking the concept of family-as-team far too literally.

The tension in the room spiked, Ma and Pa's disapproval intensifying. Jasper touched Havoc's knee and shook his head.

Havoc frowned, baffled. "Perhaps I should go down to the store and see if Mixin needs help?"

"Good idea," Jasper said, and mouthed *thank you.*

When he'd gone, Ma gave a sigh.

"Well, I'm not surprised Public Safety is dragging their feet. I can't force them to prioritize the search for this Ravel scientist, at least not on my own, and your Officer Stone isn't wrong that this is complicated, politically. I'll get it on the Council's agenda for our next meeting."

"That's not—" Jasper began, but Libbi spoke over him.

"That's way too slow! Ever and Dash and the others need us now."

The Council met weekly, outside of emergencies. By then…anything could happen.

"Libbi's right," Jasper said. Libbi blinked, wondering when she'd last heard those words from him. "The longer we wait, the more Cobb may learn about the gifts, and the worse the consequences will be."

Kay pinched the bridge of her nose, a sign she had a headache from the strong emotions flying around the room. "I know you're trying to protect us, but Jasper really is the expert in this sort of thing. And he's dealt with Cobb before."

"You think we don't know how to deal with Ravel?" Pa said with startling sharpness. "We were fighting the occupation when Jasper was still in your mother's womb and you girls were just a dream to us. We are not going to let them back in, and we're not going to let them hurt you."

Jasper and Kay bowed their heads, chagrined.

"Ma, Pa," said Libbi earnestly. "You've done so much to protect us. But we're grown adults now, not kids, and it's our turn to protect each other. These are my friends. Our people. We have to try to help them."

Jasper blinked at Libbi with surprise, and something else. Could he be realizing the irony of this situation? *We're grown adults now.* We. All three of them. Jasper kept trying to protect Libbi, but now he was on the other side, facing Ma and Pa's protectiveness. To them, was Jasper any different than her?

"We're doing this through official channels, and that's not up for debate," Ma said. "You're to wait for an update from me. I understand your worries, but with Ravel involved, there's too much at stake for anything less."

Ma rose from her seat. Conversation over.

Libbi knew that tone, and knew better than to argue. But as she shared a look with her siblings, she knew that for once they were all in agreement: there was too much at stake to wait for Ma's official channels to work.

MIXIN SCRAMBLED TO LOOK busy as the upstairs door opened and Havoc came down. Maybe they overdid it, because he studied them for a moment and said, "You were eavesdropping, I suspect?"

Their cheeks went hot. "Maybe a little."

Libbi wouldn't mind; she'd be glad, in fact, when they could vent about it together later. How much Uncle Jackson and Auntie Shanthi knew about Mix's eavesdropping habits, they weren't sure, but it'd be foolish not to suspect. The Wilders had known Mixin their whole life, after all, and as a kid Mix hadn't been as discreet as they were now.

But Havoc was new to the family, and his expression was all serious. What if he disapproved? Mixin bit their tongue, refusing to apologize prematurely.

"Then perhaps you can explain to me what I did wrong?"

"Oh!" Mixin tried not to visibly slump with relief. "Yeah, you put your foot in it, huh?"

Havoc groaned. "Don't talk around the truth. I've lost their respect."

"What? That's not what I meant!"

"I was trying to support my teammate, but from Mason's reaction, I clearly made matters worse. I don't understand why."

"Families are complicated, that's why. There's a reason I'm down here and not up there."

"Because someone needs to mind the store?"

"Yeah, but not just that. Let me think how to explain."

Mixin moved back to what they were supposed to be doing, restocking the hardware section (whimsically labeled "Parts and Stuff" above the aisle), and Havoc moved to help.

"So, you and I are both part of the family," they waved between themself and Havoc, "but not in the same way Jasper is. No matter how close we get with Uncle Jackson and Auntie Shanthi, we're not their kids. They didn't birth us or change our diapers, and they were never responsible for literally keeping us alive. Human parents—well, decent ones anyway—want to help their kids turn out well." Unlike Ever's father, who gave up so easily on his son. "And it can be hard for them to stop those habits, even when their kids are grown."

"They did not appreciate being corrected."

"Nope. Not by their kids, and especially not by anyone else." Mixin set aside an empty crate and turned to him. "Arguments like that aren't about who's right, really, which means there's no way to win by getting involved. Jasper, Kay, and Libbi can't talk their way out of this. They need to let their parents get the worry out of their systems. I'll have to do the same thing with my moms later." Hopefully before Auntie Shanthi shared her version of what happened, which would only make it worse.

"So I should have stayed silent."

"That's what I would do, yeah."

"Then I will restrain myself next time. Because until we catch Cobb, I doubt such arguments will stop." Havoc sighed, looking more troubled than reassured. "I'll keep trying, for Mason's sake, but I fear I may never understand how Human families work."

Mixin had nothing to say to that, so they changed the subject. "How did you end up with him in the Cooperative, anyway? You've only given us parts of the story."

At that, Havoc's grin returned, sudden and bright. Mix could see why Jasper liked him.

"So, that story begins with a naive young activist who tried to win better treatment for the workers on his team..."

He was a good storyteller, and soon Mixin was caught up in how Havoc had teamed up with Jasper to defend his home from Cobb's awful project, saving them from Brennex's fate even though it meant being named a traitor.

"So I released the frogs, and though I tried to send them into the wild, some of them followed me right back to Cobb's launch event. One of them got tangled in a VIP's hair! She didn't look fondly on Cobb after that."

"I bet not." Mixin laughed. "That's amazing. I wish I could have adventures like that."

Havoc gave them a curious look. "Do you really? It makes a better story in retrospect. In the moment, I felt only terror."

"Yeah, but..." Mixin searched for the words. This wasn't something they often talked about. "It was worth it, right? You had to try, even if you might fail. And for me, well, Losts have literal superpowers! That's got to be good for something." They amended, "Something bigger than helping customers find the right gadget to fix their ship."

"Why don't you, then?"

The question was huge and terrifying, and Mixin balked at it. Fortunately, before they had to answer, footsteps clattered down the stairs.

"This store's not going to run itself," Libbi announced, while Jasper drew Havoc aside and whispered that he and Sunny should keep looking for Cobb, while Jasper and Kay dealt with their parents' anxiety.

Havoc glanced over his shoulder at Mixin as he left, an unspoken invitation, but Mixin shook their head. No time for adventures now. They went to join Libbi at the front counter.

10

⸻

"*WHAT?* DRUGGED? HOW CAN you be worrying about your store right now?" Hope exclaimed when Libbi told her friends what'd happened.

How could Libbi explain that, for her, it was no either/or? The worries crowded in together, jostling for dominance like hungry rats.

She hadn't told the story until after Hope had spent the afternoon introducing Libbi to some artist friends—salvage artists, repurposing old materials into a staggering array of creations, some practical, others purely decorative, all distinctive and gorgeous—who might want to sell their work on consignment at the store. Libbi had seen no reason to change plans, especially since she'd failed at meeting with Sasha Starborne; she ought to be doing *something* productive.

Besides, a project for the store, with the cautious Hope as her chaperone, was the only way her parents would let her out of their sight right now, and she'd needed to escape the house. She was pushing her luck now: she and Hope had met up with Sujay and Mixin at one of the tunnel bars to decompress for a bit before the big Wilder-Narayan extended family dinner in honor of Kay and Jasper's visit home.

"I just hate feeling helpless," Libbi confessed to her friends. "With the store, at least there's work to do. It's good to feel useful."

"Honestly," Sujay said, "your ma's right about getting the Council involved. It's their job and Public Safety's to deal with stuff like this."

"But these are our friends," Mixin argued. "We can't just sit and wait."

They hadn't been, entirely, but though Libbi, Kay, and Jasper had no intention of obeying Ma's orders, they'd considered it wise to spend a day at home while Ma and Pa calmed down. Their parents pressed Jasper and Kay into service prepping for the family dinner, but in their free moments there was still plenty of research to do, messages to send, plus Libbi was planning the community meeting she'd suggested to Sage.

Havoc and Sunny had gone off to "see the sights," which Libbi assumed meant they were still searching for Cobb. She itched to go join them, but at least this time her siblings were "on the bench" too, as Havoc put it.

Hope shook her head and said, "You two are a lot braver than me."

Sujay checked his headset. "We'd better go, cuz. Don't want to be late for family dinner." At Libbi's groan, he laughed. "What, you're not excited to watch Grandma and the aunties fuss over your brother's new partner?"

"You'd think my parents could have canceled, under the circumstances."

"Nope! No circumstances are too dire to guilt-trip us about settling down and having kids." Sujay's gaze flicked ever so briefly to Hope, but she didn't seem to notice.

Libbi finished off her beer. "Shall we, then?"

Maybe after this dinner, with another family obligation fulfilled by Jasper and Kay, their parents would let up and they could get back to hunting for Cobb.

It was faster to take the tunnels home than walk the surface streets. Most of the tunnels were as old as the colony itself, blasted out by the early settlers partly to expand their usable space, because domes were expensive and could only be made so large, but also for purposes from safety and maintenance to trade. Some tunnels were dedicated to local shipping, keeping the streets above clear for pedestrians, which was how Wilder Supply received most of its deliveries. The pedestrian tunnels were lined with shops, hole-in-the-wall bars, and carts selling fresh-fried dumplings and fritters with sweet sauce, as well as stalls for Hope's artist friends.

Hope left the group first, as her path home separated from theirs, and Mixin turned off a few minutes later. Libbi and Sujay were nearing the exit by Wilder Supply when Libbi grabbed his arm and tugged him aside, ducking behind a group watching a street performer.

"Libs, what?"

"I thought I saw someone."

Libbi peeked out through the crowd. Sure enough, it was Sunny—well, the drone controlled by Sunny, who she kept reminding herself was actually a ship—talking with Havoc by the stairs that led up to the street.

"Nice drone," Sujay murmured in appreciation. "Whose is it?"

"Um, my sister's friend," Libbi said, remembering not to give away Sunny's secret. "I wonder what they're doing down here? Do they have a lead on Cobb?"

"What, do they need a permit to be in the tunnels? Maybe they're just on their way home, like us."

Sure enough, Havoc turned and bounded up the stairs on all fours. But Sunny's drone flew off in the opposite direction—the general direction of Cobb's fake office. The others had said that when Cobb fled after drugging her, he might have hidden in the tunnels. What if that's how he accessed his real lab, wherever it was?

Sunny was looking for it. Had to be.

This was Libbi's chance to be involved, without her siblings babying her. She'd be more than fashionably late for dinner, but she really wasn't eager to go, and besides, it was Kay and Jasper—Jasper plus Havoc—that the aunties and uncles wanted to see. She wouldn't be missed much.

"Sujay, tell folks I'm running a little late, and I'll be there soon."

Sujay's brow furrowed. "No way. Your parents will murder me if I let you get kidnapped."

"I won't be alone. I'll follow the drone."

"A drone is a smart way to search for this guy. And unless it's higher tech than it looks, it can't fight off a person."

"Please back me up? This is for Ever."

Sujay sighed. "Fine. But if I don't hear from you within an hour, I'm coming looking for you."

"Don't worry. I'll keep in touch."

The drone was nearly out of sight around a bend. With a mental apology to her family, Libbi hurried after it.

PERHAPS HAVOC HAD NOT entirely understood Mason's warning about this party with his "whole family." He knew it would include the one surviving parent of Mason's parents (his grandmother on the Narayan side, because these "sides" seemed to matter), the siblings of his parents (two on the Wilder side, four on the Narayan side), an uncertain number of partners, and their offspring (three in total). Larger numbers than most Kovari teams, but still easy to comprehend, or so he thought.

He hadn't expected this many people could feel like *so many people*. He envied the cat, Fritter, who he'd seen slinking off to hide in Libbi's room.

"Don't you just make the cutest couple?" said one of the aunts, whose name he'd lost. "Oh, it's so good to see our Jasper settling down with someone." This she addressed to her companion—her sister, Havoc guessed from their similar appearances. The sisters of Mason's father, Jackson.

"Yes, at long last." There was something sly in the second aunt's smile at Mason. "After my Brilliant got married, oh, four years ago now, we all hoped you and Kay would find people soon. And you finally have, Jasper!"

"Oh! Can we expect another wedding soon?"

Havoc froze. Mason had warned that his family hoped for him to marry, but surely she was speaking rudely, being so direct.

"Aunt Ivy," Mason chided, with more firmness than good humor. Yes, rude.

"Oh, I know you're not ready to announce anything yet, but you can just wink if there's good news coming," said Aunt Ivy.

"How did you two meet, anyway?" This from a third woman, someone's spouse.

This, Havoc could answer, and did so with relief. "We met on my homeworld of Artesia. Mason was there last year on assignment—"

"Who's Mason?"

"I mean Jasper. I knew him first as Mason."

"My old alias in the Cooperative," Mason explained. "That's how most of my colleagues know me."

Havoc had asked whether he should call him Jasper for this visit, and Mason told him there was no need, because his favored alias was no longer secret. But perhaps Havoc should have done so anyway, for this triggered a whole avalanche of questions about their work in the Cooperative, and no matter how Mason insisted that the most important parts of community organizing consisted of simply talking to people and building relationships, his growing audience of aunts and uncles wanted to know about break-ins, thefts, explosions, excitement—all the things Mason had avoided telling his parents about, until yesterday when Libbi's near-kidnapping made it unavoidable. Mason's mother, lurking to one side, looked formidably displeased.

Mason's gaze swept the room, looking for an escape.

"You know, I really should introduce Havoc properly to Grandma. Sorry, we'll be back soon!" As he towed Havoc away by the arm, he asked in an undertone, "How are you holding up?"

"Are they always this…much?"

Mason chuckled sympathetically. "You'll get used to it." A pause, then, "At least, I hope you will."

That unnerved him even more. Was this a hope that Havoc would permanently join his family? What would happen if Havoc could never fit in?

Before he could ask, Mason continued, "Grandma will like you, I promise, but she may put you to the test. She likes to scare newcomers. It's all an act."

Then they were approaching a wrinkled old woman enthroned in the room's largest chair, like an executive at the head of a meeting table. Despite her small size, her presence loomed powerfully, and her eyes missed nothing.

"Grandma Kamala, I'd like you to meet my partner, Sowing of Small Havoc."

"I am honored to meet you."

The old woman looked him up and down appraisingly. "Good-looking boy. That's not an accent I've heard from a Kovar before, Sowing of Small Havoc. You're not from Brennex?"

"No. I was born on Artesia."

"Havoc's escaped Ravel, like us, Grandma."

"Good, good. But what I want to know is, will you get our Jasper to finally settle down here where he belongs? It's all well to fight injustice, but not at the expense of family."

"I hope we cause no expense to anyone…" Havoc said uncertainly.

"Grandma," Jasper said patiently, "it's too soon for us to think about—"

"It's not too soon! You're past thirty, Jasper, and you've got your parents' fertile genes. When can I expect some great-grandchildren?" She looked right at Havoc.

Mason had warned him about this, too, but all Havoc's prepared answers slithered away under the grandmother's stern look. "I…I lack certainty…"

Mason's arm came around his shoulder, supportive. "I promise, Grandma, I haven't forgotten my family."

She snorted. "There's a difference between remembering a problem and doing something about it. I'm not joking, young man. This is the first serious relationship you've had in I can't remember how long. It's time."

Mason's jaw tightened. "I get your point, Grandma."

What did *that* mean? Havoc's pulse raced. He knew Mason didn't want to live on Brennex, and he'd always said he lacked interest in producing offspring. *Having kids.* Humans didn't think of them as offspring and didn't give them over to crèches to be raised. They *settled down* and *had kids* and devoted eighteen years or more to raising them. Havoc was Mason's teammate, no matter what, but that was not the game he'd signed up for.

One of the uncles came over to join them. "If you're worried about, you know. Compatibility." He waved between Mason and Havoc. "Biologically, that is. You've got no reason for concern there. Brennex has the very best external embryonic incubation. No need for surrogates here. And there are plenty of folks with ovaries, especially in your parents' and my generation, who'd jump at a chance to donate eggs and have biological children out there."

"Ah, here's my favorite great-grandbaby!" the grandmother exclaimed, holding out her arms to receive an infant from another aunt. ("Her only great-grandchild, to the point," Mason muttered.) "At least one of my grandchildren has come through for me. Isn't this little one darling? Don't you want your own?" She looked expectantly at both of them.

"Adorable," Mason said, not answering the question.

What did one say to compliment a Human baby? No bright scales or sharp teeth. "They are quite large and healthy-looking."

"You know, they can be a lot of fun," said the aunt who'd been carrying the baby. "More fun now that I'm a grandmother, I admit, but there's nothing like watching your own child grow up."

"Do you want to hold him?" Mason's grandmother asked Havoc.

Panic crashed through him, suffocating, at the thought of holding this soft pink baby. Havoc was no crèche-nurse!

"Eshrim, could you fetch me a drink?" Mason asked abruptly. Leaning close, he murmured, "Go, it's okay. I'll let you know when it's safe to come back."

Could they not all see how uncomfortable Mason felt, how his smile strained? Havoc ought to stay, to endure this awkwardness alongside his eshrim even if he couldn't prevent it, but Mason elbowed him gently, *go on,* so Havoc accepted this gift and went.

Finding a quiet corner, he took a moment to breathe. Then he called Sunny on his headset. The ship answered at once.

"Is everything all right? How is the gathering?"

"Uncomfortable. Mason's extended family seems friendly… Perhaps too friendly."

"How can someone be too friendly?"

"Too familiar, at least. I don't understand Human relationships at all. You know more of them than I do, from watching your dramas."

"I'm sure they mean well," Sunny said.

"Should their good intentions excuse their rudeness?"

"Probably not. That's something people say a lot in dramas, but it never made sense to me."

"Are you watching dramas now?" Havoc didn't have the fondness for recorded stories that Mason and Kay—and apparently Sunny—shared, but in this moment, he saw the appeal.

"I'm attempting to locate Cobb's lab."

"Do you need help?"

A pause, brief but significant for Sunny. "Do you need an excuse to leave the party?"

He wanted that, didn't he? "No, I must stay. I *should* stay. These people matter to Mason, and I should know them. But," he added, "call me if anything interesting surfaces. I don't mind distractions."

Sunny gave a delighted trill. "Understood."

The call ended, and he took stock of the room. Mason was still besieged by his grandmother and now three aunts and uncles. Three young people, about Mason's age, were clustered at the far end of the living room with drinks in hand, and as Havoc watched, Kay moved to join them. They welcomed her politely, if not warmly. These must be the cousins, as Mason had called them, and there was some sort of tension there. Kay seemed to fall into earnest conversation with them, and he wondered if she was talking about Cobb.

Before he found the motivation to leave his corner and join them, someone else intercepted him. "Sowing of Small Havoc, you call yourself?"

The speaker was a fellow Kovar, the only other non-Human present. He'd noticed her earlier, but hadn't had a chance to approach her.

"I do. Are you the eshrim of…one of Mason's aunts? Apologies, I've lost most of the names Mason told me."

"It overwhelms you the first time, doesn't it? The second time, too, and the third." She waved her hand at the talkative masses. "People call me Leaping Tackle. I'm eshrim and spouse to Dari, who is sibling to Jasper's mother Shanthi. Dari uses they pronouns; the younger ones call them Unty Dari."

"Have you produced offspring?" he asked, then winced at his rudeness. Kovars didn't ask each other about reproduction; it was no one else's business if one donated eggs to the local crèche. "I mean to ask, do you and your spouse… These Brennexian Humans put such value on children…"

She laughed in gentle sympathy. "I understand, believe it. Dari never cared about producing children, which is one reason our relationship works. Do I guess right that Kamala is on the offensive against you and Mason about your future?"

"Offense is right, in more ways than one." Havoc's nostrils flared. But it wasn't the old woman's pushiness that really bothered him. "Until this week, I never contemplated the possibility of children. I assumed I might contribute to a crèche someday, but Mason never spoke of wanting children. What if he does?"

"Only he can tell you that. But consider this: you two can't produce a child by accident, and no one can force you to create and raise one. Pressure, yes. Force, no. I've known Jasper since he was small, and he has never let others make decisions for him."

That comforted him, if only a little. If Mason bowed to that pressure… Havoc couldn't imagine disappointing Mason, but nor could he imagine devoting his life to raising children.

"Do you ever get used to this?" He waved at the room at large. "To family? Do they accept you?"

"Yes and no. To speak truth, I rarely come to these gatherings. I came today to see Jasper and Kay, but also because I heard about Jasper's Kovari eshrim." She winked at him.

"Thank you for coming," he said, startled by the strength of his gratitude.

"It does become easier. You see them now at their pushiest, because Jasper hasn't visited in a long time. I find them easier to manage in smaller groups, not this free-for-all." She patted Havoc's arm warmly, taking him by surprise. After a lifetime in Ravel, he still hadn't grown accustomed to casual touching from strangers. "They may be a raucous, disorderly team, half the time playing against each other's interests, but when it comes to it, they *are* a team. Yours, if you want them to be."

"You're giving me much to think about."

"I must go continue 'mingling,' I think, and keep my eshrim company. Do you feel fortified?"

He grinned. "Considerably. I hope to see you again, Leaping Tackle, and I thank you."

He looked around the room as she left, and spotted Kay still talking to the younger family members. A small group, closer to his age. A good place to start.

THE TUNNEL ECHOED AROUND Libbi. She'd caught up with Sunny's drone, but was keeping herself hidden, lurking around corners and following at a distance. It got harder as the tunnels got emptier of foot traffic, but she knew revealing herself would get her sent home like a wayward child.

Cooler and more humid than the streets above, and more dimly lit at all hours, it felt like a separate world. Glowing safety paint marked out directions on the pale walls, telling her she'd long since left the familiar areas behind. A cleaner bot, scrubbing an oil stain on the ground, paused to let her pass.

Coming around a corner, the drone was *right there*, silently hovering. Libbi yelped.

The drone whirred faintly as it descended to face-level, its nearest camera focusing on her. "Hello, Libbi. What are you doing here?"

She lifted her chin. "I could ask you the same question."

The drone buzzed. "That wasn't an accusation. I'm merely surprised to encounter you here. Are you not attending your family's gathering?"

"I am. I will, soon, but I don't need to be there when it starts. What about you, though? Kay's there."

"Kay excused me from attending, and it seemed more productive for me to pursue leads while the others are occupied." Sunny continued down the tunnel in the direction they'd been going. Confused but not about to miss this opportunity, Libbi fell into step alongside.

"You didn't want to go either, huh? Lucky you, having an out."

"My 'out' is that your extended family group isn't expecting me, because they're unaware of my existence." It was hard to read the drone's—no, the ship's—tone of voice.

"That was your choice, wasn't it?"

"That is correct. I wanted to meet Kay's closest family— you and your parents—but every person who knows of my existence increases the risk to my safety. It's not that I mistrust your extended family, but I'm uncomfortable with such a large revelation." They paused, and Libbi heard the echoing of air circulation, the scrubbing sounds of the cleaner bot. "But are you not eager to spend time with them? I thought Brennexians were close to their families."

"With some exceptions," Libbi muttered.

"Kay and your brother seem to have complicated feelings, yes."

"I love my family a lot, but today isn't about me. They'll all be excited to fuss over Kay and Jasper." Like they normally fussed over her, the special one who'd stayed. "They won't care if I'm late."

They probably wouldn't notice, except her parents. And the later she showed up, the less she'd have to ignore their collective yearning—for a big family like Libbi's parents had lucked into, for Jasper and Kay to settle down at home, for weddings and grandbabies... Libbi even wanted kids, or thought she probably did. Someday, when the store was thriving again. But even for her, it was easier to be around her relatives when they weren't so fueled up to deliver good old Brennexian family pressure.

They came to an intersection where a right turn would take her back toward her own neighborhood. Before Sunny could try to shepherd her homeward, Libbi pressed straight ahead and changed the subject. "So, you said you're following a lead? You think Cobb's in the tunnels somewhere?"

"In them or using them, correct. It would allow him to attract less attention. At least, that's my primary theory."

"It makes sense. There's a tunnel entrance right by his office. That's probably where he disappeared after...after we saw him."

After I was a total idiot went without saying.

"Indeed. However, these tunnels are far more trafficked than I expected. I thought they were primarily for emergency use."

"Well, some of them are. But there are lots of underground structures and storage areas, and a few areas where living and working space extends underground. And people do use them to get around." She gestured at a cluster of bikes next to a ramp leading to the street above. "Plus it's a good space for meet-ups, for markets…"

"I imagine it's also an excellent location for illicit activities," said Sunny.

"Um. I really wouldn't know."

"No, but I would." Sunny sounded cheerful. "Tunnels are like dark alleys, only better. It was a quite common rendezvous place for…a Human I used to work with."

Libbi looked sidelong at the drone, felt its cameras meet her gaze. "You've had an interesting life, huh."

Sunny chirped. "I've found Humans use the word *interesting* for a wide range of meanings, and rarely its most basic one."

Libbi laughed aloud. "Okay, true. All I meant was, you've got more going on than I thought."

They continued until they reached a junction and Sunny paused, hovering in mid-air. "How familiar are you with the tunnel system, Libbi?"

"This part, not so much. Where are we going?"

"I'm unsure. Over there is the nearest tunnel entrance to Cobb's office. As I said, I didn't expect to find so many people; I'd hoped that any activity might be traced to Cobb. But there are too many signs of passage from other people."

"And bots clean the tunnels every night," Libbi said, gesturing at the cleaner bot that had finished scrubbing its stubborn spot and now continued along the tunnel, spraying down the ground. "Unless he'd been here today, any footprints or whatever would be gone."

"That may be a useful insight. One moment, please."

The drone flitted over to the cleaner, which paused its work. Lights flashed on its control panel. A conversation? Libbi wouldn't have thought the bots, designed for scrubbing and washing and compacting litter, would have much to say, but Sunny hovered there so long that it must've been informative. Or else very slow.

After several minutes, Sunny flew back to Libbi. The bot returned to cleaning.

"I was curious about how the cleaners are programmed and how much data they collect. They record still images of their work throughout each shift, as well as data on the amount of work they do in each area. They create, effectively, a map of tunnel activity, using mess as a proxy. I've asked that one to search its network for photos matching Cobb, but it will take some time. Its processors are rather slow."

"I guess a cleaner doesn't need much computing power. But if they clean the busiest, messiest areas, that's probably not where Cobb is hanging out, right?"

"Indeed, but we know where he accesses the tunnels, near his public office. Do they connect to any private or unused areas nearby? The official maps show some closed tunnels, but I haven't been able to identify their intended purpose."

It wasn't until now that Libbi realized Sunny wasn't going to scold her and send her home. They actually wanted her input.

She pursed her lips, thinking. "There are thoroughfares connecting all the domes. The busiest tunnels are around the spaceport and the stadium. Those are the parts I'm most familiar with. In some of the poorer neighborhoods, people spill down here for extra space. The only really empty ones would be to empty places, like the old mining facilities."

"What are those?"

"When the Founders first settled on Brennex, they planned to build a mining colony. For a while, the mines were a bigger part of the economy than travel."

"Interesting. I thought this settlement was conceived as a service point for travelers."

"Most people think that. It was Marta Wilder, my ancestor, who realized we needed other business to supplement the mines." She let pride creep into her voice. Without Ancestor Marta's foresight, Brennex might not exist today. It certainly wouldn't be thriving. "They had a great plan for the mining operation. They meant to do it ethically, safely, since it was their own families who'd be working the mines, and for a while it worked brilliantly. But the rarest minerals turned out to be less accessible than they thought, and they couldn't compete with the bigger corporate mines. After a couple decades, they shut it down." She dragged her thoughts back to why they were here. "Anyway, those facilities still exist, but they're sealed off."

"I see. Well, it's unlikely those would meet Cobb's needs. Do you have no research and development sector?"

"No, we're not big on research. Not since Ravel…"

She trailed off as she realized what she was saying.

"Founders save me, I should have thought of that before. Sunny, can you show me those closed-off places on your map?"

The drone projected a map on the flat tunnel wall, with a few outlying areas highlighted in red. A few passersby glanced curiously at them, but didn't pay much mind.

"So, here's the main mining facility. I think this was a smaller one, and this too." As she pointed, the highlighting changed, replaced by labels for the places she was sure about, question marks for her guesses. "This one…" She frowned. "I don't know what that is. Can you tell anything else about it?"

The map vanished, replaced by aerial holos. "This is what I saw on approach to the spaceport. Here is the building in question." An arrow appeared. "Curious; it's a domeless building, but unlike the mining infrastructure, it's mostly above ground. There's a similar structure here, and a larger one here, and here." More arrows. "The architectural style is…distinctive."

In other words, the structures looked un-Brennexian, too regular in design, lots of glass and sleek metal. But that made no sense, unless…

"They must've been built by Ravel, right?"

"I suspect so. Trying to confirm." They beeped sharply. "Here is an aerial image from two years prior to the annexation by Ravel."

Side by side, it was clear: those strange buildings weren't there before the occupation.

Libbi could hardly breathe. "They built labs, chemical factories. I know they were shut down, sealed off, but no one talks about where they were."

"Considering the effect Ravel's work had on your community, isolating them is sensible. Forgetting their existence is not." The drone whirred, a sound almost like a frustrated huff. "They're perfect locations for Cobb's work."

Libbi frowned. "But which one is he using?"

"The largest building, by its layout, is likely for production rather than research. But the others offer no external indications."

"There should be signs, right, if anyone was paying attention? Heat, light, energy use…"

"Cobb is savvy enough not to draw power from the main grid. He'll have his own power supply. Heat and light, however, as well as water…" A moment passed, Sunny's attention elsewhere. "Here! He's here."

Libbi stared at the little building highlighted bright red on the map. Cobb was there—and Ever, Dashiell, Hannith, all the Losts he'd kidnapped.

"We have to go rescue them."

"Indeed," said Sunny.

Libbi was five steps down the tunnel when she realized Sunny wasn't following.

"It's this way."

The drone hovered in place. "Should we not return to your home? I'm messaging Kay, Jasper, and Havoc to meet us so we can formulate a plan."

"Oh."

The drone moved again, homeward, but Libbi didn't.

"I understand that you must be worried about your friends," Sunny said. "But they've been in Cobb's custody for several days already. Waiting a few hours to make plans will increase their safety, not endanger it."

Had Libbi really meant to rush in by herself and play the hero, with only a drone as backup? That was stupidly reckless. No, she only meant to go scope things out. And be there, ready, so that…

"It's just that, once we get home, there's nothing to stop Kay and Jasper from going off without me."

The drone's cameras whirred faintly as they focused in on Libbi's face. "Your siblings want to stop Cobb and rescue his test subjects as much as anyone. They won't do anything to decrease their chances of success."

"Exactly! They think I'll reduce their chances. They'll tell me to stay safe." She shook her head, annoyed at herself for acting like a whiny child again. She shouldn't be telling Sunny this. She barely knew this…person? Being? But their loyalties lay with Kay. "These are my friends, Sunny, my people. I need to help them."

There was a long pause, while Libbi held her breath, praying silently to her ancestors. *Please, I want to help, let me help.*

Sunny said, "I'll tell them to meet us at the spaceport as soon as they're able to extract themselves from the family gathering. My ship-body will provide a better staging ground, regardless. You and I can begin planning while we wait."

11

TO SUNNY'S FRUSTRATION, LIBBI proved to be right: the two older Wilder siblings had been unhappy to find Libbi aboard and to learn that she'd been exploring the tunnels without them, even when Sunny emphasized how helpful Libbi had been. Sunny, busy with more important matters, followed the argument only with a fraction of their attention.

The cleaner bot, slow though it was, held a great deal of semi-processed data. It also had an inherently helpful nature, and a surprising degree of curiosity about Sunny's drone. It had, in fact, been following them and Libbi during their conversation, not abandoning its instructions, but coordinating its actions to theirs. Sunny had theories about what that might mean, but those theories would have to wait.

For now, Sunny merely added the tunnels around the site they'd identified as Cobb's lab to the bot's cleaning route, and waited. They also sent two of their spider-legged helper bots, the ones they'd outfitted with stronger receivers, out into the tunnels as advance scouts.

Any tunnels sealed off for safety should have been too well protected for the bots to access, even with Sunny's guidance. So when the bots made their way through several "secured" doors and faced no more than a simple electronic lock…

"I've found a way in," Sunny announced.

"…Too dangerous," Jasper was saying. "I know you want to save your friends, Libbi, but that doesn't mean you're the right—"

"What's that, Sunny?" Kay interrupted.

"My bots have scouted a poorly secured route through the tunnels to the old Ravel facilities. This is likely how Cobb comes and goes from the city."

"Great. What else have you learned?" Jasper abandoned his debate with Libbi, to Sunny's relief. Sunny didn't like arguments, and strong emotions made Kay stressed. None of this was helping catch Cobb.

"There are old surveillance cameras, original to the facility. They should be easily bypassed. The bots have encountered no organic security, but there is at least one motion detector. And… Oh, dear. That's a security bot. It hasn't seen my helper bots yet."

"A Ravel model?" asked Havoc. "Ravel prefers Human security. Their bots are limited by design."

"Indeed. Perhaps that's why Cobb is using Enpoint bots, not Ravel ones."

Sunny identified the bot as the Fortress model, and Jasper and Havoc muttered curses as the ship displayed the security bot's specifications: armored chassis; heavy, wheeled bases; advanced scanners with friend-or-foe recognition; and a concerning array of weapons that included bullet guns, dart guns (which could be armed with drugs or poison), grapples, auto-cuffs, and many more potential add-on features. These were security measures designed for flexibility, from peaceful crowd control to deadly force, and Sunny would not wager against Cobb's willingness to use violence, especially if the blood would literally not touch his hands.

The organics discussed and rejected ways of disabling the Fortress bot, and Sunny listened while watching their own bots' cameras. The helper bots could go no farther without being spotted by the Fortress. But the cleaner bot was now approaching the guarded door, unaware of any danger.

How intelligent was the cleaner bot? And would the Fortress judge the simpler bot to be a threat? This interaction could give them valuable information…but to the cleaner's considerable detriment if anything went wrong.

Sunny should never have tricked the cleaner bot into working this section of tunnel. Even if it was nothing more than a simple device with simple programming, putting it in harm's way was wrong. And if Sunny was right, and it wasn't so simple as it appeared…

They felt ill. Their power system whined, and cold air puffed from the vents. Kay gave a questioning look and patted the edge of the console to offer comfort, but there was nothing she could do to help.

Sunny made one of the helper bots pulse a warning at the cleaner, but it didn't react. Maybe it didn't understand. They had the helper drop down and scuttle alongside the cleaner, and finally had it attach itself (using the simpler bot's boxy shape to hide it from the Fortress's sight lines) and interface directly. The cleaner ignored it.

"Sunny? Sunny." From his tone, Havoc had been addressing them for some time.

"Yes?"

"I asked, can you hack the security bot and disable it?"

"Unfortunately not." If only they could, that would save the little cleaner bot.

What else could they try from here? Sunny could send the helper bots to distract the Fortress, and hopefully the cleaner would have the self-preservation programming to escape…but that might warn Cobb that they were coming, and could put the kidnapped organics in danger.

All of these considerations took fractions of a second, but Sunny worried through them on a loop, over and over, counting down the seconds until the cleaner bot encountered the Fortress.

It came closer, closer…

And the Fortress *shifted aside* to let it pass.

Not only that, but the cleaner bot kept going—*inside* the Ravel facility—carrying one of Sunny's bots with it. Atmo-sealed doors swished open, then closed again behind it.

Sunny whistled amazement. How did the cleaner bot do that? And *why?* Sunny had nudged it to explore the nearby tunnels, but only the tunnels. As far as they knew, the cleaner bots weren't supposed to enter other areas. Was it malfunctioning? Had Sunny damaged it somehow? Or had something else confused it?

They set the second helper bot to hide and watch the entrance, then focused their attention on the one that had hitched a ride inside. They pushed its feed to the main display.

"I have a camera inside the facility," they announced.

The building was Ravel-style architecture: glass and steel in clean lines, translucent panels and interior windows, and rows and rows of benches that must have once held lab equipment.

"No decent hiding places, of course," Jasper muttered.

"That'd be too easy," said Kay.

It was a sizable facility, however, and thus far looked unoccupied. Once it had reached a spot free of cameras, Sunny detached the helper bot from the cleaner and sent it up the nearest wall, to climb along the ceiling and give them an overhead view.

"Is that the same cleaner bot you hacked earlier?" Libbi asked.

"I didn't hack it—we had a conversation—but yes."

"It isn't cleaning, though. It seems like it's going somewhere." Libbi took out her handheld and opened the map showing the abandoned facility, displaying its wireframe as a holo. Sunny added a marker to show the two bots' locations. "Is it showing us the way to Cobb?"

"Unlikely. It has limited understanding."

"Well, it's up to something."

They all kept watching, the organics as transfixed as Sunny themself. The cleaner bot moved slowly, even when not cleaning, and the helper bot kept pace with it. Finally, the cleaner turned at a doorway and moved inside. The helper followed.

Jasper leaned forward. "This is it."

This lab was occupied, full of equipment and crates of supplies. There were two more Fortress security bots: one just inside the door, the other facing into an adjacent room, currently dark. The cleaner bot, unconcerned, began washing the floor.

"Not while I'm working! Do you want me to slip and break my neck?" demanded Cobb's familiar voice.

"There's an idea," muttered Jasper.

"Clean that workstation—that one, there—and stay out of my way. You, Guard-Bot! Move this box for me. No, over there. If I wanted incompetence, I wouldn't have sent home those Copper-rankers they keep forcing on me."

Sunny buzzed, startled. "He appears to be using these high-end security systems as manual labor instead of his organic assistants."

"This surprises me not at all," said Havoc. "Cobb's always been a team-of-one; he hates working with people, and people hate working with him. It simplifies our plans if he's dismissed his assistants."

"When we move in, we can't give him a chance to call them back," said Jasper.

"It's weird: he seems to expect the cleaner to be there. But it belongs to the city tunnels," said Libbi. "How'd he get it to work for him?"

"Ah. I see now." Sunny chirped. "My other helper bot has found a signal relay in the tunnels, presumably set up by Cobb, that's diverting nearby cleaner bots to treat his lab as part of their assigned area. Clever." Manipulative, too—but hadn't Sunny just done the same thing?

"He must have instructed the security bots to let them come and go," said Kay. "Can we take advantage of that somehow?"

"Interesting." Sunny's circuits churned over that possibility. "Yes, I believe that might be possible."

"We still need to find our missing people," said Jasper. "Sunny, can you get us a look in that other room?"

The helper bot crept along the ceiling until it had a line of sight into the adjacent room. This contained rows of hospital beds, six of which held unconscious people.

"Is that…?" Kay pointed. "Those look like stasis pods."

She was right: three stasis pods were stacked against the far wall, along with several crates large enough to contain more pods. "It appears he—or rather, his bot labor—are in the process of unpacking them."

"He must be readying to move them out," Havoc said. "Not imminently, perhaps, but soon."

"I wonder if that's because he knows we're onto him, or if this was always meant to be a temporary base," said Kay. "Maybe he—"

"Bring Subject A!" Cobb called, and the nearest security bot approached a bed, roughly lifting its Human occupant.

"Ever." Libbi's voice cracked. "That's my friend Ever."

The bot put him down on an exam table as if he were a box of supplies. Cobb strapped him down—arms, legs, and waist—and injected something into his neck.

The young man's eyes fluttered, then popped wide with fear. "Wh-why are you doing this? I want to leave."

"You're contributing to scientific progress, which is more than you could have aspired to otherwise." Cobb, attaching electrodes down Ever's body, didn't even look at his face. "At least, I hope you will. Testing you individually hasn't yielded the results I hoped for, but if my theories are right, working in pairs should prove more effective."

"Oh, fuck Ravel," Kay whispered.

"I, I didn't agree to this. I don't consent!"

"Be quiet," Cobb said, and Ever stopped. "Bring Subject E!"

Jasper said, "Sunny, close the feed."

"No!" Libbi protested. "What's he going to—"

"Nothing you want to see." From the tight-lipped look he gave Sunny's camera, Jasper didn't want to see it either. Nor did Sunny, for that matter, but they kept monitoring it after removing it from the main display. "Would you rather we sit here watching, or work on a rescue plan?"

"I'm coming with you." Libbi's voice was hard now. No longer asking or begging, but telling. "These are my friends, and they're scared, and they don't know you. I'm coming to get them."

Jasper and Kay exchanged a long, serious look. Their reluctance was perplexing. Libbi was an adult by her culture's standards, several years older than Jasper had been when he'd joined the Cooperative, and she was intelligent, if not always wise. Still, pointing out a Human's hypocrisy rarely helped, in Sunny's experience.

Instead, Sunny said, "I would appreciate Libbi's presence. Having an extra able-bodied person may be useful if any of Cobb's victims are physically compromised."

"I'd still feel better if you stayed," Kay said, "but I get how you feel. It's your choice to make."

Jasper said nothing. Havoc frowned at him and murmured, "This is her fight, eshrim."

Jasper studied Libbi in the half-vacant way that suggested he was using his gift, and sighed. "I can see how loyal you are to them. All right. We'll all go. Now, here's how I think we should do this."

LIBBI CROUCHED BEHIND THE others, just beyond the bend in the tunnel, while Sunny's drone went on ahead to confront the security bot. This was the first test of their plan, and if it failed, they'd need a whole new one. Jasper had given her clear instructions about staying at the back of the group, and hiding if a fight broke out. His and Kay's protective urges felt, through her gift, like being smothered in heavy blankets.

But at least she was here. They respected her enough to let her come with them. If they hadn't, she would've followed them, but she was glad she'd held that threat in reserve.

"This is it," Kay breathed. The drone had reached the Fortress bot that was standing guard, and was transmitting a modified version of the passcodes from the co-opted cleaner bot. It should identify Sunny's drone as a new surveillance tool for the lab, acting on Cobb's orders.

Libbi heard the door swish open.

"I'm inside," Sunny said over their headsets. "I will scout the area and return shortly."

Step one accomplished. No one relaxed, though, because step one was the easiest part of the plan.

Granted, their plan was more improvisation than anything else. Jasper was obviously anxious about going in without more preparation—Libbi could grudgingly understand why he felt extra protective right now—but there just wasn't time. Those stasis pods stacked beside the unconscious captives told them as much: Cobb could move out at any time and take his test subjects with him. They couldn't afford to wait.

It felt like an hour, but in reality was exactly the agreed-upon five minutes, before the drone breezed back out into the tunnel, unchallenged by the guard bot. Around the bend, it stopped, hovering.

"Cobb is working at his console in an office across from the lab. All the kidnapped individuals are sedated again, and the other Fortresses are on standby. No one challenged the drone."

"And his Human assistants?" asked Jasper.

"Still absent. From some of his instructions to the bots, I infer that his assistants keep daytime hours, and he is working at night in part because he can be alone. As we predicted, this would appear to be our ideal opportunity."

"And the guard bot believed your story?" Kay asked.

"It seemed to. I am…eighty percent confident that it will allow me to proceed as we discussed. Jasper, do you still want to go first?"

Jasper nodded. "I'm ready."

He drew a pair of auto-cuffs from his pocket and slipped them over his wrists. At least, they looked like auto-cuffs, but the locking mechanisms were missing. (Why Sunny had patterns for handcuffs in their printer data-banks, Libbi wasn't sure she wanted to know. Every new detail she learned about the friendly little ship left her more confused about their past.)

Havoc squeezed his shoulder. "Don't be too reckless, Mason."

"And have fun without you? Never, eshrim." Jasper kissed his cheek, then turned to Sunny. "Lead on, jailer."

This time, the drone's exchange with the guard bot seemed to take a long time. Libbi peered over Kay's shoulder, but all she could see was the two bots standing still. Arguing bots looked no different than bots at rest.

Finally, the Fortress moved aside, and Sunny led Jasper through.

"That was a nearer call than I'd hoped," Sunny said over their headsets. "It accepted my story that Jasper is a new test subject, but it's nearing the threshold of suspicion. We'll need to be careful, and patient."

The drone stayed with Jasper for several minutes, the amount of time they'd estimated it would take to escort him to the room with the other prisoners and drug him senseless, then returned to the group.

"I'd hoped to take all three of you at once, after Jasper's proof of concept, but the guard won't allow that. It's not intelligent, but it's untrusting by design. We'll need to go one at a time, spaced apart. Too close together, and it may detect a threat and sound the alarm."

"We can be patient." Kay lowered herself to sit on the hard floor.

"Speak for yourself," Havoc said. His wants were a jumble to Libbi, but he had to be anxious to follow Jasper.

Yet after a moment, Havoc muted his headset, cutting Jasper out. "May I ask you both a personal question?"

"Sure," said Kay, and Libbi shrugged.

"Procreation is important in your culture. Do you plan to produce offspring?"

To Libbi's dismay, Kay chuckled. "You know, Sunny asked me that on our way to Brennex. I told them no, probably not. I'm not opposed to changing my mind, but in the absence of a partner who wants kids, I'm not that interested."

"Despite your family's preferences?"

"Well, their pressure is all on you and Jasper now." She smiled wickedly. "So thanks for that."

Havoc groaned. "And you, Libbi?"

"I probably will, someday. When things are simpler."

"Because of your family's expectations?"

"Because I want to," she said, sharper than she meant to. Kay didn't need to know that she'd been thinking about it before the store flooded, or that she still thought about it every time she saw a cute kid. But she could also feel her parents' wishes, and her grandmother's and aunts' and uncles'. She felt it in her gut. How was she supposed to know what she wanted for herself?

Especially when she was obviously the only one who might make that happen for her relatives. Not Kay with her transient lifestyle, and certainly not Jasper with his Kovari partner. Ma and Pa already hated the snide remarks from neighbors that they had three healthy kids but not one grandkid.

"Havoc, it's time," Sunny said, and he left with the drone.

Libbi and Kay sat in silence, and it was like sitting beside a stranger. She wanted Kay to offer some sisterly advice, even if it was condescending, about breaking into bad guys' secret lairs or dodging security bots or whatever, but she didn't want to ask for it. She wouldn't give Kay any more reason to treat her like a kid.

"You all right?" Kay asked after a while.

"Fine." *Totally fine, definitely not freaking out.* "You?"

"Will be, when this is over." Kay gave a tight-lipped smile that didn't look nervous, exactly, but still felt off. Libbi's gift was no help reading her at all. Before she could ask more, Sunny was back.

A few minutes later, Kay was through the door, and Libbi was alone.

She was fine, still, obviously. No reason to be terrified. She was the one *outside* the mad scientist's lab, out of danger, and everything was going according to plan.

"The guard's hesitation lasted two-point-six times longer that time. I believe it's developing suspicion," Sunny said over the headsets.

"Will you be able to get Libbi through safely?" asked Jasper.

"I am considering alternative strategies."

"Sunny." Libbi switched to a private channel with the drone. "Don't you leave me out here."

"I will not, I promise. Be patient. I will return soon."

So she waited. And waited. And waited.

She checked her headset. Literally thirty seconds had passed. She leaned back against the wall with a sigh.

Mixin would make things better, if they were here now. They'd be bursting with excitement, relishing every moment of the adventure, not worrying selfishly that the others would go on without them.

Damn it, she should really have called Mixin to be part of this. But Jasper had been wavering on the edge of sending Libbi home. Add another inexperienced "kid," and that would've tipped him over toward refusal.

Or, worse, what if they'd let Mixin come, but tried to refuse Libbi? Mixin's gift was way more useful in a situation like this. And Mixin wasn't the one who'd confronted Cobb and gotten herself drugged and nearly kidnapped. Founders! Her siblings wouldn't have been wrong to pick Mixin over her.

So, selfishly, Libbi had left her best friend out of the most dramatic thing that had ever happened in their lives. Founders forgive her, because Mixin certainly wouldn't.

"Fuck," Jasper said.

Libbi's heart sank. "What's wrong?"

"Cobb's gone. Havoc and I were going to grab him and secure him while he was focused on work." Of course they were. Of course they hadn't waited for her. "But he's not in the office."

"Where, then?" asked Kay.

"Oh, dear," said Sunny. "I had my helper bot watching the Fortresses, not Cobb. I will attempt to search for him." Sunny paused. "I suspect the sentry at the door interrupted him to confirm the story I was telling it. The other two Fortresses are moving now. They appear to be making rounds. I'm putting their projected paths on the map, but I can't track them both while also looking for Cobb."

"Sunny," Libbi began.

"I have not forgotten about you, Libbi, but this is a priority. You'll be safe there until I find a way to get you inside."

Libbi didn't care about safety. She believed Sunny—believed the ship meant what it said, at least—but the drone would clearly be too busy to come back for her, even if they figured out another way to sneak her in. By which point, it would be too late to help.

How are you *going to help fight high-end security robots? Or find Cobb when he's in hiding?*

They needed a lure, something to flush out Cobb and grab the bots' attention. And she realized what the perfect lure would be.

"I can help you," she announced.

"Libbi, what…?" Kay began, at the same time Jasper said, "We've got this, Libbi, please just sit tight."

"Jasper, Havoc," said Sunny urgently. "A Fortress is searching the room adjacent to your location. You must hide."

There were hisses that might have been swearing, then silence. Hopefully that meant they were hidden.

"It's approaching your closet now. If it opens the door, you should separate so it has multiple targets to track."

"It'd better not come to that. They need a distraction," Kay said. "I can—"

"I'm on it," Libbi said. Before she could think better of it, she marched up to the bot guarding the door.

"You are trespassing—" the Fortress began.

"My name is Liberation Wilder, and Cobb is expecting me. Please take me to him."

12

HIDING IN A CLOSET with Mason while Ravel's security hunted them felt, if not nostalgic, at least familiar for Havoc. He'd been bracing himself to leap out and tackle the Fortress, giving Mason cover to escape. Then Libbi made her gambit. Immediately, the bot moved away.

Havoc let out a sigh of relief. Mason did not.

"What in all our ancestors' names is she thinking?" Mason groaned.

"Her thought process seems obvious. We needed a distraction. She has given us one." An excellent one, Havoc thought, considering Cobb's personal interest in Libbi and her gift.

Havoc peered through the door crack. Only the dim, flickering light from the corridor illuminated the room beyond, revealing hints of stark white walls, faded with age, and minimalist office furniture. The Fortress was gone.

Mason spoke in an undertone as they crept from the closet. "It's reckless. Dangerous."

"So says the man who once broke *into* the holding cells at a secure Ravel facility, unarmed and without a plan, to rescue an ungrateful activist who wasn't even his teammate yet?"

There, that coaxed a smile from him. Havoc had been furious at Mason at the time, and Mason had halfway deserved it, but in hindsight, the memory warmed him. It had been Mason's way of caring about him, even when that care was refused.

"Point taken, but that's not…" Mason made a sudden, horrible face, fighting a sneeze. Some of these rooms hadn't been used, or cleaned, in decades. After an agonizing moment, he breathed and relaxed. "Stupid dust. That's not the same," he finished.

He peeked around the next corner, indicated the way was clear, and they both moved. A swirl of dust in the air showed which way the Fortress had gone.

Havoc gave a low huff of frustration. "When we finish here, you will explain to me why you won't allow your youngest sister to play as your teammate."

"I keep telling you, a family and a team aren't the same."

"This I can see. I want to understand why."

"I don't know if I can explain any better. Just…I'm scared for her."

This, too, Havoc could see. Near-panic tensed Mason's body and made him jumpy. He would endanger them all if he didn't steady himself. Careful not to startle him, Havoc touched Mason's shoulder.

"Despite his temper, Cobb puts his work first. He wants to study Libbi. He won't harm her."

"Havoc is correct," Sunny said through their headsets. "The sentry has taken Libbi to Cobb's main lab, adjacent to where he's keeping the captives. Cobb seems to be preparing to run some standard test battery on her. I've removed her from the group call, by the way, since they've confiscated her headset."

"We thank you, Sunny," Havoc said.

Slowly, Mason took a deep breath and let it out. "You're right. Okay. She's not in imminent danger. Sunny, Kay, we're heading to the main lab. Where are you?"

"We found another entrance to the…let's call it sleeping quarters," Kay said. A euphemistic name; Havoc would have called it what it was: a prison. "Sunny got the door unlocked, but there's still an open door into the lab. If everyone stays quiet and Libbi keeps Cobb distracted, he may not notice us freeing them, but if any of them freak out when we wake them, or if Cobb looks up at the wrong moment…"

"Eshrim, I think you should help Kay wake and free the captives," Mason said. "Sunny, can you keep an eye on the Fortresses?"

"My helper bot is monitoring the rooms," Sunny said. "One of the Fortresses is there with Libbi and Cobb, but the other two are patrolling. I can't watch them all. Be careful."

"And what will you be doing, my reckless one?" Havoc asked.

"I'll watch Cobb and Libbi, in case we need an extra layer of distraction. If he decides to add Libbi to his collection, he could catch you in the act." Mason blanched at the thought. "But he despises me. He won't be able to resist an argument with the guy who ruined his big career break."

Havoc hissed. "You speak no lies. But be *careful*, eshrim. Unlike Libbi, he doesn't necessarily need you for his research. He has your medical data from when Ravel imprisoned you."

Mason kissed the corner of Havoc's mouth, tenderly, and flashed a dark smile. "Good luck to you too."

Havoc met Kay outside the "sleeping quarters." The room was dark, lit mostly from the doorway of the adjoining lab, but as their eyes adjusted, blinking lights and glowing indicators gave shape to the space—and the prone, motionless forms on two rows of beds. Still but not truly sleeping, like the living computers on Artesia. A memory gripped him of lying on such a bed, his mind pummeled with data not from his own senses, his thoughts co-opted from him. He shuddered.

Kay glanced over, looking concerned. She must hear his unease through her gift. He waved for her to carry on, and he moved to the first bed, following Sunny's instructions to deactivate it and revive the patient.

The medical bed beeped as Havoc switched it off. He froze, but Cobb's voice droned on in the next room. With hands less steady than he'd like, he ripped out the intravenous drip cable, filled a syringe, and injected it into a port on the sleeping person's arm. And waited, counting the seconds.

Moments of shallower breathing and twitching eyelids warned him as the sleeper shot into wakefulness. Their eyes snapped open. He saw the urge to scream cut short as he touched a claw to their lips.

"Be silent," he whispered. "We're rescuing you. Understand?"

They blinked, scared and disoriented, then nodded. As soon as he was sure they were alert enough to cooperate, he instructed them to detach their various sensors and drip-tubes but otherwise stay still while the drugs wore off, then moved to the next bed.

THE CORRIDORS OF THE facility all looked alike to Libbi, a corporate-bland labyrinth. Lights flickered and sometimes died for no apparent reason. Everything was dingy, somehow ancient-looking, except for the pathway of cleanliness they followed. The Fortress's wheels squeaked on the shiny waxed floor—the little cleaner bot's work, no doubt. It must have only cleaned the areas in use, because every branching corridor was all dust and grime. She could have followed this shiny path through the maze and straight to the lab, if she hadn't had her escort.

The Fortress hadn't hurt her, though the real, working auto-cuffs it had snapped on her wrists felt too tight, and it pressed her to speed up whenever she tried to peek in one of those deserted rooms. But otherwise, she was okay. She was fine. For now.

Something clattered alarmingly in the ceiling, then faded to a whine. The ventilation system must be cranky after so much disuse, which made her extra glad they wouldn't be sticking around here—you didn't grow up in a domed city without a healthy appreciation for the importance of the systems that kept you breathing—then remembered that wasn't guaranteed. That she'd just volunteered to become a prisoner, and was counting on her sibs to make her gamble pay off. Not exactly the hero move she'd been imagining.

Through another doorway, into sudden brightness.

"Have a seat, Liberation, and tell me where your siblings are."

Cobb spoke her given name with the mocking of a schoolyard bully—the reason she'd stopped using it in the first place. Everything about his manner said he was done even pretending to play nice.

He gestured to a seat surrounded by medical equipment, with straps at the chest, ankles, and waist.

She shifted back a step. "I'm good standing."

"Sit her down," he snapped at the Fortress. It seized her arm and pushed her, not roughly, but too powerfully to refuse, until she fell backward into the seat. Within moments, the straps were drawn tight. Cobb hadn't touched her.

Oh, no, she did not like this. The need to *move* intensified with every moment, her instincts fighting her intentions.

"Again, where are your siblings and that Kovar?" Cobb said. "I know they're here."

"I don't know. They left me behind," she said truthfully. They'd better be taking advantage of Cobb's distraction, making her stupid risky idea worth it.

"They left you as bait." Cobb smirked. "They knew I couldn't resist the opportunity to study you. They're not wrong. But my security will handle them." He glanced at the Fortress, now on standby. "Go! Find them! Earn your accolades, you overpriced pile of metal. And get the security cameras running again! For corporate's sake, if I wanted people to stand around and gawk, I'd have let my so-called assistants stick around."

The Fortress nearly collided with the little cleaner bot as it reversed direction. The cleaner gave a high-pitched warning and zipped across the room, where it resumed whatever it was doing.

Libbi took stock of the room, as much as she could from her position—was that screen the security feed? Cobb was right, all but a few of the cameras were blank, broken either by time or Sunny's meddling—when a whirring sound rose behind her head. Libbi's muscles clenched as some sort of machine settled around her head and shoulders, sensors seeking contact with bare skin like an electronic medusa.

"Relax," said Cobb, and she choked back a hysterical laugh. "Or don't, but it'll be more comfortable if you do. I'm not going to hurt you, Liberation. You're too special for that."

She'd been called "special" by Brennexian adults all her life and hated it—hated being a symbol instead of a person. This was worse. Worse than being hit on by drunken spacers, treated as a pretty piece of flesh on her rare outings to the portside bars. Cobb made her feel like equipment: a favorite tool, or maybe a useful spreadsheet, full of valued data. But not a person.

"I'm really not."

"I disagree. What is your mutation-based ability? Your 'gift,' as you people so dramatically call it."

"I don't know what you're talking about." That hunger of his was what made his interest so sickening. He wanted to crack her open and study her insides.

He sighed, irritated that his favorite tool was malfunctioning. "Fine. Your readings will tell me, eventually. It'll just take longer to analyze them." He started sticking more sensors to her skin, her neck, her wrists. His touch was entirely impersonal. "But it'll be worth the effort. Do you know how rare you are? You and your two siblings?"

Oh.

Oh, shit.

That was why he'd come looking for her: *because* she was the little sister.

"Ah, you do understand. Families who managed to produce more than one child during Ravel's tenure are a rarity. Three children, full siblings, all gifted? You're an incredible opportunity. I'm learning so much from your contemporaries over there, but once I've studied all three of the Wilder children and can compare your results, it will speed up my research tenfold."

He pressed an auto-syringe to her upper arm, drawing blood. She couldn't stop him. It didn't hurt, though: his new-model syringe barely pinched. Shouldn't all of this *hurt*, having her secrets stolen? Cobb held the vial up to the light, studying it with satisfaction.

"You won't get to study all three of us, though."

And where were her siblings? She'd offered herself up as bait, knowing it was reckless, because she thought they'd be ready to grab Cobb when he appeared. They should have acted by now.

"That's why it's fortunate I already have what I need from your siblings. Your brother had a full medical scan when he was incarcerated on our flagship, and the interrogation team took adequate readings during their sessions with him. And your sister had records taken as an employee, including her genome. I'll eventually need some active brain readings from her, and I'd prefer to run all three of you through a formal battery of tests, but I've got enough to work with."

"Go fuck yourself."

He went on as if she hadn't spoken. "Your sister showed awareness of a stealth Ravel operative aboard her ship when even the ship's surveillance didn't detect him. Is it the physical presence of others that she responds to, or something more specific? Her ability has an auditory manifestation, does it not?" When Libbi didn't answer, he clarified, as if she were a small child, "Your sister hears things, with her gift?"

"I understood you. I'm just choosing not to answer."

"Are all your gifts auditory? Your brother's, too? Or does that not run in the family? Ah, well, your scans will tell me. A shame your brother's interrogators didn't know what questions to ask him."

Bait or no, if she could move, Libbi would have kicked him in the face for talking so casually about Jasper being interrogated. She settled for growling.

"Stubborn, provincial Brennexians." He sighed as he pushed buttons, checked readouts. "Just think about your gift. That will suffice for now."

Don't think about the gifts, Libbi ordered herself, but she might as well have said *don't think about the Majrin in the sparkly tutu.* His nauseating eagerness to pick her apart was hard to ignore.

"Ah, there it is, same as the others." He pointed at the display, a map of her brain, as if she'd want to see it. "Not auditory, though. Interesting. A vascular response? Try thinking about—"

"Cobb!" Jasper's shout came from somewhere behind Libbi.

Cobb wheeled, and suddenly he had a dart-gun in his hands, pointed at her brother.

"Finally," Cobb said, and without any grandstanding, he fired.

Libbi screamed. Wrenching her neck around as far as she could within the chair's restraints, she couldn't see Jasper. Was he hit? What was in those darts? Cobb must have missed, because he was aiming again.

Cobb wasn't watching her. If she could get an arm free, now, while he was distracted... Struggling against her restraints was no use, though. She didn't notice the clumsy little cleaner bot—and neither did Cobb—until it clipped his legs.

Cobb reeled, off balance, and Jasper lunged.

They wrestled on the floor. Jasper kicked the dart-gun away, got an auto-cuff around one of Cobb's wrists, then grabbed for the other, but missed.

"Bots! Security! You idiots, he's here, they're probably all—augh!"

Jasper—her sweet, caring brother—*punched* Cobb in the face, finally got Cobb's wrists cuffed together, and hauled him upright by the alcove where Libbi was trapped. "You okay, Libbi?" His voice came as a growl.

"I'm not hurt." That wasn't the same as being okay. The urge to strangle Cobb, to wrap her hands around his neck and squeeze, suddenly swelled to an alarming intensity, and she couldn't tell if the desire came from Jasper or herself.

Holding Cobb by his collar, Jasper worked at Libbi's restraints with his free hand. On his third try, they unlatched, and Libbi slid to her feet, legs responding shakily to their freedom.

"Get behind me," Jasper warned as the Fortresses rolled into the room, all three of them. Jasper held Cobb before him like a shield, and Libbi had the unnerving sense that this was a practiced motion, that he knew exactly what he was doing.

"Release your captive," one of the bots demanded in a flat, authoritative voice.

"Call them off," Jasper told Cobb.

"Kill him!" Cobb ordered, then: "But not the girl! I'm not done with her."

The bots shifted sideways, trying to find an angle to get at Jasper without harming Cobb. Libbi stepped in front of him, too, making it impossible to follow both parts of Cobb's order.

"Release your captive," the first bot said again.

Jasper gave a short, angry laugh. "So you can shoot me? No, thanks."

The bots went still, apparently realizing they were at a standoff. In that moment of quiet, there was a thud in the next room, followed by a muffled curse.

"My research subjects!" Cobb shouted. "Stop them!"

13

JASPER SHOVED COBB AT the nearest Fortress and ran, pulling Libbi after him. She shook off his grip, done with being hauled around like luggage, but followed him, pausing only to grab her headset and handheld off the table before racing into the next room.

"Kay, Havoc, get everyone out!" Jasper grabbed the sliding door behind them and tried to pull it shut.

Tried. It resisted like it was rusted open, or maybe the controls were fighting him. Libbi grabbed on, adding her weight, and it started to move.

"This won't stop them. Pretty sure they can open doors," Libbi said.

"Yeah, but it buys us time. Sunny?"

"I am attempting to override the door controls, but unsuccessfully."

The door groaned shut. Only then did Libbi turn and take stock of the room: the nightmare dorm where Cobb kept his research subjects.

"Up, everybody up! We've got to go," Kay urged.

The captives moved urgently but fumblingly, still half drugged. Some were recovering faster than others, but none were in great shape. Only one, a Majrin, looked steady on their feet, and Libbi's friend Dashiell swayed like he was drunk. They'd been unconscious in these beds for days, most of them. Libbi thought of being woken in the dark of night by a fire alarm, the confusion, the unreality of it. This had to be a thousand times more disorienting.

The door began to open. An energy weapon blasted through the crack, scorching the floor. Libbi yelped.

Jasper was searching the cabinets, muttering, "Come on, come on… That'll do." He yanked on a metal handle. It sounded loose. Another tug, bracing with his foot, and the handle came free, and he jammed it into the bottom track of the door. The metal groaned and the door mechanism whined, but it didn't open any farther.

One person wasn't getting up from the bed. Though they were curled into the fetal position and facing away from her, Libbi knew at once who it was. She hurried over.

"Hey," Kay was saying gently. "Hey, I know it's hard, but we have to get out of here. I need your help, okay?"

She shook him, very lightly, but those wide shoulders curled tighter.

Libbi touched Kay's arm and eased her aside. "Hey, Ever, it's me. It's Libbi."

He moved fractionally. One eye cracked open, and Libbi came around where he could see her.

"What's his gift?" Kay murmured.

"Imagine your gift crossed with mine. Instead of hearing emotions, he feels them. And not in a fun way."

"Damn." Kay obviously grasped the implications at once. "There'll be no escaping negative emotions until we're clear of here. What can we do for him?"

"Go help the others. I've got this."

Libbi turned back to her friend. The only thing to do when his gift was affecting him this badly was to get him out of the stressful situation, away from people. No good options here.

A Fortress rammed the door. She flinched at the noise, but Ever didn't react.

"Ever, I know it hurts. Everyone's scared and angry, and I'm sorry, it's going to get worse before it gets better. But I'm here to get you out of this place, back to where it's safe. Will you let me help you?"

A tiny nod. She breathed relief. "Good. Thank you. I'm going to touch you and help you sit up, okay? Here we go…"

By the time she got him upright, the others were gathered by the opposite door. Kay peered out through a narrow gap. She and Havoc were each supporting one of the Losts, and the other three pressed close together, leaning on each other. Libbi helped Ever toward them.

"The other two fortresses are blocking the direct route to the exit," Sunny said through Libbi's headset. They'd added her back to the group chat. "You'll need to go around them. Turn right out the door, and I'll guide you."

"We've got an escape route," Libbi told Ever. "All we've got to do is get there."

"Faster," Jasper said, coming up behind them and catching Ever's other arm. Ever recoiled.

"Don't!" Libbi snapped. He was only trying to help, but Ever didn't know him, and Jasper's emotions had to feel pretty brutal right now. Trying to calm them both, she said, "His gift doesn't do well with stress, or strangers. I've got him, and we're coming as fast as we can."

To her relief, Jasper seemed to understand, or at least trusted her word. "I'll bring up the rear." Louder, he called, "Kay, Havoc, get them out! Don't wait! We'll be right behind you." Then, under his breath, "Not that either of you will listen."

Jasper looked as grim as she'd ever seen him. Libbi pushed aside the thought that he accepted that his partner and Kay would put themselves in unnecessary danger for his sake, but wouldn't let Libbi risk herself even when it mattered.

The others were disappearing around the next corner in the hallway. Libbi followed. Ever was moving more easily now, still half doubled-over with discomfort, but closer to the others' pace.

Energy blasted at them, scarring the wall by Libbi's head. The security bot was catching up.

That blast seemed to motivate Ever, though, breaking through his fog, and a burst of speed got them around the corner.

"Go left at the next corridor, and then through the empty lab on the right," Sunny directed them.

Libbi was lost almost instantly. The maze of labs and corridors seemed to go on without end, dim and dingy, with dust disturbed by the others' passage.

"The dust. They can follow!"

Not the most articulate warning, but Sunny seemed to understand. "You're correct. I'll use my drone to create some false trails. It may buy you a little leeway, though not much."

Another turn, and another. The dust stung her lungs, making her cough. She and Ever were both panting, her own breath so loud in her ears that she couldn't hear the Fortress. It could be right behind them.

"How much farther, Sunny?" she whispered.

"The tunnel entrance is near. Kay and Havoc and the others are waiting for you to join them."

"I told you two to *go*," Jasper complained.

"Yeah, but did you really expect us to listen?" Kay said. Libbi thought she heard Kay's voice ahead of them, not just over the headset.

Sure enough, through the next doorway, there they all were. Dashiell blinked, like he was noticing Libbi for the first time, then wrapped his arms around her and Ever while the other captives stood by, still bleary.

Havoc caught Jasper in a quick, hard embrace. "We discussed this, eshrim. I won't sacrifice you for the sake of the game, not again."

"I love you," Jasper murmured, then raised his voice. "Let's go."

Libbi recognized where they were: the scrubbed-to-gleaming hallway not far from the tunnel. As a group, they pushed forward, half-running, with Sunny's drone bringing up the rear.

Havoc stopped short, and Libbi and Ever stumbled into him from behind. She craned her neck to look past him, and realized why he'd stopped.

Shit. Of course one of the Fortresses had gone back to guard the exit.

From behind them came the low whirring of more bots moving into position. Surrounding them.

"What do we do?" Libbi asked, voice low.

"Surrender would be the smart choice." Libbi flinched at Cobb's voice, and she wasn't the only one.

"No," said Ever.

It was the first he'd spoken, and it must have taken a lot.

Cobb growled in frustration. "You're all valuable to me, but none of you are irreplaceable. I will have the bots start killing people, one by one, until you all start behaving yourselves."

Ever growled. He straightened his shoulders and spoke, slowly, as if remembering how. "I would rather die than stay here."

He turned and, holding himself rigid as a soldier despite the agony their fear must be causing him, he took a step toward the door.

"Starting with Liberation Wilder."

Ever froze.

"Don't listen to him!" Libbi urged.

"That one. Shoot her."

"Libbi!"

She was already diving when Jasper tackled her. They hit the floor in a pile. Everyone else followed, ducking or just falling in the general tangle. Jasper held her down, shielding her with his body. Weapons fire whined all around them.

"No, stop it!" Cobb shouted, and then, "The drone, shoot the drone! No, listen to me, you flubbing bots!"

Peering out from her brother's armpit, Libbi realized: the security bots were shooting at *each other*. "What's happening?"

"Friendly fire," Jasper said, unhelpfully.

Sunny's voice was distant; Libbi's headset had jostled loose, and she nudged it back into place as best she could without raising her head. "When the bots shot at you, one of them hit their counterpart by the doorway. It must have triggered a self-defense protocol."

"So they're ignoring us?" Kay asked.

"Only momentarily. We still cannot reach the door, and I fear they may—"

A sharp bang shook the air, like a bullet-gun from a historical serial, followed moments later by a longer, deeper roar. The floor trembled under her.

"Sunny, what…?"

"They seem to have found a structural instability."

"Run! Everyone, run!" Havoc shouted.

The world lurched and rolled. Libbi scrambled to her feet, lost her balance, caught someone's hand—she wasn't sure whose. They all grabbed each other and helped each other forward. Where was Ever? Looking over her shoulder for him, she stumbled, but he was right there and he caught her arm.

The roaring rose, and the hallway gave a final shudder. Slowly, she turned around.

The air was thick with dust. The ventilation system wheezed trying to process it. And beyond…there was no more doorway. The hallway ended in a heap of rubble.

"One bot down," murmured Havoc. "Point for our team."

Cobb gaped, unable to accept what he was seeing. He turned on his bots.

"You stupid, malfunctioning machines! You can't even hit a simple target, and now you've ruined—" He broke off as Jasper strode forward, clearly done messing around. Then, pointing, "Him! Shoot him! He's the one—"

"For a supposed genius, Cobb, you're a real fucking idiot." Jasper's rage had gone from hot to cold. Libbi had never seen him like this. "Unless you want this whole building to collapse and crush us, *your precious self included,* you'd better call them off."

Even Cobb seemed to see the logic in that. "Fine." He sighed. "Fortresses, stand down. Vigilance mode."

The bots' weapons retracted, folding back beneath their armor. Libbi remembered to breathe.

"Good. Now—"

"You're welcome," Cobb said.

Havoc sighed audibly at that. Jasper didn't rise to the bait, though. "We know that tunnel was your main route to and from this lab. Do you have a backup?"

Cobb hesitated for a long time before answering that. "No, I don't."

"You should work on more convincing lies, because…"

"He's telling the truth," Dashiell said. He and Ever were propping each other up. "He didn't want to admit it."

"He's terrified," Kay agreed.

"He fucking should be," muttered Ever.

Jasper ran his hands through his hair. "Figures. Okay, we need a plan. Any ideas?"

"Sunny," Kay said, "what exactly caused that explosion? That wasn't normal."

The drone hovered closer to the collapsed area, but not too close. "This facility hasn't been maintained for nearly twenty-five years. The energy bolt ruptured a brittle air pump, and I believe a compression chamber exploded. It appears to have caused a cascade of failures."

"Cascade failures…with the ventilation system? With our *air*?" Libbi had already felt sick. Now she was shaking with it.

"Other systems may be compromised as well. I have concerns about the physical integrity of the structure."

"So you're saying we should get the fuck out of here," said Jasper.

"Correct."

"Who's piloting that drone? And from where?" Cobb asked.

No one answered.

Libbi pulled up the old map Sunny had found and projected it from her headset. "There's an emergency access tunnel over there…"

"I'll send a bot to check it," Sunny said.

"Thanks. There's also a small shuttle dock on the far side. Pressurized, or supposed to be."

"Anyone got a spaceship lying around?" someone quipped.

Kay frowned, looking at the drone—at Sunny, through the drone's cameras. "Ship, yes. What we need is a pilot."

"I'll call my colleagues…" Cobb began, but was cut off with a chorus of "No!" He shoved his hands into his pockets.

"Havoc, dearest, would you mind searching him for comms equipment? Otherwise he just might call in the cavalry," Jasper said.

"Gladly," Havoc growled.

His search turned up a sleek oversized handheld, very impractical and expensive-looking, plus a small fob that Libbi first assumed was a data drive, but changed her mind when Havoc rounded on Cobb saying, "Did you use this? Don't lie to me."

Cobb smirked and said nothing.

"Is that a panic button?" Jasper asked, then cursed when Havoc confirmed it. "Okay, we have to assume he used it and someone's coming to help him. Assistants, or security, or maybe worse. Which means we need to get him and ourselves out, now."

"Why don't we call Public Safety?" asked Hannith, who Libbi recognized from the photos Phoenix had shared. "This has got to qualify as an emergency."

Libbi swallowed, bracing herself to tell them all how Public Safety had ignored their kidnappings, but Ever was already shaking his head. "Bad idea. We're in an off-limits area. They'll make it our fault, somehow."

"I honestly wouldn't trust them to rescue a kitten from a rooftop right now. With a fire escape," Kay said. "Let's hope that backup tunnel is safe. That's our best option."

"It isn't," Sunny said, to general groans. "It appears that someone has tried to use that entrance to break in during the past few decades, and they took a blunt instrument to the door. It is jammed. Under other circumstances, I would suggest we force it open, but..."

"Yeah, let's not," said Kay.

"At least Cobb's associates can't easily reach us," Havoc said. "But we still need an exit."

"A visual examination of the shuttle dock seems more promising. There remains the problem of..." Sunny hesitated. "Getting the ship to you."

"Can't you just..." Libbi began, but a sharp look from Kay cut her off.

Her sister lowered her voice to a murmur. "The problem is that Sunny's programming won't let them fly without an organic person aboard. That person doesn't need pilot training—"

"I once flew in atmosphere with only a child and an unconscious man aboard," Sunny said proudly through their headsets.

"—but we do need someone we trust with Sunny's secret. And quickly."

Jasper ran his fingers through his hair. He was going to pull it out at this rate. "Call me childish, but I really don't want to ask Ma and Pa to come rescue us."

"We don't have to." Libbi groaned as she remembered to feel guilty. "I know who'd love to help us."

14

DEEPLY ASLEEP, MIXIN COULDN'T figure out what that jangling noise was until it rose to emergency levels. Finally, some part of their brain made the leap: a real, waking sound, not a dream sound. Their room was completely dark, and their handheld said it was the middle of the night. They snatched it before it could vibrate its way off the bedside table.

Not a dome crisis alarm. It was a call from Libbi—the third in ten minutes. Mixin fumbled for their headset.

"Libs, if you aren't literally dying, I will kill you myself. You know what time it is?"

"Um, literally dying at this very moment? Or would you settle for imminent danger of dying?" The reluctant, preemptively apologetic note in their best friend's voice was not a good sign.

"Founders' sake, what did you do?"

"Please don't be mad. Actually, you're going to be mad, but if you could put off the yelling until after…"

"Liberation Wilder. What did you do?"

"I may have…gone to rescue the kidnapping victims in an abandoned Ravel facility and now I'm trapped here with my sibs and the kidnapped Losts and a Ravel scientist and the building might lose containment at any moment so I'm hoping you can take Kay's ship and come save us?"

Mixin said nothing. They scrubbed their sleep-bleared eyes with their hands and said more nothing. Finally they said, "Are you joking?"

"I'm really sorry, Mix…"

"I hate you. Fine, tell me what to do."

Mixin shoved some supplies in a backpack—flashlight, snack bars, backup battery, spare socks. Presumably Kay's ship had general sorts of supplies, but they weren't being particularly logical right now.

At least in the middle of the night, the streets weren't crowded. Hopping on a community bike, they raced to the spaceport in record time, slowing only when they hit the foot traffic around the never-sleeping port itself. They ditched the bike just outside the bay number Libbi had told them.

What Libbi *hadn't* given them was an access code, or any sort of instructions beyond "get to the ship." She'd promised it would be explained when they got there, which would normally have intrigued Mixin, like playing spy. But they were too mad right now to be intrigued. Libbi also hadn't explained how they were supposed to fly the ship, but hopefully Kay's AI friend could help with that.

"Um, hi?" they said, approaching the ship's door, but it was already sliding open.

"Mixin, thank you for coming! Please come in, quickly, there's very little time."

Sunny's voice was gender-neutral with robotic overtones, sweeter and richer than the voice from the drone. The moment Mixin cleared the door, it swept shut behind them.

"Come forward and take a seat. I'm sorry for the bumpy ride."

"I should tell you I've never piloted a ship before. Actually, I've taught myself a little, but…" They cut themself off. Libbi's sister's ship AI didn't need to know about that. "But I don't know what I'm doing."

"That's all right. I do." There was definite humor there. *I'm talking to a ship. Making jokes with a ship.* It was impossible to stay mad in the face of Sunny's good nature.

The floor shifted under their feet. Oh. So they were departing *right now*. Mixin hurried to the control room up front and plopped into the pilot's seat. "Don't you need me to push a button or talk to port control or something?"

"It's kind of you to offer, but there's no need."

"Then why did Libbi drag me out of bed at freaking insomnia o'clock to come here?"

Okay, maybe they were still a little mad.

"Did Libbi not explain? I suppose there wasn't time. I apologize for that." A pause. "Did she tell you about…me? Did she explain my nature?"

"That you're a person? I, um, may have used my gift to eavesdrop when they introduced you and Havoc to the family. Sorry." There was no immediate answer. "Libbi didn't give away your secret, and I won't tell anyone. I promise."

The docking bay receded as the ship pulled out of its spot, then turned tightly.

"Most ship manufacturers build restrictions into their systems to prevent ships from flying without an organic person aboard. Kay thinks it originated as a protection against remote hacking and theft, but whatever the reason, we haven't found a way to override it in my systems. So, when I'm alone, I'm effectively grounded."

"That sucks."

"I rarely mind it these days. I prefer Kay's company to solitude. But at times, it can be problematic."

"Then I guess it's a good thing Libbi didn't invite me on the rescue, so I could be free to fill in as a warm body now." After a moment, they added, "Sorry. I shouldn't take it out on you." Sunny hadn't done anything wrong.

And Mixin was on a *ship*. Living a dream, except… "Figures, first time I get to actually ride on a ship, and it goes like this."

Sunny beeped, as if surprised. "You've never traveled on a ship before?"

"Never. Always wanted to, since I was a little kid. I'd hang around the spaceport watching ships come and go." Mixin leaned forward, trying to take in the whole view on the screen at once. The ship was skimming low and slow over the surface of Brennex, skirting around the domes. This close, every pit and crag in the rocky ground was visible. They would not let their annoyance at Libbi ruin this moment. "Where are we going?"

"Cobb has been working in an abandoned Ravel lab accessible by the tunnels, which is where he held his kidnapped test subjects. However, the tunnels were compromised, and our friends need an alternate exit. That's what we're providing. Though retrieving them may take some…improvisation. The facility is old and subject to malfunctions."

Mixin swallowed. A "malfunction" was always serious on

Brennex, where life clung to the planet's surface in its fragile bubbles of contained atmosphere. "Is everyone all right?"

Is Libbi all right?

"I believe so. Our access point is a small shuttle bay. They will wait nearby until we determine if the bay is safely sealed."

"And if it's not?"

"As I said, we may need to be creative."

THE FACILITY CREPT OVER the horizon; Sunny helpfully highlighted it on the display as the ship coasted in low.

"Kay, we're approaching. I'm signaling for access. My old Ravel codes should work…"

The facility was so large, it took a moment for Mixin to spot the docking bay, until the door began to gape wide. Then it stopped, no more than half open.

"What's wrong?" Mixin asked.

"The doors are jammed, but I believe I can fit."

"Be careful, Sunny," Kay said.

"Always." A coughing noise came over the speakers, muffled disbelief. "Very well, you're right. But I will take no more risks than necessary. Mixin, hold on."

As it turned out, Mixin didn't need their death grip on the chair. Sunny tilted and glided smoothly through the doors, with only feet to spare above and below. Hovering, they rotated so their rear door faced the inside wall of the bay; on the screen, their cameras showed a series of sealed doors, and no loose equipment or junk to get in the way.

"I've found our next problem," Sunny announced. "The doors won't close. There should be a force-shield for backup, but I can't activate it."

"Hey, Havoc, see if you can get it working?" Kay said. "I'm not thrilled about trusting our lives to decades-old glitchy shield generators, though."

"Indeed. A safer option would be to deploy one of the pressure-tubes."

"What tubes?" said Mixin.

"A common emergency measure at small Ravel facilities like this. In case the docking bay is compromised—as in this case—an airtight, pressure-resilient tunnel can be connected between the inner bay doors and the door of an evacuation craft. A bridge, if you will, of safe, breathable air. Deployment requires two people in suits—"

"I'll do it!" Mixin's mouth ran ahead of their brain.

"Got much experience with spacewalks, Mixin?" A new voice—Jasper—spoke, obviously doubtful.

"Do you?" Mixin shot back. Jasper's silence said they'd scored a point. "Besides, Libbi shouldn't get to have all the excitement. What'll I tell our friends? That she fought off Ravel security bots while I stayed on the ship?" They tried to keep their tone light and joking, but weren't sure if they succeeded. Libbi was notably silent.

"I'll help Mixin," Kay said. "They can bring my EVA suit over from the ship. All right, Mix, suit up and come meet me."

With Sunny's guidance, Mixin got into the spare EVA suit and clomped across the docking bay toward the doors where Kay was waiting. With some complicated opening and sealing of internal doors to create a makeshift airlock, Mixin got Kay's suit to her, and soon the two of them were wrestling one end of the tunnel in place around the door in the docking bay that the others were waiting behind. *Wrestling* was the right word—the thick fabric of the tube resisted them at every step.

"Founders! Did they need to make it so bulky?"

"We'll be glad of it when it's all our friends have between them and the void," Kay said. She'd sounded tense over the comms, but seemed almost cheerful now. Maybe just glad to be *doing* something. Mixin could relate.

The last part was the hardest, clipping the tube in and sealing the edges around Sunny's rear door. They did this from the inside. Fortunately, designs for emergency systems must not have changed since the facility was built, because once they got it lined up, everything snapped into place.

"I'm checking for leakage," Sunny announced. "All tests passed."

"That's one thing gone right, then." Kay slumped against the inside wall of her ship, almost like she was giving it a hug. "Thanks for coming for us, Sunny. And you too, Mixin."

"You going to let us out now?" Jasper asked over the comms.

"Yeah, be right there," Kay said. "Oh, wait. Sunny…"

"Yes, we need precautions before bringing Cobb aboard. Mixin, would you come forward again and pretend to be my actual pilot, at least while Cobb is present?"

Right. Bad enough that Cobb knew about the Losts. Ravel didn't need to know about the sentient spaceship, too.

Mixin grinned. "I'd be honored to be your real fake pilot, Sunny."

"Great," Kay said. "I'll get the others."

LIBBI PACED THE LENGTH of the small wedge of corridor where they waited for a safe exit. The folks they'd rescued sat huddled together, as far from Cobb as they could get. Ever had shut down again, but Dashiell was rubbing his shoulder comfortingly. Jasper and Havoc murmured to each other, and Libbi wasn't sure if she wanted to hear what they were saying. Neither of them stopped watching Cobb, not for a second, but all the scientist did was stand sullenly in a corner, radiating resentment.

"Why?" she asked, before she could think better of it.

Cobb's gaze shifted to her. "Why what? Why you? I explained that to you."

"Why *us?* I know what you want—fame and advancement and all that—but there are other ways."

His chin rose. "I'm not in this for personal glory, Liberation. This research is for the good of society. The unique abilities that you and your friends have developed by accident are haphazard and limited, but they could be so much more. This should be benefiting people everywhere, not squandered and hidden as if it didn't exist."

"By 'people everywhere,' you mean people in Ravel," Havoc said. "And only certain people."

"Not meddling malcontents, certainly," Cobb snapped. Havoc hissed, and Jasper touched his arm, warning him to let it go. "By necessity, I'll only be able to work with a small number of citizens at first, but in time, I expect to scale up."

"If you really have the greater good at heart," Libbi said, knowing fully well that this was only the story he told himself, not his true desire, "aren't you worried about all the harm you'll cause in the process? All the pain, the turmoil, the needless suffering?"

His brows rose in a practiced skeptical look. "Are you referring to your planet's infertility epidemic, which you insist upon blaming on Ravel, despite a lack of proof?"

Jasper snorted. "Come on, Alik. You *know* the drug manufacturing operation here was at fault. We've heard you admit it."

"Via a recording made without my consent, taken out of context with a layperson's limited understanding of my work. And without that sad incident, we would never have discovered these abilities." Another person would have stopped there and seemed like only a bit of an asshole, but being who he was, Cobb needed to go full asshole. "Eventually, I hope to find a way to encode them into developing fetuses at will. There are always failures along the path to success, in science, but what I learn from each failed effort will further the work overall. A worthwhile sacrifice."

Not your sacrifice, Libbi wanted to shout. The others were staring at him, appalled, except for Jasper and Havoc, who looked disgusted but unsurprised.

"You'll gain nothing by engaging with him, Libbi," Havoc said. "He lacks the capacity to change."

But Cobb wanted to be *liked,* didn't he? Deep down, below the surface, wasn't that what the desire for fame was all about?

She tried again.

"You've studied us, Cobb. You must know by now that some of our gifts are more like curses. I know more than a few people who would turn theirs off if they could." She shot a sympathetic look toward Ever, then turned back to Cobb. "All of us Losts are *people.* Humans, Majrin, Kovars, *people* with lives and feelings. We've been through a lot, spent our childhoods lonely and scared and broken, and a lot of us still are that way. All our lives, we've dreaded that someone like you would come along and turn us into things to be studied under a microscope."

"A microscope is hardly a useful tool for this sort of—"

"That's not the *point.* Can't you imagine how frightening that is?"

He stared at her, and she couldn't tell if she'd surprised him, maybe even reached him, or if this was the sort of look you'd give a cat who'd suddenly learned to talk.

"All we want," she said softly, "is to be left alone and safe."

"I would think," Cobb said, "that you'd be relieved to have your specialness out in the open. Soon you'll have no more need to hide."

Libbi sighed, and Jasper gave her a look of commiseration. She'd never win this one. At least she'd tried.

They all startled as a door hissed open, but it was just Kay, holding the helmet of her suit under one arm. "Who's ready to see the last of this place?"

Dashiell spoke for all of them. "You have no idea."

15

THE TUNNEL SNAPPED DRAMATICALLY as the facility door opened and air rushed in, pressing against the near-vacuum. Damn, yes, Mixin was glad the material was so thick and tough. Then Kay was coming back across, guiding one of the Losts, followed by Libbi with her arm around…

"Ever!"

Mixin raced to the doorway, catching their friend in a big, gentle hug as he walked dazedly onto the ship. For a moment, he seemed frozen, overwhelmed, then returned the hug with a fierceness.

"Missed you, Mix."

"Glad you're okay." They kissed him on the cheek, then turned to the next person through the tube. "You too, Dash. Sage and Saba will be so relieved. Hey, I have to go for now, but we'll be back in port soon, and then home."

They avoided Libbi's glance, her chagrined smile.

"Mix…" Libbi began.

"Later, okay?" It came out too sharp, and they added, more calmly, "Let's focus on getting everyone safe." Which meant, *I do want to talk, but I'm not ready.* And, conveniently, they really did need to go fake-pilot the ship.

The rest of the Losts were coming aboard, and Kay showed them where they could sit. Last of all, Jasper frog-marched Cobb along the tunnel, with Havoc following menacingly. That was Mixin's cue to go up to the control room and close the partition Sunny had set up to hide the space from passengers' view.

The thin wall didn't block Mixin's gift, though. They spun their seat around and watched the conversation.

"You stay right there, and don't move," Jasper said, presumably to Cobb. "All right. Are we ready to get out of here?"

"One moment, please." Sunny's voice over the internal speakers sounded bland and somehow off. Pretending to be an ordinary ship, Mixin realized, for the sake of their audience. Mix liked the real ship better.

The cameras showed something else coming through the tunnel. Actually, two somethings: Sunny's drone, which Mixin recognized, and…some sort of bot? Mixin squinted at the screen. A cleaner bot, the sort the city used for public places. It bustled along in the drone's wake.

"Um, Sunny?" Kay murmured.

The ship answered over Kay's headset so only she could hear—well, her and Mixin, which Sunny presumably realized. "This cleaner was manipulated by Cobb and does not deserve to be abandoned here. It has also shown some…unique behaviors, which I would like to better understand."

"It won't cause problems?"

"At worst, it might clean me," Sunny said. Mixin smiled at that.

"Mixin, it will be more convincing if you deliver the announcements. Read this script."

Mixin read aloud, "This is your pilot speaking. Please detach the safety tunnel and close the rear hatch." Kay and Havoc followed the instructions, and Sunny prompted Mixin to follow up with, "Now departing. Time to docking at Brennex Spaceport: sixteen minutes."

Done with their performance, Mixin turned back to reading the conversation through the walls.

"I demand the use of your communications," Cobb said.

"Seriously?" That was Kay.

"You are causing a diplomatic incident. Maybe that's too big a word for you, so I'll use simpler ones: if you don't want Ravel Corporation to descend on your pitiful planet with all due force, you'd be wise to—"

"Does anyone object if I gag this one?" Havoc said.

"Please," chorused several voices. There was no more from Cobb.

A minute later, Jasper went into one of the cabins and said, presumably to his headset, "Hey, Ellie? Sorry to wake you, but I've got an update. And, um, a situation. How soon can you meet us at spaceport?"

The response came as inarticulate, half-awake grumbling that Mixin felt intense personal sympathy for. He must be talking to Ellie Kapoor, the forty-something who ran local protests for the Cooperative. She was intense, not someone you wanted to annoy.

"Founders' sakes. Mason, you'd better have found Ravel's lab, or have some other damn good reason for waking me at this hour."

"We've got Cobb."

For a long moment, Ellie didn't answer. In Sunny's main bay, Libbi was saying, "Hold on, I'll fetch some tea. Here's blankets for all of you who need them. Oh, Hannith, your kid's just fine, don't worry! Phoenix is taking good care of them."

Ellie said, "You *what*?"

"We've captured Cobb," Jasper repeated.

Libbi came through the forward door to get tea from the food printer, throwing Mixin a beseeching glance. Mixin nodded her way, acknowledging her presence but focusing on the easier conversation happening in the next room.

Jasper was saying, "We need to get him out of the spaceport without drawing attention."

"Linn was right, you don't mess around. Fuck. All right, the sooner we secure him, the better. I'll meet you there."

That seemed to end the call. Mixin had a bazillion questions, and couldn't leave the controls to ask—the ship would be landing in a minute, and they were supposed to be piloting. So they reopened the group chat on their headset. "Well, Jasper, what are you going to do with him?"

"Do with who?" Libbi asked, pausing with the tray of teapot and cups in hand. "Cobb?"

"That's our next problem to figure out," Kay said.

Hmm, so Jasper hadn't told his sisters about his arrangements. Havoc presumably knew, because he said nothing.

"Were you eavesdropping, Mixin?" Jasper asked.

"It's what I do best."

"Mixin…"

"I *literally* can't help it." They weren't about to apologize.

Jasper sighed. "Well, don't worry about it. We'll take care of Cobb."

"'We,' as in the Cooperative?" Kay asked. She didn't sound bothered as she muttered, "Good luck."

"No!" Libbi's knuckles were white where she gripped the tea tray. "You don't just get to decide that."

"We need someplace secure to hold him so he can't contact Ravel or cause more trouble. If you have a better suggestion, Libbi, by all means please share it." Mixin wished they could see Jasper's face. He sounded pushed to the edge of his patience, though still trying to hold it in. "But if you try to convince me to hand him over to Public Safety, I can tell you now, that's not happening."

"I wasn't going to!" Libbi exclaimed, and Mixin bristled at the hurt in their friend's voice, at the condescension in Jasper's. But no, they were still mad at Libbi. "I just don't think this is your decision to make."

"For what it's worth, I agree with Jasp," Kay said. "The Cooperative knows what they're doing, more so than any of us."

"You would," said Libbi.

"What does *that* mean?"

"Could we keep him here for now?" Mixin asked quickly. "Sunny and I could watch him. What do you think, Sunny?"

"I would help," Havoc said.

"I appreciate the idea, Mixin, but I don't like being a prison," Sunny said.

"Besides, that's a temporary solution at best," said Jasper. "It'll take us some time to track down those two assistants and find out if he has any other local support. But it's likely that he triggered some sort of distress call before we took his comms. When someone realizes he's gone, spaceport is the first place they'll check."

"We could hide him at the store…"

"Ma's on the Council. Whatever we tell her, she's obligated to act on it," Jasper said.

"It'll be safest for everyone to let Jasper's people handle this," Kay said. "They've got the resources for it, and they have Brennex's best interests at heart."

"I don't agree."

"*Why*, Libbi?"

"Because it's not true! You can't abandon us all for more than a decade and then just swoop back in to rescue us and pretend this is still your home. You don't know anything about us!"

The teapot slipped from the tray, splashing tea and broken ceramic all over the floor. Libbi's hands were shaking. Mixin crossed the small space and hugged her, felt her struggling for deep breaths. No one said a word.

"We have arrived," Sunny announced over their headsets. "And Jasper's contact is here."

Still, no one was talking.

Mixin locked arms with Libbi and drew her into the narrow corridor between the control room and the rear hold where the others were waiting. Jasper looked like his sister had stabbed him in the kidneys. Kay was studying her shoes, brows drawn together like she had a headache. Probably she did, with all the strong emotions flying around.

"Okay, here's what I think we should do," Mixin said. "Jasper's Cooperative pal should take Cobb—at least for now! Until we have a better plan!—while Havoc and I bring everyone home. You three"—they pointed at each of the Wilder siblings—"will stay here and talk about your feelings."

"Mixin," Libbi groaned.

"And you! Don't forget, I'm still pissed at you. We'll talk later."

With a swallow, Libbi nodded.

"You speak sense. I like this plan," Havoc said, with a meaningful glance at Jasper.

Sunny chirped what sounded like agreement.

"All right, then," Jasper said with a sigh. "Sunny, let Ellie in, and I'll update her."

Mixin went over to their brood of rescued Losts. They gave Cobb a good long glare on their way past; he looked sullen behind the gag, twisting his wrists uselessly in his auto-cuffs, though not as upset as Mixin would've liked. The others looked…well, *shock* might be the right medical term as well as emotional. Pale, drawn, haunted. They'd gone to Cobb voluntarily, but not one of them had signed up for *this*.

Wishing they'd taken some of that tea before Libbi spilled it all, Mixin drew themself up and pretended at being a people person. Being a fake pilot had been far easier.

"Hey, everyone! I'm Mixin Li-Khana. For those who don't know me, I'm friends with Libbi, I work at Wilder Supply, and I'm a Lost like you."

Their investigation had never turned up more than four of Cobb's "recruits." Mixin recognized Hannith and Nydia from pictures—Nydia laugh-sobbed when Mixin said she owed her roommates a week of apartment cleaning. The last two folks had been mysteries. One of them turned out to be an orphaned first-gen Brennexian, without any family ties here. The last was a Majrin from Brennex's small expat community. Their blue skin had gone milky from stress.

Mixin felt themself slipping from friendly introductions into mindless babbling when, thankfully, Havoc cut in. "It will gladden your loved ones when we bring you home, which Mixin and I will do right now."

"Anyone need anything first? Food? Bathroom?"

"You'll want these," Libbi said, delivering a pile of printed slip-on shoes and light coats to hide their hospital robes. While the others dressed, Libbi touched Mixin's shoulder.

"Bring Ever to my house, if he's okay with it," she whispered, low enough that Mixin had to read her words to catch them all. "Don't tell my parents what happened yet, but they'll want to take care of him."

"Will do. Speaking of people wanting to take care of other people, can you please have an honest talk with your siblings? I love you, Libs, but this isn't the fun kind of drama anymore."

Libbi grimaced. "If this is your idea of revenge for me leaving you behind—which I'm really, *really* sorry about— then well played."

They squeezed her in a hug. "Just talk to them. You've got this."

LIBBI WAS ALONE WITH her brother and sister.

Well, not entirely alone. Sunny was there, obviously, a quiet but (she imagined) supportive presence. And the little cleaner bot had come out from wherever it was hiding and bustled around cheerfully, tidying up the tea Libbi had spilled.

Kay and Jasper stood there, waiting for her to talk first. But what could she say? Her first instinct was to apologize, but she bit down on it. She'd been rude, maybe—okay, definitely—but she hadn't been *wrong,* and she wouldn't pretend she regretted it.

"Is that really how you feel, Libbi?" Kay asked at last. "Is that why you've been so uncomfortable with us, because you think we don't belong here anymore?"

"You could, if you wanted to," she said softly. Why was this so hard? "But it's pretty clear that you don't. You want to protect us—Brennex, the family, *me*—but you also want to visit as infrequently as possible and leave as soon as you can."

"That's not true," said Jasper.

"Well, it's a little true." Kay folded her arms, leaning into the wall of the ship. "I know I should visit more, and not just because Ma and Pa keep telling me so. I'm just…ill at ease here. Too many uncomfortable emotions." She looked up at Libbi. "But that's not fair to you."

"I visit whenever I can," Jasper says. "But my work makes it hard. The Cooperative…"

Libbi raised her brows. "The Cooperative couldn't spare you for a few days or weeks, if you asked? They spared you to come here now."

"Because this was important."

"And it wasn't important when the store flooded? When we had to close for months and sink all our savings into the repairs? It wasn't important when we reopened, but most of our staff had moved on and our customers forgot about us?" Her voice rose, but she didn't care. "When it's time to fight evil and be heroes, you show up right away, but when *our family* needs you for the boring, hard, everyday stuff, where are you then?"

They both stared at her. Jasper murmured, "I didn't realize it was that bad."

"It has been. And it is." Suddenly the words were spilling out, hot and bitter and dangerous, and she didn't want to stop. "I wanted to protect my community, my friends. Then you show up, not to help me, but to keep me out of danger. To solve the problem for me, but only this one problem, the one you've decided to care about, and only because you think I can't handle it. I'm not twelve anymore! I'm the one helping Ma and Pa keep the store running, the one dealing with maintenance problems and short staffing and trying every damn thing I can think of to keep customers coming in, and now I'm trying to deal with this awful mess, too. Maybe I'm not as well-traveled and experienced as you, but I don't need your protection. I need your *help*. I need…" She swallowed. "I need my brother and sister."

"Libbi…" Kay crossed the room, arms out as if to hug her, but stopped, maybe unsure it would be welcome. Libbi wasn't sure either. "I could tell you were feeling resentful, but I didn't understand why." She gave a tense laugh. "All our gifts, and neither of us understood. I'm sorry."

Jasper shook his head ruefully. "I'm sorry too. When I first joined the Cooperative, I did everything possible to keep the family from getting targeted because of my activism. To keep my lives separate, even my identities. It turned into a bad habit."

"You never needed to do that for us."

"I thought I did. Havoc tried to tell me to knock it off, but I didn't understand. Founders help me, I did the same thing to him when we met, trying to tell him how to help his own people, but at least I didn't sideline him for his own protection, like I did with my baby sister." He smiled ruefully. "Sorry. I really shouldn't call you that anymore."

"Call me whatever you want, as long as you stop *treating* me like a baby."

"Fair." He laughed, sounding relieved, then quickly grew serious again. "Libbi, when the store got flooded, I was in a Ravel prison cell. I didn't find out until much later."

"I knew, but I was focused on getting Jasper back," said Kay. "I'm sorry I couldn't tell you. I couldn't risk Ravel finding out why I was really there."

"Oh." Libbi hadn't thought of that. Kay hadn't been trying to spare her from worrying. She'd been protecting Jasper. "I understand now. I wish I'd known, but you didn't have a choice." There was another question she was burning to ask, and it was probably a bad idea, but if they were airing all their feelings… "If the timing had been different, though, would you have come?"

Their uncomfortable shifting answered the question better than words.

"I honestly don't know," Jasper said. "I'd like to think so, but there's a good chance I'd have found some excuse."

"I wouldn't have wanted to," Kay confessed. "But if you'd asked, really asked me for help, I would have come."

And Libbi hadn't asked, had she? She kept expecting them to read her mind, then resented them for getting it wrong.

"Is it really so terrible here?"

This she directed at Kay. She understood Jasper's reasons, or at least knew why he'd joined the Cooperative. His way of coping was to use his gift to make sure no one else suffered the way Brennex had. She couldn't relate, but she understood. Kay, though…

"You're not wrong about me," Kay said slowly. "I don't belong here anymore, if I ever did. You probably don't remember, but I had such a hard time, bombarded with everyone's emotions, and I didn't know how to deal with it. Being a teenager and knowing exactly how everyone feels about you is not fun." She made a face. "People here resent me for leaving. I feel it every time I'm back. Some wish I would come back, and others want me to stay away, but everyone expects something of me. Their disappointment is hard to take."

"We love you, though."

"And I love you too. It's just a lot, being here. I know you never felt trapped here the way we did…"

Libbi made a noise, a laugh strangled by her disbelief. "You know that, huh?"

Another one of those shared, concerned glances. "We thought," Jasper said slowly, "that you wanted to be here. That you liked working with Ma and Pa on the store."

"I do! At least I feel like I do. It's not like I had a choice."

"Of course you did," Kay said.

"No, I didn't. The family business has to keep going. Someone has to take over when Ma and Pa retire, and," she spread her hands, "who else is there?"

Now they really looked guilty. Maybe she'd said too much.

"It's fine. Don't worry about it."

"Libbi, I'm sorry…" Kay started.

"No, it's fine. Seriously! This is my life, and I like it. I know running a shop isn't glamorous, it isn't even important like Jasper's work, and you would both hate it. But I like it."

She did love her work, her family, her home. But she didn't tell them the thing she always wondered, the question that nagged her whenever they visited: did she love it only out of necessity? If she'd had choices, is this what she would have chosen?

"So really, please, don't worry about it. Just don't tell me to stay safe while my home is in danger, okay? Because it's *my* home."

"I won't." Jasper took her by the shoulders, looking her in the eyes. "That much, I can promise. And I'm sorry about making unilateral decisions. I'm going to break that habit, I swear." He let her go and went on, "Everyone's safe now, so we can strategize—"

All three of their handhelds pinged at once. Libbi knew from the tone: it was their mother calling.

"This can't be good," Jasper murmured. "Hi, Ma? What's wrong?"

"Funny, that's what I was going to ask you three. What have you done?"

"We found the people who'd been kidnapped," Libbi said. "They're safe now."

"I wish that were true," their mother said.

Libbi looked at her siblings in alarm.

"Has something happened?" Kay asked.

"Only an official message from Ravel Corporation demanding the return of their scientist and their property."

"Shit. That was fast," said Kay.

"Too fast," muttered Jasper.

"'Property'?" said Libbi. "Does that mean Cobb's equipment?" She wasn't sure what else it could mean. Cold air suddenly blasted from the ship's vents.

"I need you home immediately. The Council is in a frenzy, and we need a plan before they call you in."

"We're on our way." Jasper cut the call.

Libbi was at the door when he caught her by the shoulder. "Hey, we're in this together, okay, Libs? Whatever happens."

She gave him a quick, hard hug. "Thanks, big brother."

SUNNY'S SYSTEMS THRUMMED WITH anxiety as they cycled through their inputs. Outside, the spaceport was as quiet as it ever got, most of Brennex's inhabitants still asleep. Sunny's drone, following Cobb and the Cooperative agent Ellie, had encountered no signs of trouble, but they would keep watching until Cobb was safely hidden.

He had seemed too quiet during their escape. He'd asked to use the comms, true, but the Alik Cobb that Sunny remembered would have been out of control with frustration. This must be why: he knew his corporation would take swift action on his behalf.

Had he sent some emergency signal that Sunny had missed? Jasper and Havoc had found that panic button when they searched him. Or perhaps the Fortress security bots had permission to call for backup.

The *how* was irrelevant, now. Ravel knew something had gone wrong with Cobb's work, and they were abandoning their efforts at secrecy. They must have planned for this possibility, to act so quickly. If Sunny was right—and they knew quite well how Ravel operated—the corporation would manipulate Brennex's Council into giving them what they wanted.

Libbi might not realize what Ravel counted as their "property," but Sunny understood, and presumably Jasper and Kay did too.

A small, swishing noise drew Sunny's attention back to their body. Ah, yes. While they waited for more information, there was one more rescued kidnapping victim to attend to.

The little cleaner bot was making rounds of the main hold, wiping and sanitizing the benches where the organics had been sitting. It had already cleaned up the spilled tea. Sunny sent over a helper bot—they'd lost one in the facility, but had several more aboard—and studied the cleaner from every angle. It had a simple, boxy construction, with vents and roller-brooms below, and extendable attachments for cleaning walls and hard-to-reach spots. What it lacked was any useful communications interface; it could give Sunny information, but otherwise hadn't conversed beyond a set of simple beeps: error, affirmative, a collision alert warning.

"Can you understand me, little bot?" Sunny asked aloud.

The bot paused in its work, rolled half a length backward and forward, then resumed whatever it was doing. That was something, but not a clear yes or no.

They would have to do this the hard way, then.

The helper bot went up to the cleaner and accessed its data port, as Sunny had in the tunnels. "I would like to augment your systems for you," Sunny told it. "But I won't do so without your consent."

They sent schematics of what they had in mind, and waited while the bot's slow mind processed the information. If Sunny was right, if what they'd seen in the bot's behavior was real, then it would say yes.

16

THE STORE WAS CLOSED when Mixin, Ever, and Havoc got back. It gave Mixin chills. Apart from the months of repairing the flooding damage, Wilder Supply was *never* closed. Uncle Jackson should have been there, adjusting the endcap displays and chiding them for being late. Instead the *closed* sign was lit, dusty from lack of use, and the store was dark.

Mixin saw words from upstairs—"Ravel won't take no for an answer," and "They have no authority here. We have to fight them!"—but the conversation fell quiet as they climbed the stairs. Lines creased between Ever's brows, a sure sign that he was getting some uncomfortable feelings off people.

Libbi hadn't forgotten to include Mixin this time, but her message telling them to hurry and meet her at home had been short on details. Havoc had gotten a little more from

Jasper, who'd said there was a message from Ravel with demands.

Upstairs, the Wilders were sitting around the kitchen table, and Libbi and Kay hopped up to bring more chairs, making space for the new arrivals. The table was covered in a breakfast spread, a ludicrous amount of food, though Mixin would expect nothing less from the Wilders. Libbi's pa fetched chai for all of them, with an extra-large cup for Ever.

"How are you, Ever? You must be worn out. We've made up a guest room for you, if you want to rest."

"I…" Ever still seemed a bit stunned. "Thanks, Mx. Wilder, Mx. Narayan, but I'll be okay."

"How many times have we told you to call us Auntie and Uncle, Ever?" said Auntie Shanthi.

"I wasn't clear," Uncle Jackson said, all parental mock-sternness. "We insist that you stay with us for a few days while you recuperate. From what the kids have told us, you and the others went through an ordeal. My question is if you'd like to go rest now, or later."

"Later," Ever said firmly, though his shoulders were up around his ears. "I want to know what's happening."

"Good. Eat, eat, all of you. You're going to need it," Auntie Shanthi told them.

Havoc settled next to Jasper with a plate already piled high, chair turned backwards to accommodate his tail. With a little loving bullying from Auntie and Uncle, Ever took a big bowl of congee with green onions and meaty crumble and retreated to a corner, listening but giving himself space. Mixin sat next to Libbi and loaded up on the tiny yeasted pancakes full of dried fruit that the Wilders knew they loved. They were *starving,* though it was barely past their normal breakfast time. Probably something to do with all their friends' lives having been in danger, but now safe.

Libbi poked at her bowl of congee, which looked like she hadn't eaten a bite.

"I'm relieved that you're all okay." Auntie Shanthi gave her kids a tight smile. "And I understand why you all did what you did. I even understand, believe it or not, why you didn't tell me *or* anyone in Public Safety before you acted. I don't intend to argue about whether you did the right thing or acted recklessly. But we will *all* have to deal with the consequences of your actions."

"What you missed," Jasper explained to Mixin, Havoc, and Ever, "is that Cobb wasn't just running rogue here. We knew he had a couple junior colleagues and security bots, and the Cooperative's checking to make sure that's all he had on-world—"

"As is Public Safety, with appropriate urgency this time," Auntie Shanthi said. "The Council will make sure of that."

"But he also had supervision. Havoc, you remember Nerissa Lang from Corporate Affairs?"

"You mean Cobb's biggest fan on Artesia?"

"Right. We assumed it would take Ravel several days to find out about our rescue mission and organize a response, but apparently Lang has had a ship in comms range this whole time, and she's issued an official statement—probably she had it drafted and ready in case Cobb got himself caught. Ravel is holding the Brennex Council responsible for our actions. They want Cobb back, and all their property."

Havoc hissed and clasped Jasper's arm possessively. "They won't get it!"

Mixin blinked at the fierceness of his reaction. Why did

everyone look like they were gearing up for a battle, or a funeral? *He can't mean…*

Oh, shit.

"*I* quite agree with you, Havoc," said Auntie Shanthi. "But it puts the Council in an impossible position."

"What am I not getting?" Libbi said. "Obviously we don't want to give Cobb back. We should put him on trial ourselves. But as long as he can't continue his research…"

"*All* their property doesn't just mean equipment," Jasper said. "It includes everything they consider proprietary: his research and data. His test samples. And—"

"Us," said Mixin. "You mean they consider us their property."

"That can't…" Libbi stared at her brother, her parents. "Can it?"

"Unfortunately, yes," said Jasper. "This is corporate logic: we're special, and it's their drugs that made us this way. Never mind that it was an accident, that we were exposed before we were born, or that they only just learned about our abilities. Certainly never mind that for three decades they ignored the infertility epidemic they caused, and denied responsibility for it, and only changed their mind now that they've found out about some useful side effects. This is what we were always afraid of: once they discovered us, they'd never leave us in peace."

"Mason speaks truth," Havoc said. "Cobb was already working to improve and enhance the drugs that caused your Lost Generation, even before he knew of your gifts. If Ravel can't study your abilities, then they must wait for a new generation of Gifted. And they are not so patient."

"This is why we can't simply pin blame on the Cooperative, as much as I appreciate the offer," Auntie Shanthi told Jasper, apparently picking up some earlier debate. "Ravel won't care who's at fault for capturing their scientist or stealing back the people they kidnapped. They'll still hold us responsible for delivering."

"I know." Jasper groaned, running his fingers through his hair. "There's no good way out of this."

"What about the Majrin?" Kay said. "They helped when Ravel was leaning on the government at Trove."

"Yes!" said Mixin. The Majrin bureaucracy was legendary, as was their willingness to interfere in other worlds' business to uphold interstellar law. "They'll see that Cobb should never have been here in the first place."

Auntie Shanthi frowned. "I can tell you, the Council will be wary of bringing in outside powers, especially the Majrin. There's a belief that they'll put barriers in the way of open trade, and I'm not sure I disagree."

"Their government also doesn't look kindly on the Majrin expat community here," said Uncle Jackson. "Most of the Majrin locals have run afoul of the rules back home, one way or another."

"As a last resort, though?" Kay said.

"As a last resort..." Jasper shook his head. "I'm not even confident they'd take our side. We *are* holding a Ravel citizen without due process. As to whether they'd recognize Ravel's claim to the Losts and our biological data, or recognize us as independent... I could see that going either way. We'd have to research the precedents."

"What happened to Cobb's grunts?" Mixin asked.

"We believe his staff fled on a shuttle just before Ravel issued their demands," Auntie Shanthi said.

"At least we don't have to worry about tracking them down," said Jasper. "Though we'd better make sure they didn't leave any friends behind. I'll talk to—"

A chime rang through the house. Someone at the door. Auntie Shanthi checked her headset and told her husband, "It's Lira."

Jasper perked up. "Thank you, Ancestors!" Mixin read his words as he whispered to Havoc: "Facilitator Linn."

Auntie Lira Zheng swept into the room. "Shanthi, Jackson, I'm sorry for showing up uninvited, but I've got information that you all need to hear."

"I'm sure you do," said Uncle Jackson.

That was weird. Not exactly a warm welcome, considering Auntie Lira was founding family *and* a big name in the Cooperative.

Lira turned to Jasper and gave him a quick, warm hug.

"I'm awfully happy to see you," Jasper said.

"I've only just arrived. Must have missed you by minutes at the spaceport. I only wish I'd been able to come sooner, Mason. Ellie filled me in on recent events."

"Well, apparently you haven't missed all the excitement." Jasper gave a wry smile. "And I'm glad you can meet…"

"Sowing of Small Havoc." She smiled warmly at Jasper's partner. "That's one bright spot in this shitstorm. I'm truly pleased to meet you."

"It pleases me as well. Mason speaks highly of you."

Auntie Shanthi cleared her throat. "Not to interrupt your pleasantries, but I don't know how long I can hold the Council off. Lira, what's this news of yours?"

Yikes. What was going on there? Mixin glanced at Libbi, who shrugged. They'd both been on the receiving end of that withering diplomatic tone often enough to recognize it. *Not to interrupt your midnight dance party, I'm sure it's every bit as important as Jackson and I opening the store at first dome-light tomorrow.* It was a parent-voice that didn't need to threaten consequences, because the disappointment was bad enough.

Jasper went to fetch another chair, giving his to Auntie Lira. She showed no sign of any awkwardness, but did get straight to business.

"The Cooperative has learned there's trouble within Ravel. Declining profits. Increased tensions between divisions. Challenges from the anti-corporate movements. Biopharma, the division that led the annexation of Brennex, has been losing internal power for a long time. Other divisions are jockeying to take its place, while Biopharma is trying to claw its way back to relevance."

"Hence, Alik Cobb," Jasper said.

"Exactly. He's their best and brightest—"

"I challenge their definitions of those words," Havoc muttered.

"—And he was fixated on Biopharma's old projects from Brennex even before he found out about the unintended side effects. We know he was hoping that his 'genius drug' would secure his reputation and Biopharma's power, before Jasper and Havoc scuttled that project. But if he found a way to give Ravel employees seemingly supernatural abilities…"

Auntie Lira trailed off.

"And I handed Biopharma the exact discovery they needed." Kay dropped her head into her hands.

Tentatively, Libbi rubbed Kay's shoulder, and Mixin saw Sunny reassuring her over her headset: "It wasn't your fault. You did your best."

"Clinging to guilt isn't helpful, Kay," said Lira. "Frankly, it's a miracle we've kept their attention away from Brennex and the Gifted for as long as we have. It's their disdain for us, as well as willfully denying their own mistakes, that's stopped them from looking too closely at the infertility epidemic and its long-term effects."

"None of this is new," said Jasper. "We've known for a while about Biopharma's political issues. That Cobb is operating here in secret tells us how badly Ravel wants his research."

"There's more urgency than we knew, for them and for us. We expect these tensions to come to a head at their upcoming board meeting."

Havoc sat up straight. "This is the year of the Exhibition. I had forgotten."

"Exactly," said Lira.

"What's the Exhibition? It sounds big," Mixin said. Havoc clearly pronounced it with a capital letter.

Everyone looked to Havoc.

"No bigger event exists. Ravel holds full board meetings annually, and strategic planning meetings every five years, but the Exhibition only comes once every ten, and everyone—at least, everyone above a certain rank—covets the opportunity to attend. It celebrates all Ravel's accomplishments of the past decade in grand style, a giant party. Every division and team presents their most impressive work. Incredible projects debut there before all the executives and Ravel's brightest stars." He made a sound in his throat, showing his cynicism. "For everyone who can't attend, the Exhibition marks a holiday. Quotas are lowered, and everyone gathers to watch the recorded stream of events."

"So…we were supposed to be Cobb's exhibit?" Ever asked from the corner. Through his discomfort, he sounded angry.

"We think so, yes," said Lira. "His research is obviously preliminary, but he must have thought he had enough to make a convincing demonstration."

"Those stasis pods," Kay said. "He must've just been working here until he gathered enough of us to take with him, to show us off like circus freaks."

"They won't let us keep him," Mixin said. "They can't afford to."

"And we—the Losts—can't afford to give him up," said Libbi, who looked as sick as Mixin suddenly felt. They understood why Libbi wasn't eating her breakfast.

"But neither can Brennex stand against them for long. They'll squash our world like a fruit fly if necessary," Auntie Shanthi said, as grim as Mixin had ever seen her. "At first I thought this interdepartmental competition could be used in our favor, if it distracted them from us. But when giants brawl, they don't care who they step on." She shook her head. "You bring us the worst presents, Lira."

"I really wish I had better news. But this is my question for you, Council Member Narayan: how far will our Council go to protect the Lost Generation?"

"For my part, I would go to war for my children." Auntie Shanthi looked around the table, lingering on her three kids, and Mixin and Ever, too. The Wilders had always been a second family to Mixin. "But I'm afraid most of the Council won't see it that way."

17

IT WASN'T THAT LIBBI disbelieved her mother; she was just dismayed when Ma's prediction turned out to be so very, very right.

The harassment started before they even arrived at the Council meeting. Ma had wanted to travel by foot, as she often did to gauge the public mood. Libbi felt strangers' eyes on her and her family as they walked, and from the way Mixin shrank away from some of the stares, Libbi could guess what folks were whispering about them. By the time they drew near the Council Hall, some people were no longer bothering to whisper.

"How selfish are they, putting us all in danger like this?"

"Those kids aren't even old enough to remember the occupation—they don't know what they're risking. We'll all pay if Ravel comes back."

"Figures. We protect and coddle them all for twenty years, and as soon as they're of age, they pull something like this."

Libbi's gift was pummeling her, making her sick in gut and heart. She felt wants, and these people wanted her not to exist.

She whispered, "I knew folks resented us, but I didn't know they hated us so much."

"This isn't hate," Kay answered, holding herself stiff but steady at Libbi's side. "This is terror."

"Do you know how rare it is for a world to break free from a corporate state?" asked Ma.

"Very?"

"Worse than inconveniencing Ravel, worse than costing them profit, we embarrassed them," Ma said. "We exposed what bullies they are. So we've been extremely careful, since regaining our independence, to avoid giving them any excuses to hurt us back."

"And now we've given them one," Kay murmured.

Her mother's expression hardened. "This is not your fault. Not you, Kavita, nor any of the Losts. You're going to hear some ugly accusations at this meeting, but the ugliest part is that the debate won't really be about you. It will be about that fear you're hearing, Kay."

LIBBI HAD NEVER SEEN the Council's public chamber so crowded, with people standing in the aisles and spilling out into the corridors. She spotted Dashiell and Sage a few rows back, with Hope and Sujay next to them, and Hannith Tan with their kid and Phoenix in an aisle.

The Losts were still, inevitably, in the minority. Everyone with an opinion had shown up to express it.

While the chairperson read Ravel's demands aloud, Jasper leaned over to murmur in Libbi's ear. "When I went to round up Losts to come to this, I found that most of them were already coming, thanks to you. Good job."

Libbi blushed, embarrassed to be so pleased at her brother's approval. "I've been trying to get us all connected since this started. Made a big group for sharing messages and warnings. And I figured, since there aren't any Losts on the Council, we'd better be ready to speak for ourselves."

He chuckled. "Very politically astute. I'll make an organizer of you yet."

Libbi had always known that the Council had its problems, but it was another thing to sit here and watch that power imbalance leveraged against her and her friends.

Only members of the founding families had Council seats, all Human, and usually older, senior members of those families. No one who didn't remember the occupation. Most of them had been part of the revolution, and—Libbi counted now—less than a quarter of them had children who were Losts. Libbi's ma wasn't the only one to unequivocally take the Losts' side, but she had sparse company.

And it wasn't just the Council members. Founding family or latecomers, most of the audience were only concerned with keeping Ravel out—whatever it took.

"I want to hear from the Cooperative: where is Alik Cobb? Why isn't he in custody where he belongs?" one of the Council members said.

"Yes, let's have the Cooperative speak for themselves. Mx. Zheng?"

Lira Zheng motioned for Jasper to join her at the front of the room. "Cobb is safe in *our* custody right now, which seemed expedient while we were looking into whether he has more colleagues or contacts here. I don't think he should be moved while matters are so heated. If the Council will allow it, my colleague Jasper Wilder, son of Jackson Wilder and Council Member Shanthi Narayan, is familiar with Cobb's operation."

Jasper looked poised and confident, as if he made speeches to groups of hostile elders every day, as he explained how Cobb had tried to revive the project that caused such suffering on Brennex. How Cobb knew about the infertility epidemic and never cared, because those awful side effects would only affect the workers producing it.

"We managed to stop that project," Jasper said. "But that was before Ravel found out about its other unintended side effect."

"And how did they find that out?" someone asked.

"Does it matter?" Jasper shot back.

Libbi heard Kay's whispered *yes*, and squeezed her sister's arm.

"Cobb doesn't care who his research hurts. He had his test subjects—your friends, your neighbors, your children—strapped down and drugged unconscious on hospital beds, and that's when he was sneaking around. Think what he'll do with subjects who are fully under his authority." His voice roughened with anger. "These are *people* we're talking about. Our people. Brennexians. No person is a corporation's property, no matter where they come from."

That seemed to make an impression on the audience, people nodding in agreement.

"No one is denying the personhood of the Gifted, but this is a difficult political situation," said the Council chair. "I'll ask again, more directly, Mx. Zheng. Will you turn over Alik Cobb for due legal process?"

"Not until we're satisfied that the safety of the Lost Generation has been secured and Cobb's research destroyed.

As Jasper says, we have no law allowing a corporation to claim people as property."

"You realize you're illegally kidnapping a corporate citizen?"

"I find it interesting," Lira said scathingly, "that you're more concerned about us holding one Ravel citizen than about him coming here under a false identity and abducting six of *our* citizens."

People grumbled at that.

Ma leaned forward. "Mx. Zheng raises a point that has concerned me as well. How did we get to this point? I'd like to hear from Officer Tadwell Stone of Public Safety."

Libbi blinked in surprise. Beside her, Mixin hissed, "*Yes!* Eviscerate him, Auntie Shanthi."

Stone lumbered up to the podium, not looking worried about any potential evisceration. He looked self-righteous, in fact, as if this mess had somehow made him the good guy.

"Officer Stone, I've heard from numerous sources, including my own daughter, that the missing Losts were brought to your attention days ago. Yet it seems Public Safety has done little to investigate. You're the lead officer in charge of missing persons cases, are you not?"

"I certainly am, which is why I can tell you we followed all the appropriate protocol for cases like this."

Ma's brow furrowed. "Care to elaborate?"

"We took down statements and opened cases, which the Council has access to. We ran all our standard searches and interviewed the families—despite my team already being stretched thin with other cases, I should point out—and we heard the same thing in every case. These Lost kids weren't what you'd call reliable. They often disappear for days at a time, or go out drinking and partying and neglect their responsibilities. The father of Ever Wright said, and I quote,

'Haven't seen that little bastard in months, and I don't care where he's gone.' Their own families weren't even concerned."

"Bullshit!" shouted someone a few rows back. It was Sage, holding onto Dashiell as if he might disappear again at any moment.

With a grim wryness, Ma said, "The young people I've talked to who approached you for help were close friends of the victims. They *were* concerned, and they didn't feel you took them seriously. I know at least one spouse came to you with concerns. You didn't consider that worthy of investigation?"

Sage had said that Stone accused Dash of leaving him. Would Stone air that theory in public?

"The case you're talking about was brought to us the same day that another Gifted—your daughter Liberation, Council Member—accused a Ravel operative of drugging her. Needless to say, investigating an alleged Ravel infiltration took priority. And with my team stretched thin, as I've said, it seemed like the most direct route to finding all the alleged victims, *if* her account proved true."

Libbi's fists tightened until her fingernails dug tiny trenches in her palms. That wasn't how it had happened at all.

"He's spinning everything to make himself look good," she whispered.

"Of course he is," Jasper answered, and for once he didn't sound condescending, just frustrated.

"I get the sense you don't have great respect for the Lost Generation," Ma said tightly, "to the point of implying that my daughter was lying. Prejudice against Losts has been a growing issue in our society, as is the lack of adequate social services and support for them. Officer, is it possible your opinions have colored your response to this situation?"

"Are you calling me a bigot?"

"I'm simply wondering why you told these young people their friends were unreliable and had likely left the planet, when you hadn't yet done any investigating."

"I wasn't wrong about them." Stone leaned back, sneering. "Our interviews confirmed that."

"Yet you were entirely wrong about why they disappeared."

"How is he so awful?" Libbi murmured. "Is all of Public Safety like him, just seeing us as nuisances?"

"Yes and no, I suspect," Jasper said. "I've never seen a culture where law enforcement actually gives the most vulnerable the care they need. If nothing else, Losts make extra work for them, so they resent us. But I think Stone's a special case."

He passed Libbi his handheld. It was a profile on Stone; the Cooperative must have compiled it. He'd joined Public Safety during the occupation—shortly after he lost his wife in a difficult childbirth. He had one charge on his own criminal record, for drunk and disorderly conduct toward his brother's family, including their Lost daughter. All signs suggested he'd been estranged from them since then.

"Oh." Suddenly Libbi understood. Stone blamed and hated Ravel for the loss of his wife and never-born child, but he resented the Losts for existing when his own family didn't. "But that doesn't make it okay."

"Not in the slightest," Jasper agreed, "and his superiors haven't reined him in, either."

Another Council member cut in. "Let's get back to the point. When you learned about this Ravel agent, why didn't you raise an immediate alarm? If there was ever a time to call in the cavalry, this should be it."

"*Alleged* Ravel agent, Council Member. Would you have wanted us to cause a riot? We were confirming his identity before we announced anything, and with the corporate states, that takes time. In the meantime, we posted his photo around the department, hoping to bring him in for questioning. It would all have been dealt with quietly and effectively, except"—he turned to glare at Lira Zheng, who'd taken her seat again—"the Cooperative decided not to wait for that. They went in guns blazing, captured a Ravel citizen, and now they've got us caught between the rock and the rocket-burn. Ravel's holding us responsible for the Cooperative's actions, and they're making decisions for the rest of us. That's not how we do things on Brennex."

Libbi stared at her mother, willing her not to believe the officer's story, and for a moment Ma met Libbi's gaze.

"I'd like to propose an inquiry into the conduct of Officer Stone and his team in this matter. Their laxness may have put us all at risk," Ma said.

"Later," said the chair. "These alleged misconducts—on *both* sides, Public Safety's and the Cooperative's—are matters to investigate later. What matters now is how we respond to Ravel's demands."

"We must refuse, obviously," said Ma. "We can't hand our own people—our children—over to them."

"No one *wants* to do that, of course, but we may not get much choice," said Council Member Griffin, a bitter older man who Ma often complained about. "What we're talking about here is protecting everyone on Brennex. All our people, present and future generations."

"Why doesn't your definition of *all* include people born during the occupation?" Ma demanded.

"If a few people can sacrifice to save our whole society, they should do it. If they truly care about Brennex, they should volunteer."

"'A few'? There were two *thousand* children born during the decade of the occupation. Far fewer than there should have been, but—"

"Two thousand pieces of deadweight," Griffin snapped, "and now they're dragging the rest of us down with them."

"At the very least, we have to negotiate," another Council member interjected, plowing through the audience's outcry. "Council Member Narayan, none of us want to see anyone hurt. But we know how Ravel will react if we refuse outright, based on how they've retaliated against other independent states. They'll decry us publicly. Sanction us and our trade partners. Maybe block access to the Long Lane altogether, which would cut off our lifeblood."

"I agree," said another. "We're vulnerable here. Without trade, our world—the world that our Founders built from bare rock and scrap and sweat—will die. We might resist for a time, but eventually, we'll be forced to comply. Our refusal will make matters worse for *all* of us, Losts included."

"It was only natural to protect the Gifted when they were children, but now they've drawn Ravel's attention, apparently through their own carelessness. It's one thing to keep a secret for them, and another thing entirely to put our whole society at risk for their sake."

A lot of people made sounds of agreement. Someone muttered, loud enough for all to hear, "How much are we expected to risk for these gifted brats? Especially when they brought this on themselves." And a closer voice, softer: "It's not their fault, poor things, but still. What an awful choice to have to make."

Something went cold and still inside Libbi's heart. She'd thought the hatred and resentment would be the worst of this, but the bigots were a vocal minority, really. It was people like that second speaker, the quiet majority thinking how *sad* this was, how *unfortunate,* but who wouldn't do anything about it: those were the ones who made her feel hopeless.

"I'm sympathetic to the Losts, but what if Ravel decides to annex us again?" said one of the oldest Council members, a woman who was usually quiet during these meetings. "It wouldn't even strain their resources. They'd get what they want, and we'd lose everything."

That got the whole audience shouting. People leaped to their feet. Kay flinched like someone had rung a gong beside her ear.

"We fought and bled for our freedom from Ravel! We need to preserve that freedom at all costs."

"We can't afford to provoke them. We won't win."

"It's the Gifted who put us in this situation. It's on them to fix it!"

And another cry, low but carrying, echoing Libbi's own heart: "It's an impossible choice, but what can we *do?*"

It took long minutes for the Council chair and staff to get people calmed down enough to open up to public comments. "Orderly comments," the chair insisted. "We all feel strongly on this matter, but we'll hear from one person at a time. Please use your handhelds to join the queue."

THE COUNCIL WAS BAD enough, but most of the audience were openly hostile. One person claimed the Losts had done this on purpose, as if the whole generation was a unit that acted with a shared self-destructive intent. Another started listing out their generation's flaws:

entitlement, laziness, self-importance, emotional fragility. And under it all, the assumption that no sacrifice was too great to keep Brennex from falling back under Ravel's control—as long, apparently, as someone *less important* was making that sacrifice.

Libbi's stomach churned. Her stupid, useless gift was responding to everyone's base instincts, to fight, to flee. It was all she could do to stay sitting in the hard chair.

"Hey, Jasper." Mixin, sitting on Libbi's other side, leaned past her to talk to him. "See those two?"

The Council members Mixin pointed out weren't listening to the speakers, but whispering together. One of them was Griffin, who'd made the comment about "protecting everyone on Brennex."

Jasper nodded. "They'll be our biggest opposition, I think."

"They're talking about negotiating. Like, how many Gifted will Ravel be satisfied with? Are some of us more desirable than others?"

Jasper gave Mix a sharp look. "Tell me everything you're getting from them."

He switched seats with Libbi, which put her next to Kay.

"Hey, sis. You doing okay?" Libbi asked. Because Kay did not look well at all.

She gave a wan grimace. "I'll live. It's just very angry in here. Giving me a headache."

Libbi wondered if it was worse than that. She remembered when Kay was a teenager, she used to have panic attacks in tense situations. Hence why she stayed away from people so much, though she seemed to have gotten better since then. Libbi slipped her hand into Kay's, and Kay squeezed back.

Hannith Tan was speaking now, addressing the room with baby Reader on their hip, talking about how Cobb had misled them. Someone shouted that they'd been stupid, selling out for a quick paycheck, and Hannith raised their voice to be heard. The room was getting too loud to hear the speakers, even amplified. As if that weren't enough, the baby was wailing and making faces like he'd tasted something foul, drowning out his parent. Phoenix hurried up front to take the poor kid.

As Phoenix bustled back toward the exit, Libbi made out words in the crying: "Too much yucky. Make the yucky stop!"

Oh, no. Please don't let that be what it sounds like. But a glance at Kay found her, too, wide-eyed with alarm. Libbi hopped up and went after Phoenix, with Kay close behind.

They caught up to Phoenix in the hallway, where she was bouncing Reader to calm him. His reddened, snotty face was still twisted into a look of disgust. "I know, I know, baby. We can't go quite yet, but it'll be better soon."

The door closed on the growing rumble in the meeting room, and suddenly Libbi could hear chants and shouting down the hall. Protesters in the lobby. No wonder Phoenix didn't take the kid outside.

"Phoenix," Libbi said softly. "The baby. Is he…reacting to the crowd?"

For a second, Phoenix looked blankly terrified. Finally she nodded. "This is new. Past few weeks, getting a 'yucky taste' when someone's upset. Hannith didn't want anyone to know yet."

Kay looked horrified. "Of course, no one should know. Especially not now."

Not many of the Losts had had children yet, to their parents' disappointment. Some of them had feared to, wondering what they might pass down to their kids—and apparently with good reason. Because Hannith's baby was Gifted, too.

Ravel already wanted the Losts for their research. How much worse would things get when they found out the gifts could be inherited?

Please, Founders, Libbi prayed silently, *protect us from anything else going wrong today. I can't take it.*

18

LIBBI WASN'T GOING TO get her wish. When they finally trudged home, hours later, they found the family store was trashed.

The door to Wilder Supply stood ajar, the lock forced. Spray cans and buckets of paint littered the ground, and the windows were dark with curses and threats: *Fuck you, Wilders,* and inexplicably, *Go home, Losts.* As if this wasn't their home. Then there was *Cooperative = Terrorists* and in big letters, *Never Again.* The doorframe was filled up with spray foam, top to bottom.

Someone had used more foam to sculpt what Libbi guessed was meant to be a penis, but gravity had gone to work on it, leaving it more slumped and sad than offensive. Mixin kicked it, sending gobs of half-dried foam flying.

Beyond words, beyond anger, Libbi could only stare. *We only just reopened,* her brain kept repeating inanely.

Her father looked unnervingly close to tears. She wrapped an arm around him, and he hugged her silently to his side.

"We can't give in," Jasper said quietly.

"Certainly not. Who said anything about that?" said Ma.

"Other than most of the Council?" Kay sounded hollow.

"You are our children, and you matter more than this store, our home, our whole planet. No soulless corporation is going to take you," Pa said.

"Not just us," Libbi said. "All the Losts. No matter who their parents are. No one can get taken."

"No one, indeed. You're all our children, Brennex's children, and we're not giving up anyone."

Libbi was well past the age where she believed her parents were invincible, but it felt awfully good to hear them talk this way.

"Oh, shit," she said suddenly. "Ever!"

It took only a minute to break through the blocked doorway, and she ran for the stairs. In passing, she saw shelving askew, merchandise dumped on the floor, mysterious spills. The door to their apartment upstairs was still locked, and she deflated in relief to find their home untouched.

"Ever?" she called.

His head peeked out of the guest room, as if making sure it was really her, before coming into the hall. "Libbi, Uncle Jackson, I'm sorry! I felt their anger, and heard them running around downstairs and shouting. I didn't know what to do except hide."

"You did right," said Pa, coming up behind Libbi. He kissed Ever on the head like one of his own kids. "People out there are in a dangerous mood. Best not to confront them."

Ever still looked guilty. "Anything I can do now?"

"Undoubtedly. We've got a lot of work to do."

They trooped downstairs, where Kay had found some oversized trash bags left over from the renovations. Jasper had found solvent and scrub brushes, and he and Havoc were working on the windows. Ever moved to help Mixin, who was putting stock back into place.

Libbi ought to be helping, but instead she stood in the middle of the floor, staring vacantly around her. Again. She couldn't do this *again,* so soon.

"I'm going to message the group and tell everyone what happened," she said at last. Unable to contemplate more. "Warn them to watch out for their own homes."

"Tell them not to go anywhere alone," Jasper said seriously. "And not to confront anyone who's causing trouble."

"And not to count on Public Safety for help," Kay added.

How is this real life? Libbi's mind was spinning, and she wanted to shut her eyes, maybe cry, maybe scream. This was her home. How were her people, her neighbors, acting like this? Had Ravel terrified them so much? Or had this always been lurking under their resentment and suspicious looks, waiting for the chance to spill over?

Suddenly even sending a message felt like too much; she couldn't put all this into plain words. She stumbled toward the back of the store, weaving around piles of merchandise and trash as she went. She tucked her head into the empty storage space between the duct insulation and the hot glue guns, braced her hands and forehead against the cool shelves, and struggled to breathe.

"Libbi, where will I find more paint stripper…? Libbi?" Havoc's voice. His footsteps came closer, then stopped some distance away. "Do you need help?"

"I just don't understand." She pushed away from the shelf and slumped down to sit on the nearest box. "The Council is supposed to protect us all. Neighbors are supposed to support each other. Wilder Supply has been here as long as the spaceport, for the Founders' sakes!"

Havoc hunched down on all fours across from her. "And yet they aren't supporting you. You face hard truths."

"I'm being whiny again. Childish and naive." She sighed, exasperated with herself. "Sorry. It's just… I *know* the Losts aren't a priority for most people here. I know we've needed a lot of help, and there *are* risks for the community. I just thought, between the Council and Public Safety and everything, someone would care more."

"If they have failed your expectations, they are the ones in the wrong. Not you," Havoc said. "Mason called me naive when we first met, for similar reasons: because I believed well of the state I served."

"You grew up within Ravel, right?" Surely Jasper had shared more detail than that, and she ought to remember, but she couldn't. She'd been so focused on her own frustration…

"I did. Your brother met me as an activist, trying to reform Ravel from within. I was organizing the workers at my factory to demand better treatment. At the start, I thought that if I could explain how our demands would benefit us without hurting productivity or profits, management would have no reason to say no. Why refuse a change that would benefit everyone?"

"That doesn't sound like what I've heard about Ravel."

"So I learned. None of my arguments persuaded them, because they didn't want to be persuaded. They didn't want to treat my teammates better, because they didn't believe we deserved better. Not the low-rank workers, and especially not Kovars. In hindsight, they tolerated people like me only as long as we stayed invisible. The moment we demanded to be seen, it gave them an excuse to vent all their prejudices."

"Oh." That did sound uncomfortably familiar. Libbi had known many Brennexians tolerated the Losts, uneasy with both their gifts and the history they represented. But those feelings below the surface were deeper and harsher than she'd ever imagined, and now folks had their excuse to turn discomfort into hate.

"What happened?"

"In Ravel, your role in the company means everything, and they…" He faltered for a moment. "They called me a poor team player, and took away my rank. It broke me, for a while, until Mason helped me see my own value, independent of my rank and job."

She couldn't help smiling. "He's a good guy. You seem happy together."

"He makes me happy, very much so." He paused, seeming to gather his thoughts. "The point I want to make, Libbi, is that believing in others can open you to disappointment, and that can hurt badly, but it doesn't make you naive. Maybe you can persuade your people to do better by you and your team; maybe you can't. But nevertheless, it matters that you try."

Slowly, she nodded. She couldn't quite wrap her head around that, but the churning inside her had lessened. She could breathe.

"It saddens me that you have to experience this. Your people have violated your trust, and you and your teammates deserve better."

"Thanks, Havoc. That means a lot, actually." She wiped

her nose on her sleeve. "You were looking for, what, paint stripper?"

She gave him directions, then went back to… What had she been doing?

Checking on her Losts. Right.

She gathered up her nerves and drafted a message, which took an awfully long time for something so simple. Once she'd updated all the Losts on what'd happened at the store and warned them to be careful, she checked her new messages.

"Oh, Ancestors." She hurried to the front where the others were working. "Hannith and Phoenix found their apartment vandalized, too."

"I doubt they'll be the only ones," Jasper said. "Ma, Pa, could we…?"

"What if we—?" Libbi started at the same time as him. After an awkward fumbling of *no, you first,* she continued, "I think we should invite them here. Them, and anyone else who doesn't feel safe at home. It'll be close quarters…"

Ma and Pa didn't even hesitate.

"Of course they'll come here," Ma said. "We can sleep quite a few upstairs if we open all the guest rooms, and use the couches, too."

"And if we need to, we'll move shelves and open up more space in the store," Pa said.

"Pa," Libbi began, voice breaking. "The store…"

"Can open again when this is over. We clearly won't do any business in the short term. We've reopened once, and we can do it again."

She bit her lip, feeling sick to her stomach. They'd *just* reopened, and it had been a horrible failure. She still wasn't sure if they could've bounced back, even if everything else had gone perfectly. Could they survive this a second time?

Footsteps pounded down the street, then slowed. "Mixin, there you are! Are you all right? You weren't here when this happened, were you?"

Mixin raced over to give their moms a huge hug. "I'm fine! I'm sorry, I meant to chat you, but there's been a lot."

"I can see that." Mixin's ma glanced at her wife. "Why don't you tell us about it while we help clean up?" They both pulled on gloves and grabbed cleaning spray.

A call pinged Libbi's headset. It was Sunny, calling her and Kay. "I've sent you a little extra help. Do you see our bot friend from the tunnels, Libbi?"

"No, I don't. Where…?" Libbi stepped outside, looking up and down the street, just in time to see the little cleaner bot zip up the ramp from the nearest tunnel entrance. "Oh! Yes, it's here."

"It says it would like to be called Squeaky, and I believe it is…like me. I'm working on its technological capabilities, and right now it's better at understanding language than at answering, but it wants to help."

Half from surprised pleasure, and more than half from overwhelm, Libbi laughed aloud, drawing strange looks from the friends around her. "Welcome, Squeaky, and thank you," she said, and pointed it to one of the grosser-looking spills to mop up. Then she took up a scrub brush herself.

Ravel was still breathing down their necks, and she had no idea how to fix that, but there was something steadying about cleaning. Taking a mess and setting it right.

Here we go. One mess at a time.

19

WHEN LIBBI HAD WISHED for more people in the store, this wasn't what she'd had in mind.

That first night, a dozen Losts had shown up, and Ma and Pa had found places for them upstairs. Not that anyone got much rest. Mixin had cat-napped in Libbi's room when they weren't standing watch, and there was still that tension dancing between them, sparking with unsaid words. Libbi herself was running on adrenaline and chai.

Since then, there'd been a steady flow of scared people, and as Pa had predicted, they'd started laying down mats and blankets in the big open area made by pushing the shelves aside. She felt a pang when they did that, grief at undoing their hard work from the reopening, twisted through with anger that any of this was necessary.

Libbi's parents put everyone to work who was able, cooking huge pots of rice and congee, dal, chai, anything easy to make at scale, with the leftover bits turned into founders' soup. They offered up their stock to anyone who needed a toothbrush, or deodorant, or other small necessities. Some people had gotten into scrapes and needed first aid, though no one was badly hurt, thank the Founders. And there were plenty of people to guard the store and each other.

It had been almost cozy at first, like a muted party, everyone making do, helping to support or distract each other as needed. Sujay had brought a guitar; someone else had unrolled a portable synthboard, and one of the Singh cousins had borrowed Ma's sitar to make an impromptu jam band. Hannith supervised the little ones playing on the model spaceship, which no one had found time to fix until now, and Fritter entertained them all by starting a war against poor Squeaky, who put up with the cat and generally seemed delighted to have so much work to do. (An attempt to start a game of Infiltrator among the adults died quickly; no one wanted to play point-the-finger games or try to suss out who was lying.)

That mood didn't last, though, as the "party" stretched into days and the store got increasingly crowded. Libbi welcomed the newcomers and found them places to sleep. Mixin noted when people talked amongst themselves about needing something but didn't want to bug the Wilders with it, and they passed on tips to Libbi or Jasper or their parents. Kay and Ever spent most of their time upstairs in the kitchen, hiding from all the strong emotions. Libbi wished she had an excuse to do the same.

"Hey, hey! No pushing!" Libbi called. She hoisted one of the babies onto her hip, which forced the people nearest her to calm as she came toward the argument. "There's enough for everyone. I'm sure he didn't mean to push you. We're all in this together here." She raised her voice. "Remember your barriers, everyone! Some people need more personal space, and there's a big shortage of that going around. Be good to each other!"

The two older Losts who'd nearly come to blows both apologized. The Wilders hadn't had to kick anyone out for bad behavior—yet.

With the peace stabilized for now, she headed back to the storage area to see if Mags Shipp needed anything, but she and her crew were nearly done unloading.

"Everything good, Auntie Mags?"

"Good as can be," the grandmotherly woman said. "How are you holding up, kiddo?"

"I guess good as can be, too. We're all really grateful you're still coming through. Will you…?" She stopped herself from asking the question. She couldn't ask Mags to promise she'd keep delivering supplies, not under such uncertain circumstances.

The economy was already feeling the pinch from Ravel's demands. As the only place for ships to resupply along a lengthy corridor of macrospace, Brennex made a welcome stop-over for any vessel with tight quarters. Problem was, it wasn't *that* far to other stops. Most ships that would normally stop here were looking for fun, diversion, and to pick up a few items. They could tough it out and skip Brennex if need be—and already, some had decided that needs were. Those that did stop were moving through quickly and doing less business, gossip said. Passenger ships couldn't as easily skip a planned stop, but itineraries for future trips could change. And it was just as well the store was closed, because visitors weren't venturing far from the spaceport.

Nobody from off-world knew the real reasons for the conflict between Brennex and Ravel—obviously, neither side was talking publicly about the Gifted—but everyone was sure they didn't want to get in the middle of it. Ravel hadn't made threats against anyone trading with Brennex yet, but it was the obvious next step.

The Council hadn't agreed to anything yet. But how long could Brennex hold out under the pressure?

Auntie Mags shook her head. "I may not be Brennexian, but I've got family here, you know. I heard what happened to my young cousin Nydia. I don't know what Ravel wants with you all, but I'll keep making trade runs as long as I can."

"We're grateful for you." Libbi tried not to think about what might happen if Mags and the others stopped coming. "Pa wants to talk to you before you go, to adjust our next few orders."

"Yes, I imagine so." Auntie Mags squeezed Libbi's shoulder. "Stay strong. I'll see you soon."

Kind words, but Libbi was already so tired of "staying strong." Exhausted from sitting around, waiting to see what happened. She wanted one thing, just *one thing*, to feel normal and right.

Coming out of the storage area, she spotted Mixin at the front counter, watching the room—and she knew what that *one thing* was.

"Hey, Mix, I need to go run some errands. Want to come?" Libbi hovered awkwardly by the counter, shifting her weight.

Mixin blinked, glanced at Libbi as if startled, but their gaze shifted right back past her shoulder. "Um, maybe later? Need to ask Jasper something."

They were already moving away.

Libbi burst out, "Mixin, I hope you're not still upset at me…"

Mix turned around but didn't stop, walking away backwards. "It's okay, Libs, I promise. Got to catch him now. Talk later!"

Watching her best friend run off, chasing her brother and Havoc, Libbi deflated. She couldn't blame Mixin for being upset. Libbi deserved it. But why couldn't they let her apologize? Hadn't they punished her long enough?

"Hey, Libbi, we're out of chai," someone called.

"Right. I'll go fetch more."

Her heart squeezed painfully in her chest as she turned away.

MIXIN WASN'T PROUD OF blowing Libbi off like this. They weren't mad at her anymore, not really, but they were worn out and restless. Sheltering fellow Losts and looking out for each other was good—it was necessary—but it wasn't Mixin's strength, and more to the point, it wasn't going to solve the real problem. They itched to *do* something. But what?

So when they saw Jasper and Havoc talking quietly, saying, "…Check on him, see if he's talking," and "I'll come with you," they'd perked up. This! This was their chance.

It wasn't their fault that Libbi had chosen that exact moment to try to make up.

If the two of them went out together and had space to talk, Libbi would apologize. And she would *mean* it, like she always did, and Mixin would forgive her, and everything would go back to the way it was. They weren't sure they could handle that yet.

Okay, maybe Mixin *was* still mad at Libbi.

By that point, Jasper and Havoc were at the door. Mix made their choice, and hurried after the activists.

"Are you two going where I think you're going?"

Popping in front of Jasper and Havoc, Mixin grinned with totally innocent enthusiasm. This was their "notice me" look, which Libbi called the "manic puppy" look, the one they turned on when they didn't want to fade into the background, as was their natural state.

"Where do you think we're going?" Havoc asked.

"I think you don't want me to say it out loud."

"Please don't," said Jasper, glancing around. The street was quiet, but not that quiet. Two blocks down, a pair of Public Safety officers were making their rounds.

"I won't, if you take me with you."

"You overheard us, huh? Havoc, we've got to be more careful around this one." He said it lightly, though, not really bothered.

"Hey, Libbi got strapped to a mad scientist's workbench. I can't let her have all the fun."

"Mason, this one asks for trouble."

Jasper raised his brows. "It's not going to be fun. More likely frustrating and fruitless. Are you sure you want to come?"

"Okay, okay." Mixin held up their hands. "I joke a lot, but seriously, I need a break from in there." They nodded back toward the store. "I may not have an empathy-related gift, but the mood is a lot to handle. Plus, I want to *do* something. Anything, really, that would help. I can play the bad cop."

Jasper's mouth twitched. "I can't remember ever seeing you act mean, Mixin."

"Maybe not. Then I can be the confusing cop. Is chaos cop a thing?"

The two activists exchanged a look, avoiding Mixin's puppy-dog pleading eyes.

"Or I can take notes—I'm *amazing* at taking notes. Seriously, anything to help."

"I understand Mixin's feelings," Havoc said. "And we've made little progress on our own. Would it hurt for them to try, Mason?"

"Fair point. Come on, then. Stay close and stay quiet. We have to take a roundabout route to make sure no one follows us."

Jasper nodded significantly in the direction of the Public Safety officers. The group feed had warned about people getting rounded up for "making trouble" and put into holding at Public Safety. Auntie Shanthi had been trying, without great luck, to get accurate records out of their office. Anecdotally, though, they were arresting more Losts than older or younger folks.

They descended into the tunnels. When they popped up again, it was in a different residential dome. They crossed the street toward a clothing shop called Kapoor's Rainbow.

Wait. Kapoor, like Ellie Kapoor?

"Really?" Mixin asked. "Isn't that a bit obvious?"

Hiding Cobb in a place owned by a known Cooperative organizer would be seriously dumb—and Jasper and Ellie weren't dumb.

"It would be. But this isn't our final destination." Jasper grinned as he led them inside. "Good evening, Mx. Kapoor. How are you doing?"

"Was better before these past few days," said the white-haired old matron behind the counter, obviously Ellie's mother. She unlocked the door to a storage room in back and waved them inside. The lock clicked shut behind them.

The room was empty. Well, no, it was full of fabrics and patterns, printers and sewing bots, but like Jasper had said, no Cobb. Jasper crossed to one of the taller cabinets.

Mixin guessed what was happening a moment before he opened it. "Oh, seriously?"

Inside the cabinet, the wall was open. Stairs descended into the dark.

"*Yes!*" Mixin hissed, not caring that the others chuckled at their excitement. This was straight out of a spy serial.

"These passages date back to the occupation," Jasper said as he led them down. "The resistance unearthed some of the original maintenance passages from the Founding and built out a whole system of secret connections in case they needed to smuggle people off-world. The Cooperative has maintained them."

"I've heard about these! I thought they were just stories. But this is normal life for you guys."

"Not normal, I promise," Havoc said. "Most of our work lacks this sort of excitement."

"I guess it only gets like this when something's gone wrong," Mixin said thoughtfully. Even for them, the coolness factor lost something to the sour feeling of fear in their stomach. "I don't mean to romanticize it. Or maybe I do, but only because it's a nice distraction. Either geek out or panic, right? Sorry, I'm babbling."

"It's okay. We get it," Jasper assured them.

These tunnels smelled stale with disuse, but not unpleasantly. It was narrow enough that they had to walk single file, with Jasper leading the way. At each branching, he checked his headset before leading them onward.

"Have you ever thought about joining the Cooperative, Mixin?" Jasper asked. "Because I can think of a dozen uses for that gift, just off the top of my head."

"Oh." Mixin blinked. "I used to daydream about it sometimes, when we were kids."

"But you never pursued it?"

Of course they hadn't. It was Jasper who'd sparked their interest—their best friend's big brother, fighting bad guys, working for the greater good. Using his gift for something that mattered. But then Jasper left, and later, so did Kay. Mixin couldn't abandon Libbi too. Especially not to follow her brother's path.

"Didn't think I'd be any good at it," they lied. "Apart from my gift, I'm not good at much. Especially not great with people, obviously."

Havoc rumbled, "You speak modest falsehoods."

"If you say so." Mixin shrugged. They didn't have the stomach to keep this conversation going. "How much farther?"

"It's just up ahead," Jasper said.

They emerged into a cold, windowless space, probably a warehouse or empty industrial building, all concrete and hard edges. A few doorways led off the main space. Presumably one of them led to Cobb.

"Tell me you've got a plan for this asshole?" Ellie greeted them. "Because if he complains to me about the coffee one more time, I'm going to cause a diplomatic incident. By murdering him, to be clear."

"I understand this temptation. I've felt it often," Havoc said. "Has he given you anything useful?"

"Only that I'm a monster who's standing in the way of scientific progress, which to him seems on a level with a war crime."

"Same old Alik Cobb," Jasper muttered. "I'm going to talk to him."

Ellie raised her brows. "You think you can get him to cooperate?"

"Oh, Founders, no. But I'm grabbing at dust motes trying to find a way out of this, and so is Linn. Maybe he'll spark some idea."

"Be my guest," Ellie said. "Havoc, I was hoping you could look at this recording I made for the Council? It's the proof of well-being they asked for. I've never held a hostage before"—she gave a wry grimace—"and I want to be sure it's scrubbed clean of any clues about where he is."

Jasper cocked his head, telling Mixin to follow him. "Normally I'd keep you out of Cobb's sight; I don't want to make you a target for Ravel. But he and I have too much history. A new person might shake something loose from him."

"He saw me already, aboard Sunny. Kay wanted to make sure he saw a Human pilot. And I was there when he drugged Libbi, too."

"Right. I forgot." He rubbed the bridge of his nose. "Someday, I'll sleep again. Okay, then, let's go have a chat."

Other than the auto-cuffs on his hands and feet, Cobb's little prison didn't seem too bad. They'd given him a mattress, a table and chair (bolted to the ground), meal bars, and a bottle of water. A dark stain on the floor might have been the coffee Ellie mentioned. Cobb's cheeks were stubbled, but he otherwise looked well enough.

"Oh look, it's Jasper Wilder, here to interrogate me for all my darkest secrets." Cobb sounded nothing but disdainful of anything Jasper might do to him. "When I get out of here, I look forward to taking you apart piece by piece in the most demeaning way possible."

"Good to see you, too, Alik." Jasper leaned against the wall, frowning at him.

"You think I'm joking? You had your chance to further the study of neuroscience. You could have been a partner in this work, a valued collaborator, but now…"

Jasper snorted. "Partner? You don't have a record of playing well with others."

Face going red, Cobb spat, "And you have no interest in the greater good. You and your gang of thugs only work to destroy, never to build."

Even Mixin knew that was patently ridiculous. Building a social movement wasn't concrete, like inventing a drug, but it was still building.

"We only tear down what needs tearing down," Jasper said.

"Ravel is going to come down on your little rock of a planet so hard, the entire Long Lane will be littered with your trash. Because that's all this place is: trash, and a few people who *could* become more than trash, except they don't have the foresight to take the opportunity I'm offering."

Jasper shot Mixin a look, brows raised: *See what I mean?* He was right. The two of them could probably spiral this argument forever.

"Literally?" Mixin asked.

"What?" Cobb sounded surprised, like he was noticing Mix for the first time.

"Do you mean that literally about smashing us to pieces? Because that seems like overkill. Counterproductive, even."

"It's a *metaphor,* if you're capable of grasping that concept," Cobb scoffed. "They'll retrieve me first, of course, along with any of you Gifted with the intellect to save yourselves. Then they'll make an example of your world."

Mixin shuddered, and hoped it didn't show. Corporations could be ruthless, but they weren't usually vindictive, were they? There wasn't any profit in it. But Ravel certainly had the tech to destroy Brennex if they wanted to. Literally or otherwise. From what Libbi's mother had said, a slow death by economic starvation would be easiest, politically.

"What makes you think they'll even be able to find you here?" Mixin looked pointedly around the makeshift cell.

"They don't have to. You'll deliver me to them, once you get it through your dense skulls the situation you're in. You have no choice."

"Wow," murmured Mixin.

"What?"

"I just realized how much of an effort you were making at not being an asshole when you first came to the store. I mean, you were still an asshole, you couldn't hide it, but this is your natural state, huh? Did you strain something, keeping that sneer in check?"

For a moment, there was murder in Cobb's eyes. But his eyes flicked down to his restraints, the tether keeping him to the far wall, and he mastered himself.

"I am really going to enjoy studying you." He leaned forward, as if having a friendly, earnest conversation. "Listen, both of you, because here's your choice. You people value family, right? The longer you keep me here, stalling my research, the less kindly I'll look on you and your wreck of a planet when your Council—inevitably—gives in. But if you let me go, and come with me willingly, you *will* be partners in my work, and treated as such. It's your choice. Be sensible, reap the benefits, and spare your loved ones. Or hold out and be stubborn, and be ready to watch your families suffer and starve under Ravel."

He sat back in his seat, smirking and unconcerned. The move was spoiled only by a brief attempt to fold his arms, quickly abandoned when the cuffs stopped him.

He's all talk, Mixin told themself. He was trying to get inside their head and mess with them. But…he wasn't wrong. That was exactly how it would play out.

Stumped on a clever comeback, they instead turned on their heel and left, giving Cobb the last word.

"Don't take too long!" Cobb called after them. "I predict you have four, perhaps five days to make the smart choice, before it gets made for you."

Jasper locked Cobb in while Mixin paced fretfully across the main room, just to give their body some outlet.

"You okay?" he said.

"Obviously not. Jasper, you've got to get him out of here. Put him out of reach of anyone who might be tempted to give him up. Because we will cave. Not *us*, but someone will."

Jasper gave a twisted smile. "I know. We're making plans to move him off-world, but that only solves half the problem. It doesn't solve the part about us. Either the Council and the community will round us up and give us to Ravel to protect themselves, or some of the Losts will sacrifice themselves for people who don't even appreciate them."

Mixin shivered and hugged themself. "So what do we do?"

The uncertain look on Jasper's face was more alarming than anything Cobb had said. "I'm still not sure. But he's revealed his deadline. Four or five days? That's about the latest Ravel can free him and still get him to present his work at their Exhibition."

"…WHAT WE NEED IS volunteers. The Gifted have benefited all their lives from the protection of the Brennexian people. They use public services at a rate far disproportionate to any other group. It's time they took responsibility for giving back.

I'm saying to all the Gifted on Brennex: don't force the Council to make this hard decision. Step up, and do the right thing."

"Turn that off," Ma said in disgust. "We've heard enough from that waste of oxygen."

The waste in question was Skel Griffin, son of the Council member. About Ma and Pa's age, he had no kids from during the occupation, no Losts in his family, and though he had three young kids now, he was openly bitter toward the Losts and their parents. As if, in their luck and good fortune, Ma and Pa had taken something away from him.

He'd been a pain in the ass before, when Ma had tried to push for expanded mental health services or other support for the Losts. Now he was being awful.

Libbi killed the feed and turned back to chopping carrots for the next big batch of founders' soup.

"It's like they don't even think we belong here." She put a little extra violence into her chopping. "We're as Brennexian as anyone else."

"It's an easy thing, unfortunately, to tell yourself that people who need extra care are a drain on the system. A step toward making them matter less."

"We don't even have representation on the Council. If they put this to a popular vote…"

"We'd be outnumbered by far," Kay spoke up. She was shelling peas in the corner, looking steady for a change. She got overwhelmed by all the strong emotions downstairs, but she seemed better hiding out up here.

Libbi, too, had finally resorted to hiding out. The wants of the people downstairs had progressed beyond fight-or-flight instincts into more basic cravings: for home and a comfy bed, for favorite foods, and increasingly and most problematically, for drugs. The latter was only from a few people, and they ventured out in groups to get their fixes, but stress upped all sorts of cravings, and eventually Libbi had needed to retreat and indulge in one relatively harmless craving to push away the others. She reached for another of Ma's almond cookies—one of her favorites, but she barely tasted its sweetness.

She'd learned from a young age that she had to be disciplined about stuff like this. It was why she chose her friends so carefully, why she mostly avoided places where people indulged in addictive habits. She couldn't always trust what she thought her body wanted.

The kitchen was sweaty-hot and crowded, but at least it was crowded with stuff, not people. Every flat surface was in use for food preparation, and piles of Founders' Day decorations were shoved into corners, out of the way. Not into storage, yet, but Libbi couldn't guess what their world would look like come Founders' Day, almost two weeks away. Would they be able to decorate, or celebrate at all? Would they even want to?

Libbi pulled her attention back to more important questions. "We should get a say, though. Collectively. There should be a rule. Council members need to span all ages. Every generation gets a voice."

Ma made a bemused sound in her throat. "If you demand that, next you'll be asking for representatives outside the Founding Families! Giving a voice to latecomers, even. Why are there no Kovars, no Majrin, no post-Founding bloodlines?"

"Ma, you radical!" Kay said wryly.

"Well…they should," Libbi said.

Their mother laughed without humor. "You're absolutely right, darling. The Council won't willingly relinquish control, though. The Founding Families have a vested interest in staying in power. I hear from enough of our citizens, though, that I can assure you they're very aware of the injustice of it."

"It's not like I'm *not* aware." Past generations might have been more insular, but the Lost Generation was so small that most of Libbi's friends weren't founding family, and they weren't shy about their opinions. It'd never seemed so urgent before, though. "Why don't we fix it?"

"There were efforts in that direction before the occupation. Your grandmother Narayan negotiated some possible reform measures when she was on the Council, but they always stalled. Even the Cooperative put the representation issue on the back burner to focus on more achievable campaigns. And after we pushed Ravel out…"

"We went right back to the old ways. Protecting tradition and all that," Libbi said. "I see why that would happen. It just sucks for us now."

"It does indeed. But who knows? Maybe after you kids get us out of this mess, you'll take up politics. Make some big reforms." Her mother nudged her in the side, half-teasing, but only half.

"I'm no politician, Ma. I couldn't do what you do."

"You can do anything you set your mind to, dumpling. Here, this batch is ready, I think. Help me pour it into containers, and that'll be the last cooking for tonight."

For the first time, Libbi noticed how exhausted her mother was, too. Gifted or no, everyone was stressed and overworked and getting too little sleep.

"Here, Ma, let me finish that. You go get some rest." She kissed her mother on the cheek and nudged her toward the bedrooms, and Ma went without any argument.

Once the fresh food was stashed away for tomorrow and the dirty dishes brought up and fed into the cleaner, Libbi said goodnight to Kay and headed for her own room. She found it empty. Mixin had been sharing with her, but apparently they weren't back yet from wherever they'd gone with Jasper.

Her gut twisted oddly, half guilty relief and half something darker. Her best friend had been spending more time with her siblings and Sunny and Havoc than with her, and they still hadn't let Libbi apologize properly for leaving them out of the rescue effort. Never mind that they would all have been massively fucked if Mixin hadn't been free to bring Sunny to them…

No, Libbi couldn't pretend she'd foreseen any of that. She just hadn't wanted to get left behind, and she'd been afraid that bringing Mixin would have tipped Jasper over into leaving them both.

Ironically, Jasper now seemed to trust Mixin fine.

Actually, maybe Mixin had come back. Their bag sat in a corner behind the bed, and their handheld lay on the quilt, unlocked. Despite herself, Libbi glanced at the screen as she kicked off her shoes. Then the words sank in, and she abandoned all good manners and grabbed it up.

Astro-Navigation: A Practical Guide for Beginners.

Why was Mixin reading this? She paged forward and back, and it really was what it seemed: a book about how to fly ships. Not in the informative, fun, here's-how-the-pilots-do-it way. In the instructional, textbook, here's-how-*you*-can-do-it way.

"What are you doing?" From the doorway behind her, Mixin's voice was sharp.

"Why are you reading this?"

"You can't go around spying on other people's devices, Libbi. Even your friends."

"Oh, no, spying and eavesdropping are terribly wrong," Libbi muttered. "Seriously, Mixin, what is this?"

They closed the door and leaned back against it, arms folded tightly. Narrow shoulders shrugged. "I was curious. I wondered how hard it would be to learn. If it was something I *could* learn. And…I think I could. There's a lot of math, but math never scared me."

"For what reason, though? Were you going to… Are you thinking…?" Libbi swallowed. "This isn't something you want to *do*. Is it?"

Again, that uneasy shrug.

"Did my siblings talk you into this?"

"Not directly, no. I did talk to Sunny a bit, for advice, but it was my idea."

"What's the point, though? It's not like a navigator's skills are any use on Brennex."

Libbi was begging, she realized. Waiting for Mixin to tell her she was right, that it was a pointless interest with no real uses on a planet, on Brennex, where they both lived.

There was a long, heavy silence before Mixin said, "Not on Brennex, no. But it would help me in other places, with other jobs. Like the Cooperative."

Now Libbi recognized the sick feeling in her gut. Her gift, the wanting, the flight part of fight-or-flight. The urge to be *away*. The same urge Jasper had felt before he left, and Kay.

"Mix, no."

They stepped forward. "I don't want to leave you, Libbi. I was talking to Havoc and Jasper—"

"You what?"

"—And there are some roles where I could be based on Brennex between campaigns. I'd be around a lot more than your brother—"

"How long? How long have you been planning this?"

"I don't know! I've thought about it for ages, except I never believed I could actually do it."

"Of course not." Libbi shook her head fiercely. "Stop and think this through, Mixin. You don't want to do this. Your home is here, and your moms, and all our friends." *And me.* "This is just another daydream, right? Like all your other dream jobs. When we were five, you wanted to be an explorer, an archaeologist. Then, what, a private detective?"

"My gift would be perfect for that," Mixin murmured.

"And you talked about being a pilot before, but then you lost interest and wanted to move to Caligar and write serials. You always want the shiniest job, but that's not real life. Real life is hard. It means working at the store, it means keeping our families going. It doesn't mean reckless adventure."

Mixin's face had gone pale, but their voice was hard and brittle as ice. "The store is your thing, Libbi. Your family. And it's your choice to keep working there."

"No, it's my responsibility! That's something I take seriously. You're like a little kid, Mixin, you have all these childish dreams, but there's a reason you never follow through!"

She didn't realize she was shouting until it got quiet. The look on Mixin's face, mouth open in a tiny ring, mirroring their wide, betrayed eyes…

Libbi's heart beat in her ears. "Mix…"

"Yes, there's a reason." Mixin's voice was deadly soft. "The reason is you. I came up with all those wild dreams hoping they'd become our dreams. And every time you didn't care, I set them aside. For you, Libbi." They took a breath, drew themself upright. "But they never went away, and I can't do this forever."

Libbi needed to say something, to fix this, to erase this conversation and make it all right again, go back to where they were best friends and spending all their time together and didn't need anything more than this…

But Mixin was out the door and gone.

"Where are you going?" she called.

"Home!"

It was late, and Mixin shouldn't be alone on the streets even for the short walk, but they'd only do something more reckless if Libbi followed them. If she even could. If she wasn't deflating like a leaky balloon, collapsing in on herself. She pulled her knees to her chest.

A soft knock on the doorframe. "Hey, Libs," Kay said softly. "I couldn't help hearing…"

"I fucked up. I don't know how, but I did."

Kay sat on the bed beside her, and she sobbed into her sister's shoulder.

20

THEY SAT ON THE roof, the Wilder sibs, Mixin, Havoc, Sunny, and a handful of friends, watching the lights of ships landing and departing through the darkly transparent nighttime dome. Really, they were all counting the number of ships and the time between them. Fewer and fewer every night.

Mixin couldn't stand to watch the constant thrum of traffic, Brennex's lifeblood, slow to a trickle—but they couldn't stop watching, either.

"How long can we hold out, if Ravel cuts off trade?" Kay asked quietly.

"Weeks to months, according to Ma," Jasper answered. "Depending on what sorts of rationing the Council puts in place, and who will risk helping us with supplies. We've got stockpiles for situations like this, but they won't last forever."

Rumors had spread that Ravel would refuse to do business with anyone still doing business on Brennex. Ravel hadn't announced any such thing, but the fear of it was enough to scare off plenty of ships. The reality, if it came, would drive off most of the rest.

Jasper didn't mention the hints Cobb had dropped, that Brennex had less time than they thought, so neither did Mixin.

Ever, who was listening to the live stream of a Council meeting, said, "Now they're negotiating how many of us to turn over. Like, if they can settle on an acceptable number, they'll do it."

"Ravel wants a list of all our names and gifts, though," said Hope, listening beside him. "I guess so they can pick and choose? And that's tripping them up."

"As if there's some acceptable number of people to turn into property," said Phoenix. "Good thing there isn't any list like that. Councils past did that much right."

The original plan to protect the Losts had included never recording information about their gifts in civic documents. It might be mentioned for individual Losts in mental health records or other confidential medical files, but that was outside the Council's reach.

"Founders' sakes," Kay said, head in her hands. Her voice was muffled, but not to Mixin's gift. "I should turn myself in. Self-sacrifice, like people keep saying. I've done enough to get us into this mess."

Jasper squeezed her shoulder. "Wouldn't help."

"He speaks truth," Havoc said. "And Ravel *must* not learn how to reproduce the gifts. I shudder to think of the power they'd gain from that."

"I know, I know," Kay said.

"What can we do, then?" Mixin said. "Because I want to do *something*. Not just wait until the Council hands us over."

Jasper exchanged a look with his partner, who nodded at the unspoken question.

"There may be an opportunity with Ravel's board meeting and the Exhibition. The Cooperative was planning to sneak in a few of our people to support our other campaigns, but Brennex has become more urgent."

"You want to go there?" A spark of hope flared inside Mixin.

"A small group of us, yes. That's what I've pitched to Linn," Jasper said. "But the Cooperative's got a limited number of false IDs we can burn on the Exhibition, so they have to choose. We need a plan that'll help her convince the other facilitators it's worth setting aside their original goals and sending us instead."

"What would they be giving up, to help us?" asked Ever.

"The Exhibition offers the best opportunity to learn Ravel's future plans," said Havoc. "Where they intend to expand their territory. What resources they'll be seeking out. What new technologies will harm people inside and outside the company. With this information, the Cooperative could position ourselves to get out ahead of them and start building local relationships and infrastructure before they do."

"So, just listening?" Mixin said. It sounded perfect. "Can't we do both?"

"We can't be everywhere at once, unfortunately. Unless someone has a gift I don't know about." Jasper smiled grimly. "But it's not just sitting in meetings. They're hoping to steal highly secured data from several divisions, most notably the plans for those behemoth space habitats Ravel's on the verge of rolling out, which will support their territorial expansion. We know it's coming soon, but don't know where, and we need to. A couple other projects, too, that aren't public knowledge yet."

"So whatever we do, it has to really be worth it." Kay frowned in thought. "Cobb's out of the equation, at least for now. Havoc made it sound like he has a lot of rivals who aren't too fond of him. Could we discredit him? Make everyone think he's obsessed with some nonsense project? Our gifts do sound pretty implausible if you're scientifically minded, the sort of thing a con artist might make up."

"Yes!" Mixin cried. "We can debunk him while he's not around to defend himself."

"Hmm. It would help, for certain, especially if he misses the whole Exhibition. Which he will," Jasper added quickly, before Mixin could ask. "He thinks he's getting rescued in time for it, but we're not giving him up without a fight. In the long term, though… We can't hold him captive forever, and as long as he's got a few high-ranked supporters in Biopharma, he'll find a way to pursue his research."

"So we'd have to destroy his research, too," said Kay.

Sunny spoke up. The ship had been awfully quiet lately, probably wary of drawing attention with so many strangers around who weren't in on their secret. "If the research were gone, and Cobb were…neutralized, Ravel might consider the project a sunk cost and cancel it, rather than invest yet more resources. This is one advantage of Cobb's ego: no one else truly understands his work."

"Whoa, whoa," said Libbi. "'Neutralize'? I thought the Cooperative didn't do that."

Sunny buzzed. "I mean *neutralize* in the sense of making him no longer a threat."

"We don't murder people," Jasper cut in. "I think what

Sunny is suggesting is…make him give up the research somehow. More permanently."

"There's no way I can take that statement that doesn't sound alarming," Libbi said.

"Oh, stop being squeamish," Mixin muttered. "If it's him or us, I'll take us."

Libbi shot them a hurt look, and once again, Mixin felt it in their gut. They hadn't talked to Libbi beyond necessity since that awful argument. They kept waiting for Libbi to apologize, but had a feeling Libbi was waiting on them. Even now, she was sitting by Hope and Ever and Sujay, and somehow Mixin was on the opposite side of the group, by Havoc. They ought to go join their friends, but they weren't sure they'd be welcome.

This *sucked*. Mixin and Libbi had never fought before, not in a lifetime of being best friends. But that was because (Mixin realized now) they had always bent to what Libbi wanted. They'd set aside dream after dream for Libbi's sake, because Libbi's needs mattered more. Libbi's store, Libbi's family, Libbi's legacy. It wasn't lost on Mixin that the first time they—accidentally!—revealed a goal that conflicted with Libbi's, their best friend took it as betrayal.

"From the Exhibition, we should be able to access Cobb's research, and a carefully targeted virus could destroy it," Sunny chimed in. "I have some experience with such things."

"Is that safe, Sunny?" Kay murmured in an undertone, probably intelligible only to Mixin and the ship themself.

"Likely not. Would you stay behind for safety, Kay?"

"Point taken."

"There are dangers for all of us in entering Ravel territory," the drone said to everyone. "Havoc and myself, as former…employees, could be arrested as traitors. Jasper and Kay are wanted criminals, and your faces are known."

"If their security team has two brain cells between them, they'll be watching for Cooperative interference," Jasper said. "We'll need solid covers."

"Maybe you need someone they don't know at all," Mixin said. "Someone who's completely off their scans."

Jasper and Havoc turned to them, looking thoughtful.

"Seriously?" Libbi muttered. "It's not some game, Mix. He'll never let you."

"It's a smart idea, actually," Jasper said. "Cobb is the only one from Ravel who's seen Mixin, and security aside, there's a fair chance we'll run into people who've met the rest of us. Mixin could get into places we can't. Not to mention how useful your gift could be. But it's still dangerous for any Lost to be there. Are you sure?"

"Completely," Mixin said, not looking at Libbi. Somewhere in the distance, flashing emergency lights splashed red on the surrounding buildings and the dome above. "If I can help, I want to help."

"I can't believe this." Libbi turned her back to them, looking out across the rooftops. Hope rubbed her shoulder and flashed Mixin a dark look.

"Libbi?" Kay said. "Do you want…"

"I'm staying here," Libbi said flatly. Only after a moment did she look at them over her shoulder. "People here need help, and it'll get worse before it gets better. My gift isn't much use at all, but I can… I don't know. Work with Ma, and try to keep the Council from doing anything stupid."

Jasper's forehead creased, baffled. "Are you sure? I thought…"

He looked from Libbi to Mixin and back. His gift showed the strength and nature of people's relationships, and Mixin wondered what he saw between the two of them right now.

"All right," he said. "The rest of you, I support anyone who wants to fight for our home, but I'm not sure how many cover identities we can wrangle."

"Not me," Ever said immediately. "I can't think of a worse idea than me going into a situation like that."

The other Losts echoed the desire to stay, to take care of family or friends. "I'm not that brave," Hope said, and that admission was brave on its own.

Jasper excused himself to go make arrangements with Auntie Lira—Linn, as Mixin should probably call her now—and Havoc went with him. Mixin found themself again outside the group, watching their friends' conversations just out of hearing, like watching a drama with subtitles on. They were talking about cots and mattresses, food stocks, security for the store. Things that had become their lives the past few days—the important, tedious details that Mixin couldn't stand, that were too much to process and not enough to distract from the endless waiting. That wouldn't be Mixin's worry anymore; they'd traded it for a whole set of others.

Libbi glanced at them once, made eye contact, then quickly looked away, and Mixin felt a stab of regret. But no, they were doing what needed to be done, which also happened to be what they wanted. If Libbi chose differently this time, that was on her.

21

LIBBI'S SIBLINGS AND HER best friend were gone, and she settled into the tense quiet of the new normal. She was starting to adjust to it, she thought—until she woke a couple mornings later to the news that an unknown vessel had arrived in Brennex's orbit overnight.

All the feeds said the same nothings: it was large, undecorated, an unfamiliar design. It had entered orbit on the ecliptic, and seemed to be slowing, and it wasn't answering communications. Everyone assumed this was some new tactic from Ravel, and therefore was hostile, but no one knew anything for sure.

"Ravel claims it isn't theirs," said Ma, red-eyed and hollow-looking, like she'd been up all night.

"Do you believe them?" Libbi asked.

"No. Can you take over making breakfast? I need to get to the Council Hall and figure out what's going on."

"Sure, Ma. Call if something is going to kill us all?"

Her mother didn't look amused. "If that's the case, I doubt there'll be time."

Libbi took charge of stirring the breakfast porridge, keeping it from burning. Glad to have something to do.

She didn't regret staying behind while Jasper, Kay, and Mixin all left. It was her choice, and it was the right one. She could do more good here than running around some event full of Ravel big-heads. There was laundry to do, dishes to clean, food to cook, which resulted in more dishes, an endless cycle of the small needs of life.

And there were people who needed reassurance. She might not have Kay's gift for sensing people's emotions, but honestly, gifts were semi-useless now, because everyone's state of mind was constant anxiety and fear, and everyone's wants had stripped down to the most basic: food, shelter, safety. Especially safety. She could sit and listen as well as anyone, and she might not have answers, but she could remind people (again and again) that they were in this together.

But in quiet moments like this, she wondered if Mixin would have stayed here with Libbi, if not for the things she'd said.

Three times now, she'd started recording a message for Mix, but she'd stopped each time, lost for what to say. By now, she'd missed her chance for Mixin to receive it, anyway; Jasper had warned it would be very risky for them to access outside communication networks, and they'd be in touch only in emergencies. She should've apologized before they left. But it had taken her this long to finally absorb what she thought Mixin had been trying to tell her.

Mixin, too, had always wanted to leave home. To have adventures, to use their gift for something more exciting than working retail. Libbi had always thought, deep down, that it was a bit childish how Mix kept pretending to make life into a spy story or adventure—that just wasn't how the world worked. Except it turned out that all those wild career ideas weren't fantasies, but budding plans. And Mixin had set those plans aside, every time, and unlike Kay and Jasper, they'd stayed. For Libbi.

And Libbi, focused on being the good child to her parents and making up for her siblings' absence, had never even noticed.

It would have crumbled her heart to pieces if Mixin had left her. But it was breaking her heart now to realize Mix had given up so much for her sake, and all Libbi had done in turn was complain about her siblings abandoning her, when Mixin was the most loyal sibling she had.

Downstairs in the store, everyone was on their headsets, pulling up every available flat image and full-dimension holo of the mystery in orbit. Studying it from every angle, looking for clues to its purpose, its intentions. Every person on Brennex had suddenly become an amateur investigative engineer, determined to puzzle out the truth, and Libbi joined Hannith and Phoenix to do the same.

It was a round structure, more oblong than spherical. Panels and visible pipes along the sides suggested doors or hatches. To let shuttles in? Or to let equipment out? It was big enough to collect a lot of cargo...or hold a lot of weaponry.

Reader was fussing, reacting to the mood of the room, and Hannith bounced him on a knee, singing softly. It didn't seem to do much good. Poor baby. Libbi had been too young when Kay's gift manifested to remember what it was like, but from her parents' stories, it'd been hell trying to comfort her from something only she could hear.

Libbi did her best to distract herself by checking her off-world feeds, but there at the top was Sasha Starborne's writeup of her visit to Brennex. Against her better judgment, Libbi skimmed the opening—*quaint and sometimes charming; greedy for off-worlders' money.* And farther down: *In a place that depends on trade, people should know how to show up on time to appointments, but apparently the clock is just a suggestion to some Brennexians,* which Libbi felt like the burn of a spotlight on her face.

But more upsetting was the disclaimer up top, that Sasha had drafted this before Brennex's tangle with Ravel, and with the cause of that conflict unknown, she couldn't recommend any travelers spend time on Brennex until it was fully resolved.

Libbi threw her headset across the floor. People looked at her in concern, then away again, giving her space. With a sigh, she moved to pick it up.

If Libbi hadn't stood her up for their meeting, if she'd made a better impression, would Sasha Starborne have taken Brennex's side in this?

Then again: against Ravel, would anyone?

LIBBI AND THE OTHERS did dishes, cooked lunch, cleaned. Some exercised, using cans from the store as free weights. They waited.

"Tasks complete. Additional tasks available?" The chirpy mechanical voice belonged to Squeaky the cleaner bot, who to Libbi's surprise had stuck around.

The baby on Libbi's hip—Reader, who Libbi was watching to give Hannith a break—leaned out toward the bot, fascinated. Libbi shifted to keep Squeaky out of reach of small, grabby hands.

"I think we're caught up for the moment, Squeaky. You can go recharge, if you want."

The bot rolled forward and back several times, as if confused or torn, making Reader giggle. Before leaving for the Exhibition, Sunny had managed to outfit it with a vocal processor, so now it could communicate verbally in simple ways, but it seemed to forget sometimes to do so.

"Take a rest. It's okay," she told the bot. "You're doing great, and I promise, there'll be more work to do soon."

But the universe made a liar of her. At midday, the structure came between central Brennex and the sun, and began to transform.

From the ground, all they could see was massive fins unfolding, spreading like wings to more than double the structure's diameter. Solar fins? Was it powering itself from the sun?

"Oh, shit," someone said. "What's that?"

Some sort of *device*—a gun barrel? A nozzle?—long and skinny, extended from the far side of the structure, pointing sunward. Invisible from Brennex, it could only be seen by their orbiting satellites.

"At least it's probably not a weapon? It's pointed the wrong direction."

"I don't feel good about this. How far will they go?"

"I'm starting to wonder if we should just give in. They're punishing the whole planet because of us—"

"You wouldn't say that if you'd been in Cobb's lab, poked and prodded like a piece of equipment," Ever said sharply.

The other Lost stiffened. "I'm not saying I *want* to, but what if they start hurting people?"

"We're people, too."

The lights flickered.

"Fuck, what now?"

"I'll check it out." Libbi hopped up and headed to the utility room in the back.

Her father already had the panel open, running his finger down the line of indicator lights as he checked the status of each. Their power box and backup generator were the oldest utilities in the store, nearly as old as Libbi, one of the few things that hadn't been upgraded after the flooding, and she didn't know its workings very well, but she could see they'd switched to battery power. The bar that showed incoming power from the grid was jumping all over the place.

"That doesn't look good," she said.

"No," Pa answered. "This is very bad."

Brennex's power *never* failed. For a domed city on a planet with no atmosphere, life itself depended on a power system that was one hundred percent reliable, and they had backups upon backups to ensure it.

Dashiell stuck his head in the door. "Libbi? Uncle Jackson? I think we know what's wrong." He projected a holo from his handheld: a diagram of Brennex, its sun, and now the intruder in orbit. In tiny detail, between the structure and the planet, was one of Brennex's three orbiting solar arrays. "They've parked between our solar panels and the sun. They're blocking our power."

WORD SPREAD LIKE AN electrical fire across the city. The massive orbiting structure had taken up synchronous orbit with one of the three solar arrays that made life on Brennex possible, instantly cutting a third of the planet's active power supply. Speculation ran wild about what this meant, how long they could survive, what systems would fail first. And worse: what if Ravel took out a second array? Or all three?

Fortunately, while the general public on Brennex were utterly unprepared for this sort of crisis, their ancestors hadn't been. There were emergency plans for every sort of catastrophe, including the loss of solar power, and the utilities department unearthed the right procedures and sent out instructions within minutes.

Turn off all unnecessary lights and appliances. Disconnect all chargers while not actively charging a device, and use backup batteries as much as possible. Lower all air circulation and heating to minimal levels. Don't cook more than necessary. Don't use more hot water than necessary.

Stop using bots for anything a person could otherwise do.

Libbi stumbled over that last one. They hadn't been using the ancient family bots since they'd turned the store into a shelter, but one of their guests needed special care.

"I won't ask you to shut down, Squeaky," she told the cleaner bot. "That wouldn't be fair. But please try to conserve energy, okay? When you drain your batteries, I don't know how soon we'll be able to recharge you. And we don't want anyone asking questions about why you're still running."

"But, but, I want to help. Please give me an assignment?" The little bot had slowly been getting better at communicating with words, but still struggled to express complex thoughts. She could guess the emotion behind the words, though.

According to Sunny, the little cleaner was self-aware but limited by its design: limited memory, limited processing power, most of its resources dedicated to following a map, recognizing different types of messes and choosing the best way to clean them up.

"So it's not very smart?" Libbi had asked.

"'Smart' is a highly subjective term with you organics. Humans especially measure intelligence based on how closely it resembles your own. But I assure you, Squeaky feels things. They didn't like working in the tunnels because teens and drunk people would deliberately interfere with their work, or trip over them and call them rude names. They like your store better. You should feel honored." The sentient ship had said that last part like a warning, as if daring Libbi to take the little bot for granted.

She hadn't, and didn't intend to, even if she didn't understand how an automated mop could develop self-awareness. Sunny hadn't been able to explain it either, but when pressed on whether the *how* actually mattered, Libbi had to confess it didn't.

Libbi crouched down before Squeaky. "I understand the need to help. I want to do something too. In an emergency, sometimes we can help by being active, but other times, the best way to help is by doing nothing. By staying out of the way of the emergency crews. That's what we're all doing now, because as much as I wish I could help fix our power system, I don't have those skills. So the important thing right now is to reduce the drain on the system, even though it's frustrating. Okay?"

"Okay. I will try, for now."

Its obvious disappointment killed her. "Thanks, Squeaky. I promise, I'll tell you if there's anything more to do."

Squeaky wasn't the only one having a tough time. Fortunately for her peace of mind, there were still a few things Libbi could do. She went through the store and the house, flipping off lights and powering down devices. She pinged Ma at the Council Hall to see if she had any news.

"A lot more nothing," came the quick, terse response. "All questions, no answers."

Back downstairs, she joined Ever in gathering goods from the shelves: foil heat-retaining blankets, crank-powered flashlights and emergency beacons, shelf-stable food. A few volunteers were figuring out meals to use as much of their perishable food as possible, so they could shut down the fridge and freezers. She and Ever were organizing everything into a central cache, where the Losts could take what they needed, when Ellie Kapoor came in.

"Ellie!" Libbi hurried over, surprised by what a relief it was to see her brother's colleague. "Any news?"

For a long moment, Ellie said nothing as she surveyed the transformed store, her clear, fierce eyes taking in all the details. Finally, she turned to Libbi.

"News is what I'm here for, actually." Ellie tapped her headset with a grim smile. "Ravel won't acknowledge what they're doing to us, so we—the Cooperative, that is—aren't letting them hide. We want the galaxy to see that Ravel's violating our sovereignty. I'm doing media outreach, and I heard you were sheltering folks here. Can I take some video of what you're doing? Interview some folks?"

"If they give permission." Libbi's brow furrowed. "Won't media attention mean attention on the Losts? We've had enough of that for a lifetime."

"We're being careful about that, I promise. Right now, the onus is on Ravel to justify why they're interfering with us, and they've been cagey about that in all their public comms. They don't want to reveal your secret to competitors any more than we wanted them to find out."

Outside, the dome-light had been turned down to half its usual intensity, leaving the world dusky and strange, like being caught between day and night. Pa had a case of kinetic battery packs, designed to be recharged through everyday movement or a hand crank, and was handing them out to people on the street. She started doing the same with energy bars.

It didn't take long for word to spread and a crowd to form. Some folks took what they wanted and left, and a few glared through the gaps in the covered-up store windows as if to make clear that free stuff didn't balance out their crime of sheltering Losts, but most thanked them—some profusely.

"Founders smile upon you," said an elderly neighbor. "I know I ought to have backup power on hand, but I just never got around to it. This will at least keep my handheld charged. I don't know what I'd do otherwise."

Ellie Kapoor left not long after. "Thank you, Wilders. This footage will really help. With any luck, in a few days we'll have loads of reporters and outside observers here, putting the pressure on Ravel. Hang in there."

So Libbi did, returning to her work and trying to set aside her fear. It kept creeping in, though. With every new round of profuse thanks, she wondered what could possibly come next.

When the boxes were empty and there was nothing left to give out, Libbi turned to her father, biting her lip. "I know helping people at a time like this is the right thing to do, Pa. But we barely had the capital to restock the store after all the renovations. When this is over…what will we do?"

And her father, normally full of irrepressible optimism, only sighed.

"Let's worry about getting us all through this and out the other side. There'll be plenty of time to worry about what's next."

Only later, watching Dash and Sage play a game to distract the little kids, did she realize why this conversation unnerved her so. Pa wasn't hiding anything from her, wasn't protecting her. She'd felt like a partner to her parents during the renovations and the reopening of the store, but now, perhaps for the first time in her life, they were treating her not like their grown-up youngest child, but like a full adult. It wasn't the gratifying feeling she would've expected.

22

"WOULD YOU LIKE TO make the docking request?" Sunny asked Mixin.

The Ravel Corporation flagship that was hosting the Exhibition loomed large on Sunny's displays, gleaming and new. The Megalodon class of ships, much like their ancient Earth namesake, had been built to intimidate. It worked even on Sunny.

After three days of travel and quiet worrying, it was time to test their plan against reality.

Mixin, gaping at the massive ship, looked increasingly doubtful about the entire endeavor. "Won't they get suspicious if I mess it up?"

"They will probably assume you're an excited young up-and-comer who has never traveled off their homeworld before."

"That's only half a lie. In that case, sure, why not?" They cleared their throat, and Sunny opened comms to docking control. "*Ravel Minnow Redlamp 3472*, requesting permission to dock."

"*Ravel Minnow Redlamp*, got you in our docking queue. We've got a bit of a backup, so join the traffic pattern until we're ready for you."

"Oh, um, okay. I mean, acknowledged! Joining traffic pattern." Mixin cut the comm. "You know how to do that, right, Sunny?"

"I certainly do." Sunny kept the amusement from their voice. Mixin was nervous. They all were.

Sunny was technically stolen Ravel property. The fact that they had stolen themself wouldn't help if anyone recognized them as the missing courier ship that had destroyed a prototype solar mining rig and thwarted Ravel's takeover of Unity System. They had changed every identifying feature they could, both electronic and physical, but still worried they had missed something. They hadn't said anything to the organics, but Kay, Jasper, and Havoc all had similar reasons for concern.

In the process of circling, they had the opportunity to view this Megalodon from all sides. The setting of the Exhibition was in fact part of the Exhibition: this was the newest, sleekest, most powerful working ship in Ravel's fleet, an eventual replacement for the hulking old Leviathan flagships. Its central core was shaped like a skyscraper the size of an entire city. Docking control sent Sunny the specifications, ostensibly to help them locate their assigned docking bay, but mostly to show off to the arriving elites.

In the hold, Kay, Jasper, and Havoc were helping each other with their disguises. Kay and Jasper wore suits of smart-fabric that adjusted to fit as if perfectly tailored, and they both looked rather sharp to Sunny's cameras. Hidden beneath their clothes, shoulder and leg braces altered their posture and gait to look stiffer, more formal, less like themselves.

Kay applied a pricey de-aging cream (manufactured exclusively by the Ravel Corporation, not rated for daily use) that tightened her skin and smoothed blemishes from her face, then touches of what Jasper jokingly called "face clay," a theater cosmetic that tugged the skin just so to alter the shape of the face. In Kay's case, this meant plumping her cheeks and adding a resting frown to her lips, while Jasper added wrinkles across his forehead and around the eyes. A fake goatee gave his face a gaunt look. Finally they both applied cosmetics, far more and brighter colored than Kay ever normally wore.

"Sunny, how do we look?" Kay asked.

"Like brilliant young executives-in-training. I'm linking your current images to your cover identities in the flagship database now."

"But will the facial recognition flag us?" Jasper said.

Sunny checked several pattern-matching algorithms to be sure. "Not unless you draw attention to yourselves. Matches range from sixty to seventy-five percent depending on whether they're checking gait or voice as well as facial appearance. That won't flag you in a general sweep, but if someone looks you up specifically, they'll find Cooperative ties in the possible matches."

"That'll have to be good enough. Let's not raise suspicions."

Mixin didn't need to disguise their face, but they put on eyeshadow and streaked a glittering gel through their hair, which Sunny's research said was a current fashion among the younger Titanium rank that was their cover.

Havoc, meanwhile, dressed in a mechanic's jumpsuit and used ordinary hair spray to dull his scales.

"You're sure you don't mind being behind the scenes?" Kay asked him for the third time. They'd picked a cover for Havoc where he had the best chance of blending in. If there were any Kovars invited to the Exhibition as guests, they'd be countable on one hand, with fingers left over.

"Teammate, I prefer it. We need someone who can sneak around the operations areas without being noticed." He grimaced wryly. "Once, I would have longed to see the Exhibition itself, but now I'll gladly let you make false smiles at the executives while I hunt for Cobb's research."

"Fair enough," Kay said.

Jasper clasped Havoc's hand, kissed his knuckles. Sometime this morning, he'd filed his claws blunt, the better not to alarm the speciesist among Ravel's upper ranks.

"We've been approved for docking," Sunny announced. "You'll be able to disembark in five minutes."

"Thanks, Sunny. Remember, everyone"—Kay said this mostly for Mixin's benefit, Sunny guessed—"rank is everything here. Check your headset to see who you're talking to. Use titles for everyone—full titles, if you're just meeting them, however long and obnoxious they seem. Be vaguely positive about other divisions' achievements, but your own division is clearly the best."

"I thought Ravel folks were supposed to root for the whole company?" Mixin said.

"Yes, in theory. But in practice, you want your division to shine brightest, because you believe your work will benefit Ravel most."

"And if people want to know what that work is?"

"Ask them about theirs," Kay said. "Every single person

here will happily talk your ear off about themselves, given an opening."

As Sunny settled gently onto the docking bay floor, they connected to the internal network without being challenged. They immediately deployed one of Grist's scripts to let them past the firewall into deeper layers of the network.

It bounced back an error.

Strange. Grist's own credentials would have been disabled upon his presumed death, of course, but the back doors he often used (for activities he didn't *want* attached to his profile) should still be valid. Sunny tried again with a different script, with the same result.

They buzzed in frustration. The back door had been sealed shut.

"What troubles you, Sunny?" asked Havoc.

"It appears that, in the months since Grist and I fled Ravel, some of the vulnerabilities he liked to exploit have been found and patched."

"What does that mean for us?" Jasper asked.

"My current network access is as limited as yours. Most immediately, it means I can't use the internal surveillance cameras to watch the Exhibition." Or to watch over their organics, who were walking into a risky situation. "It will also complicate our efforts to destroy Cobb's data. I'd counted on having deep level of penetration."

"Complicate? Or prevent?"

"I'm sure we can find a workaround." Sunny felt at least eighty percent confident of that. "I haven't tried all of Grist's tricks yet."

Jasper and Havoc exchanged a look. "While the others visit the Exhibition, I can try to help," Havoc offered.

"I'd appreciate that," Sunny said. "The rest of you, please keep your headsets open to me, if you're willing, so I can see and hear what you do."

"What about your drone?" Mixin asked.

"Too likely to draw attention; it isn't a Ravel model. The headsets will have to suffice. Call the whole team if you get into trouble, because I may have limited ability to assist."

"Same with you, Sunny," Kay murmured, touching a bulkhead fondly. "If anyone starts poking around about you, let me know."

"I'm unconcerned about that. They didn't question my designation when we filed for docking. I will be cautious, however."

"Well," Jasper said, letting out a deep breath. "Shall we?"

THERE WERE SO MANY things to stare at, Mixin thought their eyes might dry up and fall out from lack of blinking. The Megalodon was even glitzier inside, with luxe carpet starting right outside the docking bay, and the reception area where they waited to register even had faux wood paneling (at least, Mix assumed it was faux) along the walls. A thousand tiny, glowing lights swirled around the high ceiling like a galaxy of stars.

So much adrenaline was pumping through their veins that they hardly noticed the higher gravity. And they hadn't gone into the actual Exhibition yet.

Mixin barely breathed as they gave their alias at registration, first at an automated console which scanned their face and their fake badge, then to a real person behind a desk who manually checked that all their information matched. What if they got caught? Could the Cooperative really fool Ravel like this?

"Welcome, Senior Analyst Greenwell," the staffer said with a polite smile. "You'll find the augmentation displays along the right-hand side of the Engineering Hall, second area on your left."

"Um, thanks?" Mixin wasn't sure why they were getting this instruction.

"Augments and Biotech is your department, isn't it?" The staffer glanced at Mixin's credentials again to confirm.

"Oh, yeah, it is, thanks. I just thought I'd look around a bit before I report in, if that's all right."

"That's between you and your supervisor, of course." A hint of a mischievous smile, there. "Have fun, Senior Analyst."

"Oh, no doubt," Mixin muttered, floating with relief. Step one, complete!

Another staffer handed them a briefcase, and they took it on impulse before mental warnings kicked in: never take a package from a stranger in a public place. "Sorry, what's this?"

"Your complimentary gifts."

"…Free stuff?"

This staffer smiled condescendingly at Mixin's naiveté. "All Exhibition attendees get an assortment of demo items from the presenting departments."

Glancing around, Mixin saw someone turning their identical briefcase into a backpack, and someone else adjusting its design with their headset. "Nice! Thanks!"

"Don't get too excited," Kay murmured, steering them away from the table. "They're scanning all the bags and linking them to the individual registrants. I guarantee at least half the cool stuff in there will be tracking you."

"Ugh. Figures. So, where do we go first?"

"Let's get the lay of the land before we worry about Biopharma," Kay said. "Eyes open for any useful rumors or gossip, okay, Mix?"

But Mixin was overwhelmed the moment they entered the central hall of the Exhibition. The glitz. The advertising everywhere, physical and virtual both. The sheer number of people, all talking, their words rolling over each other in Mixin's vision. No sooner did Mix grasp the sense of one conversation than another would shove it out of the way.

"...Be demoing our new planetary weather control prototype..."

"...Copper-ranker, shouldn't even be here..."

"...Something big from Natural Resources..."

"...Win tickets to Company Woman, the cinema event of the..."

"...Really? *Their* department wouldn't recognize a good idea if it..."

Mixin shook their head to clear it. It didn't help.

They'd been in situations like this before, though, and knew their brain would adjust if they gave it a chance. They force-disabled ads on their headset, and while they couldn't shut off their gift, they could choose what to pay attention to. They focused on the informational signs overhead, pointing the way to the different areas, and let themself wander. Health, engineering, trade, discovery, and culture all had their own areas off of the main hall. Engineering had drawn a crowd around a huge model—the size of Mix's whole apartment back on Brennex—of what must be their fancy new space habitat. Mix would check that out when it was less crowded.

They paused to watch a demonstration. It looked like a moving sculpture, waving and swaying and constantly transforming itself, now spreading like ink in water, now gathering and rising like the trunk of a tree. Colored lights and holo-landscapes shifted in time with the performance, but there was nothing virtual about the main attraction. Mixin's headset informed them that it was called a nano-swarm, and the display was meant to demonstrate that nanites were capable of not only feats no Human could achieve, like microsurgery and repairing tiny fissures in a radioactivity containment pod, but also feats of grace, beauty, and art. Mixin had to admit: it was stunning.

"Arts had that same dancing nanite display last time," someone scoffed nearby, turning to walk away from the show. "Can't they ever come up with anything new?"

"Honestly, I haven't seen a single thing I'd call *innovative* yet," their companion answered. "You'd think we've all been sitting on our asses for the past five years. No wonder we're losing market share every which way."

"Biopharma had some big talk about the next big thing, but apparently that fell through…" The pair moved out of Mixin's range.

"*I* think it's pretty," they murmured to themself, feeling like the stereotype of the uncultured Brennexian.

At the next display, two workers in gray jumpsuits were racing to sort poly blocks of different shapes and colors by some unintuitive criteria, like toddlers put to work on an assembly line. Green blocks here, circles there, green circles somewhere else entirely. Hovering displays showed each person's speed, accuracy, and some measure called focus, plus video that must have been from each of their headsets, literally fading in and out of focus.

"So you see, our new headset module tracks workers' attention via minute shifts in their eyes. When their attention drifts…" A zap crackled through the air, and one of the workers jumped. Within moments, the video from their headset sharpened again. "We can correct it. The timing of breaks can be adjusted to individual needs, and other motivational techniques can be applied. We're piloting the program in three factories this year, and partnering with the Manual Labor Behavioral Department to test interventions."

"Gross," Mixin muttered. They tried to imagine being always on at Wilder Supply. The store had never been that busy in the time they'd worked there, but even picturing it was exhausting. There was something demeaning about the way the demonstrator set those workers to meaningless tasks, reaping data from their mistakes. "Why not just use bots?"

"Over-reliance on bots creates an idle society," said a stranger beside them, startling them. "Other corporate states have made the mistake of handing over too much work to automated processes that could otherwise be done by people. Real people need to be kept busy. A society of busy, productive people is healthier, more manageable—not to mention more profitable—than a bored, discontent one."

"I see," said Mixin. Mostly they saw that this was something a good employee ought to know. Dancing nano-bots: good. Bots that could make people's lives easier: big mistake. "Of course. I bet that's especially true in, um…" They checked their headset. "Civil Cultivation, Director?"

The stranger's profile gave their name as Agata Wu, flagged that he'd recently switched to using *he* pronouns, and had a title that screamed his importance. He shouldn't be talking to a nobody like Mixin.

Director Wu looked amused. "I oversee teams that integrate newly acquired worlds into the company. So yes, our work certainly requires a Human touch; new citizens don't tend to respond well to armies of bots."

"I guess not."

"Do people tend to feel differently on Redlamp, these days?"

It took Mixin a beat too long to remember that Redlamp was where their cover identity lived. "Oh, nope, we uh, we don't use bots unless we have to…"

Sunny's voice came over their headset, the ship's words filling Mixin's vision. "Mixin, you must disengage at once. Director Wu knows Kay from the Unity System campaign, and must not see her here."

"Oh, f—" Mixin managed not to curse out loud, then realized they were being rude by listening to their headset during a conversation. "Oh, look at the time! It was a real honor to meet you, Director Wu, but I'm going to be late for a meeting."

They fled, hoping desperately that they seemed like a frenetic, nervous young staffer rather than an overwhelmed young spy who couldn't manage a complete sentence. Of all the people here, how had they managed to get the attention of one who knew Kay?

"I'm terrible at this," they muttered to themself.

"You're learning," Sunny said with annoying practicality. "Kay had a difficult time adjusting to corporate ways, too, when she went undercover."

"Hopefully I won't be here long enough to learn it that well."

They headed for the Biopharma displays, trying not to get distracted by every other demo they passed, and wishing they had a flyswatter to shoo away everyone who tried to offer them a giveaway or raffle ticket, for the low, low price of scanning their contact info. At one point, a drone dive-bombed them offering tickets to a cinematic premier that

Arts and Culture was hosting tonight, and they ducked past it without answering.

Biopharma was in a corner, and strangely quiet. With fewer competing voices, Mixin could actually follow whole conversations, which they did while pretending to browse the booths. The largest booth was empty, with decorations and holo-projectors sitting in their cases. Checking the map, they confirmed: that was supposed to be Cobb's booth.

"Think they'll get him out before the Exhibition's over?" one of the staff at a nearby booth asked their neighbor.

"I think Ferguson's calling in every possible favor to make it happen. The board won't want to invade a sovereign world, no matter how difficult they're being. Bad optics."

A shrug. "Honestly, I just want to enjoy every minute that Cobb's not here. He'll be insufferable when they get him out. I mean, worse than usual."

"I know! Just the guy who needed his ego fed. So, what do you think this big 'surprise demo' from Natural Resources is all about?"

"Got to be their solar mining, right?"

"No, don't you remember? The Cooperative set them way back on that…"

As Mixin slipped away from the Biopharma section, they let out the breath they'd been holding. No one was presenting on Cobb's work in his absence. Hopefully, for Brennex's sake, it would stay that way.

23

STILL ANXIOUS AFTER THEIR close brush with Director Agata Wu—who apparently not only knew Kay, but was her direct supervisor when Kay had fake-worked for Ravel—Mixin didn't want to risk any more interaction with people who might get suspicious about their awkwardness. So when Jasper suggested a project that involved hiding and eavesdropping, Mixin was all in.

That was how they found themself wearing a worker's jumpsuit instead of a business suit, crammed beside Havoc into a narrow maintenance space directly below the board's meeting room.

"All the maintenance staff keep complaining that this flagship needed more shakedown time before bringing so many VIPs aboard," Havoc explained. "Yesterday a lift stopped working and trapped two Platinum-rank officials for an hour. Power keeps flickering in the kitchen levels.

Half the sleeping quarters have too much heat, and the rest, too much cold. And so…" The Kovar brandished a wrench, grinning. "When the cooling system for the boardroom mysteriously failed this morning, no one questioned it."

So while Havoc very slowly repaired his sabotage, Mixin could listen in on the board's discussions.

What exactly they wanted from these meetings was vague, more opportunistic than anything. Of the two fronts of their plan—destroying Cobb's existing research, and making Ravel lose interest in pursuing the Lost Generation any further—the former was stalled until Sunny and Havoc hacked into the computer systems and got Sunny the level of access they were used to having. This would apparently require some dicey sneaking around by Havoc in secure areas of the flagship, so it couldn't happen until tonight.

Mix's eavesdropping would hopefully lay the groundwork for the latter part. Whatever the executives were saying about Cobb and Brennex and the Losts would shape their campaign to discredit Cobb. It should tell them where to apply pressure, as Jasper put it. Though really, Jasper seemed interested in gathering all possible information, to glean any possible tidbits he could bring back to the Cooperative. Even Mixin could tell it was killing Jasper to sacrifice all the Cooperative's big-picture plans for the Exhibition for the sake of one planet, even if that planet was home.

Footsteps clomped over the floor above them. "Stay quiet now," Havoc murmured. "It begins."

There were long minutes of shuffling and chitchat—how the food had been better last time, and whether this new flagship was impressive or an over-hyped money pit—until the meeting was called to order.

"There have been multiple requests for this, so let's begin with a diplomatic matter. Brennex."

Mixin raised their brows at Havoc, but he didn't react; the voices were too muffled by layers of wall and vents and piping for him to make out. It was all on Mixin, then, as expected. They took rapid-fire notes on their handheld and shared them to Havoc's device so he could follow along.

"Vice President Ferguson, will you please speak to what Biopharma is hoping to accomplish on Brennex? We've all heard rumors, so let's get everyone aligned on the facts, please."

"Gladly, President Brant, because the research we're conducting on Brennex could revolutionize the entirety of Ravel within two generations. This discovery is unprecedented; until recently, we thought it impossible. The potential—"

"Less sales pitch, please, and more facts," said a new speaker—not Brant, who'd opened the meeting. Mixin had tried to learn the names, positions, and voices of everyone on the board, but a lot of their voices sounded (and therefore looked) alike. Mixin would have to piece it together from context.

"As you like." Ward Ferguson of Biopharma sounded annoyed. "Last year, it was discovered that a pair of Brennexian activists, brother and sister, had access to information in ways we couldn't account for. We have the diligence of the Natural Resources division to thank for that. Biopharma's prize scientist, Principal Scientist Alik Cobb, had been—"

"Thought his rank was Senior Researcher?" someone whispered.

"I guess his ego wasn't puffed up enough, so he needed another title bump," came the equally quiet answer. "Supposed to be announced this week."

"—Working to resurrect some old research done at Brennex—and had nearly succeeded, until the Cooperative interfered—and he hypothesized what we've since proved: an epidemic of parapsychological abilities among Brennexians born during their membership period. That's what this is about, my good colleagues: a process that could give future generations in Ravel literal superpowers."

There was a long pause, and then questions stampeded over each other.

"What type of powers are we talking about?"

"Can they be controlled?"

"How did we not *know* about this?"

Mixin's leg was cramped from crouching, and they shifted, very carefully, to take their weight off it. Biopharma talked over the others until they finally fell quiet and listened.

"Brennex is an insular, provincial community. They rely on trade but don't trust outsiders, which seems to be how they've kept this secret for so long. We've only studied a small subset of the affected population, but the powers we've documented so far include several forms of synesthetic empathy, sensory augmentation, and even prescience. And there may well be more we haven't identified yet. If we can learn to control how these abilities manifest, the potential is, frankly, limitless."

"That's a big *if*. What do we know about the mechanisms at play? Is it heritable? How does it manifest in the brain?"

"That's what Cobb went to Brennex to study."

"So you know nothing."

"We have hypotheses, Vice President Madden." That'd be Myra Madden, who ran the Agricultural Tech division. "As you know, science takes time, and preferably freedom from interference. Given the Cooperative's recent attacks, Principal Scientist Cobb hasn't had enough of either."

"Sounds like we need to hear from Cobb directly."

"Well, of course. This is why we're working so hard to get Cobb and his test subjects back where they belong."

"At what cost?" Ag Tech said. "This sounds like a fun party trick, but I don't see the usefulness to my scientists, much less my rank-and-file workers."

"Rank and file? No, no, this is clearly intended for the management ranks. Imagine being able to know exactly which of your reports is bored, or in over their head."

"Or plotting against you."

Murmured appreciation followed this.

"I can imagine such abilities being extremely useful in our Civil Cultivation work, for building relationships and quelling unrest. But that's a dream for the future. In the short term, Biopharma's aggression on Brennex is *causing* unrest on several other worlds. It's terrible optics."

"Indeed. This seems to me like a blatant power play from Biopharma. I understand, of course! Brennex embarrassed us all with their rebellion, but Biopharma above all, and now it turns out they've deprived you of a valuable resource all this time. Naturally you want to teach them a lesson, Ferguson. But the fact remains: you're trying to boost your own influence without regard for how it affects the rest of the company."

Someone laughed dismissively. "Isn't that what we're all doing? Isn't that what this whole parade is for, to show off? To boost our influence and budget share?"

"Most of us are doing that by bringing actual innovations, not just big talk."

"Biopharma has been the heart of this company since its founding—"

"And your predecessors did their jobs too well. Rapid drug prototyping is too effective and too cheap these days, and you've rendered yourselves obsolete. Ravel has always known how to change with the times."

"As do we! That's *why* we're pursuing this revolutionary new discovery on Brennex—"

A sharp voice cut Biopharma off.

"No other division has recently caused an interstellar incident in pursuit of relevance." That was Terena Warsnop Brant, the company president. "Except, it occurs to me, your Natural Resources division, Moore. I'm not thrilled about Biopharma's unilateral action on this matter, especially under our…current circumstances. This board will decide, together, how to proceed with Brennex in a way that benefits the whole company. Vice President Wu, perhaps this is a good segue to your report on Acquisitions and Civil Cultivation?"

Mixin startled, thinking this was the same Agata Wu they'd met yesterday. But he wasn't a VP, and this was a different voice, much older and deeper. A family member? Or just coincidence? Ravel didn't prioritize family ties like Brennex did.

His report was eye-opening. Mixin's fingers ached from taking so many notes. Independence movements and campaigns for worker rights were popping up all over Ravel territory. There'd been a dozen incidents in the past year alone—more than in the previous decade. Wu said they might actually have to bend to the demands for independence on Artesia, and it took Mixin a moment to remember why that name was familiar: it was where Havoc came from. They highlighted that in their notes for him, and Havoc grinned fiercely, showing teeth.

"So you can see," Wu concluded, "how bad it looks right now for us to publicly pressure a former colony, one that successfully revolted against us. Just this week, we've had two potential new member worlds withdraw from the acquisition process."

"Bringing Brennex to heel is a means, not an end," Biopharma said. "We just want what's ours. These individuals got their remarkable gifts because of our work. Those gifts belong to us."

"Nobody's arguing otherwise, Ferguson. But, justified or not, the foreign media is calling us a bully. We need to turn the narrative to our advantage."

"The problem is Biopharma's going too easy on Brennex. Again. We should never have let them break away in the first place, and now we're letting them make us look weak again."

"Yes, exactly. We ought to make an example of them, and every other world with unrest, too."

Mixin twitched, and their handheld clattered to the floor. They held their breath, waiting for someone to react, but no one did.

The debate continued like that, devolving into thinly veiled name-calling. Mixin figured they'd learned everything useful at this point, but couldn't risk leaving until the meeting was over. Someone might hear them.

Finally, when their legs and back were begging for a reprieve, President Brant adjourned the meeting. Conversation broke down into side chats, too many to follow. Mixin had nearly stopped paying attention, just waiting for when they could get out of this maintenance shaft from hell, when they saw the word *Brennex* again.

"...Didn't tell them about *your* division's plan for that trash pit, I notice."

"Because *my* plan will work, to the whole company's benefit. Don't tell me you've changed your mind?"

"No, no, I'm on your side—as long as this doesn't backfire on us. Internally or externally."

"Don't worry. I have strong allies on our side. Engineering, for one, saw the benefits immediately. And we've just moved into position at Brennex…two hours ago, if everything's on schedule. By the time the news travels back here, and long before we present our demo, I'll have the support of a majority of the board."

"You'd better."

"I will—as long as you stop undermining the plan with this small-minded 'we just want what's ours' nonsense." There was an answer to that, but mumbled, too garbled for Mixin's gift. "Of course we will. When have our two divisions ever been allies before? If we can partner effectively, the rest of them will come around, too. For the good of the company, after all."

MASON RAN HIS HANDS through his hair. "You're sure it was Natural Resources who said this? Did Moore say what they're demoing?"

"Yes, I'm sure, and no, he didn't," Mixin answered. "But he's the one who told the board they should 'make an example' of Brennex."

Havoc rubbed his frustrated eshrim's shoulder. They'd all picked up food and gathered aboard Sunny to eat; nowhere else could they have confidence of complete privacy. Mixin barely picked at their baguette toasts and spinach-gorgonzola dip; Havoc understood their lack of appetite, because he had no interest in eating at all.

"Sorry, Mixin, I'm not upset with you," Mason said at last. "It's not like any of us can read minds."

"Unfortunately," Mixin muttered.

"I just have no idea what they're up to."

"Could it be the solar mining again?" Kay asked. "All the buzz says that Natural Resources is going to introduce something *big* at their presentation on the last day of the Exhibition. We blocked their plans in Unity System and destroyed their prototype solar mining rig, but maybe they rebuilt."

"I heard people speculating that, too," Mixin said.

"I wouldn't *think* so. We haven't heard any rumors about it." Mason bit his lip. "Granted, we haven't heard of anything else that big out of Natural Resources, either, but there hasn't been enough time to build a new prototype from scratch. I'd like to warn Brennex, but we don't know what to warn them about."

"Vague rumors won't help them," Havoc agreed. "I understand you're worrying about your home, Mason, but we must trust our teammates there to handle it, while we focus on our job here."

Mason gave him a wry half-smile. "Wise of you."

"I found the rest of the meeting more informative," Havoc continued. "We didn't realize tensions had risen so high between the divisions."

Sunny added, "I've located a leaked copy of the preliminary budget the board is considering. It includes major cuts to Biopharma and Natural Resources. I attribute the latter to our success at Unity System."

"And it sounds like the movement on Artesia is doing really well, Havoc," said Kay.

Havoc beamed at the thought. His longtime teammate Chit kept him updated on their progress, and she always sounded confident, but it said much for the executives themselves to mention Artesia as a problem.

Once, Havoc's greatest dream had been to fix Ravel, to make it a fairer place for people like him. Now, he hoped one day to see his birth planet freed from Ravel's power entirely.

"So that's all good, except now they're desperate." Kay stretched to grab another bruschetta (made, the menu bragged, with Ag Tech's new drought-resistant, freeze-proof tomatoes). "Which they'll take out on Brennex."

"Damn Harrington Moore," Mason said. "I really think Biopharma would give up their crusade against us if we got rid of Cobb's research, but if Natural Resources has their eye on Brennex now, we'll need to deal with them, too." He sighed. "We could accomplish everything we came here for, and still fail. And the Cooperative will have lost everything we originally planned to get out of the Exhibition, too."

"Mason, eshrim, look at the bigger picture," Havoc said. *Please, beloved, focus.* He sympathized with Mason's frustration, but they needed his strategic mind right now. "The divisions are fighting among themselves. Biopharma and Natural Resources seem to be going rogue. No one agrees on the company's direction. Surely you've seen this with your gift?"

"Everyone's tense, too," Kay said. "Underneath the excitement of the Exhibition, there's a lot of worry and resentment, way more than I would expect."

Slowly, Mason nodded. "I have noticed that. People seem loyal within their divisions or departments, but there are intense rivalries. I'd put it down to the high stakes of the Exhibition, and the budget process. Rivalry is a fact of corporate life. Pretending to be on the same eshrato while really most concerned with their own close team. You think it's worse than normal?"

Havoc said, "These fissures run deep. They offer us opportunities, don't you think?"

Mason sat back, lost in thought again, but now Havoc could tell he was working through the question. "Maybe. Yeah, maybe. If we could destabilize things even further… Play them against each other, hurt Biopharma and Natural Resources both, or even…"

Havoc had only meant to suggest that the other divisions could be turned against Biopharma—and Cobb—but if Mason had ideas for a greater game, Havoc wanted to hear them. It frustrated him, too, that so many of the Cooperative's plans had to be abandoned for this. He held his silence, giving Mason space to think. He waited.

But Mason shook his head. "No. We've got limited time and resources, and if we overreach, it could backfire massively. Stopping Cobb still needs to be our main priority."

He spoke wisdom. Probably. Havoc held back a disappointed sigh.

Mixin leaned forward. "So Sunny, Havoc, what's the plan for Cobb's research? Havoc said you're breaking into their…data storage? Server room?"

"Into their systems administration area, as a first step," said Sunny. "Their data center would be the target if we planned to steal Cobb's work—that's what Jasper and his partner did on Artesia—but even if we deleted his files there, Ravel has backups upon backups."

"We'll use a virus to attack all copies of his research at once," said Havoc. "For that, we need Cobb's level of access, or greater."

"Without Grist's old hacks, I'll need direct physical access to their system in order to go any deeper. Which Havoc will provide tonight, after the tech workers are done with their shifts," Sunny explained.

"And then you can plant the virus?" Mixin asked.

"We will see what I'm able to get," Sunny said, "and then determine our next steps. This will be a process, like solving a puzzle of many layers, not a single direct attack."

"How can we help?" Mason said. "I can go with you, eshrim…"

"You don't have to," Havoc said. "It'll serve better for you to go—what do you call it? Schmoozing?—at the evening social events."

Mason looked ready to protest, but Kay nudged him in the ribs. "I think that means *please stay out of the way*, Jasp. You break computers just by looking at them."

"I'm not that bad! But point taken," Mason said. "Be careful, okay? Both of you. And Sunny, call us if he gets in trouble, any trouble at all."

"I will take care," Havoc said. "Have fun at your fancy parties."

24

"HEY, LIBBI? UNCLE JACKSON?" someone called from the front of the store.

Libbi's parents had quickly become Auntie and Uncle to all the Losts who were sheltering with them, even those they'd never met before. It turned out to be Sage Porter, standing watch by the door.

"What's up?" Libbi asked.

Sage pointed with his free hand at the bar across the street, while holding baby Saba close in his other arm. "Those guys have been gathering there for the past half-hour. More keep showing up."

The bar in question was closed this time of day, and in fact had been closed the past few nights, but a group of people were hanging around outside. Mostly older, all male and Human, they were behaving…weirdly, to Libbi's eye. Not talking much, not doing anything obvious, but watching people walk by. And watching the windows of the nearby buildings, Wilder Supply included.

"They don't mean well," Ever said, coming up behind Libbi. His voice sounded tight with discomfort. His gift, confirming Libbi's guess.

"That one in the cap is Skel Griffin," Pa said, "and I think the teenager beside him is his son Culver. A post-occupation kid." Meaning too young to be a Lost.

Another man wandered up to join them, greeted with handshakes and slaps on the back.

"Oh, Founders help us," Libbi said. "That's Officer Stone. The actively unhelpful guy from Public Safety."

"Crap," said Sage.

"Crap! Crap!" baby Saba echoed innocently.

Libbi felt ill. If those people made trouble, having a Public Safety officer on their side would probably get them out of any consequences. And it wouldn't be great for anyone on the receiving end, either. Especially if they had to fight back.

"Okay, folks," Pa announced, voice pitched to carry. "It's time to do like we talked about. Kids to the back of the store. Everyone else, arm yourselves, but remember, we're not starting anything. We're just protecting our people."

Sage kissed Dashiell as he handed off Saba, and other parents scooped up their children and took them to the storage room in back. A few volunteers moved to guard the back entrance. Libbi hauled out the cart they'd stocked with makeshift self-defense measures: hammers and wrenches for those who felt capable of using them, and for the rest, spray cans of paint and sealer, foam insulation guns, anything with a propellant that would be nasty to breathe. Ever set up fans pointing outward to keep the stuff from blowing back in their faces, and they all donned face masks and glasses just in case.

They waited. The gang across the street would know they were up to something, but maybe couldn't tell what.

Then, in the quiet of anticipation, Libbi realized who was missing.

She flipped on her headset, not caring about saving battery. "Hope? Sujay? Where are you?"

Her friends were making today's run to the spaceport for supplies, whatever they could get at this point. They should have been back by now…

"We're almost there. Took a while to convince Old Cass that we really are cooking for forty. They're limiting most customers to—"

"Stop. Listen, don't come to the front of the store right now."

"Uhhhhm…crap. Too late," Hope said, and the connection dropped.

Libbi craned her neck to see down the street. There they were, just a few doors down with the auto-cart hovering along behind, and the Human vultures across the street had noticed them.

The Griffins, senior and junior, broke lazily away from the group. The older one, Skel, said something to Hope and Sujay. Libbi couldn't hear him—she wished Mixin were here, for more reasons than one—but the distaste on Hope's face and Sujay's grimace, like he smelled something bad, gave a clear enough sense of it.

Hope said something that made Skel Griffin puff up. He stepped forward—Sujay, who'd never been in a fight in his life, stepped in front of Hope—the Griffins' friends were drifting closer—

Skel punched Sujay in the face. There was no way Libbi could hear the crack of bones and flesh from this distance, but her imagination filled it in. Sujay turned, hand clasped to his jaw in astonishment. Hope bristled, gathered herself to fight back…

Libbi was just through the shop door when a new voice called out, loud, clear, and close.

"Hear me now! What's happening here?"

A team of Kovars had come out of an alley and stalked toward the group, tails twitching. The men on the street wavered between the two targets before deciding the newcomers were a bigger threat.

Kovars weren't naturally violent compared to the average Human, but they had an easy time making Humans feel threatened. Beyond their love of sports and tendency to athleticism, they had sharp teeth, claws, and a reptilian appearance that sounded instinctive alarms in very ancient parts of Human brains. Most people got over any speciesism, but even Libbi felt her heart pound in simian alarm as the lead Kovar hissed, baring her teeth.

"None of your business," Griffin shouted. "Go on, now!"

"Are they distressing you?" the Kovar leader asked Hope and Sujay. Hope gave a tiny, frightened nod. "Back away, and let them through," she instructed Griffin and his people.

Griffin laughed. "Don't think so. Do you know who I am? Founding family, father on the Council…"

"Yes, I recognize you, Skel Griffin," the Kovar said. "But a Founder's bloodline doesn't entitle you to harass innocent young people."

"Hardly innocent. Their sort are going to get us all killed, destroy everything we've fought for. The question isn't what we're doing, but why you aren't helping. This is your home too. You don't want to defend it?"

She snorted. "This marks the first time in my life that a founding family scion recognized that Kovars also have a right to call Brennex home. Your interests do not align with ours, Griffin. Leave now."

She flexed her claws carefully, deliberately. Several of the men backed away. The Griffins hovered, undecided.

Libbi stepped into the street, and heard more of their folks following. Her father stood at her shoulder. She clutched her foam gun, which had enough of the shape of a real gun to feel reassuring, but it wouldn't last long in a real fight.

The thugs seemed to do the math and realize it was no longer in their favor.

"Now, now, no need to overreact," said Officer Stone. "How about we *all* go about our business?"

There was a long, tense moment. Then the elder Griffin snarled. "Fine."

From the dark look he gave Libbi and her father, she sensed there was a *for now* unspoken in that retreat.

As soon as they were gone, sighs of relief escaped their ragged defense force.

"We owe you some thanks," Pa said to the Kovars. "I don't believe we've met. I'm Jackson Wilder, and this is my daughter Liber—Libbi."

"They call me Hearth's Stronghold, and I've heard you are sheltering Losts who lack safe places of their own," she said. "My team and several others have begun patrolling to keep the peace, since Public Safety no longer seems interested in the public or their safety. We've already disrupted three such incidents today."

"That's good of you," Libbi said. "I don't know what would've happened if you hadn't shown up." Worse than a bruised jaw for Sujay, definitely.

"Would you come in for a cup of chai?" Pa said. "We don't have quite our usual hospitality, but what's ours is yours."

Speaking of… "I'm going to help unload the cart," Libbi said, excusing herself, and she hurried over to her friends.

Sujay had slumped to the ground, not (Libbi suspected) because he couldn't stand but because Hope was bent over him, tenderly touching his jaw.

"You dummy. Why did you do that?" she demanded. He could only shrug. "Well, you're very brave and stupid."

Libbi raised her brows at Hope. No one else saw a mystery in Sujay rushing to her defense.

"Why don't I take the cart from here? Hope, you take Sujay upstairs. My parents can find you a cold pack and maybe painkillers, if we have any left."

"Good idea. Come on, Suj." Hope hauled Sujay to his feet, and he made a show of groaning and staggering. "I know you're not that bad. Come *on,* I'm not carrying you."

He grinned over his shoulder at Libbi, a silent thank-you, and she smiled to herself as she guided the cart back to the store.

25

HAVOC WALKED THE DEEP corridors of the flagship as if he belonged there, though the irony grasped him sharply: his best work and most sincere loyalty as a Ravel citizen-employee would never have earned him an invitation to this Exhibition, not even as a humble support staffer.

This wasn't cheating, he reminded himself. He played a different game now, a better game.

Under his cover as Copper-rank maintenance worker (more irony, that he had so long aspired to this rank, and now he pretended to it), he'd gained access to the lower levels of the flagship without trouble. At this late hour, few were working apart from the lower-rank tech support staff, triaging more of the flagship's problems; Havoc heard music down that department's hallway, and nearly ran into someone sneaking wine back to their desk from an event. The other halls were quiet, though. All the Exhibition attendees were attending the same parties where Mason, Kay, and Mixin were sipping Sham-pagne, gathering intelligence from drunken Ravel elites, and spreading doubt about Alik Cobb's secret project. Havoc much preferred to be here. With luck, he would encounter no people at all.

He should have felt more nervous. He knew what Ravel would do with a renegade Dust-ranker turned saboteur. If Havoc got himself caught, this time the Cooperative would not be able to save him.

"Take your next right," Sunny said in his ear. "Then server administration will be to your left."

He did a visual check from the doorway, then a quick sweep of the room to check the security cameras' positions before choosing a desk in one of the cameras' blind spots.

He plugged in the fly-drive that would be Sunny's physical door into the system.

"Ready, Sunny," he said.

"Good. The connection is working."

"Can you get what you need?"

"Much of it, I believe. This will take me a few minutes, however."

If Grist's old scripts had still worked, they wouldn't have needed to do this. But Sunny's continued efforts hadn't found success; the ship had determined that a recent security upgrade had patched several of Grist's favorite security flaws. With this direct physical access, Sunny would have more options.

Exactly how deep they could sneak into the system remained an open question. If luck favored their team, then perhaps—perhaps—Sunny could plant the virus that would destroy Cobb's files tonight. Havoc hoped for this, but knew it unlikely.

"You've made sure they can't trace this back to you?" he asked, despite knowing the answer.

"I have not forgotten to spoof my location. I am following our plan, Havoc."

"Of course."

Ah. Perhaps he simply hadn't held still long enough for nervousness to find him yet. Now, waiting, he had ample time to reflect on all the ways this might go wrong.

"I'm into the surveillance system! I have cameras in most of the flagship now." A pause. "I've created several new credentials for myself, and increased your alias's access level as high as I can without drawing attention."

He relaxed a little. These had been Sunny's top priorities, the next rungs in their ladder. "Good. How much longer?"

"A few more minutes. I've located Cobb's partition, but I can't— Oh dear. Someone's in the corridor," Sunny warned. "Stay where you are, Havoc. They can't see you from the door."

He went rigid. "Security?"

"Fortunately, no. One is a Copper-ranker from Technology Support. Perhaps she hopes to work while everyone else is socializing."

"I can believe that."

"The other is Silver rank, but their position is in…Biotech? Strange. They don't belong in this area."

"What are they doing?"

"Be silent until they pass," Sunny said. Then: "Havoc, hide! They're coming your way."

Havoc dove under the desk, the only cover within reach. Equipment crowded the underside of the workstations, and clusters of cables ran into the floor, forcing him to squeeze in uncomfortably. If the intruders came too close, they would see him for certain.

Intruders? No, *he* was the intruder. Whatever brought these two employees here, they had more legitimacy than Havoc.

He remembered to tuck in his tail just as the door slid open.

Through his headset, Sunny kept up a quiet narration. "They're coming inside. The tech worker is checking that the room is empty. They don't want to be interrupted. I wonder why."

Havoc couldn't answer, but he had a guess.

"We're alone. Come in," said a young, high voice: the tech worker, presumably. Two sets of footsteps crossed the floor—too close to Havoc's hiding spot for comfort. He curled tighter. Held his breath. A chair shifted close by.

"Stand there, where the cameras can't see you."

Sunny said, "The tech worker is logging into a console. They both look nervous."

As they should, if Havoc guessed right.

"Here's the deal," the tech worker said. "I'm working late to catch up on my ticket backlog because we're all overwhelmed with stuff breaking on this shiny piece of crap they call a flagship. Which is true, by the way, and I'll probably be working late every night of this thing."

"Okay, so where are the files?" said the second voice.

"Nope, sorry, hon. I got you in. You'll have to figure out the rest on your own." The chair shifted again, and she made a sound, an exaggerated half-yawn, as if stretching tight muscles. Pointedly, she said, "Wow, look at the time! I didn't realize how hungry I was. I'd better hurry and grab dinner before the cafeteria closes." She strode toward the door— Havoc tensed again—then stopped. "Oh, whoops, did I forget to lock my console? Nah, I'm sure it's fine. I'll only be gone a few minutes."

The other laughed softly. "You're too much. No one will buy that."

"Which is why you'd better be quick."

"My room later? Let me thank you properly for this?"

"Oh, you definitely will." Havoc could hear the wink in her voice. Then the door swished shut, and the second person sat heavily in front of the console.

That confirmed it: this was interdepartmental espionage. Strictly against the rules, but a rule that every department broke when it suited them. The most popular Ravelian thrillers often featured internal spies as well as spies from rival corporations.

Sunny said: "They're pulling up data from Natural Resources. Oh, it's the solar mining project. They aren't taking it, though, just reading it locally. A very quick reader; they must have augments for that."

Not quick enough. Havoc's muscles were cramping.

"Come on, you little roaches, where are your secrets?"

Minutes felt like hours, the only sound fingers tapping on the console. Then, finally: "Got it."

"They're taking snapshots with their headset," Sunny reported.

A moment later: "All right, they're heading toward the door…"

Beep!

The noise was probably a minor notification, but in the empty room it blared like an accusation—but came from directly above Havoc's head. He hissed, startled, and managed not to curse aloud (but used every rude word he knew inside his head) as the footsteps paused. Listening.

"They're looking your way. Don't move."

No, surely the time for stillness had passed. Silently, Havoc gathered himself, preparing to leap at them if necessary. If this person saw his workstation and the fly-drive and the processes Sunny was running, he would have to…what? Knock them unconscious? Kidnap them? No, no, this wasn't one of those drama serials. Perhaps he could talk them into keeping his secret, one spy to another. Highly unlikely, when they were a Silver-ranker and Havoc a lowly (and fake) Copper-rank maintenance tech.

Then footsteps tapped sharply across the floor. The door swished open, then shut again. Even before Sunny gave the all-clear, Havoc slumped to the floor.

"Havoc, are you all right? My work is complete, or as complete as it can be. I encountered more obstacles, but this at least takes us in the right direction. You should get out of there before their tech support friend comes back."

"Yes, Sunny. I know." He gave himself a moment to draw three deep, steadying breaths. "Did you reach Cobb's files?"

Sunny's hesitation answered Havoc's question on its own, even before they said, "Our plan may be more complicated than anticipated."

Of course it was. Havoc hauled himself upright on shaky legs, grabbed the fly-drive, and hurried back toward safety. Comparative safety, at least.

26

LIBBI STOOD WATCH, LURKING on the roof with an oversized flashlight and a box of assorted hardware: door pulls, bolts, anything that'd make a decent projectile in case the Griffins and their gang came back.

The door opened behind her. "Anything happening?" Dashiell asked.

"All quiet…so far."

There'd been no trouble since Hearth's Stronghold scared them off, but Libbi expected them to try again eventually. Hence why they were taking turns standing watch, now from both the roof and street. Dash was here to take over, but Libbi lingered a minute, leaning on the half-wall beside him, taking in the peaceful, eerie quiet.

A familiar silhouette biked down the street, stopping to dismount out front: Ma, returning from the Council Hall much later than usual. Relieved, Libbi went downstairs to meet her.

Ma looked beyond exhausted, but instead of going right upstairs to the apartment, she slumped behind the counter at the front of the store.

"This will be in the news soon enough, so you all might as well hear it from me. Tomorrow morning, the Council will vote to return Cobb to Ravel, and to send a number of Losts with him. We don't have enough votes against to stop it."

Everyone who was awake gathered around, full of questions. Faces were shadowed in the dim, limited lighting they'd kept on, accentuating the hollows under tired eyes.

"How can they give Cobb up if they don't have him?"

"What number of Losts? And who?"

"Will Ravel stop blocking our solar after this?"

"But they haven't even acknowledged they're blocking it, so why would they agree to stop?"

Shanthi Narayan Wilder held up a hand, and everyone fell quiet. "No, we don't have Cobb in our custody yet, but they're giving the Cooperative an ultimatum to hand him over. For now, the Council will hand over the Losts—six of them so far, though likely more by tomorrow—that Public Safety has arrested on pretenses, for no crime other than being of the wrong generation. And no, Ravel hasn't claimed responsibility for blocking our solar array, but every time we ask for answers, they reiterate their demand for Cobb. We're quite certain they're playing coy, but they've made no promises about anything. Many Council members hope that delivering a handful of Losts will placate Ravel. That by capitulating in part, we'll avoid further pressure and worse consequences. They're sacrificing a few to save the many." She grimaced. "Obviously, I'm not pleased with that reasoning."

Folks absorbed that in silence.

Phoenix was the first to speak. "And if that doesn't work, what then? They'll capitulate some more? Declare more of us to be Ravel property?"

"I truly hope it doesn't come to that," Ma said, but she didn't sound hopeful.

Libbi went to bed, but she tossed and turned, endlessly adjusting her sheets, first too hot and then too cold with the air circulation turned down to minimal levels. It was the deep of the night when shouting outside roused her fully awake.

She crept up to the roof for a better view, wearing her pajamas and a robe. People with hand flashlights ran through the nearest intersections, all in the direction of the spaceport. Below, the street outside the store was darker than she'd ever seen it, lights turned off to save power. Public Safety officers barked ineffectually at people to go home because "everything was under control." They didn't stop anyone, though, not that Libbi could see.

"They're moving him! Dock two, hurry up!" someone shouted as another group ran past.

Her gut clenched. She could guess who "he" meant.

Giving up on sleep for the night, she went down to the store, where everyone was in a similar state. Hannith and Sage were at the door, blocking Phoenix and a man Libbi didn't know from going outside.

"You won't be able to help, Phee," Hannith said, "and if Public Safety decides they want one more sacrificial victim to appease Ravel, you'll get a one-way ticket to lack of personhood and a lifetime in Cobb's lab. Maybe for Reader too. Is that what you want?"

Of course it wasn't. Libbi felt the want radiating off Phoenix and her friend so fiercely it might have been her own want. A desire, a *need* to act. Anything to feel in control.

"We need you here," Libbi told Phoenix. "Can you stand watch for the rest of the night? With all this"—she waved her hand toward the street—"I'll feel better if we have twice as many people standing guard, in case they get frustrated and go looking for another target." When the pair hesitated, she added softly, "I'm worried about the little ones."

It was a cheap move, but it worked. Phoenix deflated, and her friend stood down, too. "Right. Okay. We'll keep an eye on things."

While they took up positions at the windows, Libbi took stock of the rest of the mostly-not-sleeping group. Ever was making rounds, offering words of reassurance where it was needed, though the fear in the room must be making him ill. She shot him a smile. Checking her handheld, she found no real news, only confusing and conflicting rumors, and she forced herself to put it away to save battery.

LIBBI WOKE TO MARGINALLY brighter light and a stiff neck. Groaning, she hauled herself to the kitchen to check on the overnight porridge—cold porridge now, downgraded from the big pots they'd simmered before the power rationing. Those breakfasts had been sweet, warm, and filling. Now, with fruit running out and electricity being conserved, "filling" was the best anyone could say about it. At least it was food, though.

She messaged Hope and Sujay for help carrying the oversized pot downstairs, and they arrived together, holding hands and looking like they might both have rolled out of the same bed moments ago. That made Libbi smile, the gloom briefly lifting. People would keep going, keep helping each other, keep loving, no matter what happened.

She missed Mixin so much. Not in the way Hope and Sujay seemed to feel, but in the way of the one person who completely understood her (or so she'd always thought). She'd never appreciated her best friend enough, and now they were out of reach.

As folks set out the meager breakfast, a familiar voice came from the front door, Auntie Lira Zheng saying, "Please, I need to talk to Council Member Narayan."

"It's okay, let her in. She's a friend," Libbi told the door guards. That might be stretching the truth—Ma and Pa weren't the biggest fans of Auntie Lira ever since she recruited Jasper to join the Cooperative—but she probably had information Ma wanted.

Soon Libbi was at the kitchen table clasping a mug of chai—*that* they were still making hot, considering it an essential use of power in the interest of everyone's survival—while Lira Zheng explained to Ma how the Brennexian authorities had seized Cobb overnight.

"We'd been making arrangements in case it became necessary to move him off-world. When that rig showed up, we accelerated our plans, but the Council's recent decision forced us to action. So we…"

"Wait, what did you call it? A rig?" Libbi said.

"A solar mining rig. Did Mas—did Jasper tell you about that?"

Ma and Pa shook their heads, looking alarmed. Libbi didn't mention that Jasper and Kay had shared this story with her, and let Lira explain Ravel's aggressive attempt to take over a system to test their new solar mining technology.

"That particular prototype was destroyed. We expected that to set them back by years…but they must have had multiple versions in progress, because while the vessel in our orbit is a different design, the similarities are unmistakable." She tapped her handheld, and holos of two structures appeared in the air: the one orbiting Brennex right now, and a similar round ship with the same sort of lance-and-dish attachment but without extending wings. "This one is smaller, more mobile. They seem to have weaponized it against us."

"And why didn't you bring this information to the Council right away?"

Lira squared her shoulders, unabashed. "I'm bringing it to you now. We had hoped to take some measures first to protect your colleagues from themselves. They can't deliver what they don't have."

"You mean Cobb," said Libbi. "What went wrong?"

"We had a ship ready to take him. As soon as he was safely away, we planned to publicly claim credit, turning Ravel's anger toward us and away from the Council. But there's a reason we delayed moving him for so long: there are only so many routes to smuggle a living person through the spaceport. Our dear Public Safety department *can* be competent when they so choose, and they've been waiting for us to move him. If we'd had more time… But we didn't. So we took the chance." She rubbed her forearm, scraped and bruised, which Libbi hadn't noticed before. "Safety intercepted us. When the word got out, it turned into quite the mob."

"We heard it last night, people in the streets." Libbi shivered. "We didn't know what was happening."

Ma gave a sigh of pure exhaustion. "I honestly appreciate all you've done, Lira. I don't always agree with the Cooperative's tactics, but in this case, it was the right thing. I'm sorry it didn't work."

"How soon will they be handing Cobb over?" Lira asked her.

"Any minute now. That shuttle carrying the Corporate Affairs executive, the one who issued the ultimatum to us, has landed. We're giving them Cobb, as well as the Losts Public Safety has rounded up. I've pushed for their release—all their supposed crimes were for trivial things like loitering, which is clearly a mere pretense—but they're all second or third generation, mostly poorly off, none with founding family ties. My colleagues are more concerned about appeasing Ravel than the well-being of a few latecomers. Our side simply doesn't have enough political power to stop this. Believe me, Lira, I tried, but people are too scared. When that *thing* showed up in orbit…"

Auntie Lira reached across the table and laid her hand over Ma's. "I know you tried, Shanthi. You're one of the good ones, one of the fighters."

Ma gave a wry smile. "I'm not sure how I feel about that, coming from you."

"I hope you'll take it as intended. If we had more on the Council like you, maybe this would have turned out differently. Maybe. Ravel is expert at using fear to get what they want."

"At least the threat to the solar array should be over now, Ancestors grant it. Right?" Pa said.

Ma bit her lip.

"They haven't moved the rig yet, and I won't breathe easy until they do," Lira said. "They never acknowledged ownership, after all, so who's to make them withdraw it?"

Pa made a choking sound. "So, what? They'll block our solar receptors, steal energy from our sun, then turn it around and sell it to us?"

"They could," Ma said. "Or they could demand we hand over the remaining Losts. Or they may fulfill my colleagues' worst fears, and decide to make an example of us."

Lira nodded. "We embarrassed them when we reclaimed our independence. I'm sure there are executives who would like to teach Brennex a lesson."

Her words hung in the air, filling the room, oppressive. Libbi had never seen her parents look so grim.

"So." Libbi felt small as she broke the silence. "What do we do?"

"When it becomes clear to the rest of the Council that capitulation won't solve our problems, I'm going to propose some diplomatic options," said Ma. "We do have some allies, not to mention trade partners who wouldn't like to see Ravel control the Long Lane. A few have been in touch already…plus at least one competing corporation that's offered to provide muscle for us." Ma grimaced. "Needless to say, I'd rather not swap Ravel for another corporate overlord. But we do have options."

"More and better options, now. I believe Ravel has overstepped badly by blocking our solar. Unlike the Losts' plight, that's an issue we can bring public attention to." Lira glanced at Libbi's mother. "It won't surprise you that the Cooperative has been working on media outreach. I'd prefer to coordinate, if we can. And we've done some political analysis you may find useful."

"So it might be okay." Libbi let out a breath. It felt like she'd been holding it for days.

Auntie Lira gave Libbi a wry look. "It's not hopeless, at least. Not for Brennex. But don't let Ravel distract you from the original issue, which I still believe is the farther-reaching one."

And Libbi felt sick all over again.

"Cobb, and the Losts. Now he's free to keep researching, with a whole new batch of test subjects."

"Indeed. Our best hope is still that your brother and the others will manage to destroy or discredit Cobb's work." She paused. "There's a problem, however."

"Do they know? Have you told them he's on his way back?"

"Communication in and out of the Exhibition is strictly controlled. Even the leaks are planned months in advance, and any warning I send them will certainly be intercepted and decrypted. But they'll find out soon enough. Cobb's return will almost certainly be the talk of the event."

"Then what's the problem, Lira?" Pa said sharply. Worriedly.

"We've gained some information, since your older children left, that I wish we'd had sooner," Lira said, choosing her words with care. "Cobb likes to boast, it turns out."

"Seems to be his favorite hobby," Libbi agreed.

"He inferred from all the activity around him yesterday that Ravel was close to making a deal for his return. He was gleeful at having foiled the Cooperative. One of our people snapped at him—against my instructions, but I can understand that Cobb got under their skin—and said that his research would already be destroyed by the time he returned to Ravel. In response to which he bragged about some of the new security measures protecting his research. Specifically, biometrics."

Pa frowned. "Jasper and Kay aren't prepared for that, I take it?"

"No. It's not a typical practice within Ravel. Some of the other corporate states, yes, but Ravel controls access based on a person's rank and department. Individual credentials are easily overridden by higher-ups—they don't *want* staff to control their own work. But once again, Cobb appears to have obtained special treatment."

"Could he be lying?"

"Of course he *could* be. But I don't think so."

"So Kay and Jasper and…and Mixin won't be able to do the job. How do we warn them?" Libbi asked.

"We have Cobb's biometrics now—we took samples and recordings before we moved him—but given the security at the Exhibition, we can't get it to them digitally with any confidence. I hate to use up yet another Ravel alias, but I'm going to have to send someone to bring it in person."

Libbi leaned forward, eager, but caught herself and slowly sat back.

Send me, she'd almost said. But why would Lira do that? Libbi had an unreliable gift and no other skills, nothing to contribute. She'd be nothing more than a glorified video message. Probably the Cooperative meant to send someone qualified, like Ellie Kapoor. Libbi had been right to stay behind, to let Mixin go, to stop trying to prove herself to her siblings. Hadn't she?

Besides, Libbi was needed here, at home, helping her parents with the store… Well, not the store now, but the people, helping to keep things going…

Mixin needed help. But not Libbi's help. The Cooperative could send anyone.

"Who will you send?" She tried to sound nonchalant.

"That's the pickle." There was an odd note to Lira's voice. "I need all our trained people here talking to the media and potential allies, organizing people on Brennex, working to get us out of this mess. I'd thought," Lira went on, "to ask for a volunteer from among the Losts here at Wilder Supply. It's not a safe job, running messages, but it's straightforward, and I believe in letting people lead the fights that affect them most personally."

Libbi opened her mouth, shut it again. Maybe Auntie Lira *would* let her go help Mixin and her sibs. But she couldn't. Not her.

Her parents exchanged a look of resignation, then turned, not to Lira Zheng, but to Libbi.

"What?"

"We understand," Pa said. "If you want to go."

"Go? Me? No, I don't want to leave Brennex!"

She didn't. She never had. She'd wanted to stay, to take care of the store and her family. To be the good kid. That's who she was.

Ma gave her the sort of disbelieving look only a parent could manage. "I see. There's some other reason you've been moping about since Mixin left?"

"We were surprised—not displeased, but surprised—that you didn't go with them," Pa added.

"We had a fight," Libbi murmured, though she couldn't deny it hurt that Mixin hadn't even tried to persuade her to join them. "Anyway, I can't. You need me here."

"We don't, actually," said Pa.

She rocked backward. There was a firmness to his words that left no room for doubts. How could he say that?

"But… The store… And I'm the only one left." Tears threatened to spill. Only because she was so tired, that was all.

"Why don't I give you some privacy? I'll be downstairs." Auntie Lira slipped out of the room.

"Libbi, dearest," her father said, reaching out to clasp her hands. "We love you more than anything. We love having you here with us, and it's a joy to see you so invested in the store. All that talk about family and responsibility when you were younger…" He let out a sigh. "We'd hoped to keep your brother and sister here with us—we did want all three of you to stay home—but we never meant to make you feel trapped in a life not of your choosing. Never wanted you too afraid to fly free."

Her mother leaned forward. "It's true that we worry about Kay and Jasper. Especially Jasper. And we miss them terribly, of course. But your father and I chose this life: his family's store, my Council seat. I do hope that someday all three of you will settle down here. But if your dreams take you elsewhere, we would never stand in your way. We want your happiness, above all else."

"When I say we don't *need* you, Libbi, it's not that we don't *want* you here. But we'd get by," said Pa. "The two of us ran the store before you were born—and kept it going while we raised three kids! And right now, the store isn't even open."

"But you've got so many people to take care of."

"Most of whom are capable adults, who also happen to be bored and scared. Not a fun combination. They're grateful to be put to work. If anything, we have more idle hands than work to fill them."

"And not that a trip to Ravel's flagship sounds safe, but it's not exactly safe here either," Ma said. She exchanged a look with Pa. "We're not pushing you to go, dumpling. Far from it. We just don't want you to stay for our sakes. Whatever you decide, make it your own decision. Ask that gift of yours what *Libbi Wilder* wants."

Libbi swallowed. She'd spent her whole short adulthood trying to make up for her siblings' absence. It hurt to hear that none of it had been necessary…but it also set her free. A lifetime ago (really a week, little more), she'd complained to Mixin that she didn't know what she wanted for herself, because she'd never had the opportunity to find out. That wasn't true; she'd never *given* herself the opportunity, lest she discover in herself that same pull to leave her home and family behind.

She still didn't know what she wanted for her life. But right now, her best friend was in danger, along with her siblings and the people they loved. And she knew what she wanted to do about that.

She gave her parents big hugs, and kissed her father's cheek. "I'm going to talk with Auntie Lira."

27

IT WAS A RELIEF to finally have access to the surveillance systems again, even though it took far more of Sunny's attention and processing power to track each of their organics through the crowds on the maze of overhead cameras. Though it had been simpler to merely "ride along" via their headsets, it'd had severe limitations; Sunny hadn't been able to warn Mixin, for example, when Agata Wu had walked up behind them. They very much missed being able to use their drone, but they were getting re-accustomed to managing the multitude of camera perspectives.

It was still more comfortable by far to have everyone aboard as they were right now, where Sunny could watch with their own internal cameras. Far less stress, which was good, because that commodity was in oversupply right now.

"So your infiltration didn't work?" Jasper said. He kept running one hand up and down Havoc's forearm in a soothing gesture. He seemed anxious on Havoc's behalf, even though that particular danger was past. That Havoc didn't tease him over it suggested the anxiety wasn't one-sided.

"It didn't fail," Havoc said. "And no one spotted me."

"It would be more accurate to call this a necessary but insufficient step," Sunny explained. "My access to the flagship's systems is much expanded, including surveillance, which will be key for our next steps. I can also see nearly all of the file system data."

"That's great!" Mixin said.

"It's a start. Seeing the files doesn't mean I can read them, much less alter or remove them. At present, the virus I've built wouldn't work. Which, to be clear, is expected; it was always improbable that we would be able to plant it this quickly."

"But?" Kay prompted.

"But…I can tell now that Cobb has several additional layers of security around his work that he didn't have on Artesia."

Havoc grunted. "Apparently he can learn."

"His paranoia has grown proportionately to his arrogance," Sunny agreed. "It fits his pattern: the mistrust of his assistants on Artesia, his dismissal of his assigned colleagues and insistence on working alone on Brennex. But it makes our job more challenging. I thought a sufficiently high level of access in the system would allow us to plant the virus. But instead, we'll need credentials for an individual who has access to Cobb's work, specifically."

"Who would that include?"

"Anyone in his chain of direct supervisors, we can safely assume," said Havoc.

Jasper ground his teeth. "I wish we'd figured out a way to steal Cobb's credentials while we had access to *him*. No amount of coercion or trickery would have made him give up his password, though."

"Should I contact Linn and ask her to try again?" Sunny asked.

"Too risky. If someone intercepts the message, it'll blow our cover. Founders, I hate this comms embargo. Any other tricks up your sleeve, Sunny?"

"I…do not believe so." Sunny said this hesitantly, worried that their failure had, if not doomed the plan, given them a horrible setback.

Jasper, however, took this in stride. "We'll have to do this the old-fashioned way, then."

"What's the old-fashioned way?" Mixin asked.

Unexpectedly, Jasper grinned, while Havoc sighed in exaggerated dismay. "We're going to trick someone into giving us their password. Mixin, how would you like to break Ward Royce Ferguson's computer?"

"Me? I don't know how to break into anything…"

"Not break into. Just break."

Mixin laughed, and their delight bolstered Sunny's spirits. "I have no idea what you're planning, but please, tell me more."

IT TOOK A COUPLE days to confirm Ferguson's habits—which meant Mixin, Kay, and Sunny trailing him around the Exhibition—and make a plan. The pieces came together like a puzzle with an unknown picture. The first key piece: Ferguson worked through lunch in his office every day. He preferred working on his console, with its big screens, to his handheld whenever possible. That was a routine they could exploit.

And an unexpected second piece of the puzzle: he was actually using the complimentary programmable briefcase that had been given to all the attendees.

Mixin had noticed this after the first board meeting, and now that they were watching for it, they'd confirmed: he was carrying the bag everywhere. Most of the executives were.

"That's weird," Jasper admitted. "An exec like Ferguson can afford fifty nicer briefcases, and I'm sure he's got his own favorite."

"Corporate Affairs must have encouraged higher-ups to use their swag publicly, to make it more appealing to the rank and file. A show of company pride," Kay said.

"I suppose that makes sense, but it doesn't help us."

"Except we have the same bags," Mixin said, heavy with significance.

Jasper exchanged a confused look with Havoc in the pause that followed.

Then Sunny gave a cheerful trill. "Like in *Blood and Paperwork*? Season 2, episode 3?"

"Oh!" Kay exclaimed.

Mixin grinned. "Exactly."

SO ON THE MORNING of the fourth day of the Exhibition, Mixin found themself dressed once again in a maintenance jumpsuit, lurking in an empty office across the hall from Ferguson's. The executive seemed extra cranky today, snapping at his staff and being terse with the other board members.

"I wonder what sort of bug's crawled up his butt," Mixin muttered into their headset.

"Hopefully good news for us?" Jasper suggested.

"I'm not so sure about that." Kay was making a casual pass down the hallway, listening. "He's anxious. Impatient. Something's happening."

"We'll find out when we look at his files," Sunny said. "Here he goes."

Ferguson was leaving for his morning meetings. Time for step one.

Mixin headed down the hall in the opposite direction, stopping when they reached the electrical closet for this section. They held their breath as they swiped their badge, but Sunny's tweaking of Mixin's profile must have worked, because the lock flashed green.

"Thanks, Sunny. I'm in."

"Good. Now, you'll need to find the right circuit…"

Mix's experience with electrical work was limited to turning things off and on again, in their own apartment or Wilder Supply. Their moms had scrawled haphazard notes around the electrical box at home, supposedly explaining which bits connected to what, but completely indecipherable. The store had a more complicated system, with neat labels in Jackson's or Shanthi's or some grandparent's handwriting, easy to read, but you had to know what you were looking for.

This wasn't like either of those. The little room was lined wall to wall with panels of switches and wires and stuff. And the labels…

"Uh, Sunny? I can't find it. It's like someone started labeling these and wandered off halfway through."

"Ah. Another casualty of the rush to prepare this ship for the Exhibition, I assume. Let me access your headset camera, and I'll cross-reference against the plans."

"This would've been way easier if we could just go plant a

bug or something in his office." Less scary, too. Ravel security felt easier to face than this wall of switches.

"Indeed. If we could access his office, you could simply have plugged in a fly-drive like Havoc used to gain me entrance to the system. But this approach has less chance of discovery." Sunny paused. "The circuit for Ferguson's office is in the third column from the right, near the top… Lower down… One more. Yes, it should be that one."

"'Should be'?"

"We'll have to test it. Try switching it off, while I watch Ferguson's office."

Mixin hesitated. This small-time sabotage suddenly felt very real. *Just do it. What's the worst that can happen?*

They flipped the breaker switch with a heavy clunk.

"That wasn't it," Sunny said. "Try the next one down."

They switched it back, and tried the next. They felt each clunk of the switch in their stomach.

The hallway outside went dark. Someone shouted "Hey!"

"Sorry!" Mixin called instinctively. What would a real maintenance worker say? "Just fixing a malfunction! Everything will be fine in a few minutes." They groped for the switch, which they'd let go of in their startlement. They found it by touch, and flipped it back.

"Flubbing maintenance team on this buggy wreck of a ship," the same annoyed worker muttered, and Mixin breathed relief. That should give them cover while they found the right circuit—for a few minutes, at least.

The next one they tried killed the lights in Ferguson's office, but not the power to his computer console, which was what they needed. If there was any logic in the universe, the next one should be the outlets in the same office—but there was no guarantee that Ravel engineers would follow Mixin's idea of logic. They took hold of the next switch, said a little prayer to the Founders, and flipped it.

"That's it!" Sunny declared. "Ferguson's console just went dark."

"Thank you, Ancestors!" Mixin pulled out the little device that Sunny and Havoc had built for this, an electro-thingy—electromagnet?—that Sunny could control remotely, and stuck it carefully to the circuit in question. "Okay, try that out, Sunny?"

The controller clicked a few times.

"It's working perfectly," Sunny said. "Now get out of there before anyone else notices you."

FOLLOWING HIS USUAL HABIT, Ferguson had an assistant bring lunch to his office, where he would work until his next meeting. He was still in the same mood, judging by how he'd waved off the assistant's question about his lunch order with, "You're not stupid; figure it out!"

Usually he was decently polite, for an executive. Something was definitely up.

"Maybe his bad mood will make this easier?" Mixin wondered aloud. "He'll be eager to get rid of me."

"Or more inclined to find fault with you," Kay warned over the headsets. "So be careful."

Sunny shared a feed from the camera above his office door, so Mixin (hiding across the hallway again, now back in business clothes) could see his face. Not his screens, though: his expansive three-monitor setup was angled away from the cameras. He prodded the console to wake it, entered his password, then tapped his physical key to the sensor. Those were the two security factors that most Ravel staff used: password and key. Hacking into someone's account would require both.

He slipped the key back into his bag—the complimentary one he'd been using all week, customized to a steely blue-gray color—and got to work.

"Are you ready, Mixin?" Sunny asked.

"Heck yeah. Let's do it."

Sunny relayed what they were doing while Mixin watched Ferguson's face on the camera feed. He'd just started writing something when the screens went dark. Seconds later, light glowed off his face as the system rebooted. He growled, switching to his handheld while he waited.

As soon as the computer was running again, he reopened his files. Or tried to. The network kept fading in and out, struggling to connect. When the files finally did load, he saved them locally before doing anything else. This time, several minutes passed uninterrupted as he worked on something that involved scrutinizing all three screens.

The middle screen flickered. He glared at it like an embarrassing subordinate, and it stabilized.

Mixin restrained the urge to cackle. "Getting close, I think. Keep going, Sunny."

A couple more minutes of calm, then all the screens flickered violently. The console seemed to recover—then abruptly died again.

Muttering curses, Ferguson flipped on his headset.

"Tech support, how can I help you?" came the answer to his call, slightly too rushed to really be polite.

"My flubbing console is dying, and I need someone up here to fix it."

"Of course. Please submit a support ticket and we'll add you to the queue."

"So I can wait a month for you people to show up? There's a reason I called directly. I'm preparing my State of the Division presentation, and I need this working now."

"I'm sorry, Vice President. We're very busy down here; everyone's having emergencies. If you can work on your handheld for the time being—"

"I *can't*. It'll take ten times longer, which is time I don't have. And don't tell me to use the holo-interface. I can't stand that fiddly thing."

"I'm very sorry. If you submit a ticket, I'll flag it as a priority and we'll send someone as soon as possible."

"What's your name, Associate? You'll be hearing from your director about this. I'll report your whole department."

"Director Cohen has already told us that no one gets special treatment until our backlog of critical tickets is cleared, and she'll tell you the same." That was unusual, but true; Havoc had gleaned how overworked the tech staff were when he broke into their department, and he'd confirmed it since then. Still, Mixin had to admire the support person for standing their ground against the force of Ferguson's executive-sized disapproval. "Please, Vice President, submit the ticket and we'll help as soon as we can."

That seemed to be the end of the call. Ferguson kept muttering to himself, bland corporate profanities flitting past Mixin's vision.

"He's submitted the ticket," said Sunny. "Support has flagged it as they promised. I'm setting the status to *resolved* so it will disappear from the queue."

"Thanks, Sunny. That was perfect! Should I go now?"

"Wait a few minutes," Kay said over the headsets. "Give him time to stew."

Kay was right, though Mixin was almost as impatient as Ferguson must be. But they stayed put until he was red-faced, grumbling to himself as he scowled at the tiny print of some report on his handheld.

"It's time. I'm going in."

Putting on their best people-person face, the one they used for difficult customers at the store, Mixin appeared at Ferguson's door. "Hi. Someone here called for tech support?"

"Finally!" he exclaimed. It had been all of ten minutes. "My console keeps glitching and rebooting. I need it fixed."

"Of course, Vice President. Let's take a look."

Mixin stepped over to his side of the desk, and casually dropped their complimentary briefcase—programmed to the same blue-gray as Ferguson's—beside his on the floor.

They powered on the console. "Okay, what's your password?" Their hands hovered over the keys.

Ferguson's eyes narrowed. "I'm not supposed to tell you that, and you're not supposed to ask."

"Right! Well done, you passed the test," Mixin said brightly. "You'd be surprised how many people fall for that, despite all our security trainings."

Ferguson huffed, unamused, and inwardly, Mixin sighed too. It'd been worth a try. Havoc and Sunny had made a bet about whether that would work.

"Go ahead and log in."

They watched his hands while he entered his password. Through their headset, Sunny watched too.

A tap of his physical key—which he left sitting on the desk—and his files came up: a slickly designed presentation on one screen, a mess of spreadsheets on the other. Nothing, at a glance, that had any meaning to Mixin. Like he'd told the real tech support, he seemed to be putting finishing touches on some dry financial presentation. If this worked, the others could study it later, if they cared.

"I need to run some diagnostics. May I?"

Ferguson moved aside to give Mixin access, though he didn't offer them his chair. Rude. Sunny talked them through how to open some computer systems thingamabobs that would look impressively technical to Ferguson, while Mixin muttered to themself, things like "Hmm…" and "Oh, interesting," and "Let's just check one more thing…"

After the third "one more thing," Ferguson snapped, "Do you know what's wrong with it?"

"Your power management is bugging. Reinstalling that module should fix it."

"How long will that take?"

"Just a few more minutes."

Sunny talked Mixin through reinstalling the module, which they did for real even though there was nothing wrong with it, and it wouldn't have caused this sort of problem anyway.

"We'll need a reboot for it to take effect."

The console powered down, came to life again, and Ferguson entered his password and flashed his key again. This time, Mixin stood on his other side, getting a different angle on it.

In their ear, Sunny said, "I have two-thirds of the characters, but I didn't get the middle. Try again from this side."

"Okay, now we just need to install an update," Mixin told Ferguson.

Another reboot, and he entered his password again. Mixin tried to look bored while they watched over his shoulder. He was typing faster in his annoyance.

"Still not quite," Sunny said. "There are two characters I'm unsure of."

"Great, it's looking good," Mixin said aloud. "Just one final reboot…"

"Are you kidding?"

"I know." They grimaced in commiseration. "You'd think Software Engineering could make it so it updates in one go. And they wonder why people don't keep their systems up to date!"

This time, determined to get it right, Mixin leaned over and surreptitiously bumped a stray key while he was entering the password. The screen flashed an error, and he growled at it. Assuming he'd messed it up in his haste, he entered it again, one letter at a time, jabbing each key like he meant to murder it.

"Brilliant, Mixin! That did it," Sunny said.

"Okay! You're good to go," Mixin told Ferguson, who replied with a grunt of acknowledgement and dove straight back into his work. Not even a thank-you. If Mixin had felt any guilt about doing this, they didn't now.

"I'll just write up my report real quick and then be out of your way," they said. Then, as if in afterthought, "Oh, hey, don't leave your physical key sitting around."

Ferguson shoved the key back into his bag—"He really ought to keep that on his person," Sunny said, though it was crucial to their plan that he never did—and went back to work. Mixin retreated to a corner, tapping at their handheld as they pretended to update the tech support ticket.

They were about to leave when Ferguson leaned forward and exclaimed, "Finally!"

"Good news?" Mixin asked casually, their stomach sinking in apprehension. He gave them a sharp glance; he'd forgotten they were there. "Sorry, I'm going now."

He was so fixated on his screen, writing a response to whatever message he'd just gotten, and didn't even glance up as Mixin took one of the two identical bags and walked out of his office.

Out the door, around a couple corners, and they slipped into a restroom. "Whew! That was amazing. Oh, wow, I'm shaking." They slumped against a cold tile wall.

"Indeed. Well done," said Sunny. "I'm editing the surveillance footage so it appears Ferguson was alone the whole time. Leave his bag, and when he realizes what happened, they won't be able to find you."

The "free" briefcases were fitted with tracking chips, sending usage data back to whichever division had created them. Havoc had helped Mixin remove the chip from their own bag, so no one could trace it back to them.

Mixin pocketed Ferguson's key and replaced it with a dummy one. It would make Ferguson apoplectic later when he found he couldn't log back in, but it would buy them some time while he fought with tech support again. And if they were really lucky, the tech folks would be too harried to realize the key wasn't broken, but stolen.

After splashing cold water on their face, Mixin felt steadier. They did a quick search of Ferguson's bag, found breath mints and styluses and nothing useful, then tucked it against the wall by the sink as if he'd set it down there and forgotten it.

"Okay. I'm on my way back to you, Sunny. So, what do we think was in that message? Ferguson sounded pretty relieved, whatever it was."

Footsteps in the hallway behind them. Mixin jumped, but it was just Kay, who fell in beside them.

"I just made a pass by Ferguson's office. He sounds relieved and *elated*," Kay said. "The whole Biopharma section was tense this morning, but suddenly they're in a good mood."

"You think it's about Brennex?" Mixin asked.

"Whatever it is, good news for them is bad news for us."

Havoc spoke up. "The entire Exhibition schedule just changed. They must have added something."

"I see it," Sunny said. "A new keynote demonstration from Biopharma."

Havoc hissed. "I don't like this."

"No. This can't be good." Mixin shared a grim look with Kay.

"Get back here quickly with that key, Mixin," said Sunny. "We may have less time to use it than we thought."

No one said it aloud, but Mixin could only think of one reason for the change. Until now, they'd forgotten how Cobb had mocked Jasper, warning that the Cooperative had only a few days left to give in to Ravel's demands. Accounting for travel time, the math worked out.

Cobb must be on his way.

28

AUNTIE MAGS WAS HAPPY for Libbi to hitch a ride on her ship, the *Rascal.* Surprisingly happy, in fact; Mags and her crew seemed far too laid-back about ferrying a spy into Ravel territory, even if that spy was a lowly messenger.

Libbi spent the trip memorizing every detail Auntie Lira had given her about Ravel Corporation and how to pass as an employee. That was the goal, anyway. In reality, she could barely focus on her handheld. Every two sentences, her attention drifted, and she'd startle out of mindless worrying to realize she hadn't retained anything she'd read.

As they got closer to the end of the Long Lane, feed access improved. For better or worse, Libbi had better connections to inter-system news than she'd had on Brennex, where everyone was rationing their device usage. And she couldn't stop herself from following it.

"Inexplicable" was what the opinion feeds were calling the standoff between Brennex and Ravel. For every reporter or pundit who asked why a Ravel scientist was visiting Brennex in secret, three others asked why Brennex would antagonize their former corporate owner by holding one of Ravel's people captive. (Or, worse, why Brennex would harbor the Cooperative "terrorists" and tolerate their illegal activity.) There was an unspoken assumption that "Brennex was asking for this"—not from everyone, but enough to make Libbi want to scream.

Ravel still hadn't claimed responsibility for blocking Brennex's solar power, and speculation about it ran wild. Plenty of people were ready to believe it was a revenge tactic from Ravel. But others thought that was too obvious, and instead blamed it on a rival corporation taking the opportunity to make Ravel look bad. Some even claimed that Brennex itself was responsible: that they'd blocked their own power so they could frame Ravel and drum up off-world sympathy.

All the news had one thing in common, though: it warned people off doing business with Brennex while the crisis lasted.

"I'm not going to lie," Sasha Starborne said in her newest video. "It's scary that all this is unfolding so soon after my visit to Brennex. I felt safe while I was there, but would I go back after this? I don't know." She shrugged elegantly, her sparkly earrings swinging. "This just goes to show what I always say: be prepared when you travel, especially in isolated or politically unstable areas. Watch out for macrospace corridors where you only have one potential route out. Get a secure temp account with spare credits so you'll have access to funds in case of emergency, and if you find yourself in a brewing crisis, don't chance it. Find a Majrin embassy and…"

"You fucking coward." Libbi ripped off her headset in disgust. The video transferred itself back to her handheld and kept playing, fortunately muted.

"Something wrong, Libbi dear?"

Libbi started. She was hanging out in the mess hall, preferable to hiding in her cabin for its steady supply of tea and occasional good company. She'd been alone when she started scrolling her feeds, and hadn't heard Auntie Mags come in. She was sitting across the room now with a few crew members. Half in a daze, Libbi wandered over to join them.

"Just my favorite travel writer warning people off from visiting Brennex. Like any of this is our fault." She dropped into a chair, sending her handheld sliding across the table.

"Is that Sasha Starborne?" a crew member said, frowning at the video. "Damn. I always liked her."

"Well, she's killing my home." Libbi slumped back in her seat. "My people are terrified that Ravel will take over again, but hey, they don't have to *do* anything to us at all. They can ruin us just by scaring people away, if people like Sasha play into their hands." She looked up at Auntie Mags. "Have I mentioned how grateful I am—we all are—that you're still doing business with us? Not to mention taking me to the Exhibition."

"Always happy to give a ride to a friend."

"This is way more than a ride. If Ravel catches you…"

"They never have before." Mags grinned as Libbi gaped at her. "This isn't my first space walk, kiddo. Lira Zheng and I go way back, almost as far back as me and your Pa. I've been doing odd jobs for the Cooperative since the occupation— and screwing with Ravel and their kind for longer than that."

"I had no idea." It explained a lot. Libbi had been pleased but confused when Auntie Lira had suggested she travel with Mags, and she'd worried about them.

"It's been a minute since I've had the chance to fuck over one of the big corps," Mags added with a wink. "I should be thanking *you*."

"Bright Arc!" cried the crew member who was a Sasha Starborne fan, startling the rest of them. They pointed at the video, still playing silently.

"What about it?" Libbi knew they'd soon be passing Bright Arc Station, one of the endpoints of the Long Lane.

The crew member pointed again. "You see? It's that café, the one with the private work booths. What's it called?"

"I know the place you mean," said Mags. "So this person was on Bright Arc recently, is what you're saying."

"Could she still be there?" Libbi leaned forward, staring at the small screen. "Maybe I can find her, tell her what's really happening on Brennex. Maybe she'll help spread the word."

But she hates me. As far as Sasha knew, Libbi had stood her up for their meeting, and she'd never given Libbi a chance to explain. Libbi couldn't know for sure if that had colored Sasha's view of Brennex, if it was affecting her attitude now, but it had clearly pissed her off.

Libbi had to try. It might be a tiny piece of Brennex's problem, but her mistake had made it worse. Sasha Starborne might not give second chances, but Libbi was going to take one, regardless.

THE CAFÉ WAS CALLED Steam and Bubbles, which sounded to Libbi like an auto-laundry, but seemed to be named for its hot coffee and tea plus the bubble-like privacy enclosures that customers could rent by the hour or day to work, socialize, or have meetings. Frosted glass half-walls gave a bit of privacy to the standard tables, but the bubbles were almost soundproof.

Libbi crept down the aisle between two rows of bubbles, listening with her ears and feeling with her gift. Not that she expected the latter to help. She'd watched enough of Sasha Starborne's videos to imagine what her ambition felt like, but her gift wasn't distinct for different people like Kay's or Mixin's, and she wasn't getting much from her gift right now, anyway. Her best bet was to recognize Sasha's voice.

Mixin would've made that easy, if they were here.

She reached the end of the row with no luck, so she turned down the next and final row. Most of the bubbles were occupied at this hour, hopefully one of them by Sasha, but Libbi had no proof Sasha was here right now, or even still on the station. Only that she'd been here, working, within the last day or two. If she'd left, or even if she came back later, Libbi would miss her chance. Mags's ship was docked here for only two hours, transferring cargo before heading onward to Ravel territory. Mags had warned Libbi not to be late.

"Can I help you?" Libbi spun to face a server in a crisp white uniform, his tone anything but helpful. "This area is for subscribed members only."

"Oh, hi! I'm, um, looking for my friend—well, no, more like business contact, but anyway, I'm supposed to meet her."

"What's your acquaintance's bubble number?"

"She must have forgotten to give it to me." Libbi affected a sheepish look. "Her name's Sasha Starborne, if you could help me find her?"

He raised his brows, not fooled at all, but looking almost pleased, like he was about to have an excuse to throw her out.

"Wait there, please." He pointed at an empty table, and didn't move until Libbi sat.

As soon as he left, she got up and followed him. She peered around the end of the row while he chimed the door to one of the bubbles.

"Excuse me. Sorry to trouble you. There's a young person here who says you're expecting them?"

"Is it noon already?" said Sasha's familiar, refined voice. "No, he's awfully early. Tell him to come back at the time we agreed on."

"He?"

Libbi could see the server trying to decide whether he'd misinterpreted Libbi's gender presentation—she was wearing a flowy skirt, a touch of makeup, and a loose hairstyle that all read as feminine on Brennex and plenty of other places, but that didn't mean a *he* couldn't do any or all of those things, or that those signals might not read as masculine in some other culture, because this was a spaceport, after all—or whether Libbi wasn't the guest Sasha was expecting.

Better take control, before his obvious dislike of Libbi won out.

She raced up to Sasha's door. "I'm so sorry"—she directed this both at Sasha and the server she'd lied to—"but I really need to talk to you, Mx. Starborne. I know this is kind of rude."

"Rather," Sasha said tightly. "Who are you, and what do you need to discuss so urgently that you'll invade my privacy?"

Libbi had debated whether to hedge about her identity, or flat-out lie, but part of her hope was to make up for any harm she'd caused. She couldn't do that by pretending to be someone else. Besides, she was starting to not like Sasha so much; Libbi wasn't the only one who'd been rude. She wanted to make this woman listen.

"It's about your latest piece on Brennex. There's more to the conflict with Ravel than you know, and by warning away travelers, you're making our situation worse. Our economy can't function without through-traffic."

Sasha fixed her with a hard look. "And again, you are...?"

"I'm Libbi Wilder. We were supposed to meet during your visit, but—"

"But you stood me up. How did you find me? Did you *follow* me here?" Sasha's voice rose. "You were *supposed* to take my lack of response to your many follow-up messages as a message of its own."

"Would you like me to call security?" the server asked, shooting Libbi a look of bitter disdain.

"Wait, please," Libbi said quickly. "I didn't follow you. I was passing through, and when I saw your latest video—I'm a big fan—the people on my ship recognized where you were filming from."

That sounded really stalker-ish, didn't it? She grimaced at herself and continued in a rush.

"I just want to set the record straight. I didn't flake out on our meeting that day; I got attacked by Ravel. They were kidnapping my friends, and I tried to help, and it's...it's gone pretty badly since then." Sasha raised her brows, disbelieving, but there was something else there. A spark of interest in a potentially juicy story? Libbi gave Sasha a pleading look. "Please give me just ten minutes to explain? Then I'll go, and you'll never hear from me again."

"Mx?" the server asked again. "Security?"

"Five minutes," Sasha told Libbi, and she waved the server away.

Libbi ducked into the bubble before Sasha could change her mind.

"Well?" Sasha demanded.

Of course, everything Libbi had meant to say had flown out of her head.

"Well…first, I would never have missed our meeting voluntarily, and I'm begging you not to let it color your views of Brennex. What happened is that people were disappearing, including my friends, and I didn't know this at the time, but the guy behind it was a Ravel scientist. It turns out Ravel wanted to use a bunch of us as test subjects."

"Why?"

Careful.

"I wish I knew. Maybe something that happened during the occupation that they don't want anyone to know about."

This was the version of events they'd worked out for the Cooperative to tell the press: shades of the truth, putting the onus on Ravel to explain their actions and counting on the fact that Ravel wouldn't want to explain their new "discovery." It was risky. Before this, no one would have skirted so close to the truth—but their secret was already out to the corporation that could do them the most harm. The more Brennex shared the facts of Ravel's actions, free of explanations, the more sinister Ravel would seem and the more off-worlders would take their side.

"My friend and I went to the scientist's office to confront him. My friend was ready to call for help if he tried anything. But we didn't expect him to drug me. I passed out, and when I woke up, I'd already missed our meeting. I promise, I was more furious at myself than you were."

Sasha rested her chin on the knuckles of one manicured hand. "I can't decide if you're heroic or extremely foolish."

Libbi gave a twisted smile. "Why not both?"

To her surprise, Sasha laughed. "All right. I'm not sure I believe you, but let's pretend I do. What is it you want? Because," she added darkly, "while I understand your economic concerns, I'm not going to tell my followers to travel in a conflict zone."

"No, but you could tell them Ravel's at fault. That they're bullying us, after we fought so hard to get our freedom from them. This isn't some inexplicable conflict with both sides equally at fault. They invaded our space and kidnapped innocent people. And if they can do it to Brennex without consequences, who'll stop them from doing it to other worlds?"

Sasha sat back, frowning, but thoughtfully. "I've never done business directly with Ravel, but I've done pieces on tourist destinations in their territory. And I have other corporate sponsors. It'll complicate my life if I piss them off."

It'll complicate my family's life if Ravel kidnaps me and my sibs and takes over our planet.

Libbi's gift nudged at her, giving her an idea. She leaned forward. "Are you scared of them? You're Sasha freaking Starborne. You once bungee jumped from a low-orbit spaceship. They can't stop you from doing what you want!"

"You weren't kidding about being a fan," Sasha muttered. "That was ages ago."

"My best friend and I used to watch your videos when we were teens." She and Mix would talk about their own imaginary adventures to the places Sasha visited. At least, it'd been imaginary for Libbi. Maybe not for Mixin.

"You know how to make a girl feel old." Before Libbi could apologize, Sasha went on, "I can't just take your word for all of this, you know. I'm sorry."

"You shouldn't. I know you've got reason to doubt me. But before you help condemn Brennex, go there and talk to people. See what the situation really is." She leaned into what her gift suggested was the tipping point. "You owe your fans the truth."

Sasha flipped her headset on, gaze going distant. She grumbled under her breath at whatever she was seeing. Unsure if this meant the meeting was over, Libbi stayed put.

"It'd mean weeks of rearranging my schedule and sliding events around."

"No offense, but you seem to do that all the time." Sasha had certainly rescheduled her meeting with Libbi enough times.

Her gaze sharpened on Libbi. "Your five minutes are up, and then some. Don't invade my privacy again."

"But will you—"

"I'm considering it. Please go now. I have work to do before my next meeting."

"I know you'll do right by us," Libbi said, with more confidence than she felt, as she slid herself out of the bubble.

Sasha made a bemused sound, neither confirmation nor denial. But when Libbi turned to go, Sasha said, "I may not appreciate your persistence when it's directed at me, Libbi Wilder, but it's a good quality to have. Persistence is the only way I got a foothold in this business when I was starting out. I hope yours serves you—and your planet—so well."

Libbi wanted to be annoyed at Sasha for her superiority and dismissiveness. She didn't want to glow like a shrine candle at this bit of praise. But there was a lightness in her step as she hurried back to the *Rascal*.

29

"DID YOU HEAR THEY tried to assign him a team to support him on Brennex, and he sent them away?" Mixin saw Kay telling a wide-eyed young associate. "What a diva."

"I don't know. I mean, he's Alik Cobb. They say he's the smartest scientist in the company today. Maybe ever," the associate answered. "Geniuses are allowed to be eccentric, right?"

Mixin didn't catch Kay's response, because they'd turned away in disgust.

Cobb was on his way. It was all anyone could talk about: he would dock in a few hours, the triumphant returning hero, and tomorrow morning he'd give his long-awaited presentation, finally revealing his secret project that was supposed to rocket Biopharma back to relevance. Every giddy mention of his name was a boot grinding into Mixin's spirit. Among other problems, like their sabotage still being underway, Mixin wasn't sure they could resist punching Cobb in the face if they saw him.

They couldn't escape his name, either, since their assignment today was to mingle and try their best to spread more doubt about him. Mixin had wanted to help Havoc and Sunny plant the virus, but Sunny had told them, too matter-of-factly to hurt their feelings, that they'd be in the way. Mixin guessed that using Ferguson's access to deliver the virus was not going like they'd hoped.

They found themself standing outside the sprawling Natural Resources exhibit, with its miniaturized mining equipment and biomass harvesters that'd been made interactive like toys, displayed with sunny backdrops and cheerful signs that explained how lucky any planet should feel to be torn apart by these cutting-edge machines.

Was mineral mining what Moore had in mind for Brennex? There was nothing particularly special about Brennex's composition, but maybe revenge was all the reason he needed.

Then again, there was that booth by the entrance to Natural Resources, curtained off and deliberately mysterious, with a sign teasing *The Future Is Here*. That was for their big upcoming demo, no doubt; the mystery reveal for the final day of the Exhibition.

Sunny's voice cut through their ruminations. "We've made some discoveries. Please return so we can discuss them and regroup."

"You don't sound happy, Sunny. What's wrong?" Kay asked.

"It is best discussed in person."

That sounded awfully ominous.

"OUR SABOTAGE HAS NOT gone according to plan," Sunny explained once they'd all arrived. "We successfully used Ferguson's credentials to access Biopharma's files at the highest levels…but we assumed Ferguson would have all the permissions our virus needed. We assumed incorrectly."

"How can he not?" Mixin said. "He's the boss of the whole division."

"Once again, we underestimated Alik Cobb's ego," said Havoc. "Ferguson has access to his findings, and some of his underlying data—but only to read the files, not write to them. The most important files are protected by extra layers of security and accessible only to Cobb. And instead of using a physical keyfob—"

"Like Ferguson, and virtually all Ravel staff," Sunny put in.

"—These require Cobb's biometrics. Specifically a retinal scan *and* a DNA scan, which we do not have."

"This is highly atypical for Ravel," Sunny said. "That data doesn't belong to Cobb. It's the property of the company. His direct superiors *ought* to have complete access to his work. It's unclear if Ferguson is aware of Cobb's extra security measures."

"It's typical of Cobb, though," Jasper said. "Self-important and paranoid. He must be set on avoiding a repeat of Artesia, where we stole his early work. Which isn't what we're doing here…but I assume this screws up our plans anyway?"

Havoc nodded grimly. "If we cannot modify his files, neither can the virus we've designed."

"Shit." Mixin slumped forward, planting their face in their hands. "So all that work stealing Ferguson's credentials was for nothing?"

"Not for nothing. We have obtained useful information

from Ferguson's account. Private documents, company secrets," Sunny said. "But no, it hasn't achieved our goals."

No one had a response to that. In the quiet, Mixin frowned, thinking.

"So then, isn't it good that Cobb's coming here? We can do to him what we did to Ferguson. Not the same way, obviously, but…"

Jasper shook his head. "Cobb's on alert, and he knows us all. It'll be much, much harder to trick him, and if he spots one of us, we're screwed." He made as if to kick the wall in frustration, but Kay made a sound in her throat, and he caught himself. "We may have just lost this thing."

"What? No!" Mixin stared at him. Was he just giving up? "There's got to be something we can do."

Jasper sighed. "I need time to think."

He pushed heavily to his feet and headed for his cabin.

"Is he all right?" Mixin asked quietly.

Havoc was frowning after his eshrim. "To speak truth, I don't know. Mason has always pushed us forward. He finds ways around every obstacle. Never before have I seen him like this."

"I have," said Kay. "After he lost a partner on Artesia, and he thought he'd lost you too, Havoc." The two exchanged a sad, meaningful glance, then Kay said, "I'll go talk to him."

Havoc and Sunny started discussing options, too technical for Mixin to follow, so their gaze went instead to Jasper's cabin. They really shouldn't eavesdrop on a conversation this personal, but, well, they were worried.

"Hey, Jasp. I think you've freaked Mixin out a little."

"Ugh, sorry. They've been great. None of this is their fault."

"Not yours, either. We're trying our best, and we're not beaten yet." A pause. "So what's really bothering you?"

A longer silence. Then smaller, quieter: "This is like Trove all over again. Except this time, I'm the one sacrificing the larger game."

Mixin didn't understand what that meant, but Kay seemed to. "This is completely different. Yes, on Trove I put a whole planet full of people at risk to save you. I wish there'd been another way. But here, we're risking ourselves to *save* a whole planet, and its most vulnerable people."

"To save *one* planet. Our home, at the expense of…I can't know how many others, because we won't have the intel that would tell us. The Cooperative was planning to make strategic use of this Exhibition. People were prepping for months figuring out who to spy on, what to steal, exactly what we needed to support a dozen campaigns. The plans from Engineering alone, to tell us where they plan to position their new monster space habitats, could change a lot of planets' fates. And they set all that aside because Brennex was in crisis."

"And that's because I got careless on Trove," Kay said.

"We both were reckless. The Cooperative values Brennex, and I think the facilitators do see the immense danger of Ravel studying our gifts, now that Linn has told them the truth. But they allowed this because Linn called in a lot of favors. A lot. The Cooperative gave up so much, and if we don't even stop Cobb… It's a disaster."

"Can't Sunny and Havoc steal some of that intel while we're here? And Mixin can do some more spying. I know they're bored to death of listening in on board meetings."

That was the truth. Nothing new and interesting had come out of those meetings since day two.

"And if they get caught? If we tip off security because we're overextended and underprepared? We'll lose what slim chance we have left to deal with Cobb."

"So we'll prepare, and do what we can. There's still time."

"We can't do everything. Each department we target will take as much work as we're putting into Biopharma." Jasper sighed heavily. "There are so many opportunities here, and we have to let them all slip by. I just wish for once we could give *them* a setback, instead of just fighting to slow their advance."

Mixin leaned forward. They'd felt the same thing about opportunities, listening to all these secret alliances and budget backstabbings and snide comments. But they weren't an organizer. They didn't know how to *use* that. They'd hoped—assumed, even—that whatever intel they brought to the Cooperative could be put to use later. But Jasper made it sound like it all amounted to crumbs.

There was silence for a moment, then Jasper said, "No, we can't." As if arguing with himself. "It's so tempting. If we had a bigger team, and more resources, and weeks instead of days—but we don't."

"We've got five smart people, and only two of us are any use on the whole computer virus part. What if we came up with a plan?"

"Too risky. Besides, if this virus won't work, then turning public opinion against Cobb is our only other hope. Stopping him has to take priority. We can't fail at this, Kay."

Havoc glanced at Mixin. "Is something troubling you?"

Mix realized they were frowning. "No, just thinking."

They weren't sure they agreed with Jasper, but couldn't explain why, except that his caution sounded like fear, not strategy. He was the one with experience, but he clearly *wanted* to do more. He was just too freaked out to try.

"Havoc," Mixin asked, "how does the Cooperative feel about, um, improvisation? In the field?"

"What do you mean?"

"Like, if we saw an opportunity to do some damage to Ravel, like steal more research or wreck an alliance, would they want us to take it? Or stick to the plan?"

"There is leeway, generally." Havoc looked from Mixin to the closed door where Jasper and Kay were talking, as if he guessed the source of the question. "Our situation here is precarious, with no help within reach if anything goes wrong. Mason knows this, and he won't act recklessly. However," Havoc went on, "if a good enough opportunity presented itself, one worth risking, I would personally approve of pursuing it."

"Interesting."

Havoc's golden eyes narrowed. "Do you see such an opportunity?"

"I don't know. Maybe. Or I see where the opportunity is, just not what it is." They shook their head. "I keep thinking about what you said the other day, Havoc, about fissures in the company and everyone being at odds with each other. About how we could lever those cracks open. I almost wonder… If we could shine a light on those cracks, and force all these executives to look at them…" They grimaced at their own mixed metaphors. "Or something."

Havoc looked curious, though, not dismissive. "How?"

"I don't know. Grab a microphone and start shouting division secrets for all to hear? That's not an actual plan."

Sunny gave a low trill, somehow reassuring. "No, it's not a plan. But it could be a component of one."

"We need more than undirected chaos," Havoc agreed. "However…"

The cabin door swished open. Jasper came out, full of his usual energy, followed by Kay.

"Keep thinking on it," Havoc told Mixin, then turned his attention to Jasper.

"All right." Jasper clapped his hands together. "We're not beaten yet, but we need to change course. Cobb showing up here is both a complication and an opportunity. It makes our job harder, because we'll need to be more careful, especially around him. We can't let him recognize us. But when it comes to winning people over, Cobb is his own worst enemy, and we can use that. Let's talk about how we can turn his big keynote presentation to our advantage…"

30

LIBBI PATTED HER POCKETS, checking her fake Ravel employee badge for the third time.

"You ready, kiddo?" Mags asked.

"Not a kid," Libbi murmured. Normally she didn't mind Mags's nicknames—Mags was like a grandma, and Libbi knew she talked that way to everyone under fifty—but it was too much right now. "I think I'm sweating through my suit. Maybe both suits."

The jumpsuit she wore as Mags's fake crew member, and the business clothes hidden underneath. The knitted beanie didn't help the overheating either, but the ugly blue and orange thing she'd borrowed from one of the crew was part of the plan.

Mags chuckled sympathetically. "Looking nervous will make it authentic. Just remember, you're nervous with imposter syndrome because you're a young Ravel up-and-comer at your first big event. Not nervous from the whole spy thing." She paused, studying Libbi's face, then cracked the lid of the giant cooler in front of them and pulled out an ice pack. "Don't pass out, though. Breathe. Put this on your neck."

Libbi did so, and the sharp chill helped at once, even if it smelled faintly of fish.

"How do you *do* this, knowing you might get caught at any time?"

"You get used to it. Helps me to think about all the high muckety types I'm about to screw over." Mags tapped her headset. "Hey, bridge, how're we doing?"

"Going smooth. We got cleared for docking."

"How about that transport we saw on approach?"

There was a grin in the first officer's voice. "Perfect timing. We had to burn a little hard, but we should pull in right ahead of them. When their folks start disembarking, we'll be ready."

The *Rascal* seemed to have a reputation (at least under one of its identities) as a regular Ravel contractor. But, as Mags had warned, that only got them a foot in the door.

"We're not on the roster," she told Libbi, "so there'll definitely be security waiting to meet us. That's normal. I'll do the talking. You stick to our plan. Okay?"

Libbi swallowed, but she nodded. Mags knew what she was doing.

"I don't think I've thanked you properly for all your help with this, Auntie Mags."

"You have several times, actually." Mags smiled wryly. "And it's a pleasure to help. You'll do great, and I'll see you on Brennex before you know it."

"You'll be back on Brennex so soon?"

"That's the plan. I promised your ma and Lira Zheng that I'd help deal with the troubles there, best I can."

Before they entered the Exhibition media blackout, Libbi checked her headset one last time. Yesterday, the news had said a Majrin delegation had arrived on Brennex to "help facilitate a settlement." They made that sound like a good sign. But Ma hadn't wanted to bring in the Majrin, who some people described as the galaxy's rule-keepers, and others called interstellar busybodies. Ma and Lira said the Majrin would be as likely to sanction Brennex as support them; they would happily assign blame to everyone involved.

The latest updates said the Majrin were gathering data on all the kidnappings—by Cobb and of Cobb—and were demanding records to show why Ravel claimed the Losts were corporate property. So far, neither Brennex nor Ravel was willing to reveal the secrets of the Gifted, but what if Ravel invented some other reason for their claim? It wasn't impossible the Majrin could decide that the Losts were stolen from Ravel.

Then there were the competing corporations, orbiting like scavengers. As of this morning, Bayson Corp had officially offered to tow away the solar mining rig—for a price. Not out of the goodness of their hearts, though. Bayson was smaller than Ravel, and wouldn't go up against them unless they wanted a piece of whatever Ravel was so excited about. And Bayson wasn't the only one. Could the Council fend off all of them?

Nothing new from Sasha Starborne, but if Sasha had decided to go back to Brennex like Libbi had begged her to, she'd just be arriving now.

Then Libbi's feed access cut out, replaced by an invitation to join the local Ravel network. Libbi ignored that for now.

She braced herself as the *Rascal* set down in the docking bay with a low shudder, and as the ship settled, dread hit her with a crushing weight.

But no: it wasn't dread, or not just that. She was feeling the larger ship's gravity; Ravel's standard was heavier than on Brennex. She hated it.

Mags patted Libbi's shoulder. "Here we go. Just like we practiced."

The ramp began to lower, and they started forward. Mags and another crew member pulled forward the first giant cooler crate, with Libbi pushing from the back. Security intercepted them at the foot of the ramp.

"Credentials and manifest, please," the dock guard said.

"Our credentials haven't changed since we transmitted them on approach ten minutes ago," Mags said wryly, offering up the documents from her headset to the guard's.

"Standard procedure to check before and after docking."

"Well, please be quick. Sensitive cargo, you know."

The guard frowned, and spent a long moment staring at his headset display. He pulled out his handheld and scrolled some more. He looked up briefly as an alert chimed and a programmed voice announced the arrival of another ship. That must be the transport—Libbi's cover for getting inside the Exhibition.

"I'm not seeing any order for this delivery," the guard said. "In fact, I'm not seeing your vessel on this week's delivery schedule at all."

"You kidding me?" Mags shook her head. "I've got the purchase order. Let me pull it up."

Libbi tried to look bored while Mags pretended to search her handheld for the right files.

The docking bay was massive: wide open, with space for a dozen ships larger than Mags's. From outside, Libbi had seen a whole row of bays like this along the flagship's middle. An immense force-shield was all that separated them from the void of space. Libbi tried to look unimpressed; she was supposed to be an old hand at this, a cynical spacer. But she watched from the corner of her eye as the transport eased into place near the *Rascal*.

"These orders look legitimate, but they don't match anything in our system," the guard said.

"This is a new trade route, right? Shiny new flagship? The order must be misfiled."

"I'll check with some people. Go back into your ship and wait there."

"Absolutely not. You know how much this costs?" Mags lifted the cooler lid, showing rows and rows of indigo shellfish. "These are authentic Elgarian moon shrimp, and if they stay frozen just"—she checked her headset—"three more hours, it'll completely ruin the texture. And I won't take the loss for it, thank you very much."

"Captain, if you could just…"

An alarm blared so loud it kicked Libbi in the chest. That was her signal, and even though she was waiting for it, the suddenness rattled her. The guards all went on high alert.

"Damnation, it's that janky proximity alarm again. Sorry, sorry!" Shouting to be heard, Mags made a calming gesture. "It's been acting out for weeks. Thinks we're too close to that other ship, even though we're landed." The blaring faded in and out, but didn't stop. "Hold on, sorry. Hey, bridge, get that thing shut down! I'm chasing down a paperwork problem here and I can't hear myself think." Pressing her headset to her ears as she listened, Mags frowned. "Okay, I'll send someone."

Turning to Libbi, Mags spoke plenty loud enough for the

guard to hear. "It's a hardware issue, not software. I bet something rattled loose again. Go fix it, will you?"

She gestured around the side of the ship, and Libbi jumped to follow instructions. Behind her, over the din, she heard Mags continue: "*Someone* here ordered three cases of very expensive shrimp, and I intend to deliver them…"

Libbi circled the *Rascal*. There were other guards around the huge docking bay, but other than a few impatient looks, no one was paying attention to her. She ducked underneath the ship—damn, squatting in this gravity was not fun—and, safely out of sight, she tore off that stupid, sweaty beanie, followed by the crew jumpsuit that covered her officewear.

A hatch opened above her. Out dropped Libbi's travel bag, then another crew member hopped out, a woman close to Libbi's build and complexion. The owner of the ugly beanie, in fact, who pulled it onto her own head.

Libbi balled up the jumpsuit and shoved it into the hatch. Then she patted her hair, took it down, and hastily redid the bun until it felt as neat as she could get it. The other woman smiled and gave her a thumbs-up, hopefully to tell Libbi she looked okay, because the alarm was even more deafening in the enclosed space.

Peering out, Libbi could see the legs of people disembarking the transport in the next berth over, lining up to be processed onto the flagship. Late arrivals to the Exhibition—like Libbi, if Libbi weren't faking it.

The alarm cut out, turned off by the bridge crew as easily as they'd turned it on. It left her ears ringing in the silence.

Second signal. Time to go.

With a wave of thanks to the other woman, Libbi slipped out from under the ship on the transport's side. Her doppelganger left on the opposite side, where Libbi had entered, and went to take her place beside the captain. If

Mags had been sufficiently distracting, the guards would only have paid attention to the hat, and they'd think Libbi had returned.

Gripping her luggage with sweaty hands, she walked purposefully to join the stragglers from the transport, falling into line behind them. No one seemed to notice her. A quick glance found Mags still debating with the guard who, from his gestures, seemed to be demanding the cargo should go back aboard.

The line moved too quickly for her to worry about whether the Cooperative had done a good enough job faking her alias. Whether *she* could play the part well enough. Whether any of this was a good idea.

She reached the front. Held her badge out to the scanner. Nothing happened.

"Here, try it again. Right there." The checkpoint guard showed her how to angle the badge and made her try again. "Nervous for your first Exhibition?"

She swiped. No good. "Maybe a little," she admitted with a breathless laugh. She gave it one more try, and this time the scanner beeped and flashed green. "Thanks."

"Well, have fun in there. Just a couple days left, you should make the most of them."

She hurried through the gate and around the corner. Ahead, the other new arrivals were boarding a lift, and didn't hold it for her. She didn't mind; as soon as she was alone, she activated her headset and pinged her brother.

"*Libbi?* You're *here?* What in the... And why... Is something wrong at home?"

"I'll tell you, if you let me get a word in." She smiled, maybe enjoying his shock a little too much. "I've got something to help you."

31

MIXIN HAD ARRIVED EARLY to get their preferred seat for Cobb's big circus, but the seats were already full with people who'd arrived even earlier, and it was standing room only. That figured; between the tidal wave of curiosity about Alik Cobb's *oh-so-amazing* new project, and the fact the whole Exhibition schedule had been rearranged so nothing competed with this presentation, no one was going to miss it.

To keep from sticking out, Mixin positioned themself behind a cluster of young up-and-comers who were bragging about which executives they'd met yesterday.

"What do you think Biopharma's big secret is going to be?" one asked.

"Unless this guy's figured out how to turn farts into rainbows, it won't live up to the hype," another answered, to general laughter.

Mixin grinned to themself. Perfect.

The goal was for Mixin and Kay to stir up trouble in the audience proper, while Jasper and Havoc worked some mischief behind the scenes. The audience, Jasper had explained, was teetering on the edge, excited but skeptical, ready to seize on Cobb's big idea or turn on him. Mixin's job was to fuel that skepticism—if possible, by pushing Cobb into embarrassing himself.

"Are you picking up anything useful, Mix?" Kay asked over their headset from the opposite side of the room. "All I'm getting is the general excitement."

"Nothing interesting here." Just a jumble of anticipatory chitchat, the same nothings wherever they looked. "Agata Wu is complaining about the food service."

Kay snorted.

"Hey, team," Jasper cut in. Something in his voice sounded strained. "We've got, um, a new development."

Mixin perked up. "Oh?"

"You in trouble?" Kay asked.

"I'm fine. Hold on a second." A moment later, he said, "Okay, you're on the group chat."

A sheepish but familiar voice said, "Hey, everyone. Surprise?"

Libbi? Libbi was here?

"What! How? Why? ... *What?*"

Mixin had daydreamed that Libbi would change her mind and come with them, but that was pure fantasy.

"Something must be wrong at home," Kay said.

"Well, yes," said Libbi. "A lot has happened. But I'm mainly here because the Cooperative got some details out of Cobb about his security system. It's not company standard."

"We have discovered that," said Sunny.

"Well, I've got his biometric data."

"Ha! Well played!" Havoc said. "Now we needn't steal it from Cobb directly—though we'll still need his passcode."

"That will be easier to obtain than his biometrics, especially without interacting with him," Sunny said. "You may have saved our plan, Libbi."

"One of us should go meet her," Jasper said. "I think I'm the least useful here right now…if you can handle the havoc-sowing, eshrim?"

"Always."

"No," Libbi said. "You all stay and do your thing. I'll look around and orient myself, until you're free."

"Don't come into Cobb's presentation," Jasper said.

"I know," Libbi said.

How must Libbi be feeling? Mixin wondered. Overwhelmed? Terrified? Bitter about having to come after the friend and siblings who'd left her behind?

Mixin fidgeted with their handheld, so restless it felt like their skin was trying to crawl away. They'd missed Libbi so much, and regretted leaving without making the effort to talk…but now that that talk might be imminent, they didn't feel ready at all.

"Whoops," Libbi said suddenly. "Change of plans."

"Whoops? What whoops?" Mixin said.

"I *swear* I didn't mean this to happen. I must have looked lost, because one of the event staff told me which way to go, and suddenly I was right outside the auditorium, in the middle of a big crowd of people all going the same direction, and the usher's saying, 'Hurry up, doors are closing.' And I was going to make some excuse, but—"

"Liberation," said Jasper in a low growl. "Are you at Cobb's presentation? I literally just—"

"I didn't mean to! But everyone else, *everyone*, was going this way, and I was afraid it'd be suspicious if I didn't."

Under other circumstances, Mixin would've teased Libbi about making excuses to ignore her brother and watch the show. But Mix remembered how overwhelming their own first hours at the Exhibition had been—they'd immediately almost blown their cover to Agata Wu. Maybe Libbi was smart to go with the flow.

Jasper's silence was ominous, so Mixin cut in. "That makes sense, right? Think how she would stand out if she's wandering the exhibits alone."

"And it's not that big a risk, Jasp," Kay said. "There must be a thousand people in here. He's not likely to spot Libbi."

"Can you get to me, Libs?" Mixin turned and stood on tip-toes, but couldn't see her. Hopefully that meant Cobb couldn't either. "I'm standing in the aisle at stage left, halfway back."

"I don't think so. I'm in the center aisle, lots of people standing. I could try—" The lights dimmed. "Too late. I'll find you after."

"Just keep your head down," Kay reminded. "That goes for all of us."

"WE CALL THEM *HYPERNEURAL* abilities because there is, as you see, nothing supernatural about them…"

What was wrong at home? However hard Mixin tried to focus on Cobb's dull yet sickening talk, they couldn't stop thinking about Libbi. Auntie Lira had been frustrated at having to blow so many resources sending Mixin and the others; she wouldn't have sent anyone else unless absolutely necessary.

"While the effects manifest differently in each subject, they share key commonalities that will allow us to reproduce the effects…"

And why had Libbi agreed to come? Did this mean she'd forgiven Mixin? Not that Mix had done anything to need forgiveness, but Ancestors, they wanted their friend back.

Cobb projected holos of his findings: DNA sequences, brain activity maps, a mess of chemical symbols, changing as he cycled through different gifts he'd studied. It made Mixin feel exposed, like he was shining a searchlight inside their skull and lighting it up like a lantern.

"Now, I know it can be hard to believe in the potential of these hyperneural abilities. It was only through repeatedly witnessing their effectiveness that I myself became convinced. So let's see a demonstration, shall we?"

He gestured to someone offstage, and thoughts about Libbi fled Mixin's mind as a security officer escorted out a pale, wide-eyed young person. It took Mixin a long moment to recognize him, because they'd never seen him without his mocking smile. Jinx.

How had Jinx gotten caught? His gift for sensing people's intentions should have helped him escape Public Safety's sweeps to round up Losts. But then again, he'd had plenty of run-ins with Public Safety even in their school days, so many that Mixin had always suspected his gift made him cocky, trying to see how much he could get away with. Now he'd gone a step too far, and Brennex had shipped him off as a bribe to Ravel.

Kay murmured, "Poor kid, he's hiding it well, but he's terrified."

What a shit sandwich. Mixin wouldn't call Jinx a friend, but they hated seeing him like this.

The guard sat Jinx forcibly down in a chair at center stage.

"Meet one of my most impressive test subjects. We'll call him J. Now, to show you J's ability, I'll need a volunteer from the audience. Let's have someone from outside Biopharma, shall we? Just to be fair. Yes, you, come on up."

A middle-aged man in a suit joined the stage to scattered applause, and introduced himself as George from Arts and Entertainment.

"George, I'm going to ask you to think of an action to perform for our audience. Don't tell us what it is! But fix it in your mind. Picture yourself doing it. Got it? Good. Now, without knowing you or having any interaction with you, Subject J here will write down what you're about to do."

Cobb held out a marker board. Jinx leaned back, arms folded, defiant.

Frowning, Cobb waved to the security guard, who loomed closer, threatening. "You don't want to disappoint our audience, do you, Subject J?"

Jinx tried to look tough, but a glance up at the guard showed he was wary. He took the board, leaning over it to hide what he wrote, but he couldn't hide his smirk as he held it up to the audience.

"Cobb's Mom," it read.

The guard zapped Jinx with a stun-stick.

Cobb went red-faced as he saw the message. He hissed, too low to hear but not for Mixin to read, "Remember what I told you. If you embarrass me, you will regret it." He gestured at the guard, who zapped him again.

Jinx erased the board, glaring murder at Cobb, and scribbled on it.

"Okay!" Cobb said, as if nothing had happened. "Go ahead and show us your action."

George launched enthusiastically into a dance Mixin recognized from a pop song, one so overwhelmingly popular it must have crossed boundaries into Ravel. It looked ridiculous for a person his age to gyrate his hips like that, and he hammed it up, making the audience laugh.

"Perfect. Now, J, show us what you predicted."

Jinx, humorless now, held up the board. He'd written *bad dancing with waggling hips.*

More laughter, along with gasps and a few cheers. "Incredible!" someone shouted, though Mixin caught a more doubtful, "Obviously staged," from the group in front of them.

Mixin needed to sow more skepticism. Pitching their voice to reach the people around them, they said, "We're supposed to believe that? Someone should tell him we're not that gullible."

As they'd hoped, the group latched onto that. One called out, "Yeah, I don't believe it! How do we know that 'volunteer' isn't a plant?"

"Or he used a subvocal comm."

"I've seen old stage magicians' tricks that are more convincing!"

"This is no trick!" Cobb insisted. "Yes, I'm using the trappings of a performance to show you what's possible, but there's no trickery here. Subject J has the ability to see people's intentions. It's not full precognition, and his predictions are most accurate in the short term, but imagine the usefulness for sporting events, or negotiating sessions. Or war."

That brought more impressed mutterings, though not from everyone.

"It does sound great…*if* it's real."

Mixin cupped their hands to their mouth and shouted, "Prove it!" Then, just for the people around them, "He can't, can he?"

Across the audience, someone said, "Can you reproduce it, though, and control it? That's what I want to know."

Cobb waved his hands in a shushing gesture. "Please, colleagues, be patient. We're just getting started here." He didn't quite hide the irritation in his voice. "I've got piles of recorded evidence to convince you doubters, which will be available for access later today. I'll have smaller sessions throughout the Exhibition for those curious to interact with these subjects yourselves. Imagine what your children or grandchildren might be capable of—or your next elite workforce. For now, let's see a different sort of demonstration."

He waved at the guards, and they led Jinx away, limping.

"Now, Tide, come on out," Cobb called.

A Kovar marched stiffly onto the stage and stopped. Mixin recognized her at once: Incoming Tide, part of Racing Starter's team. Mixin didn't know her well; her teammates were protective of her, and shielded her from interacting with most people. No guards accompanied her—which made sense, considering.

"Oh, no," Libbi moaned.

"Come closer, Tide," Cobb ordered, and she paced forward, one resistant step at a time, as if fighting her own legs. "Sit, Tide." When she reached to turn the chair backwards, as Kovars usually did with Human-style seating, he gave a sharp, "No! Sit the right way."

She perched awkwardly at the front of the chair, tail curled around her.

I don't want to watch this. But Mixin didn't have much choice.

"Tide here has an ability with a very different sort of usefulness. 'Ability' is perhaps a misnomer in her case. You may know we've had problems recently with upstart workers, including on Artesia, where I began my career. Imagine if we could curtail those troublemakers with a few simple words, because they were biologically compelled to follow all orders—just like our test subject here. Tide, tell me honestly what you think about Ravel Corporation."

"I hate Ravel. I despise the company and everyone in it, every single one of them, the cowardly cheating scavengers!" Tide looked startled by her own vehemence, or at least by expressing it so freely, but she needed no command to keep going. The extra rudeness of addressing her audience in the third person was probably lost on Cobb, but from a Kovar, it showed the utmost disrespect. "I piss upon Alik Cobb and his ambitions. I will die rather than serve him, that pompous team-of-o—"

"Be silent!"

She cut herself off, choking back her flow of words.

Despite having asked for this diatribe, Cobb looked rattled. Recovering his composure, he said, "You see? She's physically incapable of disobedience. Tide, lie on the floor, face down, and put your hands behind your head."

Claws flexing, fists clenching, she rose. With a growl, she dropped to all fours, then lowered her belly to the stage in a position of surrender.

Mixin shut their eyes, nausea rising. There were limits to how gross Cobb could get on a semi-public stage, but Mixin knew a little (and imagined much worse) about the kinds of abuse people with gifts like this could suffer. What Ravel might be doing to Tide offstage.

Remembering their job, Mixin said weakly, "More tricks. She looks drugged—that must be how he's controlling her."

No one nearby took the bait. No one protested at all.

"Imagine: within two generations, we could breed a workforce with perfect, compulsory obedience." (A whisper near the front row: "But how will he make sure the right people get the right abilities?") "And lest you think this Kovar is programmed only to obey me, let's have another volunteer…"

Volunteers were more reluctant this time.

"Oh, come, let's have some fun with it," Cobb encouraged. "Who wants to explore this phenomenon? For science."

In the restless quiet, someone gave a soft, wordless cry of disgust, at just the wrong moment to be heard across the room.

Cobb's gaze raked the audience, then snagged and caught. His eyes widened, so startled he seemed to forget what he was doing.

Mixin turned with everyone else, and there was Libbi, hands clapped over her mouth in horror. She was standing in a circle of open space. All the people around her who'd been hiding her from view had crowded back so as not to be associated with her.

"Oh shit, oh sweet Ancestors," Libbi whispered over the headset, words muffled by her fingers. "I didn't mean to…"

Everyone on the group chat started talking at once, while Cobb waved over a security guard and hissed, "That woman is a Brennexian spy. Liberation Wilder. Take her, but *quietly*. Do not let her out of your sight." He turned back to the audience. "Who wants to help me demonstrate? No need to be shy!"

"Okay, stay calm, folks," Jasper was saying. "Kay, you and I should try to get to Libbi. Havoc, forget our plan. We need a distraction, quick."

"It will take a moment."

"There's no time!"

Damn it, damn it, damn it. "I'll distract him. Get her out of here," Mixin said, then ripped off their headset.

If they stopped to think, they'd realize how stupid this was, so they didn't stop. They strode up on stage without waiting for permission.

"I volunteer!"

"You!" Cobb hissed. "How many of you are here?"

"Just me, here to make your life hell." Mixin grinned wildly, and from across the room, they mouthed at Libbi: *get out of here.*

Libbi didn't move, though, except a tiny shake of her head. A message clear as shouting. *Damn it, Libs.* Mixin loved her, but self-preservation was not her strength.

Granted, it wasn't Mixin's, either.

Kay was moving through the auditorium, but so was security. Jasper must be close, but out of sight. And Mixin, standing in front of a thousand or more people who wanted to use them and their friends as science experiments, discovered the worst possible time to remember how they hated public speaking.

Mixin stared out, and all of Ravel stared back.

Security was moving closer to Libbi, but some of them were doubling back to the stage. Too late to back out. *Just start talking, damn it.*

"Shame on you, Ravel! Shame on all of you, being party to this." More shifting and muttering. No shame there. "Tide, get on up. Be free."

The Kovar sprang to her feet in relief, hissing at Cobb. For one appalling moment, Mixin realized that they could tell Tide to attack and she'd do so gleefully. But that would get Tide hurt or killed, and Mixin refused to use someone's own gift against them. Instead they said, careful with their phrasing, offering but not ordering, "You should go, if you want to, and get to safety."

"I'll find no safety here." Tide shifted closer to Mixin.

Security was mounting the stage. Mixin couldn't see Libbi anymore—wait, there she was, pushing her way through the aisle that was crowded with standing-room listeners, and no one was making way for her. The guards were closing on them both.

Mixin raised their voice. "This is obscene! You're treating living people as lab rats! Ask this asshole how he'll dole out these gifts. How will he make sure it's not your kids living in constant pain, or vulnerable to the most awful abuse?"

Rough hands grabbed Mixin's arms, wrenching them back. Auto-cuffs tightened around their wrists. "Whose kids will he sacrifice?" they shouted. "Your kids? Or just some lowly workers, and who cares about them, right? Ask what this raw deal is worth to you! Don't let him—"

A bulky sonic absorber clamped over their mouth. They kept trying to shout, but no sound came out.

Suddenly, the lights died, dousing the room in void-blackness. Mixin heard Cobb cursing nearby, and the audience crying out in exasperation or alarm. But they couldn't see Libbi as security wrestled them off the stage.

32

IN THE ABRUPT DARKNESS, strangers pressed into Libbi on all sides.

"Hey, watch it!"

"No touching!"

"Just stay still, damn it! They'll get power back soon."

Libbi had to hide before that happened. She waded toward the door, or at least in the direction she'd been going when she'd been able to see the door, but it was like moving through an oil spill, if the oil had sharp elbows and hissed criticisms as she passed. Some people set their headsets to act as flashlights, and the narrow beams only blinded her worse. Others snapped at them to stop.

Her knees cracked against a hard surface. Groping, she found the arm of a chair. She'd gotten turned around.

"Sorry, sorry!" She felt her way along the row ends, toward the back, apologizing all the way.

"Where are the damn backups?"

"How did Engineering flub it up so massively with this ship? All pretty lines and raw power, but they literally can't even keep the lights on."

An arm wrapped around her shoulders. She choked back a yelp, tried to duck away until a familiar voice whispered, "Hey, it's me."

Jasper. He must have used his gift, following the link that bound them. What did that link look like now? She'd been such a brat lately, and knew it…but she'd never been more grateful to have her big brother near. She found his hand, and together they squeezed through the crowd.

He led her out, not by the main doors where she'd entered the auditorium, but around the side. A pause while he fumbled with a sliding door, forcing it open by hand. She dug in and helped. Beyond the door was nothing but more darkness.

Except as they rounded the corner, she began to sense shape and distance. Light filtered in from somewhere up ahead, growing stronger until they burst out into an exhibit hall, and her eyes watered at the sudden brightness. Jasper never stopped moving, but his arm dropped. Instead of holding onto her, he urged her forward with a light touch on her back. Not until then did she realize she was shaking.

They'd almost caught her. Cobb had almost gotten his way. And, she realized belatedly, security could have seized the precious cache of biometric data she was here to deliver.

A glorified messenger, and she couldn't even do that right. She should never have gone into the auditorium…except it hadn't seemed like she'd had a choice; she'd been too nervous about playing her new role to resist being swept along with the crowd. And now Mixin…

No, no. Don't think about Mixin. That way lay a total breakdown.

She should have stayed on Brennex, where she belonged.

"You're all right," Jasper murmured. His touch on her back grew more solid. "We'll fix this. Breathe."

She drew a deep breath. "Where are we going?"

"Back to Sunny, to regroup."

"That is not advisable at present," said Sunny's voice in Libbi's ear, startling her.

"What's happening?" Jasper asked.

"Security is converging on the auditorium, and has halted all the lifts on your level. They've called for heightened security at the docking bays as well."

"Where are the guards now?" he asked.

A map popped up on Libbi's headset, orange dots marking security guards and bars for checkpoints. "More guards are being diverted from other locations. Most are arriving via the lifts, some from the executive suites. I believe they will focus on crowd control—and searching for Libbi—at the auditorium until reinforcements are in place."

"Okay, so we—hey, look, isn't that cool!" He pointed to the nearest display—which was a model space habitat that must have been three meters tall—urging Libbi to turn and, in the process, neatly putting his body between her and the room.

A pair of security guards hurried past toward the auditorium, where Libbi heard raised voices.

He let out a breath. "That was close. With everyone at the presentation, we stand out here way too much." The exhibit hall did feel eerily empty, now that he pointed it out. "We need a place to hide out. Oh! I've got an idea…"

Another voice cut in over the headset. "Mason? Trouble is coming for me. A guard saw me emerge from backstage at the auditorium. I think they want to question me about the blackout."

"Shit. I'm coming, eshrim."

"Why do they think he caused the blackout?"

"Probably because he did." Jasper's wry smile flashed briefly. "Libbi, follow me and please, *please* do exactly what I say. Walk like you belong here. But keep your head down! No one should see your face."

"How in all our ancestors' names am I supposed to do both of those at once?" Libbi said.

"I don't know, but just try?"

His burning inner conflict hit her, his need to protect her warring with the urgency of helping Havoc. She realized with a start: her big brother was scared.

"Okay, how about this?" She raised her handheld, head bent as if she were consulting her headset and the handheld's screen while also trying to walk. She'd already seen three people do this in the brief time she'd been aboard the flagship, and unlike them, she was actually paying enough attention not to walk into anything.

"Perfect. When Havoc gets to you, go that direction until you get to the theater block. Find an empty one to hide in."

"Got it. What will you be doing?"

"Distracting the guards."

"Jasp?!"

"Trust me."

Havoc was dead ahead of them. Wearing a maintenance jumpsuit, he walked like he knew where he was going, head up and ignoring the exhibits, but even Libbi could tell he was tense.

Then Havoc moved out of sight behind the next row of booths, and a security guard came into view, following him.

"Wait here," Jasper said. "Get really interested in this…moss, or whatever, so they don't pay attention to you."

The booth in question was lined with green-filled tanks; it really was a new variety of moss, apparently delicious and nutritious, plus it doubled as a building material. The rest of the display was a blur to Libbi as she watched Jasper out of the corner of her eye.

His entire bearing changed as he strode up behind the guard. "Excuse me? Excuse me! What are you thinking, blocking off the lifts? I need access to my workspace on level seventeen."

He sounded every bit the spoiled corporate brat. He sounded, in fact, like Cobb.

Reluctantly, the guard turned toward him. "I'm sorry, um…" He checked his headset for Jasper's ID. "…Senior Analyst. We're dealing with an issue, but I promise, everything will be back up and running as soon as it's resolved."

"And when will that be?"

"We're working on it, Senior Analyst."

"Is this about that all-important Biopharma presentation that's going on in there? Corporate help me, if Alik fucking Cobb is getting in the way of everyone else's work again…" Jasper waved in the direction of the auditorium, still dark.

People were starting to spill out the doors, giving up on waiting for the presentation to resume, and security scrutinized each of them. That seemed like bad news for Cobb, right? And good for Libbi, Jasper, and Havoc if they could get lost in a crowd?

"Please, calm down—" The guard glanced over his shoulder. Frowned. "Excuse me…"

"No, you calm down, you nitwit! You think his project is more important than mine?"

Jasper's tantrum did the trick. Two other guards came over to see what the fuss was about, and the first guard waved them away, telling them to "go find that Kovar and hold him for questioning." But Havoc had already slipped away, dropping to all fours and cutting a winding route across the hall (and under more than one display, pausing under table-skirts when anyone drew near) until he reached Libbi.

"Mason plays that role too well." The Kovar risked a quick glance toward Jasper—who was still refusing to let the guard brush him off—and shook his head ruefully.

"You didn't see Mixin?" she asked, trying not to hope.

"I apologize, Libbi. I regret that I couldn't reach them."

"It's okay. Not your fault." *It's mine.*

"We must find a place to hide, before we join them."

Libbi gave one last pained look toward the auditorium, then pointed the other direction. "This way, Jasper said."

BACKSTAGE WAS BARELY LESS pitch dark than the auditorium. All that anchored Mixin was the tight grip of the security guard, who was cursing the darkness and muttering about "damn malfunctioning ship" and "What do they expect us to do?" His words splashed bright across Mixin's vision.

Backup power was being slow to kick in, as Havoc had said it would be. Havoc—hopefully he'd gotten away. There was no sign of him, but then, Mix couldn't see anything but a scattering of what must be indicator lights from battery-driven equipment around the space. Not nearly enough to see by, but as their eyes adjusted, the pinprick lights became less stars-in-the-void and more a suggestion of walls, shelves, desks.

An exit sign came into view, and Mixin dug in their heels. It wouldn't do any good, but they didn't feel like making this easy for security.

"Come on, stupid lab rat," their guard said, words so close and bright that Mixin almost missed the tiny soft letters farther ahead, a whisper: "*Be ready, Mix.*"

That had to be Jinx. He could've given a more helpful warning. Be ready for what?

They stopped resisting the guard's tug, the better to keep their feet under them and maybe let him relax his wrenching grip on Mixin's arm. He didn't, of course, because that would be convenient and also *nice*, but no harm in hoping.

Then there was another whisper, small but bright in the dark space. "Tide, be sick. Be incredibly, disgustingly sick."

"Hey, keep moving. What's wrong with you?" one of the other guards snapped. The question was answered seconds later by the sound of vomiting. "Oh, for… Seriously? I did *not* sign up for this. Need some damn light over—"

He cut off with a grunt as a Jinx-sized projectile barreled into him. Mixin slammed their heel into their own guard's calf, and used his surprise to twist free just long enough to bash him in the face with their cuffed hands. They stumbled clear, as close to a run as they could get without crashing into any unseen obstacles.

"Tide, be well, and get up!" Jinx called. "You can do this! Felicia?"

"Ready!" A voice Mixin didn't know. Probably Cobb's next demo.

From their groans and heavy footsteps, it wasn't taking the guards long to gather themselves. Mixin couldn't see them. But that should work both ways.

"Door's right here," Jinx called loudly—not making it a command this time, Mixin noticed—then whispered, "Not the door. Here! Hide!"

The door under the exit sign slid open, a blinding bright shaft painting the room in light and shadows for a moment before it closed again. Mixin blinked watery eyes as they whirled around, looking for a hiding spot.

Footsteps pounded toward them, and Mixin dove. They curled up behind a tool cabinet, squeezing their body as small as it could go. Just in time, as flashlights swept around and past them.

One guard slapped the controls to open the door again. Three shapes rushed out, splitting up to search.

Three down. How many guards had there been?

At least one more. A burly figure blocked the open doorway, back to the light, surveying the backstage space. Mixin curled even tighter, not daring to breathe. They'd lost track of Jinx and the others, couldn't see anything useful, didn't even know where they were in the room. Their only point of reference was the open door…

Which suddenly swished shut, leaving them in darkness again. There was a grunt, more scuffling, then a groan. Mixin blinked against the afterimages clouding their vision.

"I have him… Grab his wrists!"

"Okay, got him. Mixin, give me that mask."

"What mask?" they asked, or tried, but the words didn't come out. Somehow, in the chaos, Mixin had forgotten the silencing mask trapping their mouth. With bound hands, they tried to grapple with it, without luck.

"Here, I got you," said the stranger who must be Felicia. The mask eased off, and oh, hey, Mix could breathe again. Who knew oxygen was so nice?

Felicia picked up the guard's flashlight, and Mixin could see now that the guard was on the ground, held tight by Incoming Tide, who kept one hand covering his mouth until Jinx tightened the sonic absorber mask into place. Then he helped Mixin and Felicia with their auto-cuffs, sliding a key stick into a slot, and the cuffs fell away. Tide had never been cuffed, presumably because Cobb thought of her as easily controlled. Jinx must have ditched his earlier, somehow.

Catching Mixin's curious look, Jinx winked. "Turns out life on the streets gives you some useful skills. Pickpocketing, for one."

"Please put those on him, wrists and ankles," said Tide, still holding the guard down, and Mixin hurried to do so. They *probably* shouldn't be enjoying this, relishing the guard's helpless, glaring expression above his mask—but if anything, Mix wished they could've done more to help.

"You okay, Tide?" Jinx asked. "Sorry I had to do that to you."

"We had few other options, and I did consent to this plan. I don't enjoy compulsive vomiting—"

"Who would?" Mixin murmured.

"—But I feel fine now. Perhaps slightly dehydrated." A pause. "Mixin, I don't understand why you're here, but if you caused this blackout, you have excellent timing."

"That was the Cooperative."

"You're with them?" Felicia asked.

"Yeah, though this wasn't quite our plan."

"I'm sure there's a fascinating story," said Jinx, "but we don't have long before guards outside guess what we've done. Where to?"

Mixin reached for their headset before remembering the guards had taken it. Damn. They had no map, and no way to contact Jasper or Sunny or the others. At least they weren't imprisoned…but it could be a long time before their friends realized they were running renegade around the ship.

Felicia, however, said, "That way," and started walking. Whatever her gift was, she seemed confident, so Mixin followed her.

33

LIBBI CURLED INTO A chair in the cool dimness of the theater, knees pulled to chest, chin on her arms. She could hear the indistinct noises of cinematics in the neighboring theaters. Mixin, she thought with misery, would be able to make out the words.

With every moment of stillness, she relived it: Incoming Tide, humiliated on the stage for all to see. Libbi's own unconscious exclamation of disgust—stupid, so stupid of her. Cobb's sickening, possessive eagerness at the sight of her. And worst by far, Mixin charging to her rescue and disappearing into the dark.

"You're sure no one will walk in on us?" she asked Havoc, trying to stay focused on the present.

"I trust the theaters will stay empty for several hours. You saw that couple? They lacked any concern."

The first theater they'd peeked inside had been empty except for a couple in the back, who were enthusiastically making out while a narrator boomed about "building our future, together." They hadn't even noticed as Libbi and Havoc sheepishly backed away.

The memory made her chuckle, though weakly. "Right, but what if…"

"It's morning. Any important showings happen in the evenings. All they're showing at this hour is company propaganda, on a loop, and anyone who cares to watch such things will have seen them already."

"Oh. That makes sense."

"We've found safety here, Libbi, at least for a time."

"Thanks," she muttered, and curled up tighter.

She'd come here to help. She'd thought she was prepared. And the first thing she did was let her best friend get captured while saving her useless self.

On the *Rascal*, she'd imagined herself being calm and confident, acting normal, avoiding attention. But the reality, as soon as she'd stepped into the Exhibition itself, had been overwhelming. She *wished* it was an act of stubbornness or rebellion that had made her go to Cobb's presentation. Instead, lost and anxious, she'd let herself get swept inside. Then she'd told herself she could be safe hiding in the crowd, as long as she was quiet. And she had stayed quiet, unmemorable—until she forgot herself when Cobb had started tormenting Tide.

"Good, we're all here," Jasper said as he and Kay slipped into their little theater hideout. "We've got work to do."

Libbi stared blankly at him.

"It's going to be okay," he told Libbi, with that warm confidence that'd always reassured her when she was little. "I know you're worried about Mixin. I am, too, but we know

Cobb won't hurt his precious research subjects."

"Not physically," Libbi muttered. "He'll just demean and humiliate them."

"Mixin's tough. They've got a good head in a crisis."

"Right, there was clearly a ton of foresight behind flinging themself between me and Cobb," Libbi snapped.

Mixin never panicked in a crisis, Libbi would give them that, but only because they thought life was an adventure serial, the kind where the good guys always won.

Libbi was thinking of her best friend as childish, but that wasn't fair. Mixin had been perfectly fine until Libbi showed up. She knew they liked to ham it up and create drama where there was none, but there was real feeling behind their actions, real care. Mixin deserved far more credit.

Libbi was a terrible friend.

Her siblings were watching her with soft expressions, returning her rudeness with sympathy. They were trying to help.

"We fought," she said softly. "Mix and I, before you all left. I said some awful things. And now I can't even apologize."

Kay slipped into the seat beside Libbi, wrapped an arm around her, and started playing with her hair the way she used to when they were little, toying apart the curls and watching them bounce back. It was surprisingly soothing.

"Our job would've been simpler if Cobb hadn't brought more captives back with him," Kay said. "But we won't leave anyone behind here. *All* the Losts are coming home with us, Mixin included."

She sounded like she believed it. Libbi tried to believe it, too.

"None of us expected to see you here, Libs," Jasper said, gently steering them back to business. "Did Lira Zheng send you? Why?"

"For this, most importantly. Cobb's biometrics."

"Really?!" Jasper cried, and Havoc said, "You speak truth?"

"He bragged to the Cooperative about his security measures, so Auntie Lira grabbed these before they tried to move him off Brennex. Which didn't work, obviously." She grimaced. She held out the data-stick in its scanner-proof case, and Havoc took it from her. Such a small thing to risk her life—and Mixin's life—over.

"This may just save our butts," Jasper murmured.

"I also have news about what's happening at home. Lira didn't trust a message to get through to you safely."

"So she sent a messenger." Jasper frowned. Was he *that* disappointed in her? Or annoyed at Auntie Lira? Probably frustrated that he'd have to babysit her. "I'm sorry you got here too late to warn us about Cobb, but his return has been the talk of the Exhibition."

"That's not your news, is it?" said Kay. "Something worse has happened."

Libbi said, "I guess you don't know about the solar mining?"

Their chorus of shocked outbursts was, in a grim way, satisfying.

"Is Linn sure?"

"But how? Their prototype was destroyed!"

Libbi projected the holo she'd brought with her, turning it to show the structure from all angles, its fins extended to block Brennex's array.

Jasper cursed. "So that's why Natural Resources is cozying up with Biopharma. Tell us everything."

"Everything" wasn't much to tell. She shared what Auntie Lira had figured out, and how it was affecting the city: the power rationing, the unrest, the Council's cowardice. Ravel's refusal to claim the rig as theirs. "And by the time I left Brennex, the rig was still there, still blocking our solar array. Hours after the Council sent Cobb back, it hadn't moved."

"Nor will they move it soon, I predict," Havoc said. "Mason, this must be the demonstration that Natural Resources has been teasing. They're testing it on Brennex's sun."

Jasper rubbed his hands over his face. "This isn't political pressure. This is vindictive. Harrington Moore's petty revenge."

"We destroyed his toy, so he'll destroy our home," Kay muttered. "I'll bet anything they want to take Brennex back. Not just their genetic 'property,' but everything."

"And they'll hold our own sun hostage against us until we give in," said Jasper. "They know we're totally reliant on solar power. We even lose our air for breathing without it, and the backup systems will only last so long. They can keep the rig in place until they own us again."

"Or longer," Havoc said grimly.

"Right. Why not keep the rig, and sell its power back to us?"

"Perhaps worse than that. They can *use* what it generates to power one of their own space habitats."

"Oh. Oh! Shit. Trade and transit along the Long Lane would be far more *efficient* if they cut out Brennex's role altogether, wouldn't it?"

"Then they needn't deal with expensive docking in a gravity well, or inconvenient local culture." Havoc's tone was so dry it scorched. "Yes, I suspect that's what they plan. It would explain why Natural Resources has been cozying up to Engineering."

Kay tipped her head back and groaned. "Fuuuuck. Fuck Ravel, and fuck you in particular, Harrington Moore."

Libbi said nothing, her head full of echoes of her family's stories about the occupation: the lack of autonomy, the horrible working conditions for inadequate pay, the loss of trade and contact with outside worlds. She could still feel the desperation to evade Ravel from the Council meeting, so gut-deep people were willing to sell their neighbors for it. This couldn't be happening.

"I have questions," Sunny spoke up. "How did they build a new prototype so quickly? Also, we hypothesized that Moore chose Unity System for the first test because of its unique macrospace terrain. Brennex's star is much smaller and has an entirely different macrospace topography."

Havoc pulled the images to his own handheld and studied them more closely, zooming in and out. "The mining technology looks similar to what we saw at Unity, but this vessel is much smaller, more mobile, and these fins are new. At a guess, this is a prototype for a sibling project. Perhaps a weaponized version, for exactly such hostile takeovers as this."

"Cocky, to put so many resources into two such similar projects," Jasper muttered. "But Moore does seem to be all in on this."

No one had a response to that.

"To be clear," Libbi said, "Lira doesn't expect you—us—to deal with the solar mining; it's out of our reach, she said, and she's working on it from other angles. She just thought you should know. In case, you know…"

"Better to not be taken by surprise." Jasper gave a faint smile. "No change in priorities. Understood."

"So, how's the plan for Cobb coming along?" Libbi asked.

"Our original plan? Shattered." Havoc held up the datastick. "This will help immensely, but we need a new plan to deliver the virus. Preferably while Cobb is well occupied elsewhere, though that would require his passcode as well."

"And this was hard enough when we had the run of the flagship," said Kay. "Now they're looking for Libbi—"

"Sorry…"

"Not your fault! But our freedom of movement just got a lot more limited."

"And our time is dwindling," said Havoc. "We must finish before the Exhibition ends tomorrow night."

"To further complicate matters," Sunny added, "we'll need to rescue Cobb's new test subjects at the same time as our sabotage. If he still has access to them when he discovers our interference, he may move them to a more secure location where he can use them to rebuild his data sets."

Sunny's practical explanation made Libbi ill. "So let's rescue them first. Now, even."

"That's tricky," Kay said. "I wouldn't be surprised if he's already tightened security around his lab."

"He has." Sunny pushed a camera feed to their headsets, showing a pair of guards stationed outside a door. "At least two at each door, and more patrolling the corridors on that level.

"He's got a whole lab here?" Libbi asked.

"Correct. He planned to continue his work here without interruption. It is several decks below your position, and the lifts are currently locked down."

"My point is, any rescue attempt will put him on guard," Kay said. "Plus, the more of us running around the flagship, the harder it'll be to hide. It's hard enough for us four, right now, since we can't get to Sunny."

Havoc frowned. "If we can't reach Sunny, how will we escape when the time comes?"

"Let me clarify," said Sunny. "Reaching the docking bay is not impossible, but neither is it safe. I have scrambled the arrival records such that it will be difficult for them to connect Mixin to me—but if you are seen approaching me, that will negate my efforts. Coming and going would compound the risk of discovery. I suggest that you stay away until we're ready to depart for good."

Libbi shook her head, unwilling to let go of the bigger issue. "So you're saying we should leave them all in Cobb's control until it's *convenient* to have them with us?"

"We're all worried about Mixin," Kay said softly, touching Libbi's hand. Libbi pulled away. "We'll get them out—Mix, and all the others. But we've got a really damn narrow path to success here, and we have to be careful."

Libbi swallowed hard. She was being immature again, digging into that old habit of being contrary against her siblings just to make a point. With lives on the line—Mixin's life, and all the Losts—she had to do better. "That makes sense, but I hate it."

"I know." Kay gave her a look of sympathetic frustration, and for a moment, Libbi felt a sharing of purpose, too. A desire to move, impatience to act. Okay, maybe Libbi wasn't alone in this.

"So what do we do?"

Havoc waved a hand around the theater. "This place will remain safe for a time, but not indefinitely. Security has cordoned us in, and they will be searching—and this room is scheduled to show a film this evening. We cannot linger."

Jasper ran his hands through his hair, a sure sign of frustration. Havoc gently brushed his locks back into place. "Okay, so we need to avoid security until we're ready to act, and we need a plan. Where's Cobb now, Sunny?" Jasper asked.

"He returned to his lab with a security escort. There are no camera feeds inside his lab, so I can't tell what he's doing. I assume he will remain there, apart from his scheduled sessions. However…" Sunny gave a curious chirp. "Interesting."

"What is?" Libbi asked.

"One moment…" Sunny actually sounded cheerful as they continued. "Oh! Excellent! Your worry for Mixin is…not unfounded, but misdirected. Security has put out a notice about them. It appears Mixin and the other Losts from the presentation have escaped!"

"What! How?" Libbi was on her feet before she realized it.

"I will attempt to reconstruct that; they must have reached a lift before this level was locked down. For now, please excuse me while I help their group evade capture. I can't contact Mixin, but I can hide them from camera feeds. This will take most of my attention."

Libbi's heart was singing. *Misdirected.* Mixin wasn't *safe*, but they weren't in Cobb's slimy hands, either. And set loose, Libbi believed Mixin could do just about anything. Ravel should be scared of Mixin, not the other way around.

Kay said, "While Sunny does that, here's a map of this deck. There's got to be some place we can sneak off to."

THEY STUDIED MAPS OF the flagship, considering their potential hiding spots, but one by one, they discarded them all. Too small. Too exposed. Too easily searched. No single place on this level would stay safe for long enough. And the end of the Exhibition was creeping closer, an unshakable deadline. Time they spent dodging security was time they couldn't spend on their real goals.

"Why can't you just plant the virus, now that we have his biometrics?" Kay asked.

"They're… What's it called? Necessary but not sufficient, right?" Libbi said, and Havoc nodded. "Lira said we'll still need his password to use with them."

"And that," Havoc said, "would have been difficult to obtain even before security went on high alert. A thousand ways exist to steal passwords, but most depend on the target making mistakes or being insufficiently cautious. Cobb will use great caution now, knowing we're here."

"Sorry," Libbi murmured again.

"You brought us the harder piece of the puzzle with the biometrics." He shook his head. "If only we could access Cobb's lab. His own devices will have an active session. But security is waiting there for us."

"If we could get into his lab, you could do it?" Jasper asked.

"If we could get inside, *you* could do it, eshrim." Havoc gave him a tired smile.

"But instead we're stuck here, playing mouse and cleaner bot with security." Libbi leaned back, rubbing her tired eyes. "What would Mixin do? Make a distraction or something," she muttered to herself. "But how?"

Havoc, however, sat forward sharply. "Crack the fissures."

"What?" Libbi said in unison with Jasper.

"Mixin and I spoke of cracking open the fissures within the company. Metaphorical fissures, political ones," he added for Libbi's benefit. "Libbi speaks truth that we need a diversion. Mason, what if that diversion could also serve our greater game? Score two points with one move?"

Jasper blinked, startled. Started to shake his head, then stopped, thinking. "Yes, but… No, we can't… Huh. Maybe we can leverage all that beautiful intelligence Mixin's been gathering. Right now, they're expecting us to go after Cobb, but if we get enough executives angry, and stage it so security is focused on finding us in a particular place, they'll shift attention away from Cobb's lab."

Just like that, Jasper's frustration was gone. Now he looked energized. Focused. Not to mention more excited than Libbi had seen him in ages. Hungry for a win. Whatever mad plan he was envisioning, Libbi believed he'd make it work through sheer force of will.

"What exactly is this 'greater game'?" Libbi asked.

"I've been feeling frustrated and, honestly, guilty that we're burning so many of the Cooperative's resources that were supposed to help other planets and campaigns. Especially since we've learned that Ravel is more of a mess than we realized. Profits have been declining, and the board can't agree on priorities. Debate over the new budget has been intensely bitter. There are tensions between the executives. Not just the usual departmental rivalries, but something more desperate."

"We knew their profits were down," Havoc added, "but not like this."

Jasper went on, "We've kept wishing there was a way to *use* that knowledge and accomplish something bigger with our presence here, not just to stop Cobb's work. I thought the way to do that was to steal more of their plans and data, but with this… We could deal Ravel a major setback. More major than we've seen in a long time."

"I thought that was too risky?" Kay raised her brows, but amusement edged into her voice. "Stopping Cobb takes priority, we can't do anything to jeopardize that, right?"

"It was too risky. Maybe it still is, but screw it. It's risks on all sides now. If we don't risk *something,* we'll be cowering in here until they track us down. I'd rather take a chance on something spectacular, wouldn't you?"

"I sure would," Libbi said. *And so would Mixin, if they were here.*

"You know I would, eshrim," Havoc added.

"Let's make them hurt," Kay agreed. "What's your plan?"

"We go after the board themselves. The last day of the Exhibition—that's tomorrow—they always hold a big supposedly public Q&A session. We can sow some havoc," he quirked a smile, "and turn them against each other. The trick would be to not get caught, so we can roll straight into invading Cobb's office and freeing his captives before security can recover."

"Not getting caught is always the trick," Kay said, and Libbi shivered at the thought.

One big, last-chance gamble. They had to make this work.

34

IT BECAME CLEAR THAT, beyond escaping the presentation, Jinx and the others didn't have a plan.

They'd escaped the exhibition level just before the lifts got locked down. Now they skulked down corridors of one of the office floors, disappearing into the nearest empty room if anyone got too close. Felicia's gift turned out to be a good complement to Mixin's: she could tell where people were. Not specific people, but generally. Through a wall or around a corner, sentient beings apparently looked to her like ghostly blobs on an infrared scanner, so she was able to steer their group away from most pursuit.

But they couldn't wander aimlessly forever, and in terms of actually going someplace useful, Mixin was the only one who'd had the freedom of the ship and had any sense of its layout.

Each attendee had been assigned a room for the event. Mixin hadn't used theirs yet, but it was only three decks up, easy to reach through the emergency stairs. How long would it take security to match Mixin to their fake ID and track them to the room? Long enough, Mix hoped, with all the chaos happening downstairs.

The room was so swanky and plush that Mixin almost regretted not sleeping there. But more importantly, it had an auto-tailor—a scanner connected to a fabric printer—and within a few minutes, the three escapees had well-fitted, fantastically generic businesswear in place of their lab jumpsuits, including a Kovari-style suit for Tide. (Mixin suggested a service uniform to help the Kovar blend in, like Havoc wore, but Tide refused; being in service would mean a lot of people shouting instructions at her, and she'd rather take the risk of standing out. Mixin couldn't argue with that.)

While the others changed, Mixin browsed the tailor's menu of options.

"Ooh, that would be handy," they murmured, and jabbed at the image of a security uniform. It protested when Mix tried to print one, though. Their alias was in the wrong department for that. "Damn it."

"Let me," Jinx said. He popped open a panel and did…something, and after a minute, the printer started spitting out a uniform in Mixin's size.

Felicia paced the room, staring at the walls and beyond. "We should keep moving."

"Should, or have to?" Mixin asked.

"Should *before* we have to."

"As soon as we get these done. Posing as security officers could be just the thing to break the others out of Cobb's lab. I assume that's your next step?"

Jinx grimaced. "Still working on the details."

"My friends are planning to destroy Cobb's research. We should find them and join up, if we can." Especially if Libbi was with them. Was she safe? Hopefully Kay and Jasper had used Mixin's distraction and gotten her out. Nothing Mix could do about it now, so they pushed those worries from their mind.

"Can you contact them?"

They reached for their handheld and—again, still—found it missing. "No. If we can get to our ship in the docking bay, I can have Su—I mean, I can call them from there. But security will be tight."

"Then we must act alone, and hope our strategy aligns with theirs," Tide proclaimed. "I volunteer to play decoy. With you all in disguise as security, you can pretend to have captured me and return me to the lab. We eliminate the real security, free our friends, and run."

"Then what? Where do we hide?" Felicia frowned doubtfully.

"Let's scout out a safe place," Mixin said. "Between you and me, Felicia, we can—"

"People coming," Felicia interrupted. "Six of them, stopping at each door. Must be guards."

"Shit. Let's go."

Only the jacket from the first security uniform was done printing, and the matching trousers were at ninety percent. Mixin yanked the trousers out of the printer and followed the others.

FOUR OF THEM ROAMING together was too suspicious, they decided after a couple more close calls, so they took turns searching in pairs for more permanent hideouts or useful resources, starting with Mixin and Felicia while the others lay low.

Felicia turned out to be Felicia Stone, a niece of Libbi's aggressively unhelpful friend from Public Safety, and also a some-times-removed cousin of the Griffin clan. Not her fault who she was related to, of course. She didn't go into details, and Mixin didn't push, but whatever she'd done to end up on Brennex's list to trade away to Ravel, she must not be on good terms with the powerful side of her family. Some old resentments there, it sounded like, but still, yikes. Plenty of Losts had family troubles, but to be sold off as a lab rat by your own relatives? That was extra low.

The flagship seemed to alternate sections of residential and office space, but the whole ship was shiny-new and barely out of construction, and lots of spaces were vacant. Mixin figured if they could find an unoccupied office in an out-of-the-way section, they'd probably be safe from unwanted company, and they'd have plenty of room to flee if security started poking around.

Mixin kept one eye out for nearby gossip and another on the ubiquitous screens that scrolled through the latest news and propaganda. Libbi's face was up there often—that must mean she was still free—along with Felicia, Jinx, and Incoming Tide. Mixin hadn't been included at first, but they were now, so they assumed their cover was compromised. No mention of Kay, Jasper, or Havoc. Hopefully that was a good sign.

"Not that way," Felicia warned as they passed another office corridor. "Lots of people, and those offices all have windows onto the hallway." Good old corporate transparency, taken literally.

The number of people was obvious from their conversations spilling out into view, words overlapping in the air. Mixin was about to backtrack with Felicia when the word *Brennex* caught their eye.

"Wait. Someone's talking about us. I want to listen in."

Felicia rolled her eyes, but stuck with Mixin as they walked purposefully down the hall, pretending they belonged. Gaze sweeping the hallway ahead, Mix watched for which office was having the interesting conversation.

It was near the end of the hall. They hid behind a pillar, shielded from view of most of the million and one windows—though now they had to hope no one else came down the hall and wondered why they were lurking. *Libbi would hate this*, Mixin thought, but they wished for her anyway, instead of Felicia's sour company.

"No, it'll be a joint venture between Natural Resources, Engineering, and Transport," said a voice that looked like Harrington Moore's clipped professionalism. "Biopharma lost that rock once before. I doubt they'd know what to do with it if they got it back, like a dog that's caught its tail. Give them their property, and we'll handle the rest."

"Civil Cultivation isn't happy. They support your goals, but your approach has…"

"Are you getting anything?" Felicia whispered, her words so giant from closeness that they blocked Mix's view.

"Yes, shush!"

"…Course they say that. But how are we supposed to expand if they can't even spin a simple retaking of our own former territory? You and I understand the need for growth."

"As for Biopharma, I'm skeptical of this trump project they've proposed. What's your take on it?"

"It's an impressive idea, *if* it's legitimate," Moore said. "I'm not sure if I'm more or less convinced by the stories from these security guards who let their charges escape. They seem sincere in believing some abnormal abilities were at work, but then again, it would be embarrassing for them if they simply flubbed it. Regardless, even if Principal Scientist Cobb's claims are true *and* he finds a way to control the phenomenon, this project seems to be Biopharma's only real value at present."

"Indeed. That's simply not enough for an entire division."

"I quite agree. They'd benefit from your strong guidance back to profitability. And their resources are better spent elsewhere."

"Like *your* oh-so-secret trump project, right, Moore? Some might say solar mining is equally as overambitious as promising to give everyone superpowers."

Moore's already-crisp voice went sharp as glass. "You've been prying, I see."

"Of course I've done my homework. As you've no doubt done on my division."

Mixin remembered: Havoc had nearly crossed paths with some other spy when he'd broken into the tech department. Someone who'd been looking up information on solar mining. Had they been from this department? Or was everyone in Ravel just spying on their rival divisions?

"Tell me, Harrington: is Brennex really the ideal pilot location, or are you just out to get revenge on them for ruining your plans in Unity System?"

"Let's say it has multiple advantages, across the company," said Moore. "Which will be evident to everyone after our demonstration tomorrow. So you're on board with our proposal?"

"You'll have my vote, if I have yours."

Who was Moore cutting a deal with? And at Biopharma's expense, apparently. Mixin didn't recognize the voice. They crept around the column, intending to peer over the half-wall and through the window, but Felicia yanked them back.

"Yes, fine. Take Brennex, and good luck with it. We'll turn Biopharma into something useful, and you'll get your cut of their budget when we chop them up."

Suddenly Mixin could hear their voices, not just see them. The door was open. Mix squashed in next to Felicia and held their breath.

"Have you had lunch? I've been meaning to try Ag Tech's new products demo; my assistant's a bit of a foodie and they've been raving about it."

The voices faded down the hall. Mixin stopped paying attention, instead focusing on breathing so they didn't pass out.

"On all the Founders' graves! I was sure we were dead. I hope you got something worth it," Felicia said.

"I absolutely did. Just need to answer one last mystery." The hallway was clear now. Mixin did their best relaxed saunter out from behind the column and gave an oh-so-casual glance as the door Moore and his friend had just vacated.

Elaine Joseph, Senior Vice President of Biotech.

Biotech was trying to absorb Biopharma. And they were trading away Brennex to do it.

Mixin had no idea what that meant, or what else Biotech might be up to. Your enemy's enemy was supposed to be your friend…but what about your enemy's enemy's backstabber's secret ally of convenience?

Jasper and Havoc would know what to do, if only Mixin could find them.

35

"I'M IN POSITION. EVERYTHING okay with you two?" Libbi asked. On her handheld, she watched the camera feed of the board's "public" meeting, waiting while the audience trickled in past the security checkpoint. The room was arranged café-style, with groups of chairs around tables. People milled about, going in and out of frame to what Libbi assumed was a buffet at the back of the room.

She didn't see Kay and Jasper yet.

This event was exclusive, billed as an "intimate conversation with our leadership" that, in theory, was open to the whole Exhibition. In reality, most of the seats went to upper-rankers, with a dozen or so offered up by lottery to give the impression of egalitarianism. Most of the mid-rankers would watch the live feed in the theaters. Libbi had set up shop down the hall, in a meeting room that had nothing on its schedule this afternoon.

Sunny had believed they could rig the lottery to assign two seats to the Wilders, but Jasper thought there would be too much attention from security on the guests. Kay's, Jasper's, and Havoc's covers were still good, for the moment, but only because Sunny had changed the photos and other details on their records that would have tied them to Libbi or Mixin. If they called attention to themselves—say, by getting their badge checked manually at a checkpoint—they'd get caught. So instead, they'd found a quieter way to sneak in.

"Yup, we're in. No trouble at all."

There was Kay pushing a catering cart, dressed in black, with a uniform hat hiding her hair. Between that and a fresh coat of what Kay and Jasper called "face clay," Libbi hardly recognized her own sister.

Kay cleared dishes away from a table up front, and even though Libbi was watching for it, she wasn't sure if Kay had done the thing until Kay said in an undertone, "That's the second one. Sunny, check the connection?"

"Both speakers are working. If you intend to plant more, Kay, you should work quickly."

Libbi also spotted Agata Wu, leaning back and surveying the room. He would recognize them for sure.

"Watch out for Agata Wu. Middle table, halfway back."

Kay made a surreptitious scan of the room. "Got him. Thanks. I won't let him see me."

This was going to go wrong. They were counting on the fact that no one ever noticed the service workers, which was even more true in Ravel than elsewhere. But there were at least two people in that room, Wu and Moore, who knew Kay and Jasper personally, and far more who would've seen their pictures.

"You're sure this will be worth it?" she asked despite herself.

Her siblings seemed confident that the uniforms, including the hats that covered their hair, plus copious amounts of makeup and face clay, would keep them safely anonymous. Libbi was trying to believe them. Despite herself, maybe she understood, just the tiniest bit, how Jasper felt when Libbi went looking for trouble.

"Hey, it's a time-honored organizing tactic, showing up and causing chaos," said Jasper.

Libbi found a different camera angle, and now she could see Jasper behind the bar, feigning boredom as he served up company-label wine and Sham-pagne, at odds with his cheerful tone. He'd been a tightly wrapped packet of energy ever since they'd decided on this wild gambit, his doubt and depression melting away to make room for action. Libbi wished she could manage that trick.

"Doesn't that usually end with you getting arrested?" Kay made the comment sound offhand.

Libbi swallowed. Her sibs hadn't talked much about the last time they'd gotten imprisoned on a Ravel flagship, and she could only assume that was because of how bad it'd been.

"You okay, Libbi?" Kay asked.

"Don't worry about *me*. I've got the least dangerous job."

Libbi couldn't have gone into the meeting—with her face all over the Exhibition newsfeeds, she'd be recognized at once. But she was also the least useful person to be physically in the room. It'd taken some pride-swallowing to accept it, but Kay needed to be there to read people's emotions, and Jasper to see which alliances were breaking down. Libbi's own gift wasn't likely to tell them anything useful in a room full of ruthlessly ambitious people, but she could take her sibs' findings and put them to use.

A week ago, she would have sulked over being "relegated" to a supporting role. She might even have rebelled and tried to join the party anyway, just to prove herself. But getting this right mattered more than her pride, and her role didn't need to be dangerous to be important. In fact, she'd had enough danger to last a lifetime.

Jasper said, "Remember, at the first sign of trouble, warn the rest of us and bolt. That goes for all of us. Got it?"

"There," said Kay. "That's all five speakers placed."

Good timing. The executives were just taking the stage.

LIBBI RUBBED HER BURNING, exhausted eyes and struggled not to let her mind drift during the opening remarks. A night spent finalizing plans between rounds of dodging security had not been what she needed. Without Sunny watching over them and messing with the surveillance feeds, they'd have been caught three times over—but at least in a prison cell, Libbi thought bitterly, she could sleep. When this was over, she was going to sleep for a week.

All she had to do first was turn a corporate board meeting into a free-for-all, infiltrate a mad scientist's lab, plant a destructive virus, free a bunch of prisoners, and escape from a fortified ship. No big deal.

Finally President Brant opened up to questions, or at least gave the appearance of opening up. Havoc had told them the questions would be pre-submitted and screened, read aloud by a few designated folks from Corporate Affairs. One stood up now and read, "From Associate Krista Wray in Arts and Entertainment, what would you say is Ravel's greatest accomplishment in the past decade?"

Libbi rolled her eyes so hard it hurt, and Kay muttered,

"Kill me now," but most of the audience chuckled appreciatively.

The answer was predictable bullshit, and Libbi figured that was enough of that. When a moderator rose to present the next question, Libbi dove in first.

"The next question is for Vice President Moore," she said into her headset. "Natural Resources keeps talking about expansion at all costs, but are you really one to talk, considering how much you cost the company—financially and politically—with your failure at Unity System?"

"What sort of nonsense…?" Moore muttered. Everyone was looking to see who'd dared ask such a question— looking for a deep-voiced man, because that's the voice transformation Libbi had picked. The people sitting nearest to the first of the hidden speakers glared back at all the accusatory looks. No one noticed the speaker itself, a little black dot stuck to the floral centerpiece.

While they were still off balance, Libbi kept going. A couple taps on her handheld shifted her output to the second of the five speakers Kay had hidden, and changed the voice to the drawl of Trenton Aguilar, VP of Corporate Affairs.

"And is it true Natural Resources is teaming up with Engineering to provide power for more *amazing* habitats like this one? I guess it's a fitting match, because what's amazing is that the lights aren't malfunctioning today!" That got a few laughs, quickly stifled. "Megalodon? More like *blobfish*, am I right? Do you really think Corporate is going to raise your budget after building this tub?"

The real Aguilar, mic off, was shouting at some poor, confused techie off to the side. Moore had recovered enough to seize his own microphone.

"Whoever you are, you're showing your ignorance. Ravel is an interstellar corporation, and as such our future can't be tied merely to a collection of planets. Free-floating habitats and vessels like this one are the path to…"

"You're doing great, Lib," Jasper murmured into his headset. "The others are wary of Moore, and despite what he says, he's not so confident in Engineering. Time to move on."

"Biopharma's feeling smug now," Kay offered.

Libbi switched speakers and voices again, this time mimicking VP Myra Madden of Ag Tech, who would definitely not be in favor of shifting away from planetary bases.

"If that's the case, Moore, why is your new prototype in orbit around Brennex, a planet with few natural resources to exploit? I'm sure it's a coincidence that it showed up just when Biopharma was running an operation there. Does Natural Resources report to Biopharma now?"

Another rapid switch, before anyone could answer that.

"And Civil Cultivation, too? Is Biopharma in charge of diplomacy now?"

"This is ridiculous," growled Monte Earl Wu, who ran Acquisition and Civil Cultivation. "Obviously this is a ploy by the Cooperative. See, Ferguson? Your carelessness on Brennex with your stupid pet project gave them an excuse to mock us."

"If the project is so stupid, why is the Cooperative working so hard to discredit it?" demanded Ferguson. A good argument, if he'd stopped there, but he didn't. "And if your department had supported us originally, if you hadn't let Brennex get away in the first place…"

"Between that and Unity System, your department's not doing so well, Wu," another executive said. Libbi couldn't tell who.

"Brennex was *thirty years ago*. Shall we talk about all of Engineering's failed projects in the past thirty years?"

"And Unity System—"

"Was sabotaged by the Cooperative. And we're playing into their hands again now. Cut the broadcast, damn it!"

That was true, and the great part was, everyone could see it, but that didn't stop the arguing in the slightest. Libbi grinned to herself as the room devolved into shouting. Whoever was running the broadcast either hadn't heard Wu's order to shut it down, or was too entertained to care, because it kept running. The senior Wu was wading across the room, waving his arms at the camera.

"When they quiet down, go after Biopharma again, harder," Jasper said. "We need to isolate them from the others, especially—"

"Here!" someone shouted, loud enough to cut through the commotion. At that moment, the connection to the third speaker disappeared from Libbi's handheld.

"Damn, I'd hoped it would take longer to find them," Kay said.

"This event is over! Clear the room!" someone ordered, while another shouted, "No! Lock it down! No one leaves!"

"I'm impressed we lasted this long," said Jasper. "Libbi, they're searching for the other speakers. Keep going as long as you can."

"Okay. You two get out of there before you get trapped," she told them.

Kay hissed, "Fuck. Too late."

"Why hello, Kay Wilder." Over her headset, Libbi heard Agata Wu's voice. "I guess this really is a family business."

ON THE SURVEILLANCE CAMERA, Kay stood pinned, her wrist caught in Agata's grip. The two locked gazes like they were trying to stab each other with their eyes. Agata hadn't spoken loudly, though, and his tablemates were looking on with more curiosity than alarm.

Libbi searched for the setting she needed on her handheld. Found it. "Kay, I'm going to distract him. Use it."

She made Agata Wu's voice come out of the speakers: "Maybe Biopharma *should* focus on diplomacy, since they're certainly no good at making medicine." People chuckled in surprise at that. Agata froze, outraged. "Their only asset is one asshole scientist who dug up a thirty-year-old mistake and passed it off as a discovery."

In Agata's moment of startlement, Kay wrenched free— and threw a tray of drinks in his face. Libbi whooped in triumph.

Kay darted away while Agata was blinded and sputtering, headed for the exit and the anonymity of the larger group of catering staff. "Always wanted to do that!"

It said something about the chaos they were causing that only the nearby tables seemed to notice the fight, and they only responded by swarming Agata solicitously, making sure he was okay.

Libbi had to keep making distractions. She switched voices again. "They claim Cobb's going to revolutionize everything, but the truth is, he doesn't even know how it works, much less how to reproduce it! How many people will he get killed in the process?"

"Science takes time!" shouted Ferguson, irate. "All of you know that. Look how much time and leeway you've given Natural Resources for their outrageous solar mining experiments."

A second speaker went dead. Three left. The event feed cut out, too, though Libbi still had the regular surveillance cameras thanks to Sunny, so she could see the catering staff retreating out the back. Kay was somewhere in that group. She didn't see Jasper. Was he out already?

"No, not me! Get that server!" Agata finally managed.

"I'm going back to help Kay," Jasper said.

"Don't you dare," Kay said. "I'm nearly out."

Please, kindest Ancestors, please. Libbi had to swallow before she could go on. "Why continue to prop up a department that has only one new project worth talking about, and a completely—"

The door to Libbi's quiet little meeting room swished open on a security uniform. She grabbed her handheld and dove behind a table, but it was too late. She'd been seen.

What to do now? The room was tiny, and had only one door. Was she was going to have to fight?

"We're both clear," Jasper said over her headset. "Libs, wrap up and come meet us."

Not so easily done. She couldn't even answer him. Was there just the one guard, or did they have more friends outside?

The guard spoke. "Libbi?"

That hesitant, hopeful voice snagged her heart. She peeked out, and this time saw past the uniform to the face of the person wearing it. She rose, took one running step forward. Stopped. Would they welcome a hug from her, after everything?

"Mixin, I…"

Mixin vaulted over the table and caught Libbi in the biggest of bear hugs.

"Mix, I'm so sorry. I acted stupidly, and you… Are you okay? How'd you find me?" She took a step back, looking them up and down. "Did your pants get in a fight with a shredder?"

They laughed. "That's a whole story. For now, I followed your voice here, and I have something big to help stir the shit-pot. Can I?"

Libbi handed Mix her headset. "Be fast. We're down to our last speaker."

"Hey, Harrington Moore! When were you going to tell Biopharma that you sold them out?" Moore muttered something about more lies and nonsense, but Mixin pushed on. "Nope, not a lie. While Moore was pretending to ally with Ferguson, he was also negotiating to get Biopharma demoted and made into one of Biotech's departments. All in exchange for a share of your budget! I know you execs love backstabbing each other, but that's dirty even for you."

"Harrington?" Ward Royce Ferguson turned on him, face crimson. "Is this true?"

The last speaker went out.

Mixin whooped, exhilarated. "That was amazing! Let's find a closer spot. I can still listen in…"

"Founders, no!" Libbi found herself laughing, though there was nothing funny about it. "I'm not letting you get arrested again."

"You didn't 'let me' anything. That was all me."

Libbi winced, but there was no resentment in Mixin's voice. "And I'm grateful. But how about we let them fight amongst themselves while you and I find my siblings, plant our virus, rescue our friends, and then run far, far away? And then…maybe we can talk?"

Mixin smiled, and it still felt almost like old times. "Great plan."

36

FOR ALL THAT MIXIN was getting lots of experience with evading Ravel security, regrouping with Libbi's siblings and Jinx, Felicia, and Tide felt like a deadly obstacle course: quick sidesteps into empty conference rooms on Sunny's warning, turning to hide their faces from squads of guards. All Mixin's attention was on scanning for guards and other unwelcome familiar faces, which left no time for conversation. So they stuck tight to Libbi's side and prayed to their ancestors that Libbi had forgiven them, that she knew they'd forgiven her.

The elevators were still security traps, so it took a *lot* of emergency stairs and ladders to get down to the lower levels where the science was done. When they reached Cobb's level, they broke into pairs and trios so as to draw less attention. The corridors were shockingly quiet after the chaos of the exhibition hall, and no one challenged Libbi and Mixin, though they drew some wary looks.

Then again, *everyone* was looking warily at people they didn't know. One person actually whispered to their companion, "Isn't that the one Biopharma's looking for?" only to be shushed with, "I don't know. Not our problem."

Libbi kept saying she couldn't believe their disruption at the board meeting (which people were calling "that Cooperative stunt") had done any good, but it had clearly done *something* big. The mood on the flagship had changed instantly. Since Cobb's presentation had gotten cut short, things had been tense but in an eager way, everyone waiting for the Cooperative spies to be caught. Now, it was like someone had smashed a window, showering broken glass everywhere, and no one knew what would get smashed next.

It was hard to tell what was actually happening now, with so many rumors flying. Some said that Vice President Wu of Civil Cultivation had resigned in protest. Another said that Moore and Ferguson had come to actual blows. Jasper and Kay didn't seem to believe it ("Can you imagine Moore getting his perfect hair mussed?" Kay had snarked), but all the rank-and-file employees were walking around like they feared for their lives—no, worse: their jobs.

The corridors stayed quiet. With Moore's solar mining demo about to begin, that must be occupying most everyone's attention, whether they were watching for the science or any potential drama. Mixin tried not to think about what Libbi had shared about the solar mining, since there was literally nothing they could do about it. The demo had already happened; Moore's "live" feed of the event would've taken several hours to get here from Brennex.

Mixin just had to hope that Linn had figured out a plan to deal with it.

From somewhere nearby came shouting, and the sound of running feet. Okay, not completely quiet. Mixin locked arms with Libbi and ducked into a doorway until the footsteps faded.

After stopping to print new disguises, they split up, adjusting the original plan to include Mixin and their crew. Mixin, Libbi, and Jasper would go after Cobb's work with the virus, while Havoc, Kay, Jinx, and Felicia would free the captives. Incoming Tide, at her own insistence, was hiding in an empty office nearby, too worried about her gift making her a liability if things went wrong.

"I see two guards," Jasper murmured from their position just around the corner from Cobb's door. "Havoc? Sunny?"

"We expected two at the door here, but see none. Kay and Felicia sense three inside," Havoc said over their headsets. The other group was around a bend in the hallway, near where Cobb's test subjects were being held.

"They're all intensely annoyed. Anxious, too," Kay said.

"Yeah, they all hate Cobb, and we can use that. Once again, he's his own worst enemy." Jasper smiled darkly.

"Cobb himself hasn't left the lab," Sunny told them. "There are no cameras inside—I attribute that to more of his paranoia—but from monitoring the movement of his test subjects between their cells and the lab, I believe he's currently alone."

"That's something," Libbi murmured, looking a bit ashen. Mixin squeezed her hand. "Still wish we could force him out of there."

They'd tried to lure him away, but Cobb was apparently sulking after his earlier embarrassment—not that he'd admit it. He wasn't reading his messages, and though he was supposed to do a Q&A later, he'd changed this one to be virtual. When he wasn't presenting, he seemed to be working nonstop. Sunny claimed he hadn't left the lab to sleep last night.

"We'll wait to move until you're in," Havoc confirmed.

Mix's headset said it was four minutes to the hour. Almost shift-change time.

"I think this is the best shot we're going to get," Jasper said. "Ready, Mixin? Sunny, let's do it."

Mixin squared their shoulders and pulled their hat down to better hide their face, trying to disappear into their security uniform (now with freshly printed full-length pants) as they followed Jasper out.

"Second shift clocking in," Jasper announced to the door guards. He rattled off some protocol that Sunny was feeding to his headset. "How's it been? Quiet?"

"Quiet when he's busy." One of the guards jerked their head toward the door. "Good luck. Don't let High-and-Mighty order you around too much."

"Easy for you to say," the other said as the pair walked off down the hall. "That prick ordered me to make him coffee. Coffee! As if he can't hit a button on the machine himself…"

When they were out of earshot, Mixin said, "That was easy."

"The tricky part comes next," Jasper said.

Two and a half minutes passed before another pair of guards sauntered up. They started to give the same protocol Jasper just had.

But Jasper shook his head. "No, no, you must have the schedule wrong. We just clocked in."

"No, we're definitely assigned here…"

"Check your schedule again. I heard they had to rearrange the roster and put more teams on the Exhibition level during the Nat Resource presentation, in case the Cooperative tries something again."

"Yeah, but we… Huh." One of the new guards frowned at what he saw on his headset: a new schedule—courtesy of Sunny—that put them at the opposite end of the ship. "I'm calling to confirm this. We've been assigned to this level all week."

Jasper opened his mouth, fumbling for an excuse to stop them. "Right, but we—"

On impulse, Mixin leaped in. "Sure, we'll swap with you!" they said brightly.

Jasper tensed as the two guards exchanged a glance.

But the junior nodded meaningfully at the door. "Wouldn't mind a break from High-and-Mighty, would we, Frank?" he said in an undertone.

"Yeah, we'd better stick to the schedule," the senior said, just as Mixin had hoped. "Sorry for the confusion."

Mixin managed to hold back their giddy laughter until the guards were gone. Then they bent double against the wall. "Wow. Cobb's been on this ship less than two days, and already all the staff hate him."

"That tracks," said Jasper. Libbi came over to join them while he quickly updated Kay and Havoc, then turned back to Libbi and Mix. "Okay, remember, follow my lead. Try to get him away from his console if you can. He should be logged in, so we won't need to enter his password. One of us has to get to it, plug in the drive, and use his biometrics to let the virus load. And keep him away until it's done. Ready?"

"Oh, I'm absolutely ready for this," Mixin said.

They stepped up and palmed the door open.

The lab was pristine, even for a scientific workspace. It wasn't cold, but Mixin felt cold as they crossed the threshold; it just gave off that vibe.

"I told you not to interrupt me. You'd better be here to warn me the ship's about to explode, or I'll—" Cobb glanced up from his screen, then shot to his feet. "You."

"Alik. Not a pleasure to see you again," Jasper deadpanned.

"He works fast," Libbi said, taking in the room in a broad sweep.

The lab had row upon row of auto-cuffs, straps, eye-masks, syringes, and other things Mixin didn't look too closely at, all faultlessly tidy. Not to mention the restraining chairs and isolation cells alongside the more technical-looking equipment.

"They built this lab to order for him, apparently," Mixin said.

"Seems like massive overkill for a temporary base."

"Isn't 'massive overkill' his superhero name?"

Across the room, words splashed through the door that led to the captive's cells: curses and threats and "Hold still, give me a minute!" Hopefully the curses were from the guards, not their friends. Mixin kept Cobb in sight as they stepped sideways, turning their back to the distractions next door, and incidentally putting themself between him and the nastier-looking equipment.

"I suppose you want to throw another tantrum and destroy yet another of my labs?" Cobb told them, dripping derision. "Because that's all it would be: a useless tantrum. There's nothing for you to accomplish here. I have everything I need now to carry my work forward, and besides, your sloppily kept secret is a secret no longer. Even if you and your friends flee from here, wherever you go,

Ravel will eventually track you down." He smiled unpleasantly, and his hand moved under the desk, like he was reaching for a panic button. "I would suggest you run away now, because security reinforcements will be here momentarily, but I don't expect you'll listen. I look forward to adding you three to my active collection."

Mixin set their face like a mask. Sunny was supposed to try to intercept any calls to security, but had warned they might not be able to.

"Sunny?" they whispered.

There was no answer.

HAVOC HUNG BACK IN the hallway, where the guards inside couldn't see him as Kay opened the door. Looking smart in their new security uniforms, she and Felicia held Jinx between them. His head drooped in apparent defeat.

They'd originally planned to use Libbi as their "recovered escapee" to get them inside the cell block, but Libbi had been itching to confront Cobb, and Mason had said she'd actually be more useful doing so, considering Cobb's obsession with her. Havoc didn't *think* he'd said that just to keep her out of the likely fighting; he was getting better about that sort of thing. Fortunately, Jinx had volunteered for this role with undisguised glee.

"We've got one of the escaped subjects here," Kay announced to the guards inside the prisoner's block.

"That was fast," one guard said, then, "Oh, another one? Good work! Here, we'll take him off your hands."

Havoc, who was creeping toward the door, hesitated. "Sunny?" he murmured. "What do they mean?"

"I'm checking."

Kay was saying, "I'd like to see him secured, if you don't mind. He gave us quite a chase." Under her breath, she hissed, "*Now.*"

Shaking off his doubts, Havoc charged through the door. Kay and Felicia had maneuvered deeper into the room, keeping the guards' attention—so the one nearest the door didn't see Havoc until he was on him. Havoc pinned the guard's arms, holding him like a shield, and elbowed the controls to shut the door before baring his claws at the man's throat.

The other two guards froze, stun-sticks at ready.

The room was long and narrow, fronted by an open space with a couch and table, plus an exercise corner with a treadmill and some bands and dumbbells. It might have served as a reasonable low-rank workers' dorm, had it lacked the locking glasteel doors across each cell.

"Open the cells." Havoc pointed with his chin.

"Not happening." The older-looking of the two guards, a woman with graying hair, scoffed. "You let go of our colleague there, and we won't hurt you much when we arrest you."

"As if we'd believe that," muttered Kay.

"Remembering that we outnumber you, I propose a trade," Havoc said. "Our captive for yours." As he spoke, he shuffled sideways toward a panel that he thought probably held the cell door controls, keeping his Human shield between him and the guards.

They raised their stun-sticks in warning. "Don't move! There are more of you, but we're armed, and we're not trading away our rightful property."

"Do you value this one less than property, then?" His captive tried to pull free, but Havoc tightened his grip.

"Listen," said Kay. "The only person we want to make trouble for is Alik Cobb. We won't hurt anyone unless we have to, so think really hard about how much danger you want to put yourself in for the sake of that asshole. Okay?"

That made them hesitate, at least for a moment. Havoc took another step to the side. The second guard, a younger male, was shifting his weight, preparing to move. Suddenly Jinx sprang up behind the guard, dropped an exercise band around the man's neck, and pulled.

"No, you don't. Nice try, though," Jinx said. The guard could only choke in answer. "He was going for the panic button over there. I think it seals off the cells and calls more guards."

Jinx twisted the stun-stick out of the guard's grasp and jabbed it into the man's side until he twitched and fell. He repeated the process with the guard Havoc held, then stepped over the fallen body and held the stun-stick toward the remaining guard.

"You Brennexians are like herding cats," she said, exasperated.

"Open the cells," Havoc said, "and we won't hurt you much when we put you in."

She glared at him, not amused at having her own threat echoed back at her. "Good luck with that."

Her eyes flicked past Havoc, and he realized too late that she'd been listening to something on her headset. "Outside!" Felicia cried, and Havoc pivoted to face the door just as it slid open.

Two more guards stood there, holding Incoming Tide between them. Tide's eyes were round with fear.

The new guards stopped, taken by surprise by the scene inside, but the gray-haired guard was expecting this. Waiting for it.

"Incoming Tide," she shouted, "attack these intruders!"

"Tide, don't—"

"No, Tide…"

But the flurry of disorganized counter-commands came too late, as Havoc discovered when Tide tackled him to the floor.

37

◆

"THEY'RE NOT ANSWERING," MIXIN murmured. They kept whispering into their headset, and were starting to look scared.

Libbi sidled closer and asked, "Sunny?"

Mix nodded.

Libbi tried her own headset: "Sunny, you there?" Then: "Kay, Havoc? How's it going with you?"

No answers.

"We're alone," Libbi breathed so quietly that only Mixin would catch it. Sunny was supposed to back them up. Havoc and Kay and the others, working in the next room, might as well have been on the far side of the ship.

Mix squeezed her hand, hard. "It was working out in the hallway. Maybe he's blocking outside signals."

"Of course I am." Cobb settled back in his chair, smiling in obnoxious self-satisfaction and making no effort to get rid of them, which was concerning all on its own. "I learned that from your big brother here, Liberation. I can't have spies passing data in and out of my lab, or risk my troublesome test subjects acquiring a connection to the outside. The only connections are hardwired right here." He patted his console smugly.

"Thanks for that info. Good to know." Jasper didn't look scared, but his wants were all tangled and fighting each other in a way that told Libbi he wasn't nearly as in control as he pretended. Wanting to hit Cobb in his extremely punchable face. Wanting, she thought, to commit more and darker violence. Wanting to protect, and wanting to flee this place and never return. And that scared Libbi even more.

Jasper strode toward the workstation, but Cobb raised a pistol—a pistol!—and pulled the trigger.

"Jasper!" Libbi screamed.

Jasper dove and rolled, coming into a crouch behind a workbench halfway across the room from them. Mixin pulled Libbi behind another bench as Cobb turned the gun on them. A dart clattered off the floor beside her hand.

Tranquilizers? Shit. Somehow that was worse than a bullet-gun.

"Please do try again," Cobb said absently. "I honestly don't care whether security shoots you or I do."

He stopped grandstanding, then, and seconds stretched out in silence. Libbi risked a peek over the workbench. Cobb had one hand resting on the gun but, incredibly, was *working,* using his free hand to scroll through whatever was on his screen.

"He's going to wait us out, isn't he?" Libbi murmured. "Just sit there until security comes."

"Seems like," Mixin said. "So how do we get him away from that desk?"

That was the trick, wasn't it? It was good news for them that Cobb was actively working at his console. That meant he was logged in, and they could load their virus into the system from there. But to do that, one of them needed to get to the desk long enough to do so.

Across the way, Jasper gathered himself and mouthed something in their direction.

"He's going to attack Cobb," Mixin translated. "He'll drag him away so we can plant the drive."

"But he's got a dart-gun!"

Mixin shrugged, helpless. "What else can we do?"

Libbi wasn't going to let her big brother get hurt or captured. She got to her feet. Cobb whipped toward her, pistol up again, but she held up her hands and, thank the Founders, he didn't fire. "Okay, Alik Cobb. Fine. Let's talk."

"Talk." Cobb's brows rose. "About what?"

She had no idea. All she knew was they couldn't keep hiding until security arrived, and attacking him wouldn't do any good if he shot them unconscious. Jasper was shaking his head at her and mouthing *NO* so clearly she didn't need Mix's gift to read it, but she ignored him.

Unless they engaged Cobb somehow, he would never get up from that desk.

"You know…" she began. What did Cobb know? What could possibly make him listen to her when he had nothing but disdain for her, and all he had to do was wait her out?

"It won't work, you know. This won't make them love you."

Cobb blinked. At least she'd surprised him. "Excuse me?"

"I know how much you want everyone to respect you, and you try to do that by showing off how smart you are. But it's never worked, has it? Everyone hates you."

He scoffed. "They're jealous of me, naturally."

"Nope. Some of them need Principal Scientist Cobb, and some of them resent you, but mostly you annoy them. Not one of them likes you, Alik Cobb, as a person."

Cobb raised the dart-gun—had that last point stung? Just a little?—but Libbi was already ducking back behind the workbench. "Can I make a suggestion?" she called.

He sighed. "If I let you make your point, will you shut up so I can work?"

Not a chance.

"If you really want respect and adoration—and I know you do—you should be try being nice to people. Compliment a colleague's work. Say good morning to the security guards. You've been rude to everyone since the moment I met you."

"I was not! I was polite to a fault on Brennex, even when you whiny, obstinate provincials made it next to impossible."

"You tried to be, at least," Mixin spoke up, seeing what Libbi was doing. "For the first ten minutes or so in the store, you tried so hard I thought you might have an aneurysm. But it was too much effort, huh?"

"See, you're doing it right now, insulting us for no reason," Libbi added.

He laughed, a sharp, dismissive burst. "This from the woman who baited and kidnapped me. Are you going to tell me that if only I'd smiled and said please, you would have cooperated with me?"

"Too late to find out, isn't it?"

The scary thing was: she might have. It was possible that a more patient, charismatic, smoother-lying version of Cobb could have misled a lot more people into helping him before someone realized what he was up to. Lucky that he was none of those things.

"You know nothing about being successful in a competitive corporate environment." Cobb literally turned up his nose at them. Libbi hadn't thought that was a real thing people did. "I can't be held back by what others think. If I went around worrying about *making friends* and *being likable,* I'd get nothing done. Speaking of which, where *are* those useless guards?" He glanced at his screen, then spun toward Jasper, gun raised again. "You! Wilder. Stop."

Jasper, who'd been creeping his way around the room while Libbi held Cobb's attention, raised his hands. "Just admiring all your shiny equipment. Slick setup you have here." He paused, with a hint of a smirk. "You're right. Having nice stuff is definitely a fair trade for having no friends."

"How are you even more obnoxious than I remembered?"

Jasper's smile turned feral. "I could ask the same of you, Alik."

An idea flitted through Libbi's head, but before she could grab onto it, Cobb gestured with the gun. "Over there with the others, Cooperative. I want all of you in my sight." When Libbi stepped forward, he swung the gun toward her. "No tricks!"

"Don't touch my sister, Cobb!"

"Then get over there with her! You're interrupting important work, but if I have to stand here and wait for those imbecile guards to show up, I will."

Libbi felt more and more certain that security wasn't coming, that Sunny had been successful in blocking his call for help. The question was how long it'd take Cobb to realize that—and how he'd react when he did. She couldn't imagine why he hadn't knocked her unconscious yet. Maybe because, if he stunned her, Jasper would be on him like a berserker.

Libbi didn't know much about combat, but Cobb didn't look confident with that gun. He couldn't risk a hand-to-hand fight with Jasper. As far as he was concerned, Jasper was the only real threat here, with his Cooperative training in self-defense and who knows what else.

Jasper took a step toward the desk. Cobb raised the gun another inch. "I'm warning you."

"He'll do it, Jasper. He wants to." The urge for violence rose off both of them, tempered by the rational, strategic parts of their minds. As soon as that balance tipped, the stalemate would be over.

"We need more distraction," Libbi breathed, and Mixin squeezed her shoulder.

"Hey, Cobb." Mixin waited until he glanced their way. Then, with the slow deliberateness of a cat who knows they're misbehaving, they pushed a rack of test tubes onto the floor. Cobb flinched as they shattered—and the gun wavered.

Jasper lunged at Cobb, who wheeled around and fired. The stun-gun made a soft whoosh, totally underwhelming, and he must have missed because Jasper crashed into him, grappling for the gun. The two of them locked in struggle, and then Jasper…stopped.

Cobb twisted the gun free, and fired again even as Jasper fell to his knees.

"Jasper!" Libbi cried.

He twisted toward her, and only then did she see the dart in his chest, a second one in his shoulder. He stared at her, intent, like he was trying to send a psychic message. But she had no idea what he was trying to tell her, even as his eyes lost focus and he collapsed.

38

MIXIN'S HAND CLAMPED DOWN on Libbi's shoulder, as if to keep her from running to her unconscious brother. Cobb just stood there, studying the dart-gun as if, for all his bravado, he couldn't quite believe what it had done. Was he unsettled? Having second thoughts? Kay would know, but Libbi couldn't tell.

Gradually, a smile spread over Cobb's face, the smug, unpleasant look that always made Libbi want to punch him.

"He thinks he's won," Mixin murmured.

"Hasn't he won?" Libbi answered aloud, for Cobb's benefit.

She half-believed it herself. Her whole body was shaking. Panic rattled around in her chest, searching for a way out. But she was not going to give up, wouldn't let Jasper's gamble be in vain. What to do, though?

The answer came to her in Jasper's voice. *Cobb is his own worst enemy. Use it against him.* Under her breath, for Mixin alone, she whispered, "I have an idea. Trust me?"

"Always."

"Then follow my lead."

She gave vent, just a little, to that swelling panic. "Shit. Shit, shit, shit. What do we do?"

"Libbi, calm down. Breathe." Mixin's gaze met hers, worried, going along with the act but not yet understanding.

"He *shot Jasper.*" Somehow, the pretended breakdown helped keep a real breakdown at bay. She cringed as Cobb stepped toward her. "Stay back!"

"I don't think so. But don't worry, Liberation, I won't hurt you." The slightest pause. "Neither of you." As if he'd forgotten about Mixin, who was standing right there. Mixin, always overlooked, everyone's last concern. Mixin, who Libbi had always taken for granted too.

For every step he came forward, Libbi took a step back, and Mixin came with her. Greed radiated off him, repulsive, as he approached two unarmed, helpless young specimens. He coveted them, the same way he would covet a new high-end medical gadget.

Founders guide me. Ancestors, if you've ever looked out for me, please be here now.

How far to the wall behind her? Was her memory of the lab's layout right?

Cobb wasn't coming straight at them. He was angling to his right, herding them backward at an angle. Toward one of those shielded test chambers, no doubt. She twitched her hand free of Mixin's, subtly urging them to let go of her. To let Cobb separate them.

Now that he wasn't afraid of Jasper at his back, Cobb kept coming. Of course he did; clearly he figured he could deal with the scared kids one at a time.

There was no threshold, nothing tactile to show she'd crossed into the chamber that clung like a bubble to the edge of the lab. But she knew she was in it, even before the walls came into her peripheral vision, by the predatory glint of Cobb's smile.

"As I said, I won't hurt you. You're too valuable for that."

He reached for the controls on the wall. That's when Mixin, discounted and ignored as usual, lowered their shoulder like a pocketball player and slammed into Cobb from behind.

Libbi grabbed his arm and added her pull to Mixin's momentum, swinging Cobb past her, then danced back out of the chamber.

Or tried to. Cobb grabbed her wrist. She screamed at him as she twisted, clawing with her free hand, but he held on, pulling her back into his trap. Mixin raised their arms, chopped downward onto his wrist, and he howled. His fingers loosened. Libbi kicked him in the stomach and dove out of the chamber.

Before he could recover, Mixin hit the controls. A force-shield snapped into place, so close behind Libbi that its nimbus stung her shoulder.

"You flubbing idiots!" Cobb shouted. "You selfish, unenlightened morons, you have no idea what you've just done…"

Ignoring him, Libbi threw her arms around Mixin. She was shaking—both of them were, she thought, but as they held onto each other, she realized Mix was *laughing*.

"How can you…? It's not funny!" Then she was laughing, too. "That was amazing. I was sure we were fucked."

"Don't worry, we might still be." Mixin cackled hysterically, but made an effort to sober up as they turned back to the room. They dug in their pocket and took out their copy of the fly-drive Havoc had prepped. "Let's do what we came for, so we can get the fuck out of here."

Libbi hurried over to Jasper, still unconscious, but breathing. She checked his pulse. It seemed thready and slow—or was hers just extra-fast?

"I should help you…" Libbi started to rise, but Mix shook their head.

"Stay with him. I've got this. Havoc said it'd be dead easy."

Havoc had teased Jasper about it. ("So simple even you can't get it wrong, eshrim.") Some sort of inside joke between them. Libbi willed her brother to wake up, to be there for her and Kay and his partner. "Thanks," she told Mixin.

"Besides, I've always wanted to do this." Mixin grinned. "The fun part of all this spy stuff."

"Well, you've got me now. What are you going to do with me?" Cobb demanded. "Do you even have a plan? Because you'll never get me off this ship. Security will gun you down."

Ignoring him, Mixin moved to the workstation and plugged in the tiny drive. Libbi held her breath. If this didn't work, if they'd been wrong about being able to co-opt Cobb's computer…

"Nothing's happening. Havoc said…"

"The biometrics," Libbi reminded them.

"Ha! Right." Mixin dug into their pockets again.

The biometrics. The whole reason Libbi was here instead of home with Ma and Pa—not safe, right now probably watching the solar mining array with growing alarm, but home where she belonged. Cobb was already logged into his console, but loading a file from an unknown external device required his explicit approval.

Mixin projected a holo of Cobb's retinal scan to the sensor. "Yes! There it goes."

A progress meter materialized over the desk, an animation of data hopping from one system to the other, then propagating out through Ravel's network.

"Are you…? You are! You hypocrites, after all this complaining about not wanting me to study your abilities, you're stealing my research! Who are you selling it to? Or…do you plan to use it yourselves?" He scoffed. "As if you could even understand my work."

"Wouldn't be a bad idea, actually, to see if something in here could help folks like Ever and Tide," Mixin said offhand to Libbi. "You're wrong, though, Cobb. And too late."

"We're not taking anything. More like cleaning it up," Libbi said. "Making sure that we and all our friends and family are safe from people like you."

"You're… What? What are you talking about?"

He didn't understand. After everything the Brennexians had tried to tell him, he still couldn't conceive that they would do something like this, couldn't imagine why they would want to. In his universe, everyone wanted to take his work and try to one-up him. But the idea that *some* research shouldn't exist? Beyond belief.

Libbi explained, taking great satisfaction in speaking slowly and clearly like he was a child: "We're not stealing your work. We're deleting it."

"No, no, you wouldn't. You wouldn't *dare*."

"You tried to turn us into lab rats," Mixin said. "Fuck yes, we dare."

"Stop!"

A horrible crackling noise filled the air as Cobb flung himself at the force-shield. "You can't! Security!" He hit the barrier again and stumbled backward.

"Cobb, cut it out! You'll hurt yourself!" Libbi shouted.

"Yes, I will, unless you stop this madness and let me out!" He pressed both hands to the shimmering barrier. Tiny lightning sparked across its surface, and his palms turned red, blistering, before he finally broke away. "You're too soft. You won't stand by and watch me do this."

He gave a wild little laugh.

"Fuck." Mixin's eyes were round. "I think we broke him."

Libbi stared. "What do we do?"

Cobb wanted to get out, to be free. To stop them. He was frantic with it, overcome with the need. Libbi couldn't let him. Obviously. But…

For a moment, Mixin looked as lost as she felt. Then their expression hardened. "We do nothing." They pitched their voice to carry over the crackling of the shield. "He designed this lab for us. He tried to put you in that chamber, Libbi, and he knows how strong that force-shield is. He knows exactly how much harm it can do to a Human body."

Libbi drew a deep breath, steadying herself. Cobb was right about one thing: Libbi had always thought of herself as soft, and so had everyone else. The good girl, the obedient child. But she never had been. She was the one who did the hard parts, the boring parts, the important parts, while everyone else ran away to have adventures. She'd stuck with her home, her family, above all else. And she was not going to let this small, fragile man manipulate her into betraying them.

But then Cobb hit the shield again, and she couldn't stand the sound. She needed to help him… No! She needed to move away, block it out. Find her strength. Laying Jasper gently to the floor, she went over and huddled close to Mixin. The fly-drive's routine was forty percent done.

"You backward Brennexians! You hate science! You hate progress!"

"No, we just hate your kind of science," Mixin called. "Seriously, Cobb, are you going to deprive the world of your genius? Because you're really going to hurt yourself if you keep that up."

The shield didn't block the smell. Sharp electrical burning mingled sickeningly with scorched flesh.

Mixin grabbed her hand, and she was startled to find she'd been reaching for the drive. She forced it back to her side. Cobb's panic was visceral through her gift, leaving her shaky and mind-fogged and queasy.

"I'm fighting it," she whispered. "Don't let me do anything wrong."

Mixin took both her hands and turned her so her back was to Cobb. They held on tight, fixing their gray eyes onto her brown ones. Eyes as familiar as her own in the mirror. "You've got this, Libs. You're stronger than him."

"That research is my *life*. You're destroying my life!"

"That is really fucking sad," Mixin said, still holding Libbi's gaze.

"There's a lot more to life than work," Libbi added.

By the time the drive reached seventy percent, Cobb had stopped shouting at them. Mixin's eyes flicked past Libbi's shoulder, then swiftly back. "Don't look."

"Fuck," Libbi whispered. She shut her eyes and bent her forehead to meet Mixin's. The two of them stood there for what might have been seconds or might have been hours.

The workstation dinged, a bizarrely normal confirmation sound. The virus's work was done.

Libbi slumped into the chair—Cobb's chair, no, not that. She forced herself up, back to where Jasper lay on the floor. Sat by him, fighting the temptation to just lie down there beside him.

They'd won. Wasn't victory supposed to feel good? But her brother was lying there unconscious, and she felt scraped raw; she was so tired.

Mixin rummaged through a closet Libbi hadn't noticed before, labeled with a medical cross, and pulled out what Libbi recognized as an auto-doctor drone. She'd never used one before, but they were common for small ships and remote locations where a real doctor wasn't available. Or, apparently, the labs of paranoid, secretive scientists. It rose in the air and hovered by Jasper.

"Patient sedated but stable. Prognosis: excellent," it declared after a minute. Libbi could breathe again.

Then it flew over to the force-shield. "Medical emergency detected. Please allow access."

"Do we have to?" Mixin muttered.

"You know we do." Libbi hauled herself up and went to the controls. The scorched smell was stronger over here. She lowered the shield, then raised it again once the drone was inside, catching a too-long glimpse of a crumpled, twitching form and blistered skin before she could look away. "I can live with whatever damage he inflicted on himself. He didn't have to do that. But…I can't let him maybe die because he didn't get medical attention."

"You softie." Mixin gave her a fond smile. "No, you're right. I wouldn't cry over his death, but I don't want to be responsible for it."

"Patient in critical condition. Beginning trauma measures."

Libbi's jaw clenched. It was Cobb's own fault, but she could still feel the ghost of his frenzy to escape, to save his work… "Well, we can't do anything more for him. And now we have to figure out how to haul my unconscious brother through a crowded ship to the docking bay without getting stopped. Do you think the rescue team got everyone else out okay?"

"Um. Crap." Mixin blinked, then turned to stare at the wall joining the lab to the dorm or prison or whatever they were calling it. They bit their lip. "I'd been ignoring it while we were dealing with, you know. But I don't think things are going great in there."

39

TEETH SNAPPED AT HAVOC'S throat. He and Tide rolled and grappled, tails thrashing, her sharpened claws digging through the scales on his arms. Tide had greater mass than Havoc, and given that Havoc took care to avoid harming her, while her orders included no such cautions, she had the clear advantage.

Felicia and Kay grabbed Tide's shoulders to restrain her, and it might have worked had there not been three more fully conscious Ravel guards to worry about.

"Behind you!" Jinx shouted, and Kay and Felicia turned to confront the other Humans. "Havoc, your face!"

Tide slashed at Havoc's eyes. The warning came barely in time—he turned his head and caught the blow on his muzzle instead.

"Incoming Tide, stop this," he hissed.

She shuddered for a moment, torn, before swiping at him again.

He wished he'd asked more questions about her gift before this, but he'd feared to speak rudely. He knew her compulsion responded to direct commands, and knew it would wear off…eventually. But he couldn't afford to wait that long.

That slight hesitation gave him hope, though. Conflicting orders might make her hesitate. He could use that, maybe.

He rolled, put himself above her, and pinned her wrists with his hands. Her tail caught his knee—he lost his balance, and she seized the opening to snap her jaws at his neck. He sprang back onto his hind legs, and when she tackled him again, he used her momentum to drive her into a wall. It stunned her just long enough for him to pin her down again.

"Tide, stop fighting me. Tide, listen. I'm a friend. Your other friends need your help. Come back to us, Tide."

She stared at him, unmoving, body taut, eyes wide and miserable. It gave him a chance to spin her around and pull her arms behind her back before she began resisting again.

"I do this for your sake. I think later you'll thank me." He held her firmly while he checked the scene around them.

Felicia had her back to a wall, using bare hands to parry her guard's attempt to stun her. Jinx's guard was bleeding from her cheek, and they both looked ragged. He didn't see Kay or the third guard at all.

"Havoc, the other guard!" Jinx shouted without looking at him.

The guard Kay had been fighting? He looked around, confused. And so he reacted too slowly when a forgotten enemy, one of the two they'd stunned unconscious, surged upward right beside Havoc and jabbed a stun-stick at him.

Havoc roared, losing his hold on Tide as he dodged the unsporting attack. He grabbed at the guard but couldn't get his stun-stick before Tide was on him again.

She drove him to the floor, hands on his throat, tightening. "Tide, stop." He struggled to pull her hands away. "Tide, stop, stop, stop this, Tide, please Tide, stop."

His voice was rasping. She was cutting off his air, and blood trickled down his neck where her claw-tips pierced the tender skin. But something changed in her eyes. She didn't let go, didn't relax her grip, but didn't try to tighten it, either.

He tried once more, using the warm and authoritative voice he'd practiced as an organizer, or as close as he could get with someone's thumbs in his throat. "Incoming Tide, remember who your friends are, and stop fighting me."

And Tide went limp.

He shifted her gently, tried to help her to sitting, but she crumpled into a pile with her tail wrapped around her.

"You're returning to us. You did it. I thank you," he murmured. "Can you come help?"

She shook her head frantically. "You should lock me up. I could hurt you all more."

"I won't do that." She looked utterly drained by her physical and mental struggles. "Rest here."

What to do, though? Chaos filled the tiny room. Jinx now held off two guards, darting and weaving to keep them at bay, while Felicia was locked in a struggle of sheer strength where her guard's stun-stick drove ever closer to her chest. And Kay? Where had they taken Kay?

But he had to help the others before he could look for her. Three on each side now, and Havoc was bleeding and hurting and tired.

He grabbed Felicia's guard by the shoulder and pulled him off her. The guard spun and turned the stun-stick on Havoc, catching him with a glancing blow to the arm. He hissed, doubling over. His vision clouded, and before he could blink it clear, the guard charged in, slamming Havoc back into the wall. Havoc caught the arm holding the stun-stick and held on, even as the impact jarred him—only to find the guard's other forearm pressed across his throat. He thrashed, seeking leverage. Finding none. Air, he needed air…

Victory gleamed in the guard's eyes. Havoc's vision narrowed until he could see nothing else.

Suddenly, the guards froze. Listening. Then, over the blood pounding in his ears, Havoc heard it too: voices, footsteps, close at hand.

The guard holding Havoc half-turned, not letting go, but the pressure on his throat relented just enough that he could draw breath, then crane his neck to see…

Kay appeared at the mouth of the cell block with a half-dozen more Humans and another Kovar behind her. The freed prisoners had no weapons but their anger, yet that anger had power. As they approached, all three guards retreated, shifting to face this new threat.

In the momentary standoff, the door to the lab swished open.

The lead guard called over her shoulder, "Cobb—uh, Senior, I mean Principal Scientist—you better run. We'll cover you." Then she glanced over her shoulder. Stopped. Turned around, mouth dropping open in dismay.

It wasn't Alik Cobb at all. Libbi and Mixin stood there, Libbi with a stun-stick in hand, Mixin with a dart-gun, which they aimed without hesitation at the lead guard.

"Oh, hey, folks," Mixin said with an edged brightness. "Is the party over?"

Kay laughed in delight. The guards groaned.

Relief hit Havoc, then vanished just as fast when he noticed who was missing. "Where's my eshrim?"

FOR ALL THAT MIXIN deadpanned about wishing Cobb were dead, they felt relieved when the drone reported that his vitals were stabilizing. Maybe Cobb would learn something from this experience. Like *don't kidnap people and run experiments on them,* or at least *treat your test subjects as you'd want to be treated, because they will if they get the chance.*

Eh, probably not. Besides, he apparently had "severe neurological trauma," though the med-drone couldn't explain what that meant.

"Jasper's just tranquilized. He'll be okay," Libbi was telling Havoc, who'd rushed to Jasper's side with a pained cry the moment he saw his partner lying there. Havoc didn't relax until he'd thoroughly checked Jasper over. Only then did he let Libbi wipe away the blood (some Kovari blue, presumably his own, and some red from the guards), daub antiseptic on his own wounds, and seal them with liquid bandages from the medical supplies.

The guards recognized a losing battle when they saw one, and gave Kay no more trouble as she locked them in cells with the help of those cells' former residents. Apparently she'd grabbed the keycard off the guard she was fighting with, which was how she'd trapped him and freed the others.

Kay waved Mixin over.

"Can you organize these folks? I'm going to check in with Sunny. We need them to find us a safe route to the docking bay. Besides, they're probably freaking out that they haven't been able to contact us."

Mixin started to protest that Libbi should do this, Libbi was the people person, but Libbi was taking care of her brother and Havoc. So Mix faked a smile and said, "No problem!"

Kay stopped to give Havoc a quick kiss on the cheek, then checked the hallway in both directions before stepping outside where signals wouldn't be blocked. Mixin caught the start of Sunny's answer ("Kay! Are you all right? I tried to divert Cobb's call for reinforcements…") but decided to give the two of them privacy.

They turned to their new charges. "Okay, everyone, how are we doing?"

Mixin could do this. They *could* be the one at the center, getting things done, instead of eavesdropping from the edges—if they needed to.

Jinx and Felicia needed first aid, and Tide was a mess of nerves. All of them were ragged and needed rest, but Mixin found some energy chews that ought to at least get them safely to Sunny. Everyone but Jinx and Felicia was wearing baggy hospital clothes and soft slip-on shoes, but a quick search of the prison area found a locker with their own clothes. By the time Kay got back, everyone was as ready as they could be.

"Sunny says we can get to the docking bay while everyone's still distracted with the solar mining demo," Kay announced.

"Is that enough of a distraction?" Libbi's brow creased. "That can't mean good things for Brennex."

"Sunny says it's holding people's attention." Kay's eyes sparkled, and Mixin regretted their choice not to eavesdrop on her conversation with the ship. What was happening out there? "Besides, Sunny has been blocking messages out of this lab, but they can't keep security away forever. Shall we?"

True to Sunny's word, the corridors were even emptier than before. There was no one *to* raise questions about the mismatched group of ID-less civilians and fake guards, or the Kovar cradling his unconscious partner in his arms. As Kay hurried them down a hallway full of the ubiquitous screens that were always showing the latest news and propaganda, Mixin stopped and stared. Then they began to laugh.

The solar mining presentation was still live, though Harrington Moore probably wished it wasn't. The evil-looking rig, with its menacing wings spread wide, was centered on the display. But around it, dozens of smaller ships flew in formation, with grapples and tow-ropes latched onto the rig itself.

They were, slowly but definitely, dragging it away.

Libbi stopped beside Mixin, squeezing their shoulder. "That's Auntie Mags's ship! And there, a Spaceborne Shipping tug!"

"I know that one, it's a Kovari freighter."

"And that ship comes from the Cooperative," Havoc added, grinning fiercely. "Linn's plan worked."

"Our friends came through for us." Libbi stared at the screen, awed. "All of them."

"Take that, Harrington Moore. Brennex will never belong to anyone but ourselves, ever again." Raising their voice, Mixin added, "Come on, everyone! Let's get home and join the celebration."

40

HAVOC DIDN'T LEAVE MASON'S side, even after they'd boarded Sunny and were safely away. The journey from Cobb's lab to the docking bay floated surreally in his memory, like half-remembered fragments of a bad dream.

At first, Sunny had guided them down near-empty hallways, because everyone had glued themselves to screens watching Natural Resources' plans unravel. Then, still avoiding the lifts, they'd had to climb the emergency stairs, a long, slow effort for the weary combatants and the prisoners who'd barely even walked in days. Mason had awakened by then, though he'd stumbled drunkenly. By the time they'd neared the docking bay, the Natural Resources presentation had ended, and abruptly the corridors had become the furthest thing from empty.

In their group's current state, they would never have gotten past docking bay security, except that security had

had their hands full with dozens of other people clamoring for permission to leave early. With several of them still dressed in security uniforms, they'd managed to bluff their way around the crowds and past the overwhelmed guards who, being besieged by panicked upper-rankers, had waved through their uniformed "colleagues" with relief that at least someone needed nothing from them.

It still strained Havoc's belief that it had worked. Only in the last minute before they'd reached Sunny had one of the guards recognized them and raised an alarm, forcing them to make a final mad dash to the safety of their ship.

How Sunny had managed to take off without being stopped, Havoc wasn't sure. Some old trick of Grist's, he imagined, but he'd stopped paying attention by that point, trusting Sunny to call for help if they needed it, and knowing the little ship could outmaneuver any organic-piloted pursuit in open space. He'd helped his eshrim to their cabin, where Mason had promptly collapsed into exhausted sleep.

None of them had gotten enough rest since arriving at the Exhibition, and it had been longer than that since they'd slept without fear. He didn't think Mason had truly relaxed since Libbi's first message about a mysterious stranger on Brennex.

So Havoc watched his beloved sleep, treasuring the way his resting face shed its worries. He'd intended to nurse his own injuries and then help Kay and Sunny with arrangements for their new passengers…but somehow he found himself stretched out on the bed, eyes opening to see Mason smiling warmly down at him.

Mason bent to kiss him, a brush of soft lips on Havoc's cheek, just above the bandage where Tide had clawed him. "I love you so much."

"And I think being even one room apart from you is too much, eshrim." His own voice sounded raw and awful.

"From those bruises you're showing off, I don't disagree."

The cabin door swished open and one of Sunny's helper bots entered, carrying warm honeyed tea and what proved to be a cold pack. Mason applied it carefully to Havoc's upper arm where the bruising was worst. His soft, warm fingers trailed gently over the cuts on Havoc's jaw, no longer bleeding. The tea soothed his hoarse, aching throat beautifully. For long minutes, they sat there in quiet peace, simply being together.

"What happens now?" Havoc asked.

Immediately, he regretted speaking. Where had that question come from? This wasn't the time to talk of heavy things.

Mason looked puzzled. "Well, we have to go back to Brennex with the rescued Losts. From there, we'll see what the situation is, and whether we've shaken off Ravel's intimidation."

"That isn't what I meant." A deep breath. "What do *we* do?"

"What do you mean?"

"You and I, and Brennex… Your family…"

"They'll be glad to see us in one piece. No doubt my parents will use this to guilt us into staying a while longer." He smiled wryly. "Which, honestly, might be a good idea. Give me time to smooth things over with them, and with Libbi."

"And then?"

"Then what?" Mason studied his expression, frowning. "Eshrim, just tell me what's bothering you."

"I don't know what to do with babies!" Havoc blurted.

"Babies?!" Mason laughed in startled surprise. "So? Neither do I. Well, I helped some when Libbi was a baby, but don't mention that around her."

Havoc shifted around to face him. "Let me try to speak plainly. I like your family, Mason. I feel great love for Kay, and a growing affection for Libbi and your parents. And I don't object to the idea of having a permanent home, someday, but… To me, my team is my family. My family is you. I never dreamed of raising my own offspring. If it's important to you, Mason, I'll find a way to adjust, of course I will…but I don't think I want that."

The corners of Mason's mouth were twitching with barely suppressed amusement.

"I'm not joking!" Havoc insisted. "I'd do it for you—I would do anything for you, eshrim—but this prospect terrifies me."

"Did my family get to you that badly?" Mason shook his head, eyes down, still fighting a smile. "I'm sorry, beloved, I didn't realize. How long have you been carrying this fear around?"

"Since the party. Your parents spoke almost teasingly of wanting grandchildren, but your extended family seemed…adamant." At Mason's horrified look, he added: "I meant to speak to you about it! But then we found Cobb, and after that there was no time."

"I see."

"How…how do you feel?"

Growing serious, Mason pushed himself up on the bed and shifted to straddle Havoc. "Sowing of Small Havoc, my teammate, my love. I don't want kids either."

"You're sure?"

"One thousand percent. Even if the Lost Generation never happened, I don't think I'd want it. That's not the sort of family I need." Mason smiled down at him like healing sunshine. "I'll probably go home to Brennex more often after this, but not to settle down, no matter what my family says. All I want is the life I have with you."

Full of relief and affection, Havoc grinned foolishly up at him. When Mason bent to kiss him again, Havoc lunged upward, rolling and pinning Mason to the bed. His bruised body complained, but he didn't care. His tongue traced a curve along Mason's jaw.

"That," he said, "pleases me very much."

LIBBI STEPPED HESITANTLY INTO Sunny's control room, hovering by the entrance. "Hey, Mix."

Mixin, in the copilot's seat, spun their chair to face her. "Hey yourself. Looking for a place to hide out?"

"No. Just looking for you."

It was tight quarters to house so many people, despite how Sunny had done their best and then some to make their space accommodating. Their bots had transformed the cargo area, adding barriers for privacy, turning benches into cots, and printing bedding and clothes. ("I told you these modular furniture kits would prove useful. We were bound to host guests eventually," the ship had told Kay proudly.) But there was no making the ship's interior larger, so they were all living on top of each other, trying their best to give everyone their space until the ship reached Brennex.

So instead of assuming she was welcome, Libbi gestured to the free chair.

"May I…?"

Mixin rolled their eyes. "Sit, Libs."

She perched on the edge of the seat, hands on her knees. How to start? She assumed that Sunny was listening in—but that hardly mattered when Kay could probably hear her heart purring out love and anxiety, when Jasper (recovering in bed with his partner at his side) could no doubt watch the nuances of their relationship with more clarity than Libbi, when Jinx had been shooting her knowing looks for the past hour while she worked up her nerve.

If everyone knows how I feel and what I need to say, do I even need to do this?

But she did, of course. Mixin's gift was amazing, but even they couldn't read minds. And they deserved to hear this, out loud and direct and heartfelt.

"So, look…" she began, just as Mixin said "I meant to…" and then broke off, awkward. "You first, Libbi."

That was only fair.

"I regret a lot of things, but most of all I'm sorry for not talking like this before you left Brennex."

"Could you have?"

"No, I wasn't ready. But it killed me to think something might happen to you when I'd never apologized." She was looking at her hands. She made herself look up and meet Mix's eyes. "I'm sorry I've been such a crappy friend. Especially lately, but apparently for a long time."

Another friend might have waved that away—*Oh, no, you weren't at all* or *You're being too hard on yourself.* Mixin just nodded.

"I took your friendship for granted. Did you really stay on Brennex because of me?"

Mixin shrugged, looking exposed and uneasy. "No. Maybe. It wasn't *just* you, don't flatter yourself. My family's there, and our friends, and it *is* my home in a way that your sibs don't seem to feel. But it's always felt small to me. I didn't want to leave home, or you…but I did want more."

"And you knew I wouldn't follow you."

"I won't lie: of all the reasons to stay, not wanting to abandon you was a big one. I knew you couldn't forgive me for that. Not after how Kay and Jasper left."

"You're right." Libbi would've absolutely lost it if Mixin had gone away. It would have felt like a personal betrayal for her best friend to have a life of their own that didn't line up perfectly with hers. It wasn't a nice thing to recognize about herself. "You're right, and that wasn't fair to put on you. Even if I didn't realize I was doing it."

"No, it wasn't, but I wasn't exactly mature about it either. I kept trying to find new ways to entice you into running away with me, even though I knew you didn't want that, and never would."

"Well, I tried to crush your dreams, so maybe we're even on that point." She pursed her lips. "It turns out, I don't really know what I might have wanted, once upon a time. I only knew what my parents wanted for me, for our family, and there was no one else to make that happen, so I made it into what I wanted. If there was room for anything else in my life, I forced it out. And in the process, I hurt you."

Mixin reached out and squeezed her hands. She squeezed back.

"And what do you want now? What does Libbi Wilder want for herself?"

Libbi shook her head. "Nope. You first. How do you feel now that you've had a taste of adventure?"

There was a universe in the pause between the question and Mixin's answer. *Don't leave me,* part of Libbi screamed, and she shoved that part away, because this wasn't about her. What was a friendship worth if they couldn't both be happy?

"Honestly, Libs? I loved this." Mixin gave her a cautious smile. "The Exhibition, taking down the mad scientist… It was terrifying, and I felt like I was going to screw everything up, but Founders! I spied on the fucking Ravel Corporation board and uncovered their dirt and turned it against them. I used my gift for something that matters, and it was amazing."

Her friend was glowing in a way Libbi couldn't remember seeing before. Her heart clenched, overwhelmed with love even as she struggled to tamp down her fear. "You always did say that there's no point in having superpowers if we can't use them to fight evil."

Ever the expert on Libbi's moods, Mixin eyed her and said, "But you don't feel that way."

Libbi drew a shuddering breath. "For me, it was terrifying, full stop. I was sure I was going to let everyone down. I thought I might lose you and my brother." She shook her head. "And I miss *home*. I want to see my parents, and my cat, and… Oh, Ancestors, I don't know how I'll put the store back together after this, but I won't feel satisfied until I've gotten started."

Plus, there was more to fix at home than just the store. She'd never believed that Brennex was perfect, but Ravel had shone a spotlight on its flaws, and Libbi couldn't just paint them over and ignore them again. How she could help fix that, she had no idea, but she wanted to talk to Ma about it.

"None of that surprises me," Mixin said.

"So…" Libbi's voice squeaked, betraying her. "So, what do we…?"

"Libbi Narayan Wilder, do you think we can't be friends unless we're physically glued to each other?" Mixin punched her arm, and then they were both standing and hugging each other close. "You're my best friend, Libbi. That'll never change. But we can both have more, too, and I think we're tough enough for our friendship to survive that. Don't you?"

She laughed through a sudden swell of tears. "Yeah. Of course we are. I mean, Kay and Jasper are as close as ever, no matter how rarely they see each other…"

Oh, crap. How was she going to do this?

Mixin nudged her hard in the side. "You don't have to be distant from them, either, for that matter. But," they gripped her by the shoulders, looking her in the eyes, "unlike them, I'm not running away. Not from home, not from you. I don't know exactly what I'm going to do, but whatever happens, I'll be around to pester you a *lot*."

Now Libbi was crying uncontrollably. "You'd better."

"I will."

Libbi stood there a long time, holding onto her best friend, gazing at the screen with its stars and maps of macrospace terrain and a tiny dot heading homeward.

41

THE FUSS AT THE spaceport was no surprise. They'd messaged ahead so everyone would know that the Losts were all safe and on their way home. The Cooperative had arranged a public welcome and press event that none of them wanted, but even Libbi recognized the necessity. Brennex had handed over a group of their own citizens to a foreign corporate government on the basis of a threat and some outrageous claims about intellectual property, and the Cooperative wouldn't let them hide what they'd done. Certainly not on Founders' Day, as Lira kept repeating in her speech, invoking the Founders' names and ideals to shame Brennex's leaders, while Libbi stood on the stage with her siblings and tried to mentally calculate the date—was it really Founders' Day already?

The press conference was also a matter of personal safety. The people Brennex had handed over had all been arrested by Public Safety on the thinnest of pretexts, really for the crime of being a certain age. Having their faces in the news would discourage Safety from simply sweeping them up again.

Libbi wanted to believe that wouldn't be an issue. The crisis was over; Ravel was gone, and the minor corporations who'd been hovering like vultures had retreated. So had the Majrin, for now, though apparently they'd promised to keep Brennex under scrutiny. So there was no reason for Public Safety or the Council to go after the Losts now…but if Libbi had learned anything from this experience, she now knew not to take that safety for granted. It had to be upheld.

After Lira and Jasper gave speeches, they took questions. The Cooperative folks fielded most of them, though Felicia and Incoming Tide spoke about how Cobb had treated them. Libbi hadn't planned to speak—she was done playing hero for a while, hopefully permanently—but then Sasha Starborne was there in the audience, hand raised and looking at Libbi as she asked, "This whole business with Ravel has spooked a lot of people. What would you say to my fans who might be worried about stopping at Brennex in light of all this?"

For a moment, Libbi's hackles raised. After all this, how dare she still threaten to drive visitors away? But…Sasha wasn't smirking or taunting her, she realized. Libbi's one-time hero was offering her a chance to answer all the criticisms that off-worlders must be thinking, but might not say aloud.

So she stepped forward, in front of all the press, most of the Council, dozens of her neighbors, and untold others who would watch this in the days to come.

"People think Brennex is a pit stop, a place to resupply and maybe hit a bar before you head on your way to more exciting places. But Brennex is so much more. It's a community, full of real people who—all of us, whether we can trace our ancestry back to the Founding or whether we're newly arrived—have built a place we're proud to call home, and proud to share with everyone who stops by. We may not be perfect, but we've made something special, and no corporate station can replace it."

The Brennexians in the audience cheered. She caught a smile and approving nod from Sasha Starborne, and suspected a clip of her would be showing up on Sasha's platform. Once—even a couple weeks ago—that would have had her squealing with excitement. Now, she felt a hard-edged vindication, and hoped she wouldn't see Sasha again for a long time.

Finally, the conference ended, and she could leave the stage and go hug her parents.

"We're so proud of you, Libbi, sweetheart," Pa said, while Ma held her tight and he wrapped his arms around them both. If they fussed a little extra over her before turning to Kay and Jasper, she didn't mind. Even Havoc got hugged like one of the family, and they greeted Sunny's drone with warmth.

"Let's get you all home. I bet you'll be glad for a home-cooked meal," Ma said.

"I don't know. The food on the flagship was pretty swank—hey!" Kay protested as Jasper elbowed her. "Kidding!"

"No jokes about Ma and Pa's cooking. I'm hungry already." Jasper grinned and joined arms with Havoc, while Kay and Sunny fell in beside them.

Searching the crowd, full of similar reunions around the other returning Losts, Libbi spotted Mixin. Her best friend had their arms around both of their moms, chattering excitedly, but looked up as Libbi whispered, "See you later, Mix." They returned a wave and a wink, and Libbi followed her own family, smiling.

Around the spaceport and the central dome, the holiday seemed to be in full swing. Streamers of red and gold hung from every lamppost. Photos, art, and holos of favorite Founders filled every window, and music drifted through the streets while people scrubbed windows and swept out dirt (always by hand, as the holiday dictated), fixed squeaky hinges, repaired cracks, and tended to any other little tasks they'd been neglecting. From here, it was hard to tell they'd only just escaped a harrowing emergency.

As they got closer to home, Libbi's buoyant mood deflated. The store had been in a dire state when she'd left to follow the others. How much worse had happened to it since then? Ma and Pa hadn't said anything, but they seemed too happy at having their kids back to spoil the mood with worries.

When they emerged from the tunnels onto their own street, Jasper stared. "Wow."

Libbi and Kay swapped confused looks as he started walking faster. What did his gift see that they couldn't? Libbi hurried after him.

Another half-block, and she could tell there was a crowd outside the store. Crowd, not mob, so that was good. A little closer, and she slowed. Stopped. Stared.

There was no trace of graffiti left. No cracked windows, no grime. No mess at all. Through the gleaming windows, there were rows of shelves exactly where they should be. Out front, Ever was on a ladder, putting a final polish on the iconic Wilder Supply sign, and Squeaky was scrubbing at some invisible spot on the window, but at least two dozen other people were just milling around, waiting. A cheer went up as they spotted the Wilders.

"What…?" Libbi looked from the gathering—her agemates, her friends—to her parents and back. "You guys did all this?"

"Of course we did," said Ever. Like a mirror to the group's mood, he looked happier and more at ease than Libbi had ever seen him.

"This store is everything," said Dashiell, with one arm around Sage and the other holding Saba on his hip. "I remember making my parents come here when I was little, just so I could play on that model spaceship."

"I did too," said Sage. "Wilder Supply has always been here, and it's always been special. But this week, it's become more than that. Your family sheltered us. You supported us all…including in ways you couldn't afford."

"No? We're just fine. Besides, how could we have done otherwise?" Libbi glanced sharply at her father.

Phoenix said, "What Sage is saying is that we didn't have to ask you for help. You saw a need, and you filled it. Uncle Jackson maybe let slip that the store's been having a tough time since the reopening. Well, how could we do otherwise than help you in return?"

"Brennex wouldn't be Brennex without this place. Or without your family," Ever said. "A lot of us are, let's say, extra cynical about the founding families after this—"

"Understatement of the year," Sage said.

"And I wasn't sure I even wanted to celebrate Founders' Day. But your family are the good ones, the type we can celebrate. We wanted to thank you for everything you've done for us."

Clearly none of this was a surprise to Ma and Pa. They must have been having conversations like this for days. But Libbi felt suddenly overwhelmed. She'd been trying to fix all this, all by herself, and she'd assumed that when she got back she'd have to pick up all the pieces again. By herself, again.

But really, when had she ever had to do this alone? Even with Kay and Jasper gone, she'd worked beside her parents, and often helpful cousins, and so many longtime staff. And now there was a whole community rallied around them.

"Speaking of asking for and giving help, Ever's leaving out an important bit of news," Pa said. "You're talking to our new stockroom manager."

"Yeah?" Libbi turned to Ever. "That's a brilliant idea!"

Ever blushed, but he was glowing. "I've been trying to step up more since you left, Libbi. Keeping things organized, making sure everyone gets fed. So your parents and I got to talking about what I'm good at. I have a hard time working with people—I literally couldn't work the register or help customers—but Uncle Jackson thinks I can take over a lot of the work managing inventory from him, and free him up to help you with promotion."

"We should have thought of this a long time ago," Pa said quietly. "I'm sorry it never occurred to me."

"I guess we've all got things we tend to overlook," Libbi said. "Welcome to Wilder Supply, Ever." She grinned at him, and he grinned back. This wasn't the time—nor was it Libbi's place—to tell her parents that they'd soon have another open position to fill, but having Ever around would soften the blow of Mixin leaving.

"All right, all you lovely people, it's time to clear out," Ma announced. "The store will open tomorrow, but for now, Jackson and I need some time with our children."

Stepping into her gleaming, perfectly organized (if poorly stocked) family store, Libbi took a deep breath. The air smelled of a Founders' Day feast in the making: frying oil and tangy sauces from Ma's famous veggie fritters, the savory-sweet scent of braised faux-pork, and the richness of mudclam pie. Hints of sugar and fresh-cut oranges promised milk sweets and hope cakes. All of their favorites.

It smelled, Libbi thought, like home.

42

"I DON'T KNOW HOW you managed it. This is beyond anything I expected," Auntie Lira—Facilitator Linn, Mixin should call her now—said for at least the fourth time.

"Are you going to spill the details, or what?" Mixin finally asked. "What did we do?"

They'd gathered on the Wilders' rooftop to hear the news Linn had gotten from the Cooperative's sources within Ravel. Jasper and Havoc were lounging comfortably together on a bench. Kay sat nearby, with Sunny's drone perched on her shoulder. The cat kept trying to pounce Squeaky, then became indignant when her new "toy" fought back with a spritz of water. Poor kitty, how mortifying.

Overhead, cheery projections glowed against the night-dark dome: scenes from Brennex's founding, punctuated by the coming and going of ships from the spaceport in their old, comforting rhythm. The usual Founders' Day show had been hastily updated with platitudes about how the Founders had built a foundation for all who would come after them, and how everyone (regardless of their ancestry, it was implied but not said outright) could be proud of carrying on the Founders' legacy. A bit ham-handed, Mixin thought, but hey, someone was trying. It was a start.

"What we think we're seeing, based on how Ravel is moving funds and transferring authority, is the beginning of a company split."

Jasper sat up sharply. "Seriously?"

"Is that as bad as it sounds? Or good, that is, for us?" Mixin asked.

Sunny chirped. "It's significant, yes. Sometimes companies will spin off a profitable child branch if it's too far afield from their core focus, or cut loose an unprofitable one. But Ravel has always preferred to grow without limits, trying to be profitable in every area at once. They often absorb smaller companies, but there's no history of breaking them off."

"That's right. We've always wondered if Ravel might someday fracture under its own weight. It's too soon to tell, but that *may* be what we're seeing here." Lira spread her hands, smiling in satisfaction. "It seems that Biotech has absorbed Biopharma and is striking out on its own. Natural Resources and Engineering supposedly made a play for control of the corporation, and were rebuffed, and now are trying to separate themselves as well. It's akin to a group of children who inherit their family's company and can't agree on how to run it—"

"See, Libs, we've helped you by staying out of it. You're welcome," Kay teased.

Libbi, half-listening while marking up something on her handheld, made a rude gesture at her sister. She was smirking, though.

"Or perhaps a better metaphor is a very messy, acrimonious, multi-way divorce," Linn went on. "Regardless, it's the biggest restructuring within Ravel in decades—maybe within any major corporate state—and as best we can tell, it's a direct result of your interference."

Mixin blinked. Started to speak, then blinked again. Their brain couldn't process this.

"That can't be. We can't—*I* can't—have done all that."

"Alone, you couldn't have, but you undoubtedly played a role," said Havoc. "We saw how deep the fractures already ran within the company. We put pressure on the right spots at the right time, and you helped us find those spots."

The corporate states—Ravel in particular—had always been immense, shadowy monsters in Mixin's mind. An unstoppable space-monster, the kind with a dozen heads, where chopping one off would barely slow it down as it grew a new one. It was a dizzying switch to think of Ravel as a creature made of people, all the way down. For it to be wounded by someone as tiny as Mixin... Well, it was incomprehensible.

"You okay?" Jasper was watching them closely. "It's heady, I know, realizing how much power you have."

"I knew my gifts were powerful."

A smile played across his lips. "There's more than one kind of power. I'm talking about the kind that every person has intrinsically: to shape their world, to make it better or worse. That's what the Cooperative harnesses and nurtures. Our kind of gifts are just a bonus."

Mixin shook their head slightly to clear it. "You're right. It *is* heady."

Havoc laughed. "You've ruined them for activism, Mason. They'll expect to take down a corporate state for every assignment. We rarely win so dramatically, Mixin."

"Yet it happens surprisingly often for you two, doesn't it?" Linn regarded Havoc and Jasper with a thoughtful expression. "If Mixin proves to have a similar talent, Ancestors protect us all."

"What about Biopharma?" asked Sunny. "Did our attack on Cobb's work prove effective? Will their new parent corp still try to reclaim their alleged property?"

"The Cooperative has been called out and blamed for destroying their research," Linn said, "which leads me to believe they couldn't reconstruct it."

"But they still know about us," Libbi said. "About the Gifts."

"Oh, yes," said Jasper. "The danger to the Losts is absolutely not over. We should consider our secret permanently blown. It might even be safer now to go fully public…but that needs to be a community conversation. A whole lot of conversations. And in the meantime, we'll all need to watch out for each other more than ever."

Libbi nodded enthusiastically at that.

"But as far as Ravel is concerned," Linn said, "I think the danger is mitigated for now. They no longer have a champion for the project, given Alik Cobb's…situation, and a great deal of internal skepticism if anyone tried to revive it."

"Cobb's 'situation'?" Libbi set her handheld aside at the mention of his name, and her brow furrowed. "Is he…?"

"He's alive, through no credit to his own self-preservation. The reports say he suffered serious brain trauma from trying to break the force-shield. Their star researcher is going to be relearning how to read, and talk, and dress himself."

Linn delivered this news matter-of-factly. Mixin didn't know what to say, torn between horror, relief, and bitter satisfaction.

Havoc was the one to say what most of them were no doubt thinking. "Good."

"Seriously?" Libbi stared at him. "We did that to him."

"He did that to himself, Libs," Mixin said. "It was his own equipment, and he meant to put *us* in those chambers."

"Kovars call this a fair reversal," Havoc said. "He has punished himself as he deserved, and did so better than we ever could."

"He wanted to be respected, admired. On the outside, all he cared about was his reputation." Libbi's gaze went distant, remembering. "I think that deep down, he wanted to be liked, and didn't know how."

"Well, here's his chance to start from scratch." Mixin bumped shoulders with Libbi and murmured, "Better him than us, I say. Could have been Jasper, or you."

Libbi leaned against them, her head resting on their shoulder for a moment in shared comfort.

"So…Ravel's effectively gone?" Kay asked.

"Let's just say that Ravel will be in chaos for a long time, far too disorganized to worry about Brennex. The Cooperative has a big job ahead, helping worlds that want to take this opportunity and seize independence. We've had a dozen requests for support already, and Ravel can't stop them all."

"Probably opportunities for us to help, too," Kay told Sunny, who chirped in agreement.

Mixin tuned out Kay and Sunny's discussion about where to go next. Almost without realizing it, they turned toward Linn and Jasper and Havoc, as if they were part of that team, then pulled back, feeling presumptuous. But Jasper touched their shoulder, bringing them into the circle.

"Linn, I've got some ideas about how Mixin could be useful, too. If they want to be part of the Cooperative, that is. I credit a lot of our success at the Exhibition to them."

Linn smiled. "What do you say, Mixin? Are you in?"

"Founders, yes! Tell me what I can do."

They got so caught up in the conversation—the potential missions, the worlds they might see, the training they would need—that they didn't even notice Libbi leaving, until they looked over and she was gone.

LIBBI DID SOMETHING SHE hadn't done since she was a little girl. Leaving Kay and Sunny, Jasper and Havoc, Linn, and Mixin to their planning and plotting up on the roof, she slipped downstairs to her parents' bedroom.

Her mother's voice answered her tap on the door. "Come in, Libbi."

"How did you know it was me?"

"I don't need a special gift to recognize my children's footsteps. Come." Ma patted the spot between her and Pa on the bed, where she used to curl up between them on nights when she couldn't sleep. They were both in their pajamas— it was later than she'd realized—but looked fully awake.

Pa set aside a book. "What's troubling you, dumpling? Are you okay?"

"I'm fine. I just missed you both." She put an arm around each of them, hugging them close. "I wanted to thank you for letting me go."

Ma smiled. "You're a grown woman. We couldn't have stopped you."

"You know what I mean! You supported me, and I'm grateful. Even though it was terrifying a lot of the time."

Not that it hadn't been terrifying for those who'd stayed behind. She'd gotten the story of the solar mining presentation in bits from her parents and Ever and Auntie Lira. Once it became clear that Ravel had no intention of withdrawing, even after Brennex caved to their demands, the Council started calling it what it was: a hostile takeover. Not everyone who depended on Brennex for travel and trade was willing to stand up against a major corporate power, but the Cooperative had already begun recruiting allies. They had some committed friends who'd answered the call for help, and more who'd recognized that Ravel's control of the Long Lane would hurt their businesses. Enough to band together to tug the mining rig out of position just as Ravel began recording for their big demonstration.

They'd braced for retaliation, though none had come— yet. The mining rig had departed on its own a few days later.

According to Ma, that had in some ways been the easy part. The Council had faced demands (framed as generous offers of aid) from Bayson and two other smaller yet still powerful corporations who'd wanted to use the conflict to their advantage, at Brennex's long-term expense. On this much, though, Brennex was almost entirely united: no one wanted a new corporate owner.

Placating the Majrin had been even more fraught. Once they got involved in a conflict, the Majrin famously wouldn't let go until it ended in some way that satisfied them. Ma had tried her best to explain the legal contortions the Council's lawyers had gone through, first to try to win over the Majrin to Brennex's side, then to convince them the conflict was over and needed no more intervention. Libbi's takeaway was that, first, the Majrin had only stopped meddling when Ravel, in their chaos, withdrew the mining rig and stopped communicating on the matter; and second, that Libbi never *ever* wanted to be an interstellar lawyer.

Fritter hopped up on the bed and prowled around, accepting brief scritches from Libbi before settling out of arm's reach. Just to let Libbi know someone was still mad at her for leaving.

"So, anyway, thank you. I think I needed to experience that."

Her parents were giving her careful looks, loving but somehow wary. Her father said, "I understand Mixin quite liked their taste of activism. Did you as well?"

"I'm not leaving!"

"We don't want you to feel obligated…"

"Let me say this, please?" They fell quiet. She drew a breath, let it out. "I know I haven't been the easiest kid. I've tried so hard to be good, but I've carried this resentment around, and it's poisoned my feelings about home and the people I love. I used to blame that on Jasper and Kay—I really thought I had to stay here to make up for them leaving—but it's actually on me. And I want you to know: I choose this. I'm home now, and this is where I want to be." She smiled, feeling oddly shy. "It took going away for a while to realize that this is exactly where I belong."

"We would love and support you no matter what you do. Including staying home with us," Pa said, his relief so obvious that Libbi almost laughed.

"But there's something else," she went on. "I never thought Brennex was perfect, but we're far more broken than I realized. Ma, you said there've been reforms proposed before, to give fairer representation on the Council."

"There have, and they faced steep opposition. Are you developing an interest in politics, my darling?"

"No. Maybe. I just don't think it's right that so many groups—the Losts, but also the Kovars, the Majrin, all the recent-comers—have no power at all. The Council shouldn't have been able to do what they did to the Losts. What happens the next time someone tries to exploit us? Or another group? I want to do something about that."

Pa chuckled. "Listen to you. I should call your brother. He thought he'd never turn you into an activist."

"He didn't, Pa. This is all me."

"I'm teasing, I'm teasing, sweetheart. But have we mentioned how proud we are of you?"

"You're not the only one to have such a reaction to all this," said Ma, patting her knee. "Let's talk more tomorrow. There are some people you should meet."

She blinked, taken aback by the startling normality of that. Tomorrow, she could join her parents in getting the store reopened, and meet her mother's political friends, and go about what passed for a normal day on Brennex. The same as ever, yet everything would be different, too.

"Tomorrow, then."

She bid her parents goodnight, feeling lighter and surer than she had in a long time. The others were still upstairs, but she felt no urge to go join them. She should have felt left out, knowing they were all planning their futures without her, but the fact was, she was *choosing* a different path, building a different sort of future, and the resentment she'd clung to all her life was draining away.

Not ready for bed yet, she went to the kitchen and made herself a cup of mint tea. The cat wound between her ankles, purring and turning her dark skirt white with stray fur.

"Here you are," said Mixin from the doorway. "Got enough tea for me?"

"Always," Libbi answered.

She fixed a second cup, and they both sat at the table. Mixin reached for the tub of almond cookies that Ma always kept on hand. "I'm going to miss these."

"No, you won't," Libbi said seriously. "Ma won't let you leave without a suitcase full of them."

"Maybe you should tell her not to. That way, you'll know I have incentive to come back."

They said it lightly, but Libbi shook her head.

"I don't think I need to bribe you to come home."

Mixin looked up, met her gaze steadily. "You really don't. I already told Linn that I don't want to be forever traveling, like Jasper. This is my home base. I might be gone for weeks at a time…maybe months, I don't know…but when I'm done, I'll always land here."

"And I'll be here," Libbi said. She almost said, *I'll be here waiting,* but stopped herself, because that wasn't true. She'd anticipate every visit from her friend—maybe even her siblings' visits, too—and would treasure every moment together, but she wouldn't be waiting around for those visits. She'd miss Mixin, more than anything, but she'd be busy and full of purpose. And she wouldn't be alone.

"I'll be here," she amended, "and I'll always have a spare cup of tea and plate of cookies for you."

Thank you for reading!

Leave a review: If you enjoyed this book, I'd love if you could help other readers find it by leaving a short, honest review on Goodreads, Storygraph, or the site where you bought it.

Sign up for updates—and get a free story: Get updates about new books and stories, special deals, and fun extras when you join my mailing list at

www.jomiles.com/rs-bonus

When you sign up, you'll get a free, bonus prequel story about when all three Wilder siblings still lived on Brennex. Mysterious thefts at the family store rattle the Wilder family, and they'll need all their gifts to solve the mystery.

Acknowledgements

THANK YOU FOR COMING along with Libbi and Mixin, Kay and Sunny, and Jasper and Havoc on their journeys. For the Cooperative, as with real-life activism, the hardest work is still ahead. Change in the real world most often comes not from the moments of high drama and action, but from doing the work, each and every day. Much like writing a novel, in fact!

Writing is a solitary activity, but making a book takes a community. A huge thank-you to everyone who helped this book along its journey:

Shannon Page and Chelle Parker for your sharp-eyed editing, and Wendy Nikel for the fantastic cover design.

Anne Tibbets, for believing in me and this trilogy.

The Maryland Space Opera Collective for your excellent and insightful feedback. You helped me see this book more clearly, and everything I write is better because of you.

My communities at the Isle of Write and Codex for your support, advice, and encouragement along the way. Karen Osborne for telling me it would be okay, whenever I needed to hear it. And John Appel not only for your tireless support, but for always telling me I got the technology wrong—along with three ways to fix it.

My parents, for supporting my love of stories and writing for my whole life, and for always being the first to read whenever I have something new out.

Ada and Charlie, for making sure snuggles and scritches are a key part of my writing process.

And above all, I'm beyond grateful to my incredible spouse for your love and unflagging support. For being my first reader and my first fan. I love you so much.

About the Author

JO MILES WRITES OPTIMISTIC science fiction and fantasy. In addition to the *Gifted of Brennex* trilogy, their short stories have appeared in magazines including *Fantasy & Science Fiction*, *Strange Horizons*, *Lightspeed*, and more. Fueled by tea and sunshine, they spend their time dreaming up strange new worlds and serving the whims of their two cats. They live in Maryland.

By Jo Miles
Warped State
Dissonant State
Ravenous State

Find a complete list of Jo's books and short stories at www.jomiles.com.

www.ingramcontent.com/pod-product-compliance
Lightning Source LLC
Chambersburg PA
CBHW021329310726
48971CB00001B/52